TWILIGHT OF THE GODS

TWILIGHT OF THE GODS

SCOTT ODEN

ST. MARTIN'S PRESS
NEW YORK

First published in the United States by St. Martin's Press, an imprint of
St. Martin's Publishing Group

TWILIGHT OF THE GODS. Copyright © 2020 by Scott Oden. All rights reserved.
Printed in the United States of America. For information, address St. Martin's Publishing
Group, 120 Broadway, New York, NY 10271.

www.stmartins.com

Library of Congress Cataloging-in-Publication Data

Names: Oden, Scott, author.
Title: Twilight of the gods / Scott Oden.
Description: First Edition. | New York : St. Martin's Press, 2020. |
    Series: Grimnir; 2
Identifiers: LCCN 2019043132 | ISBN 9780312372958 (hardcover) |
    ISBN 9781250022899 (ebook)
Subjects: GSAFD: Fantasy fiction.
Classification: LCC PS3615.D465 T85 2020 | DDC 813/.6—dc23
LC record available at https://lccn.loc.gov/2019043132

Our books may be purchased in bulk for promotional, educational, or business use. Please contact your
local bookseller or the Macmillan Corporate and Premium Sales Department at 800-221-7945, extension
5442, or by email at MacmillanSpecialMarkets@macmillan.com.

First Edition: February 2020

10 9 8 7 6 5 4 3 2 1

For Mido and Anna:

Nulla tenaci invia est via

Brothers shall fight | and fell each other,
And sisters' sons | shall kinship stain;
Hard is it on earth, | with mighty whoredom;
Axe-time, sword-time, | shields are sundered,
Wind-time, wolf-time, | ere the world falls;
Nor ever shall men | each other spare.

—*Völuspá*, STANZA 45 (BELLOWS'S TRANSLATION)

And I saw an angel coming down from heaven, having the
key of the bottomless pit, and a great chain in his hand.
And he laid hold on the dragon, the old serpent, which is
the devil and Satan, and bound him for a thousand years.
And he cast him into the bottomless pit, and shut him up,
and set a seal upon him, that he should no more seduce
the nations, till the thousand years be finished. And after
that, he must be loosed a little time.

—REVELATION, 20:1–3 (DOUAY-RHEIMS BIBLE)

PART ONE
FIMBULVETR

I

Corpses sprawled atop a low hill, beneath a sky the color of old slate. They lay in their tattered war gear: mail riven, shields broken, and helmets split asunder by ferocious blows. There were scores of them, arranged not in the perfect windrows borne of clashing shield walls, where the dead fall like grain beneath a thresher-man's blade, but rather in heaps and mounds—as though the Tangled God himself, cunning Loki, had decided to reshape the land with the bodies of slain Northmen. Their blood mingled with other vital fluids, turning the early snow underfoot to a scarlet slurry.

A cold north wind moaned through the evergreen spruces ringing the hill. It rattled the shafts of spears that grew from bodies of the slain like corpse-flowers, their blades rooted in bellies and spines; it snapped the fabric of cast-off pennons. Some displayed a wolf's head against a white field. Others, more numerous, bore a stark black cross. The wind faded; utter silence returned.

Amid this desolation, there came a single flicker of movement. A chestnut-haired giant clad in a ragged corselet thrust himself to his feet, notched sword clenched tight in his bloody fist. His breath steamed as he panted from the exertion of battle. Blood and spittle dripped from his beard; he turned his gore-blasted face to the heavens. Unsteady on his feet, he staggered from the tangle of corpses marking the crucible of the fight and searched above for even the smallest sign of God's favor for this victory—a rent in the clouds, a

3

finger of light from the celestial realm, something. But he saw only a limitless expanse of deep gray, as solid as arctic ice. Tears welled in his eyes; he raised his sword hilt-first to the sky.

"C-Christ!" he said, voice cracking. Then, louder: "Christ!"

"He can't hear you," someone behind him purred in answer.

The man whirled.

From the same welter of the dead, a woman arose. A one-handed daughter of Odin whose left wrist ended in an iron fist made to hold a shield. Blood clotted like rubies in the links of her mail hauberk—hacked and ragged now that this spear-shattering had run its course.

"Úlfrún Hakonardottir," the man said, lips peeling back in a snarl of hate.

The woman, Úlfrún, leaned heavily on the long oak haft of an axe. With her good hand, she drew off the ruin of her helmet, its crown ruptured along the seams where it took the blow that should have killed her. Úlfrún tossed it aside. Sodden hair the color of wood ash uncoiled and fell around her shoulders. "Heimdul Oath-breaker," she growled.

"Woman, you have more lives than a cat! I saw old Guthrum deal you a mortal wound."

"That? A child's blow," Úlfrún said. "Your Guthrum thought to spare me, and he died for it."

"Then he sits in a place of glory by Christ's right hand, alongside the saints and martyrs."

She gave a bark of laughter like the sharp grate of stones. "Does that lie bring you comfort, Oath-breaker?"

"I stand, having girded about my loins the belt of truth," Heimdul said. He cracked the bones in his neck and rolled the tension from his shoulders, then struck the flat of his sword against the heel of his hobnailed boot, knocking the rime of bloody ice loose from its edge. "And having donned the breastplate of justice."

Úlfrún hefted her axe, its bearded blade forged from Spanish steel; hard iron straps crisscrossed the haft. "Let those be the rags you and all your dogs wear, who sit outside the doors of Valhöll and beg for scraps off the Allfather's board! You turned your back on him! Tore down his altars, burned the sacred groves, and for what? So your wretched king might have his crown blessed by some cross-kissing fool in Rome? No, Heimdul Oath-breaker, you will know truth soon enough!"

"Heathen bitch! There is only one Father of All, and he's not the one-eyed fairy tale we tell children! Odin? I spit on your Odin! I piss on your Odin! I am a son of God, sworn to the White Christ!" Quicker than his brutish frame belied, Heimdul struck. He swept his jagged-edged blade up in a vicious backhand blow.

Úlfrún did not flinch. She did not shy away from the whistling blade that sought to end her life. Instead, she stepped in and caught it on the knuckles of her iron fist. The sword sparked, rebounded; the clangor of impact reverberated. Far to the north, from among the cloud-wreathed peaks, came the echo of thunder as if in answer. Úlfrún tilted her head back, listening to something only she could hear; she bared her teeth in a fierce smile that did nothing to soften the hard planes of her face. "I told you," she said, lowering her gaze to meet his. Her blue eyes gleamed with a fey and terrible light. "Your Nailed God can't hear you."

And Úlfrún Hakonardottir—Úlfrún of the Iron Hand—came on like a tempest. She fought like the she-Wolf that was her namesake, her guile and finesse tempering the savage spirit woven by Fate into the skein of her life. And like that of the she-Wolf, the strength in her lean muscles and corded sinews was no less than that of any man. The blade of her axe flashed in autumn's pale light, and she rained blow after furious blow down upon the guard of her enemy. A rush of breath, a ringing crash, and the rasp and slither of steel on iron were the only sounds as she batted aside Heimdul's clumsy riposte and very nearly took off his head. A hasty backward leap was all that saved him.

Úlfrún gave him a moment's respite—long enough to feel the cold hands of the Norns as they gathered together the loose strands of his life, their shears poised. He stood in the shadow of his own doom and could not see it. It was writ plain in the deep notches scoring his sword, in the sweat that burned his eyes, and in the tremble of his limbs. So close was he to the brink that he lacked even the breath to call upon his Nailed God. Úlfrún took all this in with a single glance . . . and laughed.

That sound, the stinging rebuke of a woman, struck Heimdul as no physical blow could. It bit through mail and leather and bored into his skin. It slipped past muscle and bone; as it lanced the naked heart of his fragile manhood, Úlfrún saw Heimdul wince. In that moment she reckoned he had thought for neither the love of his White Christ nor for divine salvation.

Could he even recall the admonitions of his so-called Lord to turn the other cheek or to love one's enemies? No. Úlfrún watched as the Northman's face suffused with rage. No amount of forgiveness would suffice. Only blood would mend this hurt. Her blood. He bared his teeth in a savage grin. Whitened knuckles cracked as he grasped his sword hilt in both hands. Then, with an incoherent cry, Heimdul charged.

Úlfrún met him halfway. She did not seek to test her strength against his, for he was like an enraged bull stung to madness. Rather, she sidestepped, dancing away from a blow that would surely have split her from crown to crotch had it connected; she pivoted on the balls of her feet as Heimdul lumbered past. Before he could turn, before he could recover, Úlfrún's axe flashed in a tight arc; it connected high, near the base of his skull. Bone crunched. Blood spurted. And Heimdul's cry turned to a rasping gurgle. His sword dropped from hands gone slack and nerveless.

Úlfrún loosed her grip on the haft of the axe.

But even with her blade lodged deep in his spine the stricken Northman continued on, dragging his feet a handful of steps through the churned and blood-spattered snow. He tottered, half-turned, and finally crumpled to the ground like a child's marionette, its strings clipped.

Silence returned.

The dull echo of thunder rolled down from the north.

Úlfrún exhaled, then, her breath coming in ragged gasps. She staggered over to Heimdul's body and grasped the butt of her axe with her good hand. Úlfrún worked it back and forth; then, placing one foot on the back of the slain man's head, she wrenched the blade free.

Grunting with effort, she struck him again. And again. With each strike came the slaughterhouse sound of butchery—the popping of gristle and snapping of tendons, the soft squelch of bloody tissue parting beneath the edge of her axe, the rasp of splintered bone on steel as she drew it forth again; on the third blow, Heimdul's head came free from his corpse.

Úlfrún stooped and caught it up by its mane of blood-matted hair. "Odin!" she roared, brandishing her foe's severed head toward the northern horizon. "Odin! Look here! Look . . ."

She reeled, a sudden sick weariness robbing her of strength. The clouds overhead boiled and throbbed; the evergreen trees around her swayed like supple maidens, dancing to a tune none could hear. On the field where slayer met slayer, only the slain remained . . . and they, too, soughed and sighed before her blurring vision—a sea of red and white, of flesh and blood and riven mail, whose steel-edged combers threatened to break above her.

"O-Odin!"

Úlfrún of the Iron Hand took a dozen steps before the sun's pale light suddenly dimmed. She sank down onto the crust of snow, then toppled to the side with Heimdul's hair yet caught in her fingers. She lay still, and like a soothing coverlet the darkness rolled over her.

How long she lay there, she could not say. Time had no meaning. A minute, a day, a year, a lifetime—all were one to her, but the world spun and the wind sighed and far away, she heard the murmur of thunder like the war drums of Ásgarðr. Inexorably, Úlfrún felt life creep back into her limbs. She flexed her frozen extremities, moving muscle and sinew despite innumerable agonizing pinpricks, willing her fingers to relinquish their hold on the dead man's hair. Slowly, she rolled onto her back and opened her eyes. Night had fallen, and eerie green lights flickered through rips in the clouds.

With a start, she realized she was not alone.

Úlfrún bolted upright, her hand clawing for a weapon. A sudden sharp pain kindled in the stump of her wrist; though it had been years, the memory of the crippling blow that parted her hand from her body was strong enough to wrench a gasp from between clenched teeth. She snarled through the pain.

An ominous presence stood near, scarce illuminated by the guttering emerald light seeping down from the heavens. It bore the shape of a man, though hunched and as twisted as the staff he leaned upon; the stranger was clad in a voluminous cloak with a slouch hat pulled low. A single malevolent eye gleamed from the utter darkness within.

Úlfrún bit back a curse. She knew him; she'd known him since childhood, since he'd picked her from the others and set her upon the path to greatness. She had called, and he had come. The Grey Wanderer; the Raven-God; Lord of the Gallows; the shield-worshipped kinsman of the Æsir. "I have harrowed the earth with their blood, Allfather," she said. "The blood of these Christ-lovers and oath-breakers!"

A chuckle, low and cruel, escaped the stranger's throat. "*Niðings,* they are. Wretched and depraved. The minions of the White Christ infest this Miðgarðr like vermin." His voice was harsh and rasping. "But the hour of their doom draws near.

"When the years tally | nine times nine times nine,
again, and war-reek | wafts like dragon breath;
when Fimbulvetr | hides the pallid sun,
the monstrous Serpent | shall writhe in fury."

Úlfrún rocked back on her haunches. "It is time?"

"It is long past time, child of Man," the stranger said. "Gather the *úlfhéðnar* and the *berserkir,* the sons of the Wolf and the sons of the Bear, and make your way to the land of the Raven-Geats. The White Christ will send his own champion, and there you must join in battle against him. But be ready," the stranger admonished. "Watch for the Wolf to devour the moon, and wait for the Serpent's coils to shake the earth! Only then will what you seek be within your grasp!"

"Sárklungr," Úlfrún replied in an awed whisper.

"Aye, the mighty Wound-Thorn! Forged in the dark fires of the Dwarf-realm, Niðavellir, and given to your kinsman Sigfroðr the Volsung to avenge the dragon-slaying of his people. It rests, even now, beneath Lake Vänern's waves.

"From the depths a barrow | rises through the water,
the stone-girdled hall | of Aranæs, where dwells
Jörmungandr's spawn, | the Malice-Striker.
Its dread bones rattle | and herald an end.

"Fetch the blade forth, Daughter of Strife! Drag it from the dragon's lifeless skull and bring it against this champion of the White Christ! Tear him asunder! Peel the flesh from his spine and hack through his ribs! Haul the lungs from his riven corpse! And let his blood call down upon this Nailed God's rabble the doom of Ásgarðr!"

"Let it make an end of them, once and for all," Úlfrún said through gritted teeth as she clambered to her feet. Thunder rumbled in the distance, and ere its echo could fade the Grey Wanderer had disappeared. She was alone.

Úlfrún of the Iron Hand staggered over to where her axe lay propped on the rigid corpse of Heimdul Oath-breaker. "Soon," she muttered, her breath steaming in the cold. "Soon, all this will be over."

2

Torches flared and guttered, casting a thin orange glow over the procession as it moved through stands of ash and oak. Thrice-nine men
and women wound their way down from the fortress-crowned heights of
Hrafnhaugr—that keel-shaped bluff men called Raven Hill. They walked
in ominous silence. No cortege for wedding or funeral was this, for neither
flute nor drum nor voices raised in gladness or mourning set their pace. Only
the jangle of war-harness and the creak of worn leather; each was clad in
the barbaric splendor of a bygone age, in ancient mail of bronze and iron, in
wolf skins and skulls, in girdles of brazen scale and pectorals of hammered
copper. The pale flesh of the north was lost beneath swirling tattoos done in
cinder and woad, beneath streaks and daubs of lampblack and ash that gave
them a peculiar cast—more beast than human. Black-nailed hands cradled
axes and sheathed swords, or clutched at the feather-hung shafts of short
stabbing spears.

They followed a path that brought them down near the water's edge, to
a ramshackle dock where a small boat waited, tied fast to the timber pilings.
The shoreline, here, formed a natural bight—a deep bay called Skærvík
where the black waters of Lake Vänern lapped at the steep, snow-clad flank
of Raven Hill. As they approached the dock, the men and women parted to
allow one of their number to shuffle forward. This figure was smaller than

9

the others and swathed from crown to calf in the pelt of an immense gray wolf, its skull still attached. The blue eyes that glared out from beneath the beast's heavy brow were sullen, angry.

The eldest woman present, hale and silver-haired, a shield-maiden in her youth whose skin bore more scars than wrinkles, stepped up to the smaller figure. "Dísa Dagrúnsdottir!" she said, her voice hard as flint. "The Fates have called you forth. They bid you take your place in the shadow of the Hooded One. Do you accept this charge?"

Eyes blazed from beneath the wolf's skull; the smaller figure said nothing.

"Do you accept?" thundered the old woman, scowling.

And Dísa Dagrúnsdottir, who would enter her sixteenth year with the next new moon, drew herself up to her full height and shrugged free of the ancient beast's pelt—which stank of sweat, and smoke, and old blood. Beneath, she wore a long black tunic, belted at the waist and heavy with runic embroidery worked in silver thread. Though small and wiry, she had the sharp, hungry eyes of a raptor. Like the other women present, Dísa's right cheek bore the tattoo of a raven; it marked her as a daughter of an ancient bloodline, a sisterhood as old as the foundations of Hrafnhaugr itself. Dísa flicked her head, causing rune-carved fetishes of bone woven into her black hair to click together like impatient thoughts.

"Do you accept?"

Dísa's thin lips peeled back in a snarl that spoke less of the fire of youth than of a long-cherished dream denied. Her sharp breath steamed.

"I do."

The old woman stared at Dísa for a long and uncomfortable moment, her seamed face an unreadable mask. Finally, she nodded. "Then go, and prove yourself worthy."

The old woman stepped aside.

Glowering, Dísa Dagrúnsdottir brushed past her and stalked to the end of the dock. She sprang into the boat and arrayed herself on a bench in the bow. The old woman gestured; two from their number, a man and a woman, followed Dísa. The man clambered aboard and ran out the oars even as the woman untied the ropes holding the boat fast to the dock and shoved off; in the last possible instant, she leapt aboard and took her place at the steering tiller.

No words of farewell passed Dísa's lips; she stared daggers at the spine-rigid old woman as the oars bit into the dark breast of Skærvík and the boat shot away, the creak of wood, the hiss of water, and the guttural *whuff* of the oarsman's breath the only sounds.

And slowly, the boat vanished into the murky night.

A man came to stand alongside the old woman. Heavyset, his chestnut beard shot through with silver, he thrust his hands into his gold-threaded girdle and rocked back on his heels. "If the Hooded One rejects her, I might yet be persuaded to find a place for her in my household. What say you, Sigrún?"

The old woman, Sigrún, glanced sidelong at the man. Hreðel, he was called; the torque of twisted gold he wore around his bull neck marked him as a man of consequence. For all that he was master of Hrafnhaugr, and her chieftain, Sigrún had known Hreðel since he was a lad—soft, sleepy-eyed Hreðel, who drank too much and worried too much and coddled his only son the way southern matrons coddle their daughters. "Will you and your boy share her, then?"

Hreðel frowned. "Don't be crass. I make the offer in good faith. She has no mother, her father is dead, but my lad, Flóki, has taken a shine to her. If she returns—"

"*If* she returns," Sigrún said, nostrils flaring, "and the mantle of priestess is not hers, then she will have no place among the Daughters of the Raven."

"Surely you would not exile your own granddaughter?"

Sigrún turned her head; her fierce gaze pierced and held Hreðel like a huntsman's spear. "Exile? No, Hreðel, if the Hooded One sends her back in dishonor, nothing as fragile as kinship will save her. If she fails, that daft girl dies by my hand."

THE PROW OF THE BOAT surged in time with the oarsman's strokes. Overhead, stars peeked through jagged rents in the clouds; the night grew old. Soon, dawn would stain the eastern sky, and where would she be? Dísa sat in silence, contemplating the answer as the far shore drew nearer—looming like an ominous prophecy she could not escape. Would dawn find her a slave? Or would she even live to see the sun's rise?

In one fist, Dísa clutched a smooth stone bearing a deeply graven rune—*Dagaz*. She bore its twin inked into the flesh of her shoulder, done by her father's own hand when she was but an infant. That rune . . . this stone, these were the foundations of her doom.

Like the sacred runes, the Daughters of the Raven numbered twenty-four. Never more and never less; drawn from the ancestral families who founded Hrafnhaugr, the Daughters each bore a tattooed rune corresponding to the first letter of their name. The rune was how the Fates decided who among the Daughters would serve as priestess to the Hooded One, who was the Tangled God's immortal herald, and the law-speaker and protector of Hrafnhaugr.

Dísa recalled the anticipation, the fear that crackled through the village a week past, when hunters found the old priestess—a crone called Kolgríma—dead near the mouth of that ravine they called the Scar. As the eldest of the Daughters of the Raven, it fell upon Sigrún, Dísa's own grandmother, to oversee the selection of a new priestess. It was, Dísa thought, a very simple matter: Sigrún gathered the other twenty-three Daughters together by the Raven Stone at the center of the village. She dispatched a nimble youth to shimmy up the face of the Stone and retrieve from its niche a sealed clay pot. For fifty-eight years, this pot had rested in the carved recess at the crown of the stone, placed there when old Kolgríma had taken up the mantle of priestess. It was light, hollow, its surface scoured and pitted by the elements. Gingerly, the youth passed it down to her grandmother.

As Dísa and the other Daughters watched, Sigrún smashed the pot against the side of the Raven Stone and from the shards drew forth the graven rock the young woman now held in her hand. *Her rune, Dagaz.* And in a twinkling, Dísa's saw her hopes dashed. She did not wish to serve the Hooded One. The mantle she wanted most was that of shieldmaiden, to raid the Norse and the Danes for cattle and gold, to wield sword and spear against the enemies of the Raven-Geats; she wanted her name spoken in awe as much as she wanted to draw the eye of blessed Freyja, who had first choice from among the slain heroes of the ages. But no. The Gods had decided her fate in an instant, when this flat rune-carved river rock peeked forth from shards of dark clay, from the remains of a pot that had sat in a niche for decades. She—

The keel of the boat scraped the rocky shingle that was their destination. Dísa started at the sound. A single lamp burned on a post near the water's edge. The girl exhaled as the woman in the stern left the tiller and came to her side.

"It is time, cousin," she said, placing a reassuring hand on the younger woman's shoulder. Like Dísa, the woman had black, fetish-hung hair and a raven tattoo on her high-boned cheek. A white scar bisecting the bridge of her nose, twice broken, did nothing to soften the hard planes of her features. She'd known Odin's weather, and Dísa knew jealousy.

"Eager to get shut of me, Auða?" Dísa bridled at her cousin's touch. Shrugging off her hand, she stood and vaulted over the side of the boat. The lake was shallow, here, and its icy water lapped at her ankles. "Go, then, and leave me to it!" Dísa slapped at the boat's hull and tried to push it off the shingle, but to no avail. Flustered, she spat and made to turn away. Auða leaned down from the prow and caught her arm. Iron fingers dragged her back around.

"Go to him like this, with an anger-filled heart," the older woman hissed, "and he will send you back shorter by a head. Do you understand? These tantrums end now, or they will be the end of you."

The man at the oars, who was Hrútr, Auða's bedmate, ducked his head and looked away.

Dísa said nothing for a moment; she stared at her feet, at the foam-flecked pebbles of the shingle and the dark waters splashing and ebbing over them. Her shoulders trembled. "I do not want this, Auða," she said, her voice hoarse with pent-up resentment. "The old hag sends me to live a thrall's life, and death!"

"And more the fool you are if you believe that," Auða replied. "You think this is Sigrún's doing? That she placed your rune in a jar a generation ago, when she was but a girl herself? Do you not see the hand of the Gods in this, Dísa? They've *chosen* you, singled you out for greatness . . . or for failure. If you go to your death it's only because you did not prove yourself worthy of their gift."

"Gift? Call it what it is, cousin: slavery! The Gods have chained me to the ankle of the Hooded One! I will be no better than one who lives and dies in obscurity!" Dísa knotted her hands into fists; she wanted to smash something, to vent her rage before it filled her throat and choked the life from her. She wanted to scream. "Where is the worth in that? Where is the glory?"

"In the Hooded One's shadow, cousin, there is no room for the obscure. In her day, men from Uppsala to Jutland feared Kolgríma's name. Your name will spread even farther. You have my word on it," Auða said.

"How?"

The older woman seized a handful of Dísa's dark hair, and gave her a playful shake. "It begins by not standing here whining like a spoiled child."

Dísa drew a deep breath and squared her shoulders. She nodded to Auða, though a hundred more questions boiled around in the cauldron of her skull. Questions like: why did men fear Kolgríma? Dísa knew her as a doddering old crone who fell to an ignominious death. How had her name spread? How would her own spread, as one poised to become little more than a handmaiden to the inscrutable Hooded One? Dísa had enough inborn wisdom to know her questions would find no answers, here. Not with Auða. She glanced over her shoulder at the lamp-lit pole, its crest carved with a stylized eye—the sigil of her soon-to-be master; beyond, she could see the beginnings of a stone-paved path beneath a mantle of snow. It led inland . . . but to where? To what? Glory? Death? Immortality? Or mere servitude until the weight of her years caused her to stumble along a well-worn trail and fall into obscurity and a shallow grave?

"Maybe you're right, cousin," Dísa said, turning back to face Auða. "Maybe I am a spoiled child. But maybe I am only angry because I would at least have liked to have had a hand in deciding my own destiny."

"Wouldn't we all." Auða reached down against the strakes and came up with a cloth-covered basket that contained Hrafnhaugr's offerings to the Hooded One—slices of smoked meat and fish, barley bread and hard cheese, dried apples, flasks of last year's mead, bits of silver and gold, and scraped parchments bearing a litany of ills that needed to be addressed, from boundary disputes to blood feuds. Dísa took the basket and set it safely ashore. "Go now, cousin, and come back in the Hooded One's favor."

The two women's eyes met; a look of knowing, of understanding passed between them, and then Dísa put her shoulder into it and shoved the boat's keel off the shingle. She watched as Hrútr backed water; she watched her cousin's face, a glimmer of white in the snow-flecked darkness. She watched it fade into the night.

"Or don't come back at all," Dísa finished for her, in a voice that did not carry. She exhaled, then, her breath steaming, and turned. It was time to sort out her fate. Time to rid herself of the worry of not knowing. Nodding to herself, she slipped her rune stone into a pouch at her waist and caught up the basket. Striding to the head of the path, Dísa Dagrúnsdottir made her way inland.

SHE WALKED HALF A LEAGUE, ascending along the path through snow-clad trees and around great boulders. This trail was not unknown to her; two years before, she had followed Jarl Hreðel's son, Flóki, up this way, to see with her own eyes the boundary between their world and the Elder World. An ancient compact promised death to any who crossed it, save the priestess of the Hooded One. Only she could approach him, only she could look upon him, only she could speak to him. As far as Dísa knew, the Hooded One never set foot in Hrafnhaugr—despite being its protector. None alive, save Kolgríma, had ever laid eyes upon him. There were stories, of course. Jarl Hreðel boasted he saw him as a boy, tall and forbidding; Auða claimed she saw him near the bridge over the Hveðrungr River, at the edge of their territory—a shadowy figure wearing antlers, his face like naked bone; a dozen others shared the same tale. All save Sigrún. That old crow kept silent, though hers was the last generation to fight beyond Hrafnhaugr's borders— surely she had laid eyes upon him?

Dísa wondered: was he truly beyond mortal reckoning, as the legends professed, a deathless *úlfhéðnar,* grim and inscrutable? Or was "Hooded One" merely a title borne by a succession of up-country brawlers, a mantle em- broidered by skalds and passed from father to son? With no little trepidation, she wondered if the duties of priestess included bearing sons. Regardless, it was an arrangement as old as Hrafnhaugr itself.

The boundary stone lay at the crest of the hill, in a clearing that was open to the sky. Dísa paused and looked around her. Dawn was still more than an hour away. A heavy pall of cloud lay over the earth, and fat flakes of snow swirled down to hiss in the greasy orange flames of the remaining torch. Behind, Dísa could see the waters of the bay called Skærvík and beyond, the faint twinkle of lights atop Raven Hill; ahead, the path plunged into a deep valley. She approached the boundary stone—a waist-high eidolon that bore the faint suggestion of a squatting figure, perhaps a troll or some manner of *landvættir.* Old offering pots lay at its feet, weathered and broken; scraps of rune-etched wood and old parchment were jammed into its grasping hands. For an instant, Dísa wondered what would happen if she simply dropped her basket here and walked away, if she refused the honor of serving the Hooded One. *Come back in his favor or not at all.* How long would she survive in the wilds as one of the *vargr,* as an outlaw? *Not long enough,* she decided.

Dísa clutched her basket tighter. Then, holding her breath, she stepped over the boundary and into the shadow of the Elder World.

Nothing happened.

She exhaled.

There was no shift to her senses, no feeling of dislocation. The sky did not change, nor the ground underfoot. Indeed, none of the things Flóki had warned her about came to pass—no lightning, no thunder, no guardian spirit demanding tribute, no test of worthiness. Merely the wind off the lake and flakes of snow drifting from one side to the other with apparent ease.

"Flóki, you lying wretch." The beads in her hair jangled as she shrugged and continued on her way. Down into the valley she went; but for the poles with their guttering torches, she'd soon have been lost. Despite the thin light, Dísa picked her way with exaggerated care, mindful of eroded ruts, tangling roots, and scree. A quarter of an hour later, she heard the gurgle and splash of water, and caught the strong, earthy stench of a mire. Beneath it was a darker scent—one she had known as a child, when her father would come back from hunting: the smells of smoke, dried blood, and offal.

Her destination lay at the bottom of the valley, at the heart of a string bog that drained through crevice and cleft into the dark waters of Lake Vänern. The natural path ended and a corduroy of logs led to a small hillock. Torches lit the approach; more flared at the crest of the hillock, where an ancient longhouse stood like a sentinel from a bygone era.

Though largely lost to the cloak of night, enough ambient torchlight spilled over the structure to give Dísa a hint as to its size and grandeur. Great carved posts of age-blackened timber upheld a roof of mossy shingle, like the scales of a great serpent. Smoke leaked from the gables, and from the clerestory atop the roof. Dísa found her gaze drawn to the porch, made by a pair of beams overhanging the gable, their ends hewn into the shapes of a dragon and a snarling wolf; beneath this, a door yawned.

The young woman shivered, clutched her basket as though it were a talisman with the power to protect. A cold sweat of fear slithered down her spine, taking with it her resolve; Dísa felt eyes on her. Malicious. Unseen.

You belong here, she told herself. *You belong here. You are the priestess of the*

Hooded One. Thus, by tamping down her fear of the unknown and shoring up her courage, she was able to place one foot on the corduroy path. Then the other. Again, nothing leaped from the darkness to challenge her. Shadows danced in the flickering torchlight, and the feelings of scrutiny did not abate.

Slowly, she walked to the foot of the hillock. Stakes and spears thrust up from the damp loam around her; some flew tattered banners from clans that had long since vanished from the North. Others bore grisly reminders of the Hooded One's writ to protect the lands of the Raven-Geats: skulls of naked bone alongside severed heads in various stages of decay. She could smell the violence, like the musk from some feral beast that rose from the corpses that lay half-buried in the bog—smears of whitish-blue flesh in the dank undergrowth, rusting helmets and armor, rotting shields, broken blades.

And looking about, Dísa apprehended the truth: it would be no mere man she served.

You belong here. You are the priestess of the Hooded One. For a moment, surrounded by the sights and smells of death, that thought brought a crushing sense of despair to Dísa. *You belong here. The Gods have decreed it. Till the end of your days you will be a creature of shadows, a servant who toils for the Tangled God's herald. You will bear witness to the inhuman things that snuffle at the threshold of the world so the folk of Hrafnhaugr can sleep soundly at night.* But Dísa shook her head, beads ticking, and shrugged off her seeming hopelessness. *No!* "I will write my own destiny," she said aloud, her voice profaning the eerie silence. And with a newfound sense of purpose, she placed one slender foot on the lowest step leading up to the longhouse porch . . .

And stopped. Her spine went rigid with fear. For behind her, Dísa Dagrúnsdottir heard a cold and humorless chuckle, as harsh as the fall of stones into an open grave. The voice that accompanied it came from no human throat:

"Will you now? And what will this destiny say, eh? That you died a lost little bird, bound for the stewpots? *Nár,* after I skin you and joint you, there won't even be a stringy morsel left."

3

Dísa took her foot from the step; she made to turn, so she might put a face to the voice that left her cold. As she did so, however, unseen fingers clamped down on the nape of her neck. The young woman flinched as her ears caught a familiar sound—the sinister hiss of iron on leather.

"Move and I'll gut you, wretch!" hissed the figure at her back, its breath hot and reeking. She heard snuffling, as though it sought to divine her intent through scent. "Where's the old crow I usually deal with, eh? That's her basket you're hugging, so you must know her. Or did you steal it from her and decide just to trespass onto my lands for a lark?"

"She . . . she's dead," Dísa said, her voice trembling. "Kolgríma's dead. Our hunters found her three days past, at the bottom of the Scar."

The fingers clasping her neck tightened. Hard nails dug into her flesh. An explosive grunt, somewhere between a cough and a curse, came from a place inches above her right ear. "*Faugh!* And what are you, then?"

"The . . . the Hooded One's new priestess. I—"

She stopped as the tip of a long-seax entered her field of vision, its blade marked by the watery gray-black whorls of pattern welding. The blacknailed hand that held it was the color of old slate, knotted with dark veins and sinew; amid a webwork of ashen scars Dísa saw a single tattoo between its thumb and forefinger—a stylized eye done in faded cinnabar. With a flick

19

of its wrist the figure knocked the basket's lid askew. Dísa heard another round of snuffling followed by a low chuckle.

"You what, little wretch?"

"I . . ." Dísa Dagrúnsdottir closed her eyes; she dredged down deep, clawing through ropy tendrils of fear until she found the cold, hard core of her anger. She saw once more the disapproving stare of her grandmother, who shone like a *valkyrja* in the esteem of her people; she heard once again the whispers of her sisters, the other Daughters of the Raven, who thought her but a silly girl and unfit for this so-called honor; she saw again the look of sadness in Flóki's eyes, a look mirrored in the eyes of old Hreðel, who had had his high hopes—that he might wed his son to Sigrún's granddaughter—dashed. She seized that core of anger and held on to it. Dísa opened her eyes. "I am here by Fate's own hand, you lout!" she said. "Release me and stand aside! Better yet, release me and show me into your master's presence!"

"So-ho! My *master,* is it?" the figure said, its tone dripping mockery. "My *master* is the one you seek? By all means, then. You'd best leg it, little bird, and double quick! Don't want to keep my *master* waiting!"

The hand around her neck gave her a shove forward. She stumbled, catching herself before she could fall. Of the figure, all she saw as it shouldered past her and bounded up the steps to the longhouse was a swirling cloak of wolf pelts and a mane of black, plaited hair worked with beads of bone and silver.

Dísa cursed under her breath and followed, albeit more slowly. She reached the porch beneath the gable, upheld by carved posts, and found the door to the heart of the longhouse standing open. She paused in the ruddy light of the threshold, wincing at the stench that flowed forth. It was a mix of sweat and smoke, the coppery tang of blood mixed with the feral stink of unwashed animal pelts. Dísa exhaled.

"Halla!" She heard the figure bellowing from inside. "Halla, Ymir take you! Where are you?"

Carefully, like a warrior crossing into enemy territory, Dísa entered the longhouse. It was not all that different from the longhouses of Hrafnhaugr. Posts of rough-hewn timber ran in two rows down its length, supporting roof beams thick with cobwebs and dust. The floor beneath her feet was hard-packed dirt carpeted in old ash, bits of slag, and flaked hammerscale, while raised platforms to the left and right provided places to sit, sleep, or eat. A long stone fire pit ran half the length of the longhouse. Stifling heat bled from its bed of glowing embers.

By that dim and sanguine light, Dísa beheld the Hooded One's domain. She expected something more ordered, more formal, like the sacred enclosure at Old Uppsala—now nothing but ashes and memory thanks to the Nailed God's followers. Her mind had constructed a temple-space; the reality was closer to a troll's lair or the bolt-hole of some hoard-hungry dragon: on each side, gold and silver shimmered in the ember-glow—torques and arm-rings, fine-wrought chains and mint-stamped coins, bent offering plates and broken altar pieces; bronze there was, too, and the red gleam of hammered copper. Among this spoil lay the trophies of war: swords and daggers with simple hilts, great maces, Frankish axes on hafts of aged oak, and spears so old their ash-wood shafts had warped; shields leaned against the central posts, some round and others shaped like inverted teardrops; hauberks of rust-spotted mail lay draped over ancient breastplates etched with the eagles of a dead empire; the skins of wolf and bear, silk gambesons torn and stained with blood, myriad belts, scabbards, sheaths, and girdles—all taken from centuries of dead foes.

"Halla, damn you!"

Dísa found the figure who had accosted her outside. He stared back at her from across the fire pit, his head tilted, his right eye like an ember that burned with a light of its own; his left eye was the color of old bone. His saturnine face was as sharp and lean as a starveling wolf's, with a jutting chin, heavy cheekbones, and a craggy brow. A jagged scar bisected the bridge of his nose, crossed his left eye, and continued up until it vanished beneath gold-and-bone beaded braids of coarse black hair at his left temple.

"You . . ." Dísa said. "You're no man!"

The creature's thin lips peeled back over sharp yellow teeth. "For which you dunghill swine should be thankful," he replied. He sprawled back in a throne-like chair that sat at the center of the longhouse, bandy legs knotted with muscle thrust out before him. He wore a Norseman's hobnailed boots, a kilt of russet linen and iron-studded leather strips, and a bronze breastplate gone nearly black with age—its muscled belly cut down below mid-sternum and replaced with a riveted drape of mail and leather. The war-belt of a Saxon prince, made of fine wide leather with clasps of carved copper and red gold, held his sheathed long-seax and a Frankish axe.

"What are you?"

The creature leaned forward, nostrils flaring. "Your master, little bird."

Dísa blinked. "You're the Hooded One?"

"Halla!"

"I am here." An eerie voice answered from the shadows behind him. Dísa caught the pale glimmer of flesh as a hunchbacked crone inched closer, an outcast hag who kept to the gloom at the edges of the longhouse. She wore a ragged green dress and no shoes, her black-soled feet inured to the cold of the bog. A grimace twisted her thin-lipped mouth as her eyes, two opaque orbs framed by fey locks of ashen gray, fixed Dísa in an unblinking stare. When she spoke again, her voice was that of a girl barely out of childhood. "He is called many things, child," she said. "Corpse-maker, Life-quencher, and the Bringer of Night; he is the Son of the Wolf and Brother of the Serpent. You bear witness to the last of the *kaunar,* child. The last son of Bálegyr left to plague Miðgarðr. He is Grimnir, and he is all that stands between you and the hymn-singing hordes of the Nailed God."

And Grimnir—whose name meant "the Hooded One"—leaned back, grinning at the young woman's discomfiture.

Dísa was at a loss for words. Indeed, she wondered, then, if she'd crossed into the realm of nightmare when she stepped past the boundary stones at the crest of the hill. Nothing was as her elders had told her—though now she understood why only one person served this thing that called itself the Hooded One. Would the men of Hrafnhaugr have countenanced a beast protecting them? And would they keep their swords sheathed even now if they knew what it was that settled their disputes and squabbles? She stared, gaped, and tried to assemble the pieces of what she knew, what she'd seen, into an answer she could grasp.

"He's . . . You're the Tangled God's immortal herald? You're who defends Hrafnhaugr, who serves as our law-speaker? You?"

Grimnir's grin turned to a snarl. "Aye, me. And scant thanks I get from you lot! A few scraps of food, a bit of gold, and for what? So you sniveling wretches can sleep at night?"

"Then, why do you do it?" Dísa glanced from Grimnir to Halla. "Why protect us if there's nothing in it for you?"

At that, Grimnir *harrumphed.* He shifted his weight; one black-nailed finger idly traced an old carving on the arm of his chair. "Stop your yammering and bring me that basket, little bird," he said, after an uncomfortable silence.

"And be quick about it! Got a craving for something besides that old hag's toadstool soup and maggoty bread!"

With halting steps, Dísa approached his chair and held out the basket. She was close enough to see the tattoos snaking across his gnarled and knotted arms, serpents and briars twisting among a webwork of old scars, runes that spelled out his enemy's doom in cinder and woad. Rings of gold, silver, and wrought iron decorated his thick biceps. Grunting, he snatched the basket from her hands.

Grimnir set it on the floor before his seat and hunched over it, his good eye agleam as he riffled through its contents. The rolled parchments he tossed to Halla without a second thought, and then went straight for the mead and the smoked pork.

He uncorked a flask with his teeth, spat the wooden stopper into the fire, and took a long pull—lowering it only after half the flask's contents had gone down his gullet. Grimnir loosed a gusty sigh; he wiped a rivulet of mead off his chin with the back of his hand and sat back, gnawing on a knuckle of smoked hock.

Dísa felt Halla's leathery fingers plucking at the back of her tunic. She scowled at the old woman and brushed her hand away.

"Kolgríma's dead?" Halla said.

Dísa nodded. "We found her three days ago, at the mouth of the Scar, where it empties into Skærvík. From the spoor it looked like she'd been seeking something." The young woman did not miss the sharp look Grimnir shot the old crone. A hint of a frown creased her forehead. *What were they hiding?*

"And the rune you bear?"

Dísa took the rune stone from the small pouch at her waist and held it out to Halla. The crone took it in her palm; she hunched over it, her long fingers twitching, never still.

"*Dagaz . . .*" she breathed; her milky eyes rolled back into her head. She hissed in a hypnotic voice: "The rune of Day, a harbinger of cataclysmic change—the light burning away the darkness. The endless winter is drawing to a close. The Wolf whose name is Mockery nips at the heels of Sól, who guides the Chariot of the Sun! Soon, the Serpent will writhe! The Dragon—"

"*Nár!*" Grimnir snapped. He flung a pork knuckle at Halla's head. "Get ahold of yourself, witch!"

The crone shook and turned away, still muttering, still staring down at the rune stone cupped in her trembling hands. "The Dragon . . . the bones of the Dragon . . ."

Grimnir's good eye rested on Dísa; for her part, she glared at the two of them as though they were nothing more than cheap mountebanks who had struck gold by playing the simple folk of Hrafnhaugr for fools. He sniffed in disdain and looked away, saying: "Wipe that snarl off your face, little bird, before—"

"Dísa," she cut him off. Suddenly, Auða's words of warning, her counsel for Dísa to school her temper lest she pay with her head, fell off like an anchor rope; like a raft tossed by a tempest, her long-simmering anger came unmoored. She would not be their silent accomplice. Not like Kolgríma; not like the score of other so-called priestesses who had come before her. "My name is Dísa, you black-hearted wretch! I am the daughter of Dagrún Sigrúnsdottir, who was slain fighting the Danes and their Christian paymasters in the surf of the Skagerrak! My mother died to keep those wretched hymn-singers at bay because that was the Tangled God's will—or so Kolgríma told us. But that was just another lie, wasn't it?" The younger woman thrust an accusing finger at the parchments Halla had set aside. "Like the lie that you are the law-speaker of Hrafnhaugr, when you cannot even be bothered to look at the complaints of my people! And our defender? Was that a third lie? Scavenger, more like! Did my mother die just so you could pick clean the corpses of more dead Christians?" Even as she spoke the words, Dísa felt the icy talons of fear close about her throat. Her eyes grew as round as stones; she dared not move, dared not even breathe.

The air of the longhouse grew chill and silent. Smoke hung frozen in the air. Grimnir's neck tendons creaked as he slowly turned his head in Dísa's direction. The dead yellow bone of his left eye bore a circle of deep-etched runes inlaid with silver for an iris; his right blazed with fiery wrath.

Grimnir sucked his teeth and spat. "I see your tongue works, little bird, but do your legs?"

"I—" Dísa shivered. "I d-don't . . . ?"

But it was Halla who answered. "Run, child."

"Aye, run!" Grimnir snarled. "I'll even make it sporting! I'll give you to the ten-count."

To her credit, Dísa did not need to be told a third time. Though fear crackled down her spine, knotting in her stomach like a fist clenching her entrails, it did not root her to the spot. Nor did it cloud her mind.

"One," he said through gritted teeth. "Two."

Dísa spat at Grimnir's feet, turned, and bolted for the door. She paused at the count of three and snatched a Frankish axe from a pile of discarded weapons by the door. Its oak haft was the length of her forearm, with a flaring head no larger than a man's fist. She risked a glance back at Grimnir, who leaned forward in his seat and clutched at the armrests like they were the limbs of an enemy.

"Four."

Dísa allowed a hint of a smile to flirt with the corners of her mouth, and then she was gone. She would write her own destiny. And if she had to die, she would not go easily into the grave.

"FIVE," DÍSA MUTTERED, TRYING TO mimic Grimnir's cadence. She descended from the porch of the longhouse at a run, her feet barely touching the steps. She paused at the bottom, the axe clutched in both hands. Dawn was less than an hour off; atop the nearest pole another torch had gone out, its smoking head still reeking faintly of sulphur and lime.

"Six."

She knew in the pit of her belly she could not outrun him. Grimnir had the deep chest and rawboned limbs of a born predator—and the wide, snuffling nostrils of a tracker. For a heartbeat, she allowed self-pity to surface. *Damn me and my foolish tongue!* But she tamped that down before despair had a chance to take root. If she could not outrun him, she'd have to outfox him.

"Seven."

Though they loathed one another, her grandmother had nevertheless raised her not to be a victim. She knew how to escape and evade human trackers, how to lay ambushes, and how to hit a man hard before he could hit her—knowing she would only have one chance. Dísa plunged to her right, into the well of darkness left by the extinguished torch, and followed the base of the hillock along a path choked with dead weeds and nettles.

"Eight," she gasped, reaching the halfway mark.

The bog's stench was thick, mud and vegetable decay warring with rotting meat and waste. Without pause, Dísa scuttled up the side of the hillock. An ancient ash tree grew near the foundation of the longhouse, its trunk gnarled and bent like an old man; using its roots and tussocks of grass, she dragged herself up and into its shadow.

"Nine."

Dísa fell prone. The damp cold and the stench, the tall grass and the knotty ash tree, the inky darkness before first light—all these things worked to make her nigh-upon invisible. Her eyes watched the front of the long-house. She controlled her breathing, from gasping to slow and measured exhalations. Her breath steamed. For a moment, she wondered if Sigrún's hard lessons would be enough to save her.

"Ten."

And in the cold darkness, axe in hand, Dísa Dagrúnsdottir waited.

"TEN." GRIMNIR SPAT OUT A gobbet of gristle and heaved himself up. He drained the mead; cursing, he slung the empty pottery flask into the heart of the fire pit. Embers exploded. Halla watched them swirl up into the damp air as though they were sibylline stars.

Grimnir put a hand on the hilt of his seax. "I'll send them her head, and maybe those dunghill rats will send me a priestess who knows the value of respect!"

Halla caught his arm. "You mustn't harm her," she said.

"Oh, must I not?" Grimnir tore his arm free from her grasp. "I'll not sit idly by while some motherless whelp insults me!" Bronze rang as he rapped his knuckles against his armored chest. "Me! And after all I've done for them? They serve me! I do not serve them, and it's high time I reminded them of that!"

"Kill her," Halla said, "and you kill us all."

Grimnir's brows beetled; his good eye smoldered like a banked forge. "What are you yammering on about?"

"She is *Dagaz*!" Halla hissed. The crone leaned forward, her milky eyes burning with a passion of their own. She had the witch-sight, a gift made more potent by the blood of the *troldvolk*—the troll-folk—seething through her veins. "She bears the final rune! Do you not see it? The circle ends with her. Kill her, and the circle is broken ere the prophecy comes to fruition!"

"Bugger off, you old wretch!" Grimnir snorted and turned away. "You and your cursed prophecy! I've told you time and again that the age of prophecies and portents is over! The Old Ways are gone! This is the Nailed God's world now. The rest of us . . . we're just monsters who dwell in the gloaming, awaiting their blasted god's reckoning!"

"Then answer the girl's question, *skrælingr*," Halla said, using the derisive name given to Grimnir's people by the ancient Danes. He stopped, turned slowly. Halla continued, unabashed. "For thrice-times-ten-score years you've haunted the shadows of Raven Hill, you and old Gífr before you, slaying their enemies and accepting their sacrifices. You've played the part of their Hooded One, and for what? If the Old Ways cannot be resurrected, why do you stay?"

"You know why," he growled.

"I want to hear it from your lips!" Halla's childlike voice took on an even eerier quality, a guttural chant that echoed about the longhouse:

> "When the years tally | nine times nine times nine,
> Again, and war-reek | wafts like dragon breath;
> When Fimbulvetr | hides the pallid sun,
> The monstrous Serpent | shall writhe in fury."

Grimnir started forward. "Hold your tongue, hag!"

Halla, though, drew herself up to her full but unimposing height; wild silver locks framed the resolute crags of her face as she pressed on:

> "Sköll bays aloud | after Dvalin's toy.
> The fetter shall break | and the wolf run free;
> Dark-jawed devourer | of light-bringer's steed.
> And in Vänern's embrace | the earth splits asunder.

> "From the depths a barrow | rises through the water,
> The stone-girdled hall | of Aranæs, where dwells
> Jörmungandr's spawn, | the Malice-Striker.
> Its dread bones rattle | and herald an end."

"I said shut your stinking mouth!" Two steps brought Grimnir within arm's reach; he lashed out. The back of his knotted fist struck Halla across the cheek. A human woman would have reeled away, nursing a broken jaw at best . . . or a broken neck. But Halla, who sprang from the loins of Járnviðja, the troll-queen of ancient Myrkviðr, the dark wood of legend, took the blow in stride. Her narrowed eyes bled milky fire as she turned her head slightly and spat out a blackened fragment of tooth.

"You know the last stanza, son of Bálegyr," she said, wiping her mouth with the back of her hand. "How does it run?"

"Faugh!" Grimnir snarled and turned away. But then, in a voice as tuneless as a broken chanter pipe, he added:

"Wolf shall fight she-Wolf | in Raven's shadow;
An axe age, a sword age, | as Day gives way to Night.
And Ymir's sons dance | as the Gjallarhorn
Kindles the doom | of the Nailed God's folk."

Halla nodded. "You stay," she said quietly, "because you know the prophecy is true."

"True? Aye, I know there's a bit of truth to it, hag," Grimnir replied. "But I also know there's a damn sight more to it than what's in that wretched scrap of doggerel! You think I chose to live among these swine, to play protector to a village of half-wits, because some *skald* cobbled together a prophecy from a tale he half-heard? Ha! You're a daft old bat!" Grimnir stabbed a finger at the open door. "Now, cease your prattle. I have a little bird to hunt."

"Let her be," Halla said. "She is *Dagaz,* you fool. She is the Day who gives way to Night—"

"Fool, is it?" Grimnir rounded on her. "Let me tell you something that maybe even those worm-riddled curds inside your skull can grasp. Your precious prophecy? It might be true, but that doesn't mean it will ripen and bear fruit! There are other things at work here, besides a bit of old verse."

"Like what?"

An ancient hate gleamed in Grimnir's eye. "Like oaths," he hissed. "Oaths sworn in blood and on bone. Sworn in the name of the Sly One, Father Loki, and of frost-bearded Ymir, sire of giants. Oaths of vengeance, woven long before some dunghill swine muttered about years tallying nine times nine times nine again. Grim days are coming, witch. And with them come justice and a reckoning . . . justice for Raðbolg, my kinsman, and for Skríkja, who gave me life. And a reckoning for that slippery eel you're pinning your hopes on, that so-called Malice-Striker!"

Halla's face turned to a mask of rage. "You would betray your own kind? Side with the vermin of the Nailed God?"

"My kind? So-ho! Where were you and the other troll-spawned whores of Myrkviðr when your precious dragon came against Orkahaugr, eh? In the days after Bálegyr fell at Mag Tuiredh?" Grimnir spat, recalling the cataclys-mic battle in distant Ireland where his father was slain fighting the *vestálfar*, the West-elves of Èriu. "Oh, aye, I remember: hiding in your caves, with your potions and your brews! I side with my people, hag, though I may be all that's left of them.

"As for the hymn-singers and their Nailed God, the whole wretched lot are dug in like maggots! Kill one and five more spring up!" He snorted in derision. "They are here to stay and no prophecy is going to change that. You'd best get used to it."

Halla turned away, her eyes fixed on the rune she clutched in her gnarled fingers. "We shall see. The prophecy is truth. Oaths or no, it still has the power to remake the world."

Grimnir stared at her a moment, his gaze inscrutable, then ducked his head and spat. Nostrils flaring, he loped from the longhouse to pick up the trail of the little bird who'd fled.

"Do not harm her, *skrælingr*!" Halla bellowed after him. "Do you hear me? She is a part of this!"

DÍSA REACHED THE TWENTY-COUNT, THEN thirty; she was fast approaching the count of fifty when she finally decided to rise. The ground's cold damp-ness had seeped through the fabric of her tunic; that, coupled with the sick palsy that followed on the heels of panic, left her feeling brittle and hollow, like an ice-bound reed.

She wondered, as she rose to a crouch: had this all been in jest? The beast's idea of a joke? Only a healthy inborn sense of skepticism kept her from rushing out and confronting the so-called law-giver of Hrafnhaugr. Instead, she inched forward, intent on peering around the porch-front of the longhouse; that's when Dísa heard their voices. She crept closer. She was careful of her footing. Through a narrow window above her head, the young woman heard Grimnir's harsh accent, ancient and distinct; she heard the weird crone's voice devolve into singsong chanting. She drew herself up, straining to hear the words, when she heard the meaty thump of a fist striking flesh. Dísa froze.

Had he killed her?

The haft of the axe clutched in Dísa's fist grew slick with sweat. She changed hands and wiped her palm down the thigh of her tunic. That crone was his ally, she reckoned, perhaps even his friend. And if that wretched monster could kill a friend without second thought . . .

Dísa cursed. She should have skinned out when she had the chance. *Aye, she thought, I could have been halfway to the boundary stone, by now. Instead, I'm standing here like a damnable fool, waiting for death.* That revelation brought a snarl to the young woman's lips. She bared her teeth, her face settling into a mask of resolve. She would wait no longer.

Dísa crept to the corner. There, she crouched in the well of darkness left by the extinguished torch. Ruddy light spilled out from beneath the porch, its wolf-and-serpent carved posts throwing long shadows over the head of the steps. To Dísa's credit, she felt a momentary sense of relief when she heard the old woman's voice once more. It rose to a hard-edged shriek: "Do not harm her, *skrælingr*! Do you hear me? She is a part of this!"

And though Dísa Dagrúnsdottir was glad the crone was alive, it did nothing to lessen her resolve. The die was cast. She let the axe drop to her side, her grip on its haft firm but not rigid—just as Sigrún had taught her.

Grimnir's shadow preceded him. Dísa watched it stretch into the night; she held perfectly still, not even daring to breathe as his apish body filled the doorway of the longhouse. Chuckling with anticipation, he crossed the threshold and took off at a slow lope. Grimnir grabbed one of the carved posts supporting the roof of the porch as he went by, using it to swing himself out toward the head of the steps. There, he stopped and bent nearly double, sniffing and snuffling as he sought Dísa's trail.

Dísa heard her grandmother's voice in her head: *You will have one chance,* Sigrún had told them last autumn as she and Auða schooled the younger Daughters of the Raven on how to handle themselves. Scant few of the others would become like the pair of them—*skjaldmær,* grim and deadly maidens into whose hearts the Gods had decanted the wine of slaughter—but they all had to know how to use axe and knife, to defend Hrafnhaugr against the depredations of the Norse, the Christian Swedes, or the hymn-singing Danes. *One chance! You must put your man down before he can lay his hands upon you. Strike fast! Strike hard!* Dísa recalled Sigrún's shoulders rising and falling in a fatalistic shrug. *Or die.*

Strike fast. Strike hard. Or die.

Dísa Dagrúnsdottir did just that.

She forced aside every shred of fear, every scrap of doubt. Shoved it down deep and locked it away. What grew in its place was rage, black and icy. Why should she run in fear? She sprang from the loins of Dagrún Spear-breaker; she was a Daughter of the Raven, bearer of the rune *Dagaz*; she was the Day-strider, chosen of the Gods. She was *skjaldmær*, shieldmaiden.

The call of her blood stung Dísa to action. She came off the wall and rounded the corner; she crossed through the bar of light spilling from the interior of the longhouse, heedless of shadows. The young woman's stride lengthened until she moved at speed, but as silent as a hunting cat.

Strike fast.

Dísa angled for Grimnir's blind side. A tiny voice deep within warned her that she risked committing blasphemy by slaying the Tangled God's herald, but her pride crushed it. If she could slay him then he was no immortal, and if he was no immortal . . .

Strike hard.

Dísa was on him a heartbeat later. She came on in a rush; the head of her stolen axe whistled through the chill air as she aimed its killing edge for the back of the beast's skull. Breath hissed between clenched teeth. She threw her right shoulder into the blow, adding the weight behind her right leg as it touched the earth. Dísa imagined that blow landing; she imagined the jarring moment of impact, the wet crunch. She imagined his skull coming apart in a welter of blood and brain. All of this Dísa saw in the twinkling that remained. Triumph swelled in her breast . . .

Or die.

And then, he moved.

Like a serpent, Grimnir twisted to his right; he ducked under her arm, letting the axe-head skim so close to his skull that it clinked against the bone and silver beads woven into his hair. He spun around and came up behind her. And while this change in fortunes left her confused, to her credit Dísa did not falter and pitch forward on her face. No, she did as Auða or her grandmother would have done—she adapted.

With a grace and speed she did not know she possessed, Dísa recovered from that missed blow and reversed her momentum. Sinew creaked as she wheeled to her right, the axe in her fist coming up in a backhand strike. And while she thought she was fast, Dísa still moved a fraction too slow.

Her wrist slapped into the palm of Grimnir's black-nailed hand.

For an age of the earth, it seemed, they stared at one another—one eye as bright and red as a forge-glede boring into two as deep and blue as lake ice. Dísa saw nothing human in that gaze. No fear, no apprehension; neither pity nor kindness. Only hate. Hate as ancient as Yggðrasil, itself, and as long as Time. Hate that knew no border or boundary. Here was a creature of the Elder World, who wanted nothing more than to see the doom of Ragnarök come to pass. And as the elongated span of time drew to a close, for the briefest instant Dísa fancied she saw the glimmer of something familiar in Grimnir's darkling visage . . . the pale shadow of respect.

The tableau held a moment longer, and then it was gone. Dísa had time to apprehend a slow and malicious smile twisting Grimnir's thin lips; his nostrils flared as he drew a deep draught of air. Fingers like steel cords tightened around her slender wrist.

And then, she felt an explosion of pain below her ribs that wrenched a scream from her. Twice, Grimnir punched her in the right kidney—quick jabs that sent waves of nausea rippling up through her frame.

Still, Dísa did not crumple.

With an incoherent cry of fury, the young woman twisted in his grasp and struck across her body. She put everything into that blow: every scrap of rage and fear, every hurt done to her over the span of her short life, the weight of every grief-shed tear. All of it, she thrust into the knuckles of her left hand even as she drove her fist into the bridge of his nose. She felt the crunch of cartilage. Grimnir's head rocked back; ropes of black blood, thick and reeking of wet iron, dribbled from his nostrils and down his chin. But as he recovered from the blow the beast's smile widened, lips peeling back over sharp yellow canines.

From somewhere behind them, Dísa heard the eerie voice of the witch, Halla: "*Skrælingr!* Hold—"

If Grimnir heard, he gave no sign. His eye never flickered toward the sound; the bloody smile he wore turned to a snarl. His free hand snaked up from behind and clamped down savagely on the nape of Dísa's neck.

She struggled, expecting death to come with a sharp twist.

And still, she fought. But before she could so much as draw her arm back for that final, futile blow, Grimnir responded with a sharp forward snap of his head, laughing as he smashed the hard bones of his forehead into her face.

Dísa heard the dull crunch of impact before her world went white and silent and she knew nothing more.

4

*S*he wakes to smoke and to ash and to the heat of crackling flames. Clad in tattered mail, her limbs feel heavy and useless, weary from fighting. Her dark hair is scorched; her silver beads and bone fetishes have long since turned to slag and charred coal. Blood smears her face. She touches it, feels naked bone beneath her questing fingertips. A flap of skin hangs there by a slender thread of flesh. And her heart breaks, for she apprehends what it is—her raven tattoo, given to her as a child and made larger each year as she grew into a young woman. It is the mark of her people. It is her identity—and the edge of some hymn-singer's knife blade has flayed it from her skull. With exaggerated care, she pulls it free and cradles it in her hands.

It is a dead thing, all pale flesh and lifeless ink. But it has served her well and it deserves more than a shallow grave. With solemn purpose, she lays the tattooed half of her face on one of the myriad fires burning close at hand. She watches that scrap of flesh crumble to ash; she watches as the raven imprisoned within flies free on wings wrought of ink and dreams. She watches as it rises into the fiery heavens to join the conflagration that is Ragnarök.

The young woman sighs and clambers to her feet, missing already the ethereal part of herself her raven had embodied. Without it, she is nothing more than flesh, bone, and mud—like the corpses that surround her. They lie amid the burning wreckage of Hrafnhaugr. Pale and bloody-limbed Geats intertwine with bearded Danes and dark-eyed Swedes, their ragged surcoats emblazoned with the Nailed God's cross. She cannot

33

speak. The weight of a broken lance pulls at her rib cage. She has no recollection of how it got there, or whose hands wielded it; she did not know which wretched bastard among the dead had planted the iron head deep in her guts. That she could not feel it was both a balm and a concern.

The young woman holds the splintered remains of the lance's shaft tight as she limps back from the ruined gates, down streets she has known since she was a child. Despite the heat, the exposed bone of her face feels cold. She wipes away a gobbet of blood. Near the center of the village, where the great rune stone that has stood since the days of her forefathers has toppled, she beholds an eerie sight: a giant cross rises from the rubble; nailed to this, arms outstretched as if to embrace the suffering of the world, she sees a pale man with hair the color of milk. He laughs at his own agony, muttering:

> "Miklagarðr twas called, | where kings wore purple,
> And men begged in the street;
> Broken, our oaths were, | though sworn by the Cross,
> When the dogs of St. Mark sought payment."

The young woman twists the lance shaft and draws the blood-slimed weapon from her side. With a scrap of cloth, she binds her injury—though it pains her not; then, she clambers up the pile of rubble and touches the white foot of the hanging man. His laughter ceases as he looks down at her, reddish eyes reflecting madness and a thirst for death. Nodding, she drives the broken lance up under his ribs.

He dies with a shudder and a long drawn-out sigh . . .

She staggers down from the rubble and moves on, past a thin, bearded man who drops an ancient sword, calls upon his Nailed God for succor, and takes up a length of ragged iron chain. This, he uses to flense the flesh from his knobby spine. With each blow, he cries out: "Eloi Eloi lama sabachthani?"

The young woman picks up a sword from where the so-called holy man had dropped it—its long, dwarf-forged blade reflecting the cruel light of the heavens. She is poised to strike this madman down when a flicker of movement catches her eye. She turns. A familiar figure approaches, stoop-shouldered and bandy-legged, the sworn protector of Hrafnhaugr. The Hooded One. He is stripped to the waist and sweating as he pulls a laden cart behind him, its contents hidden by a blood-smirched square of canvas. She wants to berate him for the destruction, but her voice is lost to the keening wind over the battlefield. Instead, the young woman watches as he stops by a welter of corpses, kicks them apart, and draws an axe from his belt. Stooping, he hacks their heads off, seizes them by their hair, and carries them to his cart. She drifts closer.

He grins at her, winking, as he draws the canvas back to reveal a mound of severed heads. Hundreds of them. Familiar faces stare up at her with dead, glassy eyes. She sees ancient Kolgríma beside young Bryngerðr, whose inked raven is barely dry; Hreðel is there, with his son, Flóki; the two Bjorns, Svarti and Hvítr—the Black and the White; Auða is there, as is hard-eyed Sigrún, her features severe even in death. Resting atop the others is a face she does not recognize—harder than Sigrún's, with ashen hair and eyes as pale as the winter sky. But not a face she fears. A name rises unbidden to her lips: "Úlfrún." And for her, the young woman feels a pang of . . . love? The love of a daughter for her mother? Or is it guilt? Guilt arising from knowing she has replaced her mother in the young woman's esteem?

The Hooded One tosses the other heads atop the pile, dislodging the woman's. It rolls down the heap and falls over the side, landing at her feet. Carefully, she picks the head up and returns it to the cart.

"Best leg it, little bird," the Hooded One growls, gesturing with his axe in the direction he had come. "And leg it quick, ere he finds you."

She turns and walks in the direction he'd indicated, the sword dragging a furrow in the earth behind her.

"Don't be a fool, you dunghill wretch!" he calls after her.

Ahead, a figure waits. It bears the shape of a man, though hunched and as twisted as the staff he leans upon; he is clad in a voluminous cloak with a slouch hat pulled low. A single malevolent eye gleams from beneath the brim.

She reckons he is the cause of this, like a spider in human form who sits at the heart of a vast web, waiting for the perfect time to strike. All things under heaven are but mere strands of this web, spun and stretched taut and linked to other strands. It has no pattern she can discern, this web, but she knows that to cause ripples across it is to court death.

But she is not afraid.

Slowly, she walks across the scorched ruin of Hrafnhaugr, her sword scraping stone. She will end it.

She, who springs from the loins of Dagrún Spear-breaker; she, who is a Daughter of the Raven, bearer of the rune Dagaz; she, who is the Day-strider, chosen of the Gods. She, who is skjaldmær, shieldmaiden.

She is not afraid.

She will end it.

Here.

Now.

She raises her dwarf-forged sword . . .

"Niðing," the stranger says in a voice deeper than Vänern's heart.

> *"From the depths a barrow | rises through the water,*
> *The stone-girdled hall | of Aranæs, where dwells*
> *Jörmungandr's spawn, | the Malice-Striker.*
> *Its dread bones rattle | and herald an end."*

And with a sound like the rattle of immense bones, the stranger's cloak is borne up as by a hot breath of wind. There is only darkness, beneath. And that darkness grows and spreads, becoming monstrous wings that blot out the burning sky. The darkness crawls like a serpent across the ruin of Hrafnhaugr. It snuffs the flames and robs the air of its breath; it slays the living with a pestilence that rots the blood in their veins. It crushes and destroys.

She turns to run as the darkness engulfs her. And in its hideous embrace, she opens her mouth to scream . . .

DÍSA WOKE WITH A START. A scream gurgled in her throat. She coughed and struggled against the harsh liquid burning its way down her gullet. A blurred silhouette loomed over her, red eye agleam. She wanted to turn her head and spit that foul-tasting liquor out, but a swarthy hand clamped over her mouth kept her from it. Dísa's gagging redoubled as the liquor hung at the back of her throat.

"*Nár*, swallow it," Grimnir muttered.

With little choice, Dísa ground her teeth together and bore down, forcing herself to swallow. Suddenly she could breathe again, and she felt a not-unpleasant warmth spreading out from her belly. Her clouded vision cleared; her aching face felt hot and swollen, and she could not draw air through either nostril. She had expected to wake up half-submerged in the bog—if, indeed, she had woken up at all. But, near as she could tell, she was back inside the longhouse. Dísa saw the fire pit again, and the drifts of gold and silver, weapons and armor; all of it lit, now, by shafts of pale gray light filtering down from the clerestory. She lay on one of the side platforms, on a pallet made from old pillows and ragged moth-eaten skins of fox, marten, and deer.

Grimnir crouched alongside her. Black blood still stained his face from where she'd broken his nose. He took a pull from a clay flask wrapped in a protective web of rope, sucking his teeth as he stoppered it. He wiped his lips with the back of his hand. "That'll put hair on your arse!"

"Wh-what was that?" Dísa said.

Grimnir straightened and stood. "*Mjöð,* brewed after the fashion of my kinsmen, those wretched *dvergar.*"

"It's got teeth." Dísa struggled into a sitting position.

"Aye," Grimnir agreed. He turned and dropped from the edge of the side-platform, hammerscale grinding beneath his heels. "You got a bit of a bite, yourself, little bird. It's been an age since anyone's managed to rap me on the beak, much less a scrawny little ape like you."

"Little good it did me," Dísa said, gingerly touching her face. Her own nose was broken, of that she was certain, and maybe the socket of her left eye—her vision jumped and twitched, blurring and then clearing once again. She tasted blood.

He glanced back at her, scowling. "You're alive, aren't you?"

"But for how long?"

Grimnir didn't reply at first. He hopped up on the edge of the fire pit, and balancing there, he started walking toward his chair. She could tell he was mulling over her question. When he reached the end of the pit, he leaped off and sprawled into his makeshift throne.

"That depends on you, doesn't it?"

"Me?"

Grimnir leaned forward, jabbing an accusing finger at her. "Don't play the fool now, little bird! The rest of you lot, all who've borne the raven, have thought serving me to be some great honor. Old Kolgríma, Mæva before her—twenty-three generations of you, all the way back to Iðunn Bragadottír, who was a witch and an outcast before we came along, Gífr and me. They traded on our names to keep their sons and husbands, brothers and fathers alive—aye, let the Tangled God's so-called herald shoulder the burden! When those dunghill swine from the Danemark came ravening into Geatland, who'd they let take the brunt? Who'd they let blunt the axes and break the shields of the whoreson Norse and the idiot Swedes?" Grimnir hawked and spat before leaning back in his seat. "To them, the Hooded One was their lord and savior—and they were proud to be our priestesses. Oh, how they cried their crocodile tears! How they crossed their fingers when they bound themselves to us with oaths none of your wretched lot would dare otherwise break. But not you! No, you take it as some mortal insult! Are you so much better than those other drabs?"

Now it was Dísa's turn to mull over his question. This, she reckoned, was the end of the rope. Her face and head ached, and she had no patience left to dissemble with him. She would speak the truth, and either hang or start climbing. "I am no better," she replied after a moment, "but I am no worse, either. I do not have the stomach to be any man's slave, and you are no man, to boot. Those others? They wanted this. They craved your protection above all else. Perhaps they were wiser than I, or had more to lose. But me? I crave freedom, and the will to protect myself, is all."

"Skjaldmær," Grimnir said.

Dísa glanced sharply at him.

"You talk in your sleep, runt. That's what you meant, out there, when you boasted that you'd write your own destiny. You think you have the sand and fire in your belly to be one of the skjaldmeyjar, those cursed shield-maidens."

"Perhaps," Dísa replied, feeling the color rise in her cheeks.

Grimnir mocked her. "Perhaps? Ymir's blood, little fool! Either you think you do, or you don't! Which is it?"

"I do!" She jutted her chin out as if daring him to strike. "My mother was skjaldmær, and her mother before her! I was born for Odin's weather, for the strife and clamor of shield-breaking, not for bowing or scraping!"

"Were you now," said Grimnir, his eyes narrowing. He tilted his head to pierce her with his ruddy gaze. After a moment, he snorted. "Well, you're an honest one, at least, though too full of yourself by half. You're what? A hundred pounds, soaking wet? The scrum of the shield wall would chew you up and spit you out." He drummed one black-nailed finger against the arm of his seat.

"I bloodied your nose," she shot back defiantly.

Grimnir bristled. "You were desperate and lucky! That's a piss-poor bet if you're wagering your wretched life."

"Men have wagered with less and still won the day," Dísa said.

Grimnir chuckled and stroked his jaw with the back of his left hand. "And swine have wagered not a thing and still ended up on the spit."

"Then kill me!" Dísa snapped. Tears of anger, pain, and frustration welled at the corners of her blue eyes. "Kill me and have done, for I'd rather be free and dead than alive and in thrall to you!"

"Don't tempt me, little fool." Grimnir fingered the hilt of his seax. He gave her one last look, long and hard, while he considered his next words. Finally, he said: "Fine, you've got a bit of skill and an arm you'll likely brag about till the end of your miserable days. But you've got no meat on your bones. Makes you quick, but it means you're never going to stand in a wall of men, shield to shield like a proper *skjaldmær*."

"*Jævla fitte!*" Dísa hissed, employing a curse she'd heard a Norse trader level at Auða last year, when they'd gone into the borderlands of Eiðaskógr to scout—one that provoked Auða to take up the knife he was trying to sell her and cut the bastard's throat. "And how would you know? What monster has ever stood in a wall of men?"

The corner of Grimnir's lips crept up in a sneer of contempt. "Fool! By what lights do you judge me? By your years? Or by the well from which you dip out your knowledge? When I tell you you'd be dog meat in a stand-up fight I speak from what I have seen, across more lifetimes than your wretched little brain can imagine! I last stood among men at Chluain Tarbh, outside the walls of Dubhlinn-town, where the Gaels broke the back of the Norse. Before that . . ." Grimnir sucked his teeth, making a dismissive *tsk*-ing noise. "Too many to count."

"So I should just give up, then, and accept my lot? Serve out my time here and die like Kolgríma—a doddering old fool, destined to slip on a patch of moss while hunting for the Gods only know what?"

Grimnir chuckled again. "If I had my way, I'd just slit your throat and be done. Sink your skinny carcass in the bog and go on about my business. But no. My luck doesn't run that simple. You're destined to be a thorn in my arse, little bird. Damn my eye, but you're quick, you've got a good arm, and there's sand in your belly. Spear and axe, those are your weapons. Maybe a bit of blade-work, a dirk, or a good long-seax."

Dísa's eyes widened; she blinked, her jaw hanging open. "What . . . What are you saying?"

"I need a priestess, not a slave," Grimnir replied. "But if I followed my gut and just staved your fool head in, your lot would likely send me another old crow, fawning and false. So, we make a compact of our own, you and I. You serve me, keep your damnable trap shut, and keep out from under my feet. In exchange, I'll make a throat-slitter out of you. What say you?"

"I'll be *skjaldmær*?"

"Call yourself what you will, little bird," said Grimnir, rising from his seat. "When I'm done with you, you'll be like the corpse-makers of old! Now, what say you?"

Dísa Dagrúnsdottir exhaled. Then, almost as if she expected this to be some cruel jest on his part, she nodded. "Yes."

Grimnir reached into the small of his back and drew forth a thin-bladed knife. He flicked it, point down, into the wood beside her. "Make your oath, then." He drew his seax; with the tip, he pricked the thumb of his off hand and let his black blood well and ooze. He sheathed his seax, then, and smeared the fresh blood into the palm of his blade hand.

Dísa rose on unsteady legs. She worked the knife free and mimicked Grimnir's gesture, smearing her blade hand with rich red blood. She thought for a moment, recalling an ancient oath she'd heard her mother utter ere she set out for the shores of the Skagerrak, to find glory and death fighting the Danes. "Hear me, Tangled One, O cunning-wise Loki!" Dísa said, slowly at first. She hesitated. "Bear witness, O Ymir, sire of giants and lord of the frost!" Grimnir thrust his blade hand out; Dísa took it in hers, wincing as he clamped down. Their blood mingled. "By this blood, I swear myself to the Hooded One! I will serve him as my kinswomen did, of old! But bind him to his word, Friend of the Raven-God, lest he and his people be forgotten and their bones ground underfoot!"

Grimnir hissed sharply at that last bit and nearly crushed her fingers into kindling. Still, both of them heard it—distant and faint: the dull rumble of thunder from the far-off north, where the Nailed God's influence did not reach. She thought of an ancient giant, nodding in its sleep.

"It's done, then," Grimnir said, letting go of her hand. "Halla!" He turned away.

The old woman emerged from the depths of the longhouse, skirting the shaft of gray light falling from the clerestory. In her hands, she carried Dísa's basket—empty now, save for the rolled parchments, bundled together and tied with knotted twine, and a sealed clay jar like the one that had held her rune stone for a generation. Halla also bore a hooded cloak of wool, trimmed in wolf fur, and a seax in a wood and leather scabbard. Its hilt was fashioned after that of a sword, with a thick cross-guard, a grip of leather and copper wire, and an acorn-shaped pommel. Halla balanced the basket on one hip and offered her the seax.

Dísa took it, avarice agleam in her blue eyes. She drew it partly from its scabbard; steel rasped against the copper throat, etched with runes to protect the blade within from harm. She aired a hand-span of single-edged gray steel, thick along its spine—steel that would carve through mail, flesh, and bone like an oar through water.

"Every bird needs a talon," Grimnir said, resuming his seat. He wiped his bloody palm down the thigh of his kilt. "Even a little sack of bones like you. And you'd best learn to keep an edge on it!"

Dísa nodded. She sheathed it again and tucked the seax into the belt at her waist. Halla then handed her the cloak, which she fastened about her shoulders with a smile. She was grateful for its warmth. Finally, the crone passed the basket to her.

"Take this back to Hrafnhaugr," Halla said. She touched the clay jar. "Instruct them to place this back atop the Raven Stone." Her wrinkled hand moved to the parchments. "And pass these to your chief. See to your injuries and then return here with the new moon. Do you understand?"

"Yes," Dísa replied.

"Then go."

Dísa turned to Grimnir and started to utter her thanks, but he cut her short with a sharp gesture. "*Nár!* See that your legs work, this time, you miserable little runt."

And with that, Dísa turned and fled from the longhouse.

HALLA WALKED TO THE DOOR and peered out. Her milky gaze followed the girl as she all but leapt down the steps and ran across the corduroy of logs connecting the hillock to the valley trail. Nothing could dampen her spirit. Not the nasty knock to the head she'd suffered, nor the broken nose, and surely not the thin rain that pissed from the overcast sky.

She felt Grimnir's presence behind her.

"You wanted her alive?" he said, his voice a scornful hiss. "She's alive and beholden to me now."

"You were awfully charitable, *skrælingr*," Halla said. "If someone didn't know you, they might think you'd taken a liking to this girl."

Grimnir grunted but said nothing. He leaned against the doorjamb and crossed his arms over his chest. His nostrils flared as he snuffled the damp air. Despite his silence, Halla could almost hear the gears grinding away in his skull.

"But I do know you." She turned, her seamed face wrinkled in a fierce scowl. "What are you playing at, with this talk of making a throat-slitter out of her?"

Grimnir kept his counsel for a long moment, long enough for Dísa to climb the valley trail and vanish into the trees along the ridgeline. Finally, he said: "You heard her, that headstrong little fool! Maundering on about how she'll do this but she'll not do that like she knows what she's about? Well, I learned a long time ago that you can't snare the likes of her with vinegar. Oh, no! They got too much pride for that. They need coaxing. Tease them with a bit of honey. Let them take a nibble off the comb. Dangle what they desire most just within their grasp and there's not a hoop made by god or man they won't jump through."

Halla nodded slowly. "She desires to be like her mother, but is that wise?"

"You remember her, do you?" Grimnir sucked his teeth and spat.

The old troll-woman glanced sidelong at the distant ridgeline, where Dísa had vanished. "I do, but the Dagrún I remember did not die fighting the Danes on a Skagerrak beach . . ."

"*Nár!*" Grimnir replied. "Curiosity's what done her in. Listened to too many *skalds* bang on about heroes and monsters. Saw her chance a few winters back, when she got Kolgríma blind stinking drunk and pried a few choice bits from her—like how a monster lived right in their midst. Well, the little swine thought she'd make a name for herself, then, as a *skjaldmær* and a slayer of beasts if she brought my head back and stuck it over the mantel!"

"It wasn't you who killed her, though."

Grimnir *tsked*. "She never made it to my doorstep. Was her own mother that done it. Knifed her in the back, then pressed Kolgríma into helping her cart the corpse out here and sank it in the bog. She probably added her to the tally of the dead from Skagerrak to keep the peace, not realizing how the lie would grow."

A chill wind gusted into the valley. Halla gathered up a few of the logs stacked by the door and laid them atop the bed of embers in the fire pit, which she stirred to life with an iron poker. "And the girl knows nothing of what her grandmother has done."

"A cold fish, that Sigrún." Grimnir turned from the door and stalked back to his seat. "And I'd bet my good eye she did Kolgríma in, as well."

"Cutting her threads and burning the loose ends? But why? Conscience, or is it something else?"

"Find out. Bend your art to the shadows." Grimnir leaned back in his seat, one elbow on the carved arm rest, and propped his chin on his fist. His gleaming eye stared into the heart of the burgeoning flames. "Put the screws to the *landvættir* of the wood. Send your spirits down to the fences surrounding Hel's cold realm. Find answers. That little wretch was nattering on about something in her sleep, calling out names. Made no sense at first. But then she said something about a spider sitting in a web. *Sæter*, she called it."

"One who lies in ambush," Halla said.

Grimnir drew his seax and drove it point-first into the other armrest. "We've been sitting pretty up here, minding our own business, but my gut tells me we let something slip. Some cross-kissing rat, I'll wager. Some poxy bastard with a gilded tongue has crept in and set up shop among them."

"You think Sigrún's turned to the Nailed God?"

"Maybe. Maybe others."

Outside, the rain sheeted down; inside, shadows danced. The firelight lent Halla's features a sinister cast. Her milky eyes darted back and forth as she plotted and schemed. "And the girl?"

Grimnir thumbed the blade of his seax, testing its edge against the thick callus of his finger. He grinned as it cut the skin. Holding up his thumb, he studied the welling blood as though it were a harbinger, all black and glistening. "Oh, I'll make a slayer out of her, all right," he said, pressing his thumb against his index finger and forcing more blood from the small laceration. "Hammer her into shape like copper on an anvil. Make her sharp. Put an edge on her." He squeezed again and held the globule of blood steady, keeping it from trickling down his thumb. "And then, maybe, tell her what really happened to her precious Dagrún."

The smile flirting at the corners of Grimnir's lips turned to a snarl as he stabbed his thumb against the flat of his seax. There, etched deep into the steel, was the stylized eye that was the symbol of the sons of Bálegyr. Black blood filled the grooves in the metal. It spilled over the incised edges, giving the sigil the illusion that it wept for the Old Ways, for a world long gone . . .

5

Though Hrafnhaugr was only a little more than two miles distant, across the dark waters of Skærvík, Dísa had neither wings nor a boat. She followed the shoreline of the bay, along game trails and through tangled copses of spruce and birch. It was a six-mile journey that should have taken her only a couple of hours despite the rocky and forested terrain; instead, it took the better part of the day.

Excitement had given way to a bone-aching weariness. She stopped by a small stream to clean the blood from her face and to drink handfuls of water—the *Mjöð* Grimnir forced into her had left her throat raw; she stopped again as spasms of overexertion racked her limbs. Dísa found a thicket near the trail where deer bedded down, the bracken underfoot warm and dry despite the rain. She limped into the nest. And with the cloak Halla had given her wrapped around her like a swaddling cloth, Dísa drifted off to sleep . . .

. . . *a figure waits. It bears the shape of a man, though hunched and as twisted as the staff he leans upon; he is clad in a voluminous cloak with a slouch hat pulled low. A single malevolent eye gleams from beneath the brim.*

"Niðing," the stranger says in a voice deeper than Vänern's heart. "I am coming. Tell your folk to choose, and choose well. No man can serve two masters."

And with a sound like the rattle of immense bones, the stranger's cloak is borne up as by a hot breath of wind. There is only darkness beneath. And that darkness grows and spreads, becoming monstrous wings that blot out the burning sky . . .

Dísa woke with a gasp. Her seax was in her hand, its trembling blade leveled at nothing. Outside, the day had waned into late afternoon. Water dripped from leaves, and she could hear the soft splash of waves striking the rocky shore of Skærvík. No darkness loomed over her; no figure in a slouch hat with a single burning eye. Slowly, Dísa relaxed. Prophetic dreams were not unheard of among the Daughters of the Raven, and some—like Kolgríma—even sought out herbs and barks that, when burned, would bring on such a state. For Dísa, though, the experience was unique. She wondered what it meant. Was it truly as dire a warning as it seemed? Or did it owe something to the influence of the Hooded One? With more questions than answers, she sheathed her seax and made ready to leave.

Dísa clambered out of her warm nest. The rain had given way to a fine mist, like a drifting fog, and the air was even colder than it had been. Cursing, she caught up her basket and trudged on her way. Before the hour was up, she knew she was nearing home. She passed a handful of outlying steadings—solitary longhouses surrounded by fallow fields and wattle hurdles woven from hazel branches that served as fences for livestock. Smoke drifted from chimney holes to join the icy mist. Dísa walked on, an unaccountable sense of unease stealing over her . . .

. . . in the wreckage of Hrafnhaugr, pale and bloody-limbed Geats intertwine with bearded Danes and dark-eyed Swedes, their ragged surcoats emblazoned with the Nailed God's cross.

Dísa lengthened her stride, suddenly desperate. The game trails she followed fed into a rutted track that was the only road to Hrafnhaugr, wide enough to accommodate log wains though overgrown now, and rarely traveled. As far as Dísa knew no prince or king laid claim to this corner of Geatland, or if they did they left it well enough alone. A few Norsemen had tried, of course, as had a handful of enterprising Swedes over the years. One even made it as far as the inlet called the Horn, at the mouth of the Hveðrungr River, where he laid the foundations for a fortified town. Since the Geats claimed the Horn as their southern border this incursion could not stand. Flóki told the tale best, for he was quick-witted and blessed with a *skald*'s sense of the dramatic. He would act out the parts of the aggrieved Geats, led by an old chief called Hugleikr, who rose up, burned the Swede's ill-fated ring-fort to the ground, and sent its master back in pieces. That—according to Flóki—was the Hooded One's doing. "Though the Norse and their Dane allies still raid into Geatland and prey upon our folk," he would say, nodding respectfully to Sigrún and Dísa in remembrance of the latter's mother, "no cursed Swede has dared step foot over the Horn since."

And Dísa hoped that would hold true for many years to come.

Approaching from its landward side, one came upon Hrafnhaugr almost without warning. The road plunged into a thickly tangled belt of ash and willow, and emerged at the lip of that deep ravine, the Scar—hewn through the ages by the endless struggle of the *landvættir* against the *vatnavættir* who lived in its depths, the spirits of the earth against the spirits of the water. Twenty yards at its widest, the Scar made an island of Hrafnhaugr. A bridge of thick ropes and planks traversed the Scar; at its edge, Dísa touched the base of a spirit pole her ancestors had erected, its upper carvings cracked and weathered, its lower carvings worn smooth from countless hands. The echo of water surging and lapping in the Scar's lightless deeps sounded like ghostly laughter—Kolgríma's laughter, she was sure—as she crossed the bridge. But on the far side the ground underfoot grew steep, the trees vanished, and there it was—limned against a cloud-racked sky: a rocky bluff of shale and black limestone that commanded the throat of Skærvík, crowned by a fortress with earthen walls reinforced by a timber palisade.

Thrice the road zigzagged before reaching the gates of Hrafnhaugr, heavy oaken timbers banded in rust-spotted iron set between a pair of thirty-foot-high square wooden towers. Dísa could not recall a day or night when the Jarl had ordered the gates closed, and this evening was no exception. They stood open a dozen feet, wide enough to allow a wagon to pass; above them, on the parapet that ran between the thatch-roofed towers, a single sentry leaned on his spear, wrapped in a thick sealskin cloak with its hood pulled forward so that only the beaked nose of his helmet and his bushy beard showed. He watched her, his weight shifting as he moved his spear from off hand to blade hand. At first Dísa thought it might be Hrútr, her cousin's bedmate, but in the twilight she could barely discern the silver in his beard—she knew, then, that it was Askr, Hrútr's kinsman.

Dísa drew her hood back and raised a hand in greeting.

"God's teeth, girl!" he bellowed in reply, leaning out over the serrated wooden bulwark. "We thought you were done for!"

"I will be if I don't get out of this blasted weather," she replied. "Do you have your horn, Askr?" The man nodded, holding up a silver-bound horn on a fine leather baldric. "Wake them up, then. It is time to send Kolgríma on her way. She's lingered in this world for too long."

Dísa passed beneath the gate as Askr sounded the horn. Its deep-throated roar echoed among the scores of buildings. Hrafnhaugr spread upward across three shallow terraces. The first, level with the gates, held the clustered houses and workshops of the hundred-odd families who called the village home. All had wooden walls on foundations of local stone with steeply pitched roofs of thatch or shingle; deep carvings decorated their corner posts, and the beams that crossed to form the peaks of their roofs bore snarling wolves, dragons, sharp-beaked ravens, and trolls—every manner of beast from the legends of their folk.

Dísa threaded between the houses on streets cobbled with smooth lake stone and ascended the rock-cut steps that led to the second terrace. Here, the ground was open, dominated by an ancient upright stone—the Raven Stone, black and glossy and carved with age-worn runes. A pyre lay prepared before the Raven Stone, topped by a linen-swaddled corpse. Kolgríma. Dísa did not know much about her duties, but she knew this: only a priestess of the Hooded One could light the fire that would consume her predecessor's mortal remains.

Beyond, the longhouse called Gautheimr, the Geat-home, occupied the smaller third terrace. Though larger than the houses below, it followed the same pattern, with a steep-pitched roof of age-darkened thatch and corner posts that curled like dragons; beyond its intricately carved doors, countless thegns and *skjaldmeyjar* had passed their days, plotting and scheming, drinking and brawling. Light spilled out now, as the doors burst open. A second blast from Askr's horn brought two-score men and women out onto the terrace, all armed and hastily armored. Dísa saw Jarl Hreðel flanked by his rawboned son, Flóki; the two Bjorns were there—Bjorn Hvítr, the White, whose hair and beard were like snow despite him being in his prime, and Bjorn Svarti, the Black, whose face and hair were as saturnine as Grimnir's—as well as the Manx-Geat, Íomhar, and Kjartan Sigurdsson—snake-eyed Kjartan—who spent more time among the Norse reavers than among his own people. She saw the gentle face of Berkano, who claimed kinship with the birch and the rowan; beside her, her younger sister, Laufeya, stern of mouth and quiet—

both sisters had fled the land of the Otter-Geats after the Norse razed their village. The Daughters of the Raven came last, twenty-three in number, led by Auða and Sigrún, her eyes burning with a fey light.

Upon seeing Dísa beside the Raven Stone, the assembled men and women fell silent. Others joined them from the houses of the first terrace, until it seemed every last man, woman, and child was jammed cheek by jowl around the black stone. Someone kindled torches, and by their orange light shadows danced. Dísa heard her name muttered time and again. Finally, Jarl Hreðel raised a hand for silence before directing his gaze to Sigrún.

"Dísa Dagrúnsdottir!" she said after a moment. "The Fates sent you forth from us. They charged you with finding your rightful place in the shadow of the Hooded One. Do you return to us now, in favor or in disgrace?"

Dísa put the basket down, straightened, and squared her shoulders—a hint of defiance in her stance. "I return in favor," she replied. "And I claim what is mine by right, as chosen priestess of the Hooded One."

"Let the Gods bear witness." Sigrún nodded to Auða, who fetched the torch that Bjorn Hvítr held aloft and carried it to Dísa. The older woman crinkled her brow at the state of Dísa's face as she handed the flaming brand over. In answer to her cousin's unspoken question, Dísa gave a barely per-ceptible shrug. She turned to face the pyre, its oil-soaked logs beaded with moisture; the body that lay atop it looked so small, almost childlike. "Kol-gríma Guðrúnardottir!" she said. "What was yours in life, I, Dísa Dagrúns-dottir, now claim as my own! What debts you owed are now my own! What was owed to you now is owed to me!" The torch guttered as she held it aloft. "Hear me, Tangled One, O cunning-wise Loki! Bear witness, O Ymir, sire of giants and lord of the frost! I free Kolgríma Guðrúnardottir from the prison of her flesh and send her unto you! She is Daughter of the Raven, priestess of the Hooded One . . . let her name be spoken from the walls of Ásgarðr to the fences of Helheimr!"

Dísa thrust her torch into the heart of the pyre. The wood, though satu-rated with oil, was slow to light. It crackled and popped, blue flames dancing in its depths. Dísa glanced about, unsure of what to do. Auða came to her rescue. She snatched a torch from one of the onlookers and carried it to the pyre. "Kolgríma Guðrúnardottir!" she said, adding more flame to the pyre.

Still it guttered and spat.

It was Flóki who fetched more torches, and who passed them to the

Daughters of the Raven, while Black Bjorn brought forth a brazier of coals from Gautheimr. Then, one by one, the women with their raven tattoos stepped forward, kindled their torches in the coals, and carried them to the pyre. Each one added her voice to the growing conflagration. "Kolgríma Guðrúnardottir!"

Sigrún came last.

The pyre was a proper blaze now, as flames greedily consumed the wood and its earthly burden. Smoke rose into the nighted sky. Sigrún kindled her torch. She walked slowly to the edge of the inferno. Jags of light reflected off the pommel of her sword, off the silver wire of its hilt and the silver chasings adorning its scabbard, off the dull rings of the mail she wore; the silver beads woven through her gray locks gave back the fire's ruddy glow as she stepped up and tossed her torch into the heart of the pyre.

"Kolgríma Guðrúnardottir," she said, her voice pitched low and full of grief. "I will see you soon, my sister." Sigrún spoke something else, then, too low for others to catch. Even Dísa, who stood close at hand, could not be certain what it was she said, as the words were lost to an explosion of crackling resin. But when she looked up again, Sigrún transfixed Dísa with her dark and feral stare—a gaze known to make even the most seasoned warriors tremble. Dísa felt her scorn, though she knew not where it came from; she felt her rage, her jealousy, and her disgust. And Dísa knew for certain, then, something she had always guessed: given the opportunity, Sigrún would go back to the hour of her birth and plunge the mewling thing from her daughter's womb into a bucket of water until it ceased to move.

But Dísa Dagrúnsdottir was no longer a mewling thing. She was no longer a motherless orphan; no longer a spare mouth to feed. The Gods had singled her out. The cloak of the Hooded One's favor stoked the fire in her belly. And the weight of the seax he had given her lent steel to her spine. She met Sigrún's gaze, her blue eyes as bright and hard as ice.

"Tell me," Dísa said as Sigrún leaned close to her. "Tell me, woman to woman, why do you hate me so?"

Sigrún's smile was the smile of a predator. She clasped her granddaughter's hand hard enough to crush bone and peered into the bruised depths of her eyes. Dísa did not flinch; instead, she conjured Grimnir's snarl and curled her lips in the same manner.

"You are no woman," Sigrún replied. "Not yet. Still a foolish child.

Enjoy this night, for it was well-earned, and your words well-spoken. Tomorrow, your real trial begins." The old woman pulled Dísa into an embrace that was without warmth; as the village looked on, she kissed her granddaughter's cheek.

"Let none say I did not offer you a chance," Dísa hissed. "I see you for what you are, hag, and rest assured *he* sees you, too."

Sigrún broke their embrace, her face an unreadable mask. "I hope he does," she replied. "After all I've done for him, all I've sacrificed for him . . . I hope the Hooded One sees me as clearly as his master, the Tangled God, does."

And with that, Sigrún turned and walked away. Dísa lost sight of her grandmother as a swell of villagers converged on the Raven Stone, leaving the young woman to puzzle over the meaning behind her words.

THE BALANCE OF THE EVENING passed in a blur. There were songs and toasts, words of congratulations and questions. Dísa recalled being raised on the broad shoulders of Bjorn Hvítr, so she might place the jar Halla had given her in its niche atop the Raven Stone; she remembered handing over the bundle of parchments to Jarl Hreðel, who was already deep in his cups. The sharp pain of Auða setting her broken nose contrasted with the mellow, numbing taste of Berkano's bark-infused mead. Exhaustion left her snappish, though even she grew silent as a long-simmering argument between Jarl Hreðel and Flóki erupted into blows. The two Bjorns hauled father and son apart; Hreðel went back to drinking among his sworn men while Flóki left with Eirik Viðarrson and his brother, Ulff.

"What was that about?" Dísa said. She sat with Auða and Hrútr, watching as sure-handed Askr tattooed the *kenaz* rune on the shoulder of his daughter, Káta, who would take her rightful place among the Daughters of the Raven, bringing their number back up to twenty-four. She cursed and drank horn after horn of mead, despite being a year younger than Dísa. "I've never heard Hreðel or Flóki say a cross word to the other."

It was Hrútr who answered. He took a long draught of ale, wiped the foam from his mustache with the forearm of his tunic. "Boy's itching to go off and earn his beard," he said. "And who can blame him? He's old enough, by Ymir."

Askr paused, wiping blood from the ivory needle he was using to prick the design in his daughter's skin before smearing it with a paste of black ash, verdigris, and oak gall.

"Soon, it will not matter," he said, adding to his daughter: "Sit still, girl. It's almost done."

Dísa frowned. "Why not?"

"*Fimbulvetr.*"

"Here he goes," Hrútr said, shaking his head. Auða smiled.

Fimbulvetr, Dísa knew, was the endless winter that would herald the coming of Ragnarök and the breaking of the world. "You think *this* is the Great Winter?"

Askr paused; he gestured with the point of his ink-stained needle. "Laugh all you want, brother, but this is the third year with no spring thaw. The end is coming, I tell you! A time of fire and blood! The Wolf-age, the poets called it—brothers shall fight and fell each other, ere the world ends." Even Káta looked askance at her father.

Hrútr and Auða glanced at one another, and both shrugged. "Does it matter?" Auða said. "The Norns, those weird sisters who weave the fates of all, have measured and cut our lives. Every good or ill the Gods saddle us with, the Norns draw these things upon the loom at our birth. Why worry? If it is our fate to witness the Twilight of the Gods, no hand-wringing or hymn-singing can change it."

"Besides," Hrútr said. "She'd know, wouldn't she?"

Dísa glanced up; saw all four of them looking at her. "Would I?"

"Surely the Hooded One would reveal such a thing to you," Auða said.

Dísa frowned. Something Halla had said bubbled up from the soup of her memory, something that fit with a deeper recollection—that of a hard voice, crooning softly . . .

The endless winter is drawing to a close. The Wolf whose name is Mockery nips at the heels of Sól, who guides the Chariot of the Sun! Soon, the Serpent will writhe! The Dragon—

Dísa closed her eyes.

"Hard blows Gjallarhorn | over Miðgarðr's shores,
And Jörmungandr | twists in mighty wrath;
Yggðrasil trembles | to its Fate-washed roots;
The dread Wolf howls | and slips its chains.

"Now from the East, | over the sea-waves,
Naglfari comes, | the Ship of the Dead;
And from the South, | the jötunn are loosed;
On their swords shimmer | the lights of slaughter.

"Vígríðr is the field | where the enemies meet;
Wolf and Serpent against | the sons of Ásgarðr;
The rock-crags crash; | the fiends are reeling;
Heroes tread the Hel-road; | Miðgarðr is cloven.

"The sun turns black, | earth sinks in the sea;
The hot stars down | from heaven are whirled;
Fierce grows the steam | and the life-feeding flame,
Till fire leaps high | about Yggðrasil itself.

"From below the dragon | dark comes forth,
Niðhöggr crawling | from the roots of the Ash;
Against the East-king, | thorn-crowned savior,
The doom of mankind | in his jaws he bears."

A cold wind swirled through Gautheimr; the fire in the broad pit flick-ered, as though some cruel and cunning *jötunn* crept past on an errand known only to the Gods. Dísa opened her eyes and saw dozens of faces staring back at her with a mix of awe and fear.

Askr grunted and nudged his brother in the ribs. "Told you, didn't I?"

Auða leaned forward. "Did you return with the gift of prophecy, cousin? Is what Askr speaks of true? Is this *Fimbulvetr*?"

The younger woman went scarlet to the ears. She waved Auða away. "That was just a bit of doggerel," she stammered. "Something Kolgríma used to sing is all. It's nothing."

"I never heard her sing such a thing," Auða said, frowning.

"Nor me," Hrútr added.

"That wasn't Kolgríma," Sigrún said from across the room. "I sang that to you, and your mother before you, though I'm surprised you remember it. Those are the words of the *Iðunnarkvitha Bragadottonar,* the Lay of Iðunn the Daughter of Bragi, who was the first of our line." Sigrún took a pull from her mead horn; with it, she gestured at the sisters, Berkano and Laufeya. "We were like *them,* in Iðunn's day: outcasts from a dozen different Geatish clans, driven from our homes by war, by pestilence, by crimes that called out for a blood-price—a *weregild.* That was how the Hooded One found us, witches and outlaws and broken men, living in squalor like rats. He likely would have killed us all had Iðunn not prevailed upon him. She begged his mercy, and in exchange she pledged herself and her daughters to his service. Thus was our compact forged—one priestess, chosen at random from the descendants of Iðunn, would serve him until death. He permitted no others to cast their eyes upon him. He granted us this land, and from the Raven Stone Iðunn named our people. We became the Raven-Geats of Hrafnhaugr."

Sigrún drank again, more deeply this time. "But time makes us forget. It's been years since the Hooded One has lit the war beacons. When my mother was a girl, she told me the Raven-Geats would fare forth every season— bound for the borders of our lands to repel invaders from the lands of the Swedes or from the Norse. How long since we've seen the wolf-cloaked figure in his mask of bone, prowling the edges of our shield walls?"

"Do you doubt he exists?" Dísa said. She felt Sigrún's eyes on her, as hot and sharp as an auger; she glanced over her shoulder and caught a glimpse of her grandmother's sharp cheekbones with their faded tattoo and her narrowed black eyes. The room held their collective breath, waiting for an explosion of ale-fueled temper.

"I know he exists, child," Sigrún said, after a moment. "I have seen him, a shadow lurking in the trees, a night-skulker under our walls. No, the Hooded One exists. I doubt that he cares, anymore, about what becomes of us."

"He cares," Dísa replied quietly, more to convince herself of this than others. "In his own way, after the fashion of his own kind, he cares."

Sigrún's eyebrow arched. "Are we not his kind?"

The younger woman felt herself skirting at the edges of Grimnir's long-held secrets. "He is the Tangled God's *immortal* herald—and that is no embroidery; it is telling no tales to remind you he is not like us. We are not his kind."

Sigrún shrugged, but kept her own counsel.

"So what does it mean?" Auða chimed in. "This song?"

"Just what you heard. Iðunn *did* have the gift of prophecy, and she foresaw a time when the world would end. She saw Ragnarök."

"See?" Askr hissed. Auða's reply was a thunderous scowl.

The sudden silence stretched on, as crisp and fragile as a skin of ice on the surface of a puddle. A moment longer . . . and then, Hreðel swore. "Ymir's blood! You witches and your prophecies! Give us a song of mead and whores, or get your pox-ridden arses out of my hall!"

His outburst prompted a peal of laughter. Berkano staggered upright—gentle Berkano, her face ruddy from the combination of the fire and mead. She clapped her hands. "I know a few songs," she slurred. "Give a listen, you wretched Geats!" And before long-suffering Laufeya could intervene Berkano snatched up a lyre and managed to strum out a tune as she sang in a voice as strident as a cat in heat:

> "I dreamt a dream last night,
> of silk and fine fur . . ."

But whether by accident or by design, the effect was the same. The cloak of doom was stripped away; slowly, conversation resumed, as did the gusty laughter of the thegns and the calls for more ale and mead. "Like I said, it's nothing," Dísa repeated, for Auða's benefit as much as for her own. Hrútr glanced away; Askr sucked his teeth and returned to his handiwork, leaning over Káta's shoulder as he wielded needle and paste. Káta pulled her father's horn cup to her and drained it, wincing with every prick of the ivory. Dísa shook herself and yawned. "I'm weary, cousin. I'm for bed."

Though Auða yet watched her with a jaundiced gaze, she nodded. "Aye, you need it. You look like day-old shit."

Dísa smiled. "Can I stay with you?"

"You have a place to stay already."

But the thought of trying to sleep under the same roof as her grandmother rankled. She wanted to curse and rail about how the old hag wanted her dead, and that dawn would find one or the other laid out on a bier with a belly full of cold steel, but Auða couldn't—or wouldn't—see it. Dísa's lips thinned, flattening so they would not betray a tremble of frustration. Since their kinship ran through the blood of Dísa's father, twelve years in the grave, Auða never saw the secret face of Sigrún. She never witnessed the fury, the scorn, the callous neglect. Even if she did, Auða would likely admire it. *The world is an anvil,* she would say, *and you are virgin steel. Your grandmother is the hammer, sent by the Gods to mold you . . . and it takes a strong arm to forge a sword.*

But Auða must have heard something in her silence—some echo of melancholy. Softly, she nudged Dísa in the ribs with one sharp elbow. "Did you forget? You laid claim to all old Kolgríma possessed . . . would not such a claim also include that rat-hole she called a house?"

A smile twitched at the corners of Dísa's mouth. "It would, wouldn't it?"

"Go on, then," Auða said. "Me, I'm going to try and get this great hairy heathen," she nudged Hrútr, "to show me his sword. What say you, warrior? Care to show a lady your goods?"

Hrútr glanced around, a smile tugging at the corners of his bearded mouth. "There's ladies about?"

"I've never had a lady," his brother, Askr, said.

"And you'll not have this one, either! You think I'm one of your trollops from Frankia?"

Still smiling, Dísa rose and went her way. She left Gautheimr with far less fanfare than when she entered. A few folk shouted their good nights before returning to their cups; Jarl Hreðel made a halfhearted wave and then went back to trying to convince Laufeya she needed a man like his son—stubborn wretch though he was—to protect her. Her grandmother marked her departure with a scowl. Dísa shivered at the malice in Sigrún's gaze, hiding the gesture as she made to straighten her cloak. She hitched reassuringly at the seax in her belt and stepped out into the night.

A cold wind blew fat flakes of snow down from the North. It was well after midnight, and flickering green lights illuminated the clouds as unseen *jötnar* struggled and strove between the worlds. Dísa averted her eyes. There was not much in this world she feared, but those weird shimmering curtains that illuminated the northern sky filled her with an unreasoning terror.

The young woman made for the first terrace; thence to an alley near the gates. Wedged into a space behind Kjartan Sigurdsson's house and smithy—its forge cold and dark more often than not—Kolgríma's ancient hovel had the look of a huntsman's shack to it, with animal skulls and antlers nailed to the roof timbers and half-rotted skins draped across a fence out front. Though Dísa saw a similarity between this moldering heap of timber and straw and the Hooded One's longhouse.

As she crossed the fence and approached the door, Dísa wasn't sure what to expect. Here was the Niflhel of her childhood, the misty abode of trolls and witches; it was to Kolgríma's lair that the women of Hrafnhaugr pointed when they sought to cow their unruly sprats. And Kolgríma played the part, gimlet-eyed and twisted, clad always in black, with gray locks that knew nothing of the comb or the braid. More than once, she threatened to hang Dísa from the rafters like a Yule boar and drain the blood from her.

"How long till I'm the same, a twisted old crone that brats taunt and their mothers use to keep them in line?" Dísa muttered.

"What?" came a soft voice at her back. Dísa whirled, her hand falling to the hilt of her seax. A familiar figure stepped from the shelter of the porch where Kjartan had his anvil.

"Flóki, you bastard," she said. "What are you doing lurking about?"

"Waiting for you," replied Flóki. At eighteen, he was taller than his father and possessed the lean frame and fine features of his mother's people. She had died bringing him forth into the world; rather than souring Hreðel's feeling toward him, the price he paid to have a son and heir caused the old Jarl to hold Flóki close. He remained clean-shaven, the mark of a youth untested in battle. "Tell me what you said, just now."

Dísa waved him off. "It was nothing. Do . . . Do you want to come in?"

"Are you sure?"

"Who knows how many dead children I'll have to move to sit down? You've a strong back."

Flóki smiled at this.

Exhaling, she braced herself and opened the door. Eerie green light flickered in, revealing nothing. Dísa stepped over the threshold. Near the door, she found flint and steel and an oil lamp. She struck a light . . .

It was not what she expected. No throat-slit children hung from the rafters, no carpet of bones obscured the floor, no fathomless sigils chalked the walls. It was . . . neat. Almost tidy: a cold stone hearth with its next fire set out, a bedstead covered in reindeer pelts, a chest for clothes, an old birch-wood loom, a cluttered table and chair. By the lamp's warm glow, she saw details of an otherwise quiet life; a life spent mediating between a folk who did not appreciate her and the beast who ruled them from the shadows. Suddenly, Dísa understood. This was Kolgríma's refuge. This was where she escaped to when Grimnir's presence became too much to bear—and it was a reflection of Kolgríma's own dream for herself, a young girl's desire for a life of peace.

And Dísa found she did not feel like an interloper. She felt welcomed, encouraged by the resonance of humanity she discovered. *I survived decades like this,* Kolgríma's spirit said to her, *and so can you.*

Behind her, she heard Flóki's grunt of surprise. "Not what I expected."

"No," Dísa replied. She placed the lamp on the table, alongside scavenged bits that were like pieces of a puzzle. A broken spindle in need of mending, an old cracked scabbard with a broken chape, bundled herbs and oak galls that awaited the grinding pestle. "But it will do."

Dísa turned. She drew the sheathed seax from her belt, tossed it on the bed, and discovered Flóki staring hard at her from the threshold, brows drawn together. "What happened out there?"

"You first. And, you should know, your father is after Laufeya to warm your bed."

"That old sot can hang," Flóki snapped with more heat in his voice than Dísa had ever heard from him.

"Hrútr said you're itching to be out from under Hreðel's thumb. Is this true?"

Flóki rubbed his bare chin. "It's high time, damn him! He grooms me to take over from him when he's old and gray, but he's forgotten that I must make my own name ere the Raven-Geats see me their Jarl. I asked for his blessing, to go with Eirik Viðarrson and his brother, Ulff, to raid down past the Horn. Perhaps even journey down to Eiðar and take ship with the Danes. He refused to give it. I've given him eighteen years, Dísa. It's time I go my own way."

"Then go," she replied. "Make your own name, and come back to Hrafnhaugr bearing Irish gold and tales of sea-demons. Unless he marries you off to Laufeya, I'll be needing a bedmate."

"Do you command me, as the Hooded One's priestess?"

"As your friend, you daft bastard."

Flóki fell silent, his dark eyes reflecting the eerie lights in the heavens as he glanced out the door. "Maybe you're right. Now, your turn. What happened?"

Dísa clenched her fist, felt the ache of bruised knuckles; thrice she did this, her attention focused on the play of muscle and sinew, on the abrasions left by her struggle with Grimnir. She rubbed at a fleck of black blood trapped by a fold of skin between her middle finger and her ring finger. "I went to him," Dísa said at length. "I went to the Hooded One with anger in my heart, ready to die rather than live on in the shame of slavery. I provoked him. And when he came for my head, I did not back down. Can you believe that?"

"You were always like your mother," Flóki said, leaning against the doorjamb.

"I wish I had more of a memory of her." Dísa sat on the edge of the bedstead. She dragged the seax over to her and drew the blade half from its scabbard. "He gave this to me, the Hooded One did, after he nearly cracked my skull. He said, 'Every bird needs a talon.' This is mine. This is how my fame will spread." Metal rang as she thrust the blade back into its scabbard. "But I must play my part."

"You do not sound sure."

Dísa looked up. "No, I am sure. It's just . . ." She searched for the words to explain how she felt without betraying her oath. Finally, she gestured about, encompassing Kolgríma's hidden refuge. "Why do you think Kolgríma fashioned this place in secret? Why did she want none of us to see past her grim countenance, to see that there was a woman of flesh and blood behind the black guise of a witch?"

"For effect," Flóki said. "Her name was built upon whispers of sorcery."

"But there was more to her," Dísa agreed. She looked up. "What if there's nothing more to me? What if I am like this scabbard, empty and useless unless filled with iron and the drippings of battle?"

But Flóki only chuckled. He took two steps into the single-room house, caught Dísa's head in his hands, and kissed her with the passion of a man who had seen his way laid out before him. A man who had far to go, but someone to wait for him by the hearth. "And you call me daft," he said, retreating to the door. "You beggar belief. Hand you the thing you've dreamed of since you were in swaddling clothes and you will find a way to suffer over it. As for me, I'm for Eiðar, Ireland, or Valhöll. When you see me again, it will be atop a ship made of gold!"

Dísa shed no tears. She smiled. "I just want to see you with a beard, you daft bastard."

Flóki cast an eye to the heavens. The eerie lights had faded, leaving nothing but scudding shoals of cloud and a bright gibbous moon. He winked, and then closed the door.

Dísa heard his footsteps recede into the night, losing them as he passed the silent forge of Kjartan Sigurdsson. She sat at the edge of the bed. Her face ached. Her vision blurred; she yawned, looked at the cold hearth, with its logs and kindling awaiting only the spark of flint on steel. She knew she should rise and see to the fire, but exhaustion had its claws in her so deep she could barely move. Dísa managed to kick her shoes off. She managed to burrow under the furs covering the bedstead—furs that smelled faintly of old herbs and dust. And as she slipped into a dreamless slumber, she managed to catch the hilt of her seax and pull it into a lover's embrace.

After that, Dísa Dagrúnsdottir knew no more.

6

The sun was fully up when the pounding started. At first, Dísa thought it merely in her head, the effect of too much mead, too little rest, and a dire crack to the skull. She groaned and burrowed deeper into the warm pelts. But it kept on, despite her every effort to ignore it.

And with it came a man's voice bellowing her name.

"Dísa! By Odin's lost eye, girl! Dísa! Rouse yourself!"

Her door rattled on its hinges as a dagger pommel struck it half a dozen times in quick succession. Snarling and spitting, Dísa threw back the furs and rolled off the bedstead. Disheveled, with bruised eyes nearly swollen shut, she staggered to the door and flung it open. Light spilled in, and with it the shadow of two interlopers.

"What do you want, you dung-bearded pot-licking whoreson starver of ravens?"

"Mind your tongue, girl." Dísa heard her grandmother's harsh voice. She was in no mood, though. Her eyes watered; her head ached far beyond anything she thought possible.

"Mind yours! What do you want, I said?"

Dísa squinted, focusing one eye on the man who stood before her— heavyset and barely a head taller than she. It was Jarl Hreðel, she realized; like her, he was still bleary-eyed from the night before. The golden torque he wore around his neck caught the watery midmorning sun and reflected it—jags of light Dísa found too painful to look at. He sheathed his dagger. With trembling fingers, he smoothed his silver-flecked beard.

"My son, where is he?"

Dísa shrugged. "How the devil should I know? I'm not his minder!"

Behind him, Sigrún smote the frame of the house with one balled fist. "Stupid girl!" she snarled. "Your Jarl—"

But before Dísa could give voice to the salty curses that were poised to fall from her lips, Hreðel intervened. "Be silent!" he said, glancing over his shoulder. "Fetch water for the girl, and see that food is brought." Then he turned back to Dísa. "May I come in?"

Dísa knew better than to chuckle at her grandmother's discomfiture. The look in Hreðel's eyes was one she knew well—a barely suppressed need to do violence. And that look reminded her, then, that though he was not the largest or the fiercest warrior in Hrafnhaugr, there was a reason Hreðel Kveldúlfsson was its Jarl.

Sigrún withdrew to do Hreðel's bidding. Dísa motioned for the Jarl to come inside. He did so haltingly. She could tell by his expression that he had never stepped foot inside Kolgríma's hovel. Dísa offered him the chair while she sat on the edge of the bedstead. The young woman palmed her aching forehead, ran the same hand through her tangled locks, and ended the motion with her cheek resting on the heel of her hand. "And so?" she said, suppressing a yawn.

"Flóki has gone," Hreðel replied. The thick fingers of his left hand twittered with a ring he wore on his right. "Snuck out sometime before dawn. The sons of Viðar, Eirik and Ulff, and Sigræfr the Bastard, have gone with him."

There came a soft scratch from outside. Hreðel cursed at the interruption; Dísa took it as a chance to gather her thoughts. She rose, opened the door, and saw the downcast face of Bryngerðr—one of the youngest of the Daughters of the Raven. She offered Dísa a basket with a flask of water, another of ale, bread, a crock of butter, and a smaller dish of honey. Dísa smiled at the girl, took her burden, and sent her on her way.

"Do you think I have him hidden away? Stashed under my bed?" Dísa said as she resumed her place.

Hreðel's eyes narrowed, but he held his anger. "My son loves you," he said, ignoring the color rising in her cheeks. "I thought, perhaps . . ."

"You thought perhaps he would not make good on his oath to fare forth and earn his beard, did you?"

"That's none of your concern," Hreðel said, his voice hard and cold.

"You've made it my concern," Dísa snapped. She sat upright and pointed an accusing finger at the Jarl. "You want something from me, I take it? So, tell me what you know!"

Hreðel chewed his lip; finally, he said: "He's been worried that a third long winter in a row might spell famine. Last night, he sought my blessing to lead a band of raiders south and west, past the Horn. And if they could find no prey, he wanted to push on to Eiðar and spy upon the Swedes there. Maybe take ship to the Danelands or to Ireland. I saw through him, of course. A lad's foolishness, it was. An excuse to—"

"To earn his beard?" Her words struck the Jarl like a blow. Still, he took it. "You refused, and he gathered a few trusty lads and went anyway." Dísa sucked her teeth. She weighed her next words very carefully. "Have you considered," she said, "just letting Flóki have his way in this? Send a couple of your thegns after him—warriors you trust—if you must, but tell them to stay out of sight. He wants space, Jarl. Space to stand on his own and be his own man."

"So now you know my son better than I?" Hreðel said, his rage boiling over. "You watched his brothers die, did you? One by one? You watched his mother bear one last son then fade away from heartsickness? You know all this, which is why you dare lecture me about my son?"

Dísa winced. "No," she said after a moment. "No, but I do know he's not some little boy who has wandered away from home. He is eighteen summers, soon to be nineteen, and you do him no favors by coddling him. Why have you come to me? What do you want, Jarl, if not my advice?"

Hreðel looked up, his fierce eyes damp and agleam with unspoken regrets. "I have served the Hooded One all my life. I have asked nothing of him. I have always put the needs of Hrafnhaugr above my own. But now, I ask a boon of him. Go to him, girl! Ask him—beg him if need be—to fetch my son back to me! Flóki is all I have left . . ."

Dísa shook her head. "I was told not to return till the new moon."

Faster than Dísa thought possible, Hreðel's long fingers wrapped around her throat; the Jarl lifted her bodily from the bedstead, twisted, and slammed her up against the stone hearth. The impact caused the hut to creak, and set stars to dancing before Dísa's eyes. Her seax clattered to the floor.

"Fool!" Spittle flew from Hreðel's lips as he leaned in close, his breath hot and reeking of sour wine. "You *will* do this! You will go to him and you will convince him to help! If he does not—Odin, witness my oath!—if he does not, then I swear I will send my warriors against him and we will burn even the memory of him from this land!" He let go of her.

Gasping, Dísa slid to the floor. She rubbed her throat, the marks of his fingers still livid against her flesh. "And you think threatening him will bring the Hooded One around to your cause?" she said, after a moment, her eyes flickering to the hilt of her seax. She very nearly dove for the blade and drew steel on her chief, consequences be damned. Instead, Dísa winced and rose on unsteady legs. "You know better than I, the Hooded One is not the . . . the *giving* sort. A lad who has run off with his mates to make their war-names might not warrant his attention. There may be a price."

"And so?" Hreðel snarled, gripping her arm. "Tell him I will give all I have to see my son safely home again, if that puts him on the trail to Eiðar, to the Danelands, or to Hel's fences! Or, tell him I will come for his bastard head if he refuses! I care naught for how you do it, girl! Just get him to fetch my boy back!"

Dísa twisted free of his grasp. "I will tell him, Jarl," she hissed. "He will understand. You have my word on it."

Hreðel nodded. He stepped back and shook himself like a bear coming awake. The image of the desperate father sank from view. Soon, he was the Jarl of Hrafnhaugr once more. Lord of the Raven-Geats. He thrust his hands into his richly worked sash and waited for Dísa to open the door for him. Outside, out of earshot, she could see Sigrún and a few others marking time and waiting for Hreðel to emerge. The Jarl stood on the threshold. He nodded to his followers, then turned and met Dísa's gaze. His eyes were cool and brown, but the madness that lurked in them glimmered just below the surface, held steady by a chain forged of will. The smile that touched his lips knew nothing of warmth. "Men think me soft in the head," he said, his voice barely rising above a whisper. "Women think me weak. I saw your eyes, girl. I saw you calculate how fast you could draw that pig-sticker and ram it through my guts. I can see why my son admires your courage. But remember this and remember it well: if you even think of drawing a blade on me again, not even the Hooded One will be able to protect you."

Dísa's smile matched his own; her eyes were like chips of ice. "And if you believe that," she said, "you're more of a fool than you seem. Have your men ready a boat. I'll leave within the hour."

Without waiting for Hreðel to answer, Dísa closed the door in his face.

It was quiet inside. Motes of dust swirled in the light that slanted through a horn-paned window. Dísa stood still, her back against the door, and listened. She heard Hreðel walk away, heard her grandmother's harsh voice: "Well?"

And then, nothing. A bird pecked on the eaves of Kjartan's smithy; a dog barked nearby.

Well, indeed, Dísa thought. She went to the basket. Her trembling hand hovered over the two flasks, one of water and the other of ale. She shook the fear from her hand, cursing under her breath, and then seized the flask of ale. She drained it in half a dozen gulps. The bite of the alcohol helped steady her. Dísa wiped her lips on the forearm of her tunic. She had an hour and more to come up with a good argument for why Grimnir should involve himself in this spat between father and son, for a reason not to relay Hreðel's threat to him. And she knew—by the dull ache in the pit of her belly—this would not end well.

Still, it was not all bad. Hreðel's petition gave her a reason to return. And though a part of her loathed the Hooded One, she was eager to begin her weapons training. As Dísa attacked the loaf of bread, in her mind she started laying out what she would need. Her seax, of course, and a change of clothes; food, and perhaps a bribe in the form of mead . . .

HREÐEL LEFT NOTHING TO CHANCE. The two Bjorns, the White and the Black, bundled Dísa into a *færeringr,* a four-oared boat that resembled a miniature longship, and set out across Skærvík. An old, weather-beaten Geat sat in the stern, his leathery hand on the steering tiller as the two Bjorns plied the oars. Dísa knew him only as Hygge—Old Hygge—and by their reckoning he was near a hundred years in age, making him the eldest man in Hrafnhaugr. Though he might have been older than some trees, Dísa watched him transform from the moment his fingers caressed the spruce wood of the tiller. The years shed from his limbs like the leaves of an oak. Strong white teeth shone through his tangled gray beard as Old Hygge guided them across Vänern's dark waters.

The two Bjorns made quick work of it, even towing a smaller boat in their wake. This last was Dísa's idea, to bring a *keipr* along. She could hide the two-oared canoe at the lake's edge, she told Hreðel, and once she had the Hooded One's answer she could be back in Hrafnhaugr within an hour.

The keel ground against the shingle; Old Hygge leaned back on the tiller, his seamed face the picture of serenity in the midday sun. Bjorn Hvítr lifted Dísa bodily from the boat and carried her ashore while Bjorn Svarti dragged the *keipr* up on the shingle and laid it keel-up under a veil of evergreen shrubs, its oars underneath it.

"We will wait here for you," Bjorn Hvítr said, handing Dísa her leather knapsack. He glanced to the sky, where clouds were beginning to gather. "There's weather on the way."

"That's not necessary," she said, nodding to where Bjorn Svarti was putting the finishing touches on the *keipr*'s hiding place. "It may take a while to coax an answer from him. But tell the Jarl I'll be along as soon as the Hooded One decides."

Bjorn Hvítr looked dubious, but finally agreed. In short order, the two Bjorns said their farewells and shoved off, Old Hygge coming to life as soon as the oars bit the water.

Dísa watched them a moment before shouldering her knapsack and heading inland. Unlike the day before, this time she was prepared: she'd drawn her hair back into a braid, gathered at the nape of her neck and secured with whalebone combs; she'd changed into a fresh tunic, dyed the same shade of green as the boughs of a spruce and worked in black thread. Dísa wore a man's trousers of undyed wool, gathered by swathing bands to the knee, and stitched leather boots with hobnailed soles of tough ox hide. Over this, she wore the cloak of wool and wolf fur Halla had given her. And riding her hip—supported by a broad leather belt with buckle and fittings done in hammered bronze—was her sheathed seax.

She made good time, reaching the boundary stone at the crest of the hill, half a league from the beach, before the hour was out. As she came abreast of the carved stone, though, she slowed, and then stopped. Something stirred the hackles on her neck. Something unseen. Dísa dropped her hand to the hilt of her seax. Her eyes raked the line of trees ahead, their roots wreathed in a thin mist that drifted up the slope from the bog-land below. An eerie silence gripped the woods around her. Images from her dreams welled unbidden in her mind: *a figure waits; it bears the shape of a man, though hunched and as twisted as the staff he leans upon. He is clad in a voluminous cloak with a slouch hat pulled low. A single malevolent eye gleams from beneath the brim.*

Slowly, she turned . . .

And there was Grimnir. He squatted on his haunches in the lee of the boundary stone with his shoulder leaned against it, his black hair a tangled veil through which his good eye shone like an ember. His nose wrinkled, nostrils flaring; he sniffed the air above the ground.

"Scared, little bird?"

Dísa relaxed—but only by a fraction. "I . . . I thought you were someone else."

"Did you now?" Grimnir snorted. "Who else but you would be fool enough to wander up to the fences of my lands uninvited? Are they here now? Call them out, so I might peel the wretched skin from their bones and hang it on a bramble!"

Dísa cursed under her breath.

"What was that, rat?"

"I said: does everyone have an oar up their ass, this day?" She gestured ahead of them. "I did not see anyone, nor did anyone follow me up here! The . . . The air grew . . . I cannot explain it. *Silent,* perhaps? Silent and alive at the same time, like the way it feels before a storm breaks. It reminded me of a dream I had, is all."

Grimnir cocked an eyebrow. "And you were ready to fight, little bird? Ready to draw your talon and rip out the eyes of your unseen foe?"

"Eye," Dísa said. "He only had one, in the dream."

Grimnir rose to his feet, chuckling. "So you're not blind, which is good news. The bad news, though, is you're too stupid to count."

Dísa blinked. "What?"

"You heard me! Did no one teach you your numbers?" Harness jangled as Grimnir sprang down to the path. "Because by my reckoning you're nigh on twelve days shy of the new moon. So I ask myself," he said, jabbing a finger at Dísa, "why *are* you traipsing about, little fool?"

"Jarl Hreðel sent me."

Grimnir sniffed in disdain. "And what does that filthy sot want now, eh? Another throat slit? Another enemy stabbed in the dark and sank in a bog? The whole useless lot of you seems to have forgotten who is servant and who is master, here."

Dísa made to take a step toward him but hesitated. "He's not forgotten," she said. "He has served the Hooded One, served you, faithfully all his life. What he asks now, is a boon. Payment for his loyalty."

"Payment, is it?" Grimnir squinted. "What is he asking?"

"His son, Flóki. He's run off with a couple of his mates, to either hunt around the borders of Geatland or raid the folk of Eiðar, at the southern end of the lake."

"Eiðar, eh?" Grimnir sucked his teeth. "I know it. Soft little squat filled with cheeseparing Swedes and the miserly Danes who trade with them. Skinflints, the lot of them. If I had a few trusty lads from the old days, I'd have long since lanced that boil and squeezed it dry. Your chief's lad is no fool, but he's a mite full of himself if he thinks three milk-blooded Geats fresh off the tit will do more than piss off that nest of pikers. Does that wretch, Hreðel, want me to show those lads how it's done?"

Dísa shook her head. "He wants you to stop Flóki. Stop him and fetch him back." But even as she said it, Dísa knew she'd chosen the wrong word. Grimnir's face darkened; his single eye blazed.

"*Fetch?* The sot thinks me no better than a dog, does he? Wants me to *fetch* his boy back to him like a cur playing at sticks?" Grimnir hawked up a gobbet of phlegm and spat it at the boundary stone. "There's my answer! Tell your precious Hreðel if he's lucky and his idiot boy isn't killed outright, the Swedes might sell what's left back to him!"

Dísa stared at him, unsure of what she'd just heard. Had Grimnir just consigned Flóki to slavery or worse over a single word, a perceived slight that wasn't there? The young woman's choler rose. She spluttered and stamped her foot. "You . . . you bowlegged dribbling shortwit! Ymir's beard! That wasn't how he meant it! Flóki's a good man! One of the best! Hreðel doesn't want to see his son die needlessly, you black-toothed sack of offal! Flóki's meant for greater things than licking the boots of some fishbelly Swede!"

Grimnir's nostrils flared. His eyes narrowed; the ghost of a sneer teased the corners of his mouth. "So that's it, is it? Aye, it makes sense now. You should have just told me the truth, little bird."

"Truth?" Dísa scowled. "What truth? What are you blathering on about?"

Grimnir turned away; as he did, his sneer turned to a full-on smile—the toothsome grin of a cat toying with its prey. "You should have just said you fancy the lad."

The accusation hung between them for a moment. Though nearly sixteen, Dísa had lived among men long enough to realize when she was being baited. Grimnir wanted to provoke her, to make her flustered and embarrassed because that amused him. And while the bastard was no man, he shared enough traits with them that she recognized how to take the piss right out of him. "So what if I do?" she said after a moment, her chin rising in defiance. "He's quick-witted and hard-handed, as befits a young lord of the Geats. He will be a man of parts, one day. I could do much worse. Does my fancying him tip the balance in his favor?"

Grimnir shrugged. "It makes the game more interesting." He glanced sharply at her. "Does the lad fancy you in return?"

Again, she didn't react to his goading; she hid her feelings. "I think not," she lied. "Oh, I'd wager Hreðel wanted the match, since it would strengthen his hold on my grandmother through bonds of kinship. But Flóki . . . ?" She made a half-shrug that turned to a wince. "I do not know."

"But you would see him spared?"

"I would."

"All safe and snug and back under the thumb of his useless sot of a father, eh?"

Dísa swallowed. If she were honest, she'd rather see Flóki make a name for himself away from Hreðel, but . . . she nodded. "I would."

Grimnir circled her; his eyes narrowed. The ivory and silver of his false one caught the light, inlaid runes flaring. "What would you give to make that happen, little bird?"

Dísa sensed a trap. Her pointed gaze matched his own as she followed his movements. "What do you mean?"

"You know what I mean. What would you give to see your sweet little Flóki safe and whole again?"

"I . . . I have nothing."

"You have a pound of flesh, do you not?" Grimnir said. "You have the blood in your veins? The sweat from your brow? The salt-sweet tears of agony you will shed?"

Dísa hesitated, and then replied: "I have those things, yes."

"And you would give them?"

"Yes, but—"

Grimnir stopped circling. One sinewy hand rested on the hilt of his seax. Dísa heard the *tick-tick-tick* of his black-nailed finger tapping the pommel. "Here is the wager, little bird: you want me to fetch your precious Flóki? I'll do it . . . but only if you can draw blood on me, first."

"I drew blood on you yesterday," she replied. Even so, her off hand drifted down toward the scabbard of her seax.

"That? That was luck," Grimnir snarled. "Let's see you do it for real, this time!"

"And what happens to Flóki if I kill you by accident?"

At this, Grimnir threw back his head and roared with laughter. He coughed and spluttered, wiped his eyes with the back of his hand. "What a tender little fool! I see why you like this wretch, Flóki—he's as full of himself as you are. Do not worry about me. If after twelve centuries I can't defend myself from some lickspittle whelp like you, I'm not fit to live."

"So, one cut," Dísa said. Subtly, she shifted her weight onto her lead foot. "One cut is your fee for helping my friend, my Jarl's son? The son of a man who has served you without fail?"

"Draw blood and he is as good as back home, snug in his bed," Grimnir replied. He held up a cautioning finger. "But you'd best not hold back, little bird. If I sense even a shred of hesitation, I'll take that sticker from you—"

And before Grimnir could finish, Dísa attacked. With scabbard held steady by her off hand, she drew her seax in a single fluid motion and slashed up and out. The tip of the blade streaked for the point of Grimnir's chin. He did not move his body; Grimnir merely swayed his head back out of reach as her blow swept by. Before she could recover, though, he stepped into her guard and punched her in the face.

Dísa went down, doubled over, her seax clattering from nerveless fingers. She clutched at her face. Hot blood ran from her already-broken nose— blood she choked on as she drew breath to scream. The young woman spat and cursed; blinded by the rush of tears, she scrabbled for her fallen seax.

Whereupon Grimnir kicked her in the ribs for good measure.

The blow of his booted foot caused a bloody froth to explode from her lungs; she gagged and writhed, gasping for breath.

Grimnir leaned over her. "I want my pound of flesh, little bird. I want every drop of blood, every ounce of sweat, every tear you shed. Show me your mettle, daughter of swine. You want your darling Flóki spared? Prove it! Come after me. Draw my blood, if you can." And with that, Grimnir bounded over and caught up her knapsack. With a derisive chuckle, he loped off down the trail toward the longhouse.

Dísa lay there a moment. Then, gritting her teeth against a wave of nausea, she rolled to her knees. She fished her seax from the leaf mold, sheathed it, and struggled to her feet. The world swam. Her head felt like someone had struck her in the face with the flat of an axe. But she stayed upright. The young woman spat blood then scrubbed her mouth with the sleeve of her tunic.

And with a murderous light dancing in her eyes, Dísa followed in Grimnir's wake.

7

Grimnir reached the top step leading to the longhouse—where they'd had their little altercation the night before last—even as Dísa emerged from the trees at the crest of the ridgeline. He grinned, watching as she slowly made her way down into the valley.

He sat. While he waited, Grimnir rooted through her knapsack. The little bird had nothing of any value to him. No coin hidden in among her spare tunics; no jewelry tucked into the coarse linen bag holding a loaf of bread and hard cheese; no ivory or silver hiding in a small purse that held her combs and bone hair pins, bronze needles and bobbins of thread. Only her woolen socks held promise. These Grimnir hefted, feeling their weight and hearing the slosh of liquid. He smacked his lips as he tugged down the wool to reveal two crockery bottles sealed with cork.

Grimnir worked the cork free and inhaled the musty reek of fermented honey. With a nod of his head, he toasted the girl as she reached the level of the bog and the corduroy of logs that led to the longhouse, then raised the bottle and drained off half its contents in three long swallows.

He grimaced. Their mead wasn't what it used to be. Back when Gífr ruled this roost, after the battle in the Jutland fen that left Grimnir's brother dead and the fortunes of his people broken, the Geats round about had more freedom to travel and to trade—not surrounded, as they were now, by the Nailed God's wretched lapdogs. Geats ventured out into the world, back then, and brought home honey from the west of England, from the vales of the River Rhône, and from as far afield as Árheimar on the banks of the Dnieper. More than honey, Grimnir recalled, they also fetched home incense and silver, glittering gems and gold, steel and fine leather. And from it all, they made proper gifts to the Tangled God's herald, Hrafnhaugr's protector, who kept their homes safe and their women unspoiled while the men fared forth.

Those Geats of old, they knew how to brew a proper mead—and how to show reverence for their betters. But this lot? Grimnir hawked and spat. *Nár!* All this lot knew how to do was whine and moan. And what do they offer for his troubles? Draughts of this honeyed dog's piss they called mead! Grimnir considered upending it, pouring the swill out where it might kill his weeds and poison the soil. But this was likely to be the best he'd get, and the son of Bálegyr was no wastrel. He tossed his head back and drained the bottle without letting it linger on his tongue.

Things changed, Grimnir reckoned as he cradled the now-empty bottle. Nothing now was as it had been. The Elder Days were a memory; less than a memory. They were the stuff of legend—heathen tales ripe for plunder at the hands of the Nailed God's folk. Fools, the lot of them! Oh, they wanted their White Christ's salvation! They panted for it like curs after a bitch in heat! But when it came time to teach their children the Nailed God's traditions, to recount his deeds and the deeds of his sworn men, they came up empty-handed. Did that stop them? No, they just stole what they needed from the Elder Days, changed the names, and made saints from swine.

With a snarl, Grimnir shied the empty bottle down the steps as Dísa reached the bottom. The crockery struck, shattered, peppering her with dregs and shards. Her curses were as salty as any of his lads of old.

What will they steal from me to recast into this world of theirs? A monster they'll make of me, no doubt; a beast of moor and fen. Good only for blunting the blade of some milk-blooded, cross-kissing hero. Faugh! Him *they'll make a saint and sing his death-song for a hundred generations to come.*

But who will sing mine?

That question vexed the son of Bálegyr. Who would sing his deeds? Not old Gífr, his mother's brother. He was four hundred years in the grave, slain fighting alongside a band of pagan Saxons against that Frankish dog-king, Karl

Magnus. Grimnir made his death-song in a burned-out village at the mouth of the Elbe River. Its crescendo was the sacrifice of the local priest, a wiry man with weather-beaten features and a salt-brown beard; his throttled corpse was the last to go atop Gífr's pyre. The sweet smoke of burned flesh drew the shades of the dead from dark Nástrond—that forsaken hall where the Nine Fathers of the *kaunar* schemed and plotted their revenge against the cursed Æsir. They heard Grimnir's song and knew who it was that came among them.

But he was the last of his people. The last of the *kaunar* left to plague Miðgarðr. *Who will sing mine?* Étaín? No, the foundling he'd left in Ériu had long since gone on to her Nailed God's halls. Would Halla summon the shades of his kin from Nástrond, or this wretched little scrap, here? He eyed Dísa, who was coming hard up the stairs, hot for his blood. *Perhaps,* Grimnir thought, rolling to his feet, *perhaps I will sing my own song.*

Grimnir came up in a fighting crouch; steel rasped against the iron throat of his scabbard as he aired the edge of his long-seax.

Dísa reached the level of the longhouse; she was out of breath, still bleeding from her twice-broken nose. Even so, she did not pause. The moment her foot touched the top step, the young woman launched herself at Grimnir.

And Grimnir met her blade to blade.

Steel scraped and whispered, grinding together then ringing apart like murderous chimes. Dísa came on like a tempest—though she hesitated to let herself get caught wrong-footed within reach of Grimnir's long arms. She danced in, hacked at his blind side or thrust for his belly, and danced back again.

Grimnir sneered. The little rat had played with a blade before; she knew enough to parry and recover, to not leave herself open, but she had no art. Fighting her was like fighting a willow branch in a gale. She was quick and unpredictable, but her blows lacked weight.

And she was slowing. Dísa made a wild cut across her body, fairly flinging the blade at him in hopes it might connect. Grimnir parried it hard. Their cross-guards met, and the impact all but jarred Dísa's blade from her hand. She stumbled back, eyes wide.

"Fool!" he hissed. "Quit your cursed flailing. You're not chopping wood! And stop all this dancing about. Move with purpose." Grimnir swayed from side to side, each step bringing him closer. He tossed his seax from hand to hand; the movement drew Dísa's gaze. The moment she took her eyes off him, Grimnir feinted—his posture and movement that of a deep thrust. Dísa leaped back, parrying nothing. Grimnir chuckled. "Make the wretch you're about to kill see what isn't there."

Dísa nodded, brow crinkling. She drew breath . . .

And quick as a snake, she stabbed something on the ground and flung it up at Grimnir. He recoiled as a woolen sock bounced off his chest; a heartbeat later, he felt the tip of her seax skitter across his mail-clad belly.

Close. The little wretch almost had me.

Dísa exhaled, her breath wrapped around a sulphurous curse. Her eyes flickered over his frame, searching.

Almost.

Grimnir used that slight pause, that wavering loss of concentration she exhibited when she sought any trickle of blood her blows might have caused; he exploited it, and he did so without mercy.

Flipping his grip so that he led with the heavy blunt spine of his seax, Grimnir feinted left; Dísa moved her blade out of line with her center, to parry what she thought would be a high backhand slash. Instead, Grimnir batted her blade hand farther left with his open palm even as he struck her across her right temple, above her ear. There came an audible *crack;* Dísa gasped. She dropped her seax as her eyes rolled back into her skull. The young woman swayed and toppled to the left, face-first into the grassy sward before the longhouse porch. There she lay, still as death.

Grimnir sucked his teeth. "Soft-skulled little fool," he muttered, sheathing his seax. Going to her side, he seized her by the arm and roughly flipped her onto her back. Dísa lay like a rag doll, eyes half-open and blood drooling from her hairline. He hadn't hit her *that* hard, and then the thick mass of her hair had taken some of the impact, or so he thought; even still, he knew the sound of a broken skull when he heard one.

Grimnir straightened. He hawked and spat, then called over his shoulder, into the longhouse.

"Halla!"

He heard the shuffle of the troll-woman's bare feet as she came to the door but did not emerge. Though hidden by a veil of clouds, the sun still had the power to turn her back to the stone from whence her kind came. Grimnir heard her pause as she peered out, then: "What have you done?"

Grimnir snorted. "She's weak, old hag! Like all their kind. Weak and useless."

Halla made a scornful hissing sound. "Bring her inside, and be quick about it."

BENEATH THE FOUNDATIONS OF THE longhouse, down twenty-seven steps of damp stone carved from its earthen mound, lay a cellar. No storeroom, this; nor was it some ragged and lightless hole where a lifetime's worth of detritus was left to molder, out of sight and out of mind. No, this cellar's measurements were precise: eighteen slabs of rune-carved stone, each a foot wide, lined the length of its walls; nine more lined its width at either end. Beams of fire-hardened ash formed a vaulted ceiling, with heavy posts carved from the same wood at each corner. A single stone slab rested flat in the dirt floor of the cellar. All of this was Gífr's handiwork—Gífr, who was the eldest son of Kjallandi and brother of Skríkja, Grimnir's mother; Gífr, who had been wise in the ways of seers and of sorcerers.

Here was where Grimnir brought Dísa. He placed the girl on the stone slab. Her body trembled, wracked by convulsions, and the whites of her eyes showed through half-open lids. *"Faugh!"* he muttered. "I didn't hit her that hard, I tell you."

"You fool," Halla snarled. Her tone brooked no argument. "Go. I will do what I can, and pray it will be enough. Go, I said!" The troll-woman sucked her teeth; she dismissed Grimnir with a terse wave as she hurried about, collecting the things she might need. She heard the cellar door snick shut, then went to Dísa's side and sat with her knees folded under her. The blow to the girl's temple had cracked her skull; healing such an injury was beyond Halla's art. She would linger in this state and be dead by nightfall, unless . . .

Unless . . .

Around them, a constellation of deeply-cut runes, silver-wrought and glowing, provided an unearthly light. By this faint radiance, the troll-woman sang in a lilting voice:

"Under the eaves sat | an old woman of Myrkviðr,
Who nurtured there | the offspring of fruit and bole."

And as she sang, she used a stone pestle to crush together ingredients in a skull-sized mortar. Hemp seed and amber, first . . .

"They nurtured her | in exchange,
  Shielding her from | Sól's hateful light."

Then, waxy green verdigris scraped from a bronze ingot soaked in vinegar . . .

"Remember this compact, | *landvættir* of yore,
  Who gave me succor | in the days gone by."

And filings of iron from fiery black rocks the Gods themselves hurled down from the heavens . . .

"Nine worlds I know, | the nine in the tree
  With mighty roots | beneath the mold."

Finally, Halla poured a measure of raw, uncut wine from an ancient pottery jar, brought over land and sea from the vineyards of the Greeks, and stirred the concoction together with a wand of rune-carved ash.

"Hear me, spirit of this land, *vættr* of root and bole," she said, raising the mortar over a patch of bare earth. "I seek your help. Come forth. Partake of the Wine of Gunnlöð and let us speak together." Halla decanted half of the potion into the earth and waited.

At first, nothing happened. The mixture of wine and arcane sediments dampened the soil; it pooled in divots and ran from furrow to furrow until slowly the earth drank it in.

Halla watched. Her brows met in an impatient scowl. She poured out just a bit more . . .

There! A pale, wriggling thing broke through the mantle of soil—like a worm, only fibrous. It sought out the dampness, questing through the loam until it reached the wine-soaked earth. Another followed. Then another. Halla knew them for what they were: tree roots.

"Yes," the troll-witch said. "Come forth, great *vættr*. Come and drink."

Suddenly, the ground around the stone slab writhed. Hundreds of roots—ash and oak, willow and rowan—boiled up from the earth. They knit themselves together, twisting and creaking, cracking and rubbing, until an eerie shape took form . . . a homunculus, a manikin wrought in parody of the human form and suspended fetus-like in a bier of tangled roots. Halla recognized the suggestion of a spine, the braided rootlets that hinted at ribs, the knotted skull-like protuberance atop narrow shoulders. The cellar smelled of damp earth and rich sap as the *vættr* opened its hollow eyes.

When it spoke, its voice was the rustle of leaves:

> "Why do you vex us | daughter of Járnviðja?
> The land is cursed | that lies hard by;
> And we shall ever | in deep Miðgarðr dwell,
> Till the Dragon answers his master's call."

"I seek your help, great *vættr,*" Halla replied. She put the mortar down in the soil at the edge of the slab. "And the Wine of Gunnlöð is my gift to you. Will you hear me?"

Tendrils of root crawled up the sides of the mortar and into the slurry of wine and sediment. The homunculus creaked and swayed in its bier.

"Speak."

"Through root and bole, stock and stone, you feel the shifting of the earth. You taste the wind on leaves beyond number and feel the rain on countless limbs. You know the time of the Dragon nears. This child of Man who lies here"—Halla placed Dísa's limp hand on the earth, where tendrils of root caressed it—"is a Daughter of the Raven. The prophecy speaks of her. She is the Day who gives way to Night. But she is wounded, great *vættr,* wounded unto death. The healing of this hurt is beyond me. Can you save her?"

There was a long silence, punctuated by creaks and sighs, by the rustle of unseen branches. The homunculus rocked as though buffeted by a phantom wind. When it finally spoke, its rustling voice bore the crackle of autumn and impending frost.

> "No measure of hurt | is beyond our ken,
> Troll-born child of Myrkviðr;
> Well we remember | the ancient compacts
> Twixt spirits of bole and stone.

"But a carrion-reek | hangs about you
    And its seed is hate eternal;
    Too long have you dwelt | in the Wolf's shadow,
    Who soon must be brought to heel."

Halla understood the *vættr*'s reluctance. Long and deep was the feud between Grimnir's folk and the spirits of Miðgarðr; the *skraelingar* honored
none of the ancient pacts, kept none of the ancient strictures. Men at least
could plead ignorance. Not so the bastard sons of Loki.

"She is not part of that feud, great *vættr*," Halla said. "She bears your kind
no malice. What's more: if she dies, we are all lost. The axes of the Cross-
men will seek out every last root and bulb of the Elder World."

"Bough will burn | and root will burn,
    And even stones turn to ash;
    What cannot burn | are the tangles of Fate
    Spun by the hands of Urðr."

Even among the *vættir*, all things were foretold; every life was apportioned
by the Norns, those weird sisters who dwelled at the base of Yggðrasil; every
triumph and every doom woven from birth. None within the Nine Worlds,
not even the Allfather, were beyond their reckoning.

"Look to your own threads, | Járnviðja's daughter,
    Free you are not from reproach;
    The *skrælingr*'s taint | drapes your eyes and ears
    And hides the nearness of doom.

"From beyond the fences | of this Miðgarðr
    One comes to collect his due;
    The Grey Wanderer, | enchanter of old,
    Whose eye has marked you as foe."

This revelation by the *vættr* caught Halla off guard. The Grey Wanderer—
one of the Allfather's myriad epithets, a guise he assumed when traveling

among mortals—was coming *here*, for her? "But that's not possible," Halla said. Her milky eyes narrowed. "Not anymore."

It started, she reckoned, with the Nailed God; the divine made flesh, his arrival, death, and eventual influence over the sphere of Miðgarðr had thrown off the old order of things. This was why the prophecy was so crucial: the Nailed God's dominance was strangling the world, a ligature around Miðgarðr's neck that slowly throttled it. Already its effects were profound: the sorcery that permeated the Elder World was all but dead; even the Ash-Road, those points where the limbs of Yggðrasil pierced the veil between worlds, had withered and died. Without these two forces, without the Ash-Road and the magic that powered it, the so-called false gods could no longer walk the earth. That was what Grimnir meant when he called Miðgarðr the Nailed God's world.

What's worse, Halla knew what the death of sorcery meant for those creatures who thrived from it: creatures like herself, or Grimnir, or even this *vættr*—creatures who failed to heed the harbingers of doom and flee Miðgarðr—were destined for the shadows. They would diminish and become a mere mockery of their former selves, until madness and eternal death claimed them. Or until the prophecy came to pass, with Ragnarök and the breaking of the world.

"The ancient ways are closed," she muttered. "Even to the Grey Wanderer." She blinked, her brows knitting together in a frown of concern. "Unless," she said, licking her lips. A cold tightness gripped her chest. "Unless he's chosen a vessel to bear his *hamingja*?"

Hamingja was a word most men translated as *luck*. Halla, however, knew it as far more than that. It was that part of the Self that encompasses wit, mettle, inborn skill, and strength; it was an entity in its own right, living beyond death until a worthy descendant was born, a name-bearer or some other of its blood, destined for Glory. And all beings possessed a *hamingja*—even the lord of Ásgarðr. If the Allfather had chosen a mortal to bear this part of himself, that was a gift far beyond measure—and a cause for concern. The *hamingja* would grant its bearer a measure of the Allfather's power; power they could then use to take an active part in the affairs of Men, either to guide and shape the future of the North or merely to settle old scores.

And if he's coming after me, Halla thought, *I'll lay my wager on the latter.* She shivered again, and came back to herself. "I know what fate awaits me," she said. "It was ever thus: my folk sprang from the loins of Ymir, the Primordial One, first and greatest of the frost giants slain by Odin and his brothers. The stones beneath our feet are the bones of my mighty ancestor:

"Out of Ymir's flesh | was fashioned the earth,
 And the ocean out of his blood;
 Of his bones the hills, | of his hair the trees,
 Of his skull the heavens high.

"Miðgarðr the Gods | from his eyebrows made,
 And set for the sons of men;
 And out of his brain | the baleful clouds
 They made to move on high.

"I have seen the ages of the Gods, the ages of heroes and of myth. Those days are all but gone. Despite your hatred for *skræling*-kind, it is their sorcery which has kept this small corner of Miðgarðr rooted in the Elder Days. The sacrifice of Raðbolg Kjallandi's son, the witch-sense of his elder brother, Gífr, and the swift blade of Grimnir Bálegyr's son has made this a haven for the likes of us, great *vættr*. But even this enchantment cannot hold the Nailed God at bay forever. These are the days of prophecy, of Fimbulvetr and the deep cold before the world-consuming fires of Ragnarök. If my end is woven into the fabric of the world and I am to be judged by my associations, then grant me one last boon: help her, if you can," Halla said. "She is the Day who gives way to Night. Let her live so she might fulfill the promise of our kind, to strike a last blow before the ending of our world."

The homunculus shook, branches rattling.

But in answer, hundreds of roots and tendrils crawled up Dísa's arm. Serpentine, they wriggled over the edge of the stone slab to wrap themselves around her torso, her legs. The homunculus floated over her then slowly came apart as the roots that created it descended and wrapped themselves around Dísa's broken skull. An eerie green light suffused the cellar; an odd smell rose from the root-bundled form—a smell of honeysuckle and fresh-turned soil, wet grass and hyacinth. A tremor ran deep beneath the earth, a faint temblor that touched even the deep-delving roots of Yggðrasil . . .

Halla rocked back on her haunches. Grimnir was right when he'd said something had slipped. Something had . . . but his suspicions were wrong about from whence it came.

The Grey Wanderer is coming.

Halla closed her eyes. And in this place of magic, she prepared herself to fight the chosen avatar of a god.

8

SKARA, IN THE PROVINCE OF WEST GÖTALAND, SWEDEN

The man with the colorless eyes shuffled down the nave of the cathedral at Skara, and the dead followed.

No one could see them. Not by the pale light filtering in from the clerestory overhead, nor by the flickering glow of immense candelabra. Even to the man, they appeared as half-sensed shadows, ripples of darkness glimpsed out of the corner of his eye. But he knew they were there, even if the smoke coiling from copper censers and the steam of every breath had more substance than these grim and tattered wraiths. Motes and jags of light marked their stern gazes. And from them, the man did not quail. For if he did not have the courage to face his victims—all the half-remembered men, women, and children he had put to the sword at Constantinople, on the long and fruitless road to Jerusalem—he feared they might try and claim him.

The man shivered; despite the cold, he wore only a moth-eaten pair of breeches, unbelted and ungaitered. Hair the color of milk hung about his shoulders, framing a face that bore the same haughty grandeur as the bust of a Caesar—broad forehead, falcate nose, and strong beardless chin, all rendered in flesh as cold and lifeless as Carrara marble. Only in his colorless eyes was there life, feverish and bright; they caught and reflected the reddish gleam of the candle flames.

If his face was a sculptor's work, then the canvas of his body belonged to

85

a different sort of artistry, for it bore the brushstrokes of war: purple braids and red craters and pale trenches of scar, a scumbled veneer wrought by blade and dart, whip and ember.

The man staggered on. The naked sword in his fist scraped the stone tile underfoot as he lurched from column to column. Frost rimed the cathedral's sandstone walls. Its benches of dark polished wood stood empty. And yet, sound filled the vast open spaces, plainsong rising from throats unseen. The man did not understand the chanted words, but the eerie echo hammered home the realization that he stood in the presence of the Almighty.

There, in the shadow of the great altar, the man bent his knees and collapsed. Only his hands, draped over the cross-guard of his sword's hilt, kept him upright. "Why?" he said, voice cracking as he raised his face to the altar. "Why, O Father of Heaven, do you send these fevers to torment me? Have I not repented? Have I not suffered for my crimes? Have I not done all that you have asked, O God? Have I not taken up the Cross? Why, then? Why have you forsaken me?" The man's chin sank to his breast; he closed his eyes . . .

No answer came from the heavens, though all of a sudden the multitude of spirits rustled and moaned around him. Their cold breath set the candle flames to flickering as a hundred voices assailed him at once. The man's shoulders slumped; he cocked his bowed head to the side and listened as they told him things he could not know. *Someone had come.*

"Do not be shy, my friend," he said, after a moment. "You are . . . Father Nikulas? Yes?" A dim silhouette moved in deep shadow beneath the arcade. "You've come from . . ." The man paused, brow furrowed as he sought to make sense of the myriad voices only he could hear. "From Lund. You're the Archbishop's man. Come to save my soul, eh?"

Indeed, the newcomer who stepped into the light wore the cassock and cape of a priest. His every movement was a swirl of rich black wool, soft as silk and trimmed in fox fur; of black cloth, too, was the sash girdled about his waist, and gold glinted from the small pectoral cross resting on his breast. "Lord Konraðr," he said with a faint bow, smoothing his beard to hide his discomfiture. "Your spies are clever, indeed, if they warned you of my coming. I told no one . . ."

The man called Konraðr clambered to his feet. He turned to face Father Nikulas, a smile flirting with the corners of his colorless lips. "Spies? No, my ecclesiastical friend," he said. "I heard your name spoken on the wind, whispered in the crackle of ice. Nikulas of Lund comes, it said, and he brings a request from that insipid wretch, the Archbishop. Tell me, does he still lick my cousin, the King's arse?"

Nikulas blinked; with aplomb to spare, he merely shrugged and nodded. "Daily, lord."

"I am no lord." Konraðr turned back to the altar.

"As you said, you are the cousin of the King, lord. To address you otherwise would be disrespectful."

"Title by association, by the thinnest claim of blood, is no title at all. I am Konraðr the White, priest." Konraðr turned and leveled his sword at Father Nikulas; the priest's eyes widened. "I am the Ghost-Wolf of Skara, and I need neither association nor blood to take what is mine!" He stared down the length of honed steel at the goggle-eyed priest a moment longer before the tip of his blade wavered and then fell. "But you are not my enemy."

"I am not, lord."

"No." Konraðr gestured with his sword. Steel rasped on stone as the blade's tip dipped and scraped the floor again. He staggered back a step, his brow damp with sweat. The dead rustled; they moaned. They spoke to him of secrets and plots, harbingers of dooms yet written. Konraðr swayed, disoriented. "But soon . . . you will be my ally."

"Here, lord," Father Nikulas said, putting forth an arm to keep the pale man from falling. "You're burning with fever. Come. Sit here while I go and fetch your servants. You should not be out of bed."

The dead whispered, and Konraðr listened . . .

"Lord? Konraðr?"

"Your errand," he said, after a moment's pause.

Father Nikulas shook his head. "It's of no importance at the moment, lord. Please, sit, at the very least."

Konraðr allowed the priest to guide him to the nearest bench. He sat, shivering, his sword locked in his fist; with a flourish, Nikulas unfastened his cape and draped it over his naked shoulders.

"They tell me your master is devising an army," Konraðr said.

The priest, who'd turned away and was on the verge of calling out for aid, stopped. He came back around to face the thin albino, his eyes narrowing. *"They?"*

"They tell me the Livonians, the Brothers of the Sword, have called for aid in their crusade against the pagans of Estonia, on the shores of the Baltic Sea. The Holy Father in Rome has given God's blessing. Now your master, the Most Reverend Anders Sunesen, Archbishop of Lund and Advisor to my cousin, the King, wants my support—and the five hundred men at my command. I will give him neither."

Father Nikulas sniffed. Though his careworn brow and full beard lent him the aspect of age, he was perhaps a score of years Konraðr's junior. "If someone had told me your spies were so accurate, I would not have bothered making this journey. Your refusal could have been dispensed with a letter and I could have stayed warm and dry in Lund . . ."

"I told you, I have no spies."

"Then how—"

Konraðr caught the priest's wrist in an iron grip and pulled him down beside him. "The same way I know your mare is a bay roan with a hard mouth who favors her left front hoof; or that she was a gift from your mother's brother, who supported your desire to take Holy orders. The same way I know the truth of your heart: that you despise your master as a politician rather than a devout man of God. And the same way I know he sent you here, to me, to get you out from under his feet—your righteousness sickens him, for he is a man of politics despite all his posturing. He . . . He hopes you will offend me and I will kill you, then he can seize my lands—"

"What sorcery is this, lord?" Nikulas, his face gone as pale as Konraðr's, tried to pull away. The fever-stricken albino held him close with a strength that belied his thin frame.

"The dead," Konraðr hissed. "*My dead* . . . they wait just there, beyond the veil. The dead of Constantinople. Christian dead, killed by mine own hand. They speak to me, priest! They tell me things that would make a sane man blench . . ."

The priest looked up; he scanned the nave of the cathedral with eyes that gleamed like lamps of righteous fervor. Though he saw nothing amiss, he did not doubt the broken lord of Skara. "And what do these Orthodox heretics want, eh? Retribution? Surely not justice, for you were absolved of those killings in the eyes of God—"

"Be silent," Konraðr commanded. "They want you to listen: an evil wind is poised to blow from the north. On it will be borne the stench of pestilence and death. An apocalypse, carried south upon pagan shoulders:

"Sköll bays aloud | after Dvalin's toy.
The fetter shall break | and the wolf run free;
Dark-jawed devourer | of light-bringer's steed.
And in Vänern's embrace | the earth splits asunder.

"The end is coming. An end not seen since the days of Noah."

"*'But there were also false prophets among the people,'*" Father Nikulas quoted in earnest, "*'even as there shall be among you lying teachers, who shall bring in sects of perdition and deny the Lord who bought them: bringing upon themselves swift destruction.'* The heretics are wrong, lord. There is no pagan apocalypse. Cleave to the words of the blessed Saint Peter, himself. The Lord Most High has made a covenant."

Konraðr's reply rose barely above a whisper: "True, but the Gods who came before made no such bargains:

"Wolf shall fight she-Wolf | in Raven's shadow;
an axe age, a sword age, | as Day gives way to Night.
And Ymir's sons dance | as the Gjallarhorn
kindles the doom | of the Nailed God's folk.

"I know what the Scripture teaches, but I also know this to be true! An end is coming."

"And you think I could be ally to this?" The priest's brows beetled into a thunderous scowl. "Your words reek of blasphemy!"

Konraðr laughed then; he laughed until his voice trailed off into a coughing fit. "You think me blasphemous?" he said after a moment. "Then what I say next will put me beyond redemption in your esteem, priest. For in the circle of the world, there are but two men who can stop this. I am one. You are the other, Nikulas of Lund."

The priest tore himself free from Konraðr's grip and stood. "You would do well not to patronize me, *lord*! You can barely walk. By appearance, alone, you seem neither to sleep nor eat. 'The mind's inclination,' as Galen put it, 'follows the body's temperature.' You are choleric and sanguine, lord, feverish and imbalanced. There is but one savior of this world, our Lord Christ, and it is blasphemy to suggest otherwise. Let me fetch your servants and I will leave you to your delusions!" The priest turned away and made to leave, but a sudden weight on his left shoulder forestalled him. He looked down; in the razor-edged length of steel resting there he saw his own fear-widened eyes reflected back at him.

"Sit." Konraðr's tone brooked no dissent. "Sit and I will tell you precisely how you become ally to this blasphemy, as you call it."

Father Nikulas opened his mouth to protest, but the diplomacy of steel—the position of a hard honed edge mere inches from the apple of his throat—scattered his arguments. The priest did as Konraðr bid.

The albino said nothing for a moment. He sat with sword in hand, blade across his lap, and shivered. Nikulas watched as he bowed his head—though whether deep thought or in prayer, he could not say; pale hair veiled Konraðr's face.

"Do you recall Magnus of Saxony?" he said, at length.

"No, lord. I was but a boy when he took the Cross and left for Outremer."

"Aye, I was little more than a boy, myself. I was his squire. Our company took the Cross at Halberstadt, in the year old Archbishop Absalon passed."

"You have surely been through a great ordeal, lord," Father Nikulas said. "Without a doubt. But I don't see what—"

Konraðr rapped the priest across the knee with the flat of his sword. "Patience! Is that not one of the virtues you priests tout? Then be silent, be patient, and attend."

Nikulas bit back a decidedly un-Christian curse as he sat straighter on the bench, clutching his knee with white-knuckled fingers. He said nothing, preferring to stare straight on; his eyes focused on the play of candlelight and shadow, on the half-sensed forms milling just beyond his sight. He watched, and he listened.

Konraðr's voice grew soft and heavy. "We joined the crusade in Venice the next summer . . ."

A city of murky canals and gilded domes emerged onto the canvas of Nikulas's imagination, painted there by Konraðr's words. A city of rot and intrigue. In the swirling shadows, he saw tall-masted ships filled with the warriors of God, black crosses sewn to their rich surcoats. Earnest men, they were, with eyes that shone as bright and clear as their swords. And behind them, across the broad Piazza San Marco, crept the sinister figure of the Doge, the de facto king of the Venetians—aged and blind and as cunning as the old Adversary of Heaven. He spoke words of venom, words reeking of false piety, and shackled the Crusaders to his will with chains forged from penury and debt. And though the Pope forbade it, the wily Doge pierced the armor of faith shielding the Crusaders and guided them against his Christian rivals.

"Rather than succor Jerusalem," Konraðr said, "it was to Constantinople that we fared. I thank God Magnus did not live to see my shame. He fell ill and died at Andros, where I became Count Baldwin's man—his *'Revenant,'* as he called me, for I was akin to the restless dead who ravened after the living with bile and hate to spare. Deeds were done . . ."

Father Nikulas dropped his gaze to the hilt of Konraðr's sword. Sweat and old bloodstains discolored its shagreen wrappings, held fast by coils of tarnished silver wire, while nicks and scratches marred its acorn-shaped pommel. They were like runes, these markings, and they told a tale akin to the sagas of old. In the shimmer of candlelight on steel, the priest watched the destruction of an ancient city, a city of cyclopean walls and sprawling palaces. He saw faces reflected in the sword's blade—snarling, screaming, young, old, male, female; he saw children cowering in the wrack of war, lit by the glow of Greek fire. And he saw an old man, gray-bearded, one-eyed, clad in the faded finery of a Varangian lord. Albino hands smeared in blood tended the old man's wounds, though there was not a leech or chirurgeon under heaven who could help him. The killer's hands folded in prayer. Haltingly, the old man spoke . . .

"The old graybeard was talking out of his head," Konraðr said, stroking the blade's hilt as he would a cat, his attention drawn into the past. "Talking about a saint called Teodor, whose sword was lost in the lands of his ancestors."

"Saint Teodor?"

"You know of him, then?"

Father Nikulas leaned forward; he clasped his crucifix with both hands, raised it to his lips, and kissed it. "A Christian soldier of Rome in the days of great Constantine. He swore an oath to God to slay a dragon that had plagued Bithynia, devouring whole villages and making off with gold and women. He followed the wyrm north, into the forests of Germania and beyond. None now know where blessed Teodor caught up to his quarry, whether it was in the bogs of Jutland or the grinding ice of the Kjolen Mountains, but their battle was said to have lasted a year and a day—and when Saint Teodor triumphed, the wyrm's death shook the earth."

"And the saint?"

"Slain, as I recall," the priest replied, "crushed by the dragon's death-throes. It is presumed his bones—and his sword, which was blessed by the blood of Christ—lie among the beast's coils to this day, wherever those coils may lie."

"The old man knew."

"The old man knew he was dying, lord." Nikulas rose and paced in a tight circle, hands clasped behind his back. His cassock rustled with every turn. "You said it yourself: he was talking out of his head. The deathbed mutterings of an old heretic. If that's what you seek to stem your so-called pagan apocalypse . . . well, you might as well wish for a piece of the True Cross or the Spear of Longinus. Saint Teodor's sword is lost to us. It—"

Konraðr cut him off. "It is in the land of the Raven-Geats, along the north-western shores of Lake Vänern." The Ghost-Wolf of Skara stood and padded to the young priest's side. "It is a pagan land, men say, the last bastion of the Old Ways." Konraðr clapped Nikulas on the shoulder; he drew him closer, his voice a seductive whisper. "This is how you become my ally: you and I, we will scour the land of the Raven-Geats, burn their heresy from our midst, and recover the sword of Saint Teodor. That done, we will join my cousin, the King of the Danemark, ere his campaign against the Estonians reaches full bloom. Imagine it: Father Nikulas, soldier of Christ—ever in the shadow of his unworthy master, the Archbishop—stepping forth to bring his liege a mighty gift! For would not the sword of Saint Teodor make a potent symbol, if carried at the head of a crusading army? Would that army not be assured of victory?"

Father Nikulas bit back a scathing rebuke. Indeed, he could find no fault in Konraðr's logic. Nikulas was ambitious, though he allowed a love of Christ and the good of His Church to motivate him rather than base desire for temporal power and the myriad sins it could buy. *That* he left to Arch-bishop Sunesen. But to possess a sword anointed by the blood of the Savior of Mankind . . . how far would he go? Would he betray his archbishop? Most assuredly. But would he betray his king?

"An army under the aegis of God, protected by one of His saints, would be indomitable," he said quietly. "But we needs must strike quickly, before your cousin, the King, declares your refusal to attend him an act of treach-ery. Spies must be dispatched with all haste, armed with coin and good sense. And we must not falter. Our lives, if not our souls, depend on it."

The lord of Skara's face was bloodless and damp; his thin frame shook from the renewed ague. "With my five hundred household troops, my sworn men, seven hundred and twenty-nine more men have flocked to my banner since Yule. And my spies have already returned. We seek a place called Hrafnhaugr, Raven Hill. I lack only the blessings of a priest. So I ask you, Father Nikulas of Lund, will you help me? Will you carry the light of Christ into the last dark corner of Sweden?"

Flickers of movement caught the priest's eye. In the shadows of the cathedral—beyond the shafts of pale winter's light filtering from the clerestory overhead, away from the glow of a hundred candles—Father Nikulas sensed a ghostly presence. There were scores of them, the restless dead, led by a figure of an old man, hunched and twisted and clad in the faded cloak of a Varangian lord. A single eye gleamed from beneath the brim of a slouch hat.

They waited.

They waited for him.

And though Father Nikulas shuddered at the thought of joining their ranks, he did not quail. He was a soldier of Christ, faithful and devout. So it was with a trembling hand that he made the sign of the Cross and let that gesture stand as his answer.

"In Nomine Patris, et Filii, et Spiritus Sancti."

9

Nothingness, shot through with jags of green light, and then . . . voices, distant and muffled as though heard from under the earth—one is harsh and grating, the other smooth and silky:

"Nár! What do those rootlings know?" says the harsh voice. A name floats from the aether, flirts at the edges of her consciousness, and is gone before she can grasp it. Anger percolates through the darkness; hate and loathing that stretches back an eternity.

"The vættir don't lie," hisses the silky voice. Halla, the green-shot void around her says, trembling. Her name is Halla. "He is probably already here, in Miðgarðr."

"Then find him! If some mortal bears that one-eyed bastard's luck, then how hard could it be?"

The silky voice, as smooth and cold as a fresh coverlet of snow, curses in a language she does not comprehend. Then: "Impossible, if he chooses not to be discovered. I think he's been sent to stop whatever it is you've got planned. To protect the prophecy. He'll be drawn to you . . ."

"Let him come, then!" The harsh voice laughs, and the void convulses with barely contained rage. "God or no, I'll send him back to Ásgarðr in pieces. That dragon is mine!"

Dragon. The dragon. The bones of the dragon . . .

The nothingness rustles; light seeps in from beyond the veil—green and gold, red like flames; by its wan illumination she can see a figure. It bears the shape of a man, though hunched and as twisted as the staff he leans upon. A single malevolent eye gleams from beneath the brim of his hat.

But he is no god.

Her voice profanes the silence. "What is the dragon?"

The stranger smiles.

> *"From the depths a barrow | rises through the water,*
> *The stone-girdled hall | of Aranæs, where dwells*
> *Jörmungandr's spawn, | the Malice-Striker.*
> *Its dread bones rattle | and herald an end."*

And with a sound like the rattle of immense bones, the stranger's cloak is borne up as by a hot breath of wind. There is only darkness beneath. And that darkness grows and spreads, becoming monstrous wings that blot out the pale light between worlds. The darkness crawls like a serpent. It robs the air of its breath; it slays the living with a pestilence that rots the blood in their veins. It crushes and destroys.

She does not flee as the darkness engulfs her. And in its hideous embrace, she opens her mouth to curse . . .

DÍSA DID NOT AWAKEN BY fits and starts, nor did she bolt upright and thrash about as though trapped by her dreams. No, she simply opened her eyes. She knew where she was; the beams overhead, the furs beneath, the smells of oiled iron and rust, incense and old blood, the smoke coiling through shafts of gray daylight that stabbed down from the clerestory—all of this was familiar to her. *The Hooded One's longhouse.* Thus it came as no surprise, as she looked around, to see Halla sitting cross-legged nearby, a mail hauberk draped over her lap and a wooden bucket of tools and scrap mail beside her.

Dísa stretched, tendons cracking and joints popping. "I was dreaming," she said. "I died and went into the earth—but not my body. Just . . . me. The earth was like water and I swam through it. Deeper, I went. Always deeper, to where I heard the roots of trees singing. They told me stories. Stories of dragons . . ."

"A fine dream." Halla nodded, cutting her eyes sharply at the younger woman.

"How long was I out?"

The troll-woman put down the tool she'd been using to remove links from the hem of the hauberk. "Nine days," Halla replied.

"Nine? Ymir's blood!" Dísa said. "Has anyone from Hrafnhaugr come looking for me?"

Halla shook her head. She did not rise and come to check Dísa's injuries; indeed, as Dísa took stock of herself she realized she had none—no pain in her face or her head, no swelling in her nostrils and cheeks that would have made breathing a labor. Halla asked, "What do you remember?"

Dísa frowned. "I remember . . . I remember it was my fault. I nearly had him, but my concentration slipped—I let my guard down—and he dealt me a crack to the skull." She touched her hairline by her temple, feeling . . . nothing. No lumps or lacerations. No contusions or bruises. She should have been a mass of aching muscles, her skull on fire and her every breath like a fish gasping its last on the bank. But she felt fine . . . better than she had in many days. "Or did I dream that, as well?"

"That was real enough." Halla took up the mail hauberk once more. She used an awl and pliers to remove rings, drawing up the garment's hem. Those she removed went into the bucket with a metallic *clink*. "The old fool nearly sent you on to the next world."

"Remind me to return the favor someday," Dísa replied, half in jest. "Where is he?"

"Gone hunting." Halla gestured with the awl. "Tell me of this wager of yours."

Dísa rolled onto her side, her legs drawn up; she raised herself up on one elbow with her head propped on her right hand. She tried with her other hand to untangle the beads and disks in her hair. She told Halla of Flóki, the Jarl's son—whom she'd known since they were children; she recounted the falling out between father and son, Flóki's departure from Hrafnhaugr, and Hreðel's desperation to see his son returned. "Though he's a horse's arse, and a fool to boot, Hreðel has been loyal to the Hooded One. To fulfill this boon would not have taxed him overmuch. But he's made his decision. He'll help, but only after I draw blood from him." Dísa's brows knitted. She muttered, "And this is proving more difficult than I imagined."

"Because you're wriggling around like a worm on a hook, that's why," Halla said. She opened a mail link, prized it free, and dropped it into the bucket. *Clink.* "You rise to his taunts, allow your anger to get the better of you, and put your inexperience on display for all to see." *Clink.* "Think, child. Has your Jarl not men aplenty? More than enough to fetch his wayward son back to him? Of course he has." *Clink.* "This is a test of your loyalty, to see how far you will go for him. To see what you will risk." *Clink.* "Grimnir's no fool. He knows what your Jarl is about, making threats, testing the limits of the Hooded One's patronage to see if things have changed." *Clink.* "What seems a small matter to you, a reasonable request balanced against a lifetime of fealty, is nothing less than an attempt to break an ancient compact that limits the Jarl's power." *Clink.* "And you are right in the middle of it, flailing about like you know the score."

A long silence passed between them. Dísa lay back and closed her eyes. She wanted to hear again the ethereal singing of the trees, the hum of root and bole, the shiver of limb and leaf, the thrum of the heartwood and the rasp of the bark. Instead, she heard only the patter of a cold rain, the rustle of a breeze, and the distant rumble of thunder in the mountains to the north. "Am I to be nothing but their pawn, then?" Dísa said, finally. "Some useless piece in this game they play?"

Halla shrugged. "That choice is yours."

"Choice?" Dísa's cheeks grew hot with pent-up rage. "What choice? Unless I can convince Grimnir to help, Flóki risks death or worse. But if I ignore my Jarl and leave Flóki to rise or fall on his own merit, I risk losing everything if Hreðel decides to rebel against the Hooded One."

Clink. "That is their game, child. What is yours?"

"Mine?"

"Aye." *Clink.* "Yours. You can be the pawn in their game or the queen in your own. You need only decide what rules you play by, if any, and what your endgame is."

Dísa hesitated. "I . . . I want to be a shieldmaiden. That is my endgame."

"Good," Halla replied. She put her tools aside, took up a cloth, and polished the hem of the hauberk, feeling for burrs in the metal. When she found one, Halla drew an iron rasp from the bucket and filed the burr down. "Then how do you get there? By bending to your Jarl's demands? By shadowing Grimnir? By recklessly attacking him every chance you get in hopes of scoring his hide and drawing blood?"

"I want to learn his war-art," Dísa said. "And I'd probably learn it faster if I were conscious and not always trying to sneak up on his blind side. But Flóki . . ."

"You fancy this lad?"

Dísa nodded.

"And you want to see him succeed, be his own man, and earn the praise and respect of the Raven-Geats?"

"I do."

"Then he must be left to his own devices. You do not make steel by plucking iron from the fire ere the heat burns it. It must taste the flames and either master them or be destroyed by them. None of you lot get out of this world alive and unscathed. Your Hreðel has forgotten this, I think." Halla held up the mail shirt. It was mid-thigh rather than knee-length now—a haubergeon rather than a hauberk—its butted rings of dark iron interspersed with rings of copper and silver. The troll-woman nodded.

Dísa sat up. "How do I begin? I can't imagine the Hooded One will want me tagging along after him as he goes about his day."

"Do precisely what you are doing now, child, but do it smarter." Halla tossed her the mail shirt. "Protect yourself. Become accustomed to the weight and wear of mail." She waved at the interior of the longhouse, which was equal parts treasure hoard and armory. "Root through this and find yourself a good gambeson, a helmet, greaves, a shield . . . enough armor where you can take a blow from Grimnir's blade without risking your neck. Find yourself an axe and a spear, as well. Then go, try and draw your blood—but be conscious of how he moves, how he attacks, how he taunts you first. Understand *why* he does this. And emulate him. Become him."

"Make the game my own," Dísa said, as a new resolve kindled in her eyes. "Be the queen, rather than the pawn."

GRIMNIR RETURNED TO THE LONGHOUSE with the setting of the sun. Wary, he emerged from the deep twilight of the forest and into the open only after he was certain no one followed him. All day, after Halla's warnings about that wretched Grey Wanderer, he'd borne the sensation of scrutiny—the crawling of his scalp, the flicker of movement glimpsed from the corner of his eye. It was enough that he came back from the hunt through the heart of the bog, laying traps in his wake. Now, mud fouled his boots; grime and blood mucked his limbs. His hair hung sweat-damp across his saturnine brow. Over his shoulders, he carried the gutted carcass of a roe deer as though its weight were nothing. One hand held the scrawny beast's leg; the other cradled a hunting spear.

Grimnir reached the foot of the stairs and turned back the way he had come; nostrils flared as he snuffled at the air. His good eye, gleaming in the darkness like an ember, swept across his back-trail.

Nár! Look at you! Grimnir snarled at himself. *Starting at shadows like that old git who raised you! Gífr'd laugh to see you now!* He hawked and spat. Then, dropping any pretense at stealth, he ascended the steps with the swagger of a conquering king. Grimnir reached the head of the stairs; from there, he could see that the doors to the longhouse stood ajar. Light seeped out, a glow that striped the gathering dark with a broad swatch of orange. He smelled the smoke of his hearth, the warmth, the ancient stink of soot-stained beams.

And he heard an intermittent *thock,* like a stick striking a wooden post.

Scowling, he sidled close and nudged the door with one booted foot. Hinges squealed in protest. Grimnir shifted his weight. What he saw, however, only deepened his scowl.

Halla sat to one side, a helmet of blackened iron in her lap and a bucket of smith's tools at her elbow. She was busy repairing the leather liner, where it met the drape of mail at the neck and the cheek guards. Grimnir recognized it by the silver-inlaid half-face guard—he'd taken it from a dead Norse prince barely older than the girl.

He saw Halla's eyebrows arch, apprehending that she'd seen him in return. With subtlety to spare, she glanced from him to the girl. Dísa stood with her back to the door, her attention riveted on the post in front of her. On it, Halla had hung three iron rings from nails. The tallest stood at the height of a tall man's face, a good twelve inches above the crown of Dísa's own head; the second was at heart level, while the third was gut or groin level.

The girl was clad now in a haubergeon of good mail over a gambeson of padded leather that reached to mid-thigh; an apron of leather and bronze scale protected her hips, and she had wrapped her lower legs, between knee and boot, in old leather belts with plaques of hammered copper and bronze decorating them. She wore her hair pulled back and tied beneath a thick wool arming cap. Dísa held a shield in her left hand, while in her right she balanced a blunt-headed spear—its shaft cut down to where it was barely longer than Grimnir was tall.

As he watched, Dísa dropped to a crouch and shuffled into range of the iron rings. She feinted at the middle ring with her shield rim—striking the wooden pole with a dull crack—and thrust over-hand at the uppermost ring. *Thock*. She backed up, stood upright, rolled a kink from her shoulder, and then repeated the movement. *Thock*.

Grimnir grunted and tossed the deer carcass off to one side. Turning, he stepped back into the chilly night and stripped off his filthy boots, his war-belt, his armor, and his kilt; soon he was naked but for a loincloth. Grimnir shattered the thin skin of ice covering the surface of a butt of rainwater and used a leather bucket to draw and sluice the grime and blood from his limbs, from his face, and from his stringy hair.

Thock.

He heard Halla rise and rummage among the drifts of coin and gear. A few minutes later, the troll-woman brought him a fresh tunic, trousers, thick-soled boots, and a sleeveless leather coat that buckled across the chest—a brigandine, heavily embroidered and reinforced with rings of bronze and iron. Grimnir dried himself off with the tunic before tossing it aside, heedless of Halla's disdainful snort. The rest he donned quickly. He left the coat open, securing it with his war-belt and hitching the hilt of his seax around until it rested in easy reach.

Thock.

Halla hoisted the deer's carcass as effortlessly as he had. She would skin it, joint it, and cut it from the bone before salting it and hanging it in the smoke shed at the rear of the longhouse. Grimnir's stomach growled as he thought of the savory stew the troll-woman would make from the deer's marrow-rich bones.

"What's that one about?" Grimnir gestured with his sharp chin, indicating Dísa.

"She's seen the light."

Grimnir snorted. "Guess that crack on the head did the little wretch some good, then."

Halla remained silent. She fixed Grimnir with a withering stare before turning and stumping off to the rear of the longhouse. Still chuckling, he followed the troll-woman inside.

Dísa barely glanced in his direction as he passed her and took up his accustomed seat. She had donned the helmet Halla had been repairing, cinched the chinstrap tight, and turned her head from side to side, looking up and down and rolling her neck around to test the fit. Satisfied, she dropped back into a fighting crouch. Dísa feinted low with her spear then cracked her shield rim across the highest ring.

Grimnir eyed her with grim amusement as she repeated the movement. Finally, she straightened and looked at him with an exasperated sigh.

"What?"

"You fight like one of *them*." Grimnir jerked his head in the direction of Hrafnhaugr.

Dísa frowned. "I am one of them."

"No, little fool!" He jabbed one black-nailed finger at her. "Forget what that hag of a grandmother taught you! You're too slight for it. A shield wall? Bah! Those louts would roll right over you and not look back. Be like the wolf that prowls at the edges of the battlefield, or be dead." Grimnir shrugged and sat back. "The choice is yours."

Dísa stood for a moment, head bowed as she measured the weight of Grimnir's words. Finally, she glanced up. "Show me."

The son of Bálegyr's lips peeled back in a jagged yellow smile.

EVEN BEFORE SUNRISE THE NEXT morning, Grimnir drove Dísa from her bed with kicks and curses. Her complaints fell on deaf ears as he led her through a series of stretches, loosening muscle and sinew in preparation for the day's exertions. "You're going to run, little bird," he growled. "Up into the hills, around the valley, and back again. And I'll be at your heels with a whip, if that's what it takes. Run until your sweat turns to blood! Until your lungs burn and your leg bones crack!"

But as she nodded in stoic silence and made to set out, Grimnir jabbed one finger into her sternum.

"Do we fight in naught but our skins, wretch?"

Dísa stammered. "I thought . . . we're just running, aren't we?"

"You want to learn the war-art of the *kaunar*? Here is the first lesson: we live as we fight. We are hated, and we hate in return, so every wretched breath we draw is drawn under a promise of death. Old Gífr taught us to make that death as hard as nails. We live in this, in our war garb!" Grimnir slapped his brigandine-covered breast. "It is the iron blanket that keeps us warm at night, and the iron shroud that will cover our axe-hewn corpses.

If you take a piss, little bird, you take it in your war rags! Fetch them—and your weapons!—and stop your dawdling!"

Dísa did. And they ran. Grimnir pushed her at a punishing pace, through the woods to the edge of his territory, then along the ridgelines to the promontory overlooking the dark waters of the Skærvík, then down the steep, rock-strewn incline to the lake shore. From there, they followed the shore until they reached the small creek that drained the bog. Scrambling up rocks and through tight clefts, over islands of peat and through shallow meres of black water, they came once more to the longhouse.

At the end, Dísa could barely breathe. She lay on her back for a time, gasping like a fish; her chest burned. Every joint in her body ached, and the spasms twisting her guts forced her to roll over and dry heave. She tried to spit, to clear her throat, but her tongue felt like a strip of dried-out leather.

But Grimnir did not give her much respite. Using the same tactics as before—nudges from a booted foot peppered with curses—he chivvied her inside where Halla waited with a flask of water and the morning repast.

"Not hungry," Dísa muttered around mouthfuls of water. The troll-woman was adamant, however, and soon she had the girl gnawing smoked venison slices and slabs of a dense bread baked with seeds, nuts, and dried fruit. Finally, Halla poured her a measure of *Mjöð,* that harsh herb-infused liquor that gagged her going down but soon turned to a hot fierce glow that lent new vigor to her limbs.

And she would need it, for the rest of the day Grimnir—in his own inimitable style—taught her the intricacies of the long-seax, of the Frankish axe, of the short thrusting spear, and of the shield. Nor did he spare any wisdom. "Slice that sticker of yours across some whoreson's thigh, right up by his bollocks, and if you get it just right he won't last a dozen heartbeats."

"And if I miss?"

"Ha! Go after some bastard's jewels and he'll go after your damn fool head if you miss! So make sure you don't, little bird!"

Before sunset, they returned to the longhouse where Halla had a bite of sup prepared—meat pies spiced with cumin and garlic, or stew made from pork or venison with carrots, mushrooms, onions, and cabbage; even simpler fare was Grimnir's favorite, such as skewers of roasted meat, a bowl of beans and hard barley bread, or *baggi,* a thick porridge of barley and organ meats mixed with parsnip and onion. After they ate, Grimnir would break out the ale and regale Dísa and Halla with tales as they mended armor or repaired weapons.

This became their daily routine: run and fight. When meat ran low they hunted, using the same skills to kill a deer as to kill a man; Grimnir taught her the art of the ambush—the hard, fast strike designed to cripple an enemy and leave him ripe for the picking. She learned the rudiments of Sarmatian archery, a skill Grimnir himself learned during his sojourn in the East with Gífr, his mother's brother. She was no crack shot, but her aim was steady enough to at least nick the target. "You'll make the wretches duck, at least," Grimnir snarled as one of her arrows whizzed past the target's head. And by night, she stared into the fire and listened as Grimnir related threads from the long tapestry of his life. She heard the tale of how he came to be at the Battle of Chluain Tarbh outside Dubhlinn, some two hundred years ago; how he'd hunted Bjarki Half-Dane from the grinding ice of the far north to the pleasant valleys and vineyards of the Franks. "I chased that wretched maggot for nigh upon five hundred years! *Faugh!* Always a step behind him. Then, I lost all reckoning of him for fifty years or so, until a blasted Christ-Dane and his little foundling put me back on his scent." Grimnir continued on, telling Dísa how he'd snagged himself a Christian hostage in a cave on Sjælland in the Danemark, walked the perilous branches of Yggðrasil to reach England, and bartered with the lord of the *landvættir* to break the walls of Badon after they'd stolen his hostage. He paused, then, to drain a horn of ale.

"So, you found this hymn-singer in a cave," Dísa said. "What was her name?"

"Étaín," Halla murmured. There was a mischievous twinkle in the troll-woman's milky eyes.

"Aye, you found this Étaín in a cave, snatched her up, and dragged her along . . . you say because she knew the lay of the land and could speak the tongue of the English?"

Grimnir lowered the empty horn and wiped foam from his lips. His nostrils flared. "What's your point, little bird?"

Dísa motioned with her hand, hoping to stave off Grimnir's ire. "Don't be cross. I'm just trying to understand, is all."

"She knew their wretched land!" Grimnir punctuated each syllable with a short, fierce rap of his knuckles against the wooden armrest of his seat. "She spoke their wretched tongue! Which of these is too much for that empty space between your ears?"

Dísa risked a sidelong glance at Halla, seeking support. The troll-woman, though, gave her nothing; her seamed and wrinkled face remained impassive as she worked her embroidery needle through the hem of a tunic. "Well." Dísa licked her lips and swallowed hard. "Both, to be honest. You say you needed this Étaín, but you also spoke the language well enough, in a pinch. You knew enough to find your way around, and you'd have twisted the head off any Norse swine that crossed your path to get the information you needed. And yet, on a lark you snatch some kneeler from a cave and drag her across the branches of Yggðrasil for . . . for no good reason?"

Hearing this, Grimnir's single eye blazed with wrathful fire. "No good reason, eh? You're a precious sort of fool, little bird. No good reason, is it? It's the same reason I plucked a wretch like you out of the muck! Why I decided—against my gut, mind you—to show you the war-art of the *kaunar*!"

"What reason?"

Grimnir leaned forward. The shadow and light rising from the embers lent his sharp, wolflike face a decidedly sinister cast. He slowly enunciated each word of his reply, fangs bared in a jagged yellow snarl. "Because I can!"

In that moment, the tension in the air felt murderous, like a strangler's cord looped around Dísa's throat. It would have made good sense to simply keep her mouth shut, to accept Grimnir's answer with a silent nod and let it be. But she could not deny the unspoken taunt in his harsh voice—he was daring her to speak her mind. Dísa licked her lips. Good sense be damned! But even as she rose to meet his taunting, Halla interrupted.

"And that," said the troll-woman, "is the lesson for this eve. Rejoice, child, for you have learned a truth few mortals are privy to."

Suddenly, Dísa felt a slackening of the tension; its knots loosened, and she found her breath. She watched Grimnir sit back in his seat, lips thinning with barely suppressed derision. He snorted. Dísa frowned as she turned to Halla. "What truth is that?"

"There are three words inscribed on the grave stone of every *kaunar*. Three words that sum up the breadth of their existence. Three words passed down from the lips of the Tangled God, himself, Father Loki. Question a *kaunr*'s motives, child, peel back the layers and you will see these three words burned upon their black hearts: *because I can!*"

At this, Grimnir only nodded. He remained silent for the rest of the night. And as Dísa fell asleep, her last waking image was of Grimnir's silhouette—hunched and immobile, brooding over a landscape of ash and embers like a defeated king over the remnants of his domain.

10

By the second week, Dísa's endurance had improved enough that Grimnir began to change up their routine. He named landmarks along the path to give her a sense of awareness—the trail began at an outcropping he called Two-Goat Rock, then through the woods to where an ancient, moss-bearded ash called the Jötunn Tree stood sentinel over the naked ridges; the promontory, more or less the halfway mark, Grimnir called the Tooth, while the rocky and precipitous path down to the lake's shore he named Hel's Stairway. The creek mouth he called the Pisser, and the narrow clefts that led to the bog were the Ball Breakers. "Make it to the Jötunn Tree without being seen," Grimnir would tell her. Or "Try and stop me from reaching the Tooth."

Their runs became running brawls, ending only when Dísa stumbled back to the longhouse, winded and bleeding. She came to Halla with lacerations and bruises, broken fingers and pulled muscles, blisters and abrasions; once with broken ribs and another time with a dislocated shoulder. These Halla stitched or set, slathered with herb-laced unguents or covered with poultices. The troll-woman also treated the sores and rashes that erupted on Dísa's shoulders and flanks from wearing her armor for too long. And as she worked, Dísa—like a *skald* reciting the deeds of the mighty—would tell her the tale of the day's struggle.

Then, one evening near the end of the fourth week she came to Halla strangely quiet. She remained pensive as the troll-woman washed the blood away from a cut across her left cheek; then, with deft fingers, she drew together the ragged edges of the wound. "No blade did this," Halla said. She eyed the girl, the ghost of a frown crinkling her forehead. "A pommel?"

"A branch," Dísa replied. The young woman flinched as Halla undertook the careful stitching of the cut; the sensation of pain seemed to rouse her from her lassitude. "*He* was lying in ambush between the Jötunn Tree and the Tooth, ready to put an arrow in me if I showed myself on the ridgeline. So I stayed low, kept to the trees . . . one of them did not much like my intrusion, it seems. Thought it was trying to gouge my eye out."

A ghost of a smile touched Halla's lips. "You must be wary, child. Some *landvættir* remain in this world. They sleep and dream of the Elder Days and are dangerous when woken."

"Like you," Dísa said. She paused a moment, then: "Halla, is it true you cannot leave this place?"

Halla's gaze flickered from her flesh-knitting to meet Dísa's frank stare. "Grimnir told you this?"

"He said your blood keeps you prisoner here."

"*Prisoner?*" The troll-woman sniffed. "More the fool is he if he thinks I am anyone's prisoner. But he is right on one count: the blood of Járnviðja, who was my mother's mother, runs through my veins—and for the daughters of Járnviðja, Sól's hateful light will return us to the cold stone from whence Ymir fashioned us. So if I journey, I must do so at night and seek shelter by day. I simply choose not to."

"Why?"

Halla said nothing for a moment. Her fingers wielded the thin golden needle lightly—pierce and draw, pierce and draw. Then, quietly, she spoke: "There is nothing for me out there. Not anymore. Gone are the days when the great forest of Myrkviðr spread across the world—the mighty Darkwood, my home. You should have seen it, child! Trees like moss-bearded titans, towering over glades and vales where no man had ever set foot. There were only spirits in those days—spirits of wood and water, sky and stone. My troll-sisters and I could journey from sunset to sunset for nights on end and never see the edges of Myrkviðr. Nor did we worry overmuch about seeking shelter. For as we walked, we sang the songs of ancient spirits, who were as

TWILIGHT OF THE GODS

gods upon the earth. In payment, the *landvættir* opened their arms to us. We shared their hollows under root and rock, or were hidden from venomous Sól in the trunks of those mighty trees." She finished stitching Dísa's cheek, tied off and cut the thread, and wiped away the remaining blood. The troll-woman reached for a jar of cobwebs and from its contents made a poultice that would stop the girl's cheek from bleeding. "Alas, as I said those days are long past. I could fare forth from here—one night, perhaps two—but to what end? To meet the vanguard of our destroyers?"

"The Nailed God's folk?" A frown creased Dísa's brow.

"Yes. But they cannot bear all the blame, alas," Halla said. "They were not the first to take axe and fire to our precious Myrkviðr. All manner of men hacked at the edges of the forest, or struck into its heart. The trees that offered us succor in the Elder Days went to make the keels of great ships, or the spines of mighty longhouses, but the men who did this offered the *land-vættir* recompense: the first fruits of the harvest, the first wool of the shearing season, the first blood of the hunt. But when the Cross-men came among them, preaching their hate for the Old Ways, the hearts of men hardened against the spirits of Myrkviðr. No longer did they offer fair payment. They set their rapine axes against oak, linden, and sacred ash because their god told them that was their right."

Halla rose and shuffled back through the longhouse to the front doors, Dísa in her wake. Outside, night had fallen. A cold breeze blew through the open door, its breath setting the flames in the fire pit to flickering. The main room was empty; Grimnir was gone on one of his sleepless wanderings that took him beyond the edges of his land. Halla sat in her accustomed spot. Shadows streaked the troll-woman's face as she took up the thread of her tale. "The *landvættir* could have survived the loss of their haunts, like Myrkviðr; they were in water and stone, in the soil underfoot and the air we drew into our lungs. What threat could another god pose, even one that drives men to madness?" Halla *tsked*. "The men of the North have many gods, after all. What is one more? But the Cross-men would have none of that. Their Nailed God was a jealous god who demanded sole dominion over the lands of Miðgarðr. They preached that there was only one world, not nine, with a heaven above and a hell below. They taught the Dane and the Swede and those among the Norse who would listen that they are born in sin and imperfect, made to suffer. And if they suffer enough, their Nailed

God will allow them into his hall to serve him—but only if they keep his law: *Thou shalt not have strange gods before me.*" Halla shivered; her milky eyes sought the heart of the fire, as though the bright flames could burn away the last vestiges of that hateful commandment.

Dísa shrugged out of her mail and stripped off the gambeson she wore beneath. This was her third since Halla had counseled her to wear armor. Though it protected her from the mail's hard edges and gave her an added layer of protection, the fabric acted like a sponge, soaking in every last drop of sweat and blood each day's exertions wrung from her. The garment quickly grew sodden, heavy, and it reeked. Dísa chucked it out the open door—she'd sink it in the bog tomorrow—and snatched up another one from the pile of old gambesons she'd looted from the Hooded One's hoard. Her limbs were hard with muscle, her flat belly ridged now, like Grimnir's sculpted cuirass; once pale flesh had a yellowish cast, and an array of bruises, knots, and scabbed sores warred with gooseflesh from the cold air to create an uneven veneer. She gritted her teeth and drew on the fresh gambeson, made of purple-dyed quilted linen and worked with gold embroidery on the breast and the sleeves. Its previous owner had died from a spear thrust that took him in the back, between his shoulder blades—no doubt splitting his spine and tearing into his lungs and heart.

Lacing the gambeson, she turned back to Halla. "Why did the Gods not intervene?" she said. "Surely they could have driven these Cross-men away."

The troll-woman stirred. "The Gods of the North are a harsh lot, child. Only grudgingly do they take notice of us, so wrapped up are they in their own affairs. And when they do take note, it is often only to heap more misfortune upon us. They looked away, and when their gaze returned to this Miðgarðr they discovered the Cross-men had done with ink and parchment what no Jarl could with axe and sword: unite men under a common banner—a banner made from the scraped skins of sheep and decorated in oak gall and iron with the words of their Nailed God. They had brought their holy war north, under our very noses, and we did not realize it for what it was until too late."

"What do we do, then?" Dísa said, shaking her head. "How do we settle the score?"

"Grim days are coming. It is Fimbulvetr, the Endless Winter. The Gods of the North gird their loins and look to their steel, for there is the reek of war upon the winds of Miðgarðr. Even the spirits of the land have fled, taking

with them the sorcery of the Elder Days. And soon," Halla's voice dropped
to a whisper:

"When the years tally | nine times nine times nine,
  Again, and war-reek | wafts like dragon breath;
  When Fimbulvetr | hides the pallid sun,
  The monstrous Serpent | shall writhe in fury.

"Sköll bays aloud | after Dvalin's toy.
  The fetter shall break | and the wolf run free;
  Dark-jawed devourer | of light-bringer's steed.
  And in Vänern's embrace | the earth splits asunder.

"From the depths a barrow | rises through the water,
  The stone-girdled hall | of Aranæs, where dwells
  Jörmungandr's spawn, | the Malice-Striker.
  Its dread bones rattle | and herald an end.

"Wolf shall fight she-Wolf | in Raven's shadow;
  An axe age, a sword age, | as Day gives way to Night.
  And Ymir's sons dance | as the Gjallarhorn
  Kindles the doom | of the Nailed God's folk."

Dísa listened, a hard set to her jaw. She nodded. "Good. This dragon,
this Malice-Striker, he will be our vengeance. He will bring death to the
Cross-men."

"To all things," Halla said. She did not look up from the fire. The ruddy
light burnished her crag-set features, so like carved stone, and illuminated the
wisps of hair growing from the point of her chin. "Malice-Striker will scour
the earth with fire and with pestilence, and war will follow it like a shadow.
Stones will crack and trees shatter; seas will boil and the skies burn! And from
what scraps it leaves behind, the Elder World will emerge again, reborn."

"How long?" Dísa said after a moment. "How long do we have until the
end comes?"

The troll-woman glanced sidelong at the girl, who sat shivering despite
the heat rising off the fire pit. "None can say, child. Seven hundred and

twenty-nine years have passed since the prophecy was first spoken—nine times nine times nine again—and we are in the throes of the Endless Winter. The rest?" She shrugged. "There is no guarantee it will come to pass. Especially if Grimnir has his way."

Dísa straightened. "How could *he* be against this?"

From the shadow at the rear of the longhouse came a harsh snort. "Aye, tell her why, you gobby old hag." While Halla did not so much as flinch at the unexpected sound of Grimnir's voice, Dísa reacted as though stung; she came to her feet, her seax partly drawn from its sheath. The girl relaxed only a little as Grimnir rose from where he'd been crouched on his haunches and came around to his throne-like chair.

"What are you on about with all this peaching sneakery?" Halla said.

"Don't change the subject! Answer the little bird's question. Tell her how I could be at odds with this precious fantasy you lot have concocted."

Halla lapsed into silence for a long moment, deep in thought; Dísa resumed her seat. From the fire pit, embers crackled and spat. A breeze that reeked with the cold promise of snow moaned through the doorway.

"Don't be shy," Grimnir goaded. There was a hard and sardonic edge to his voice. "Tell her what I believe, since you seem to know my mind better than I do!"

Finally, Halla stirred. She jabbed a gnarled finger at Grimnir. "The Old Ways . . . the old prophecies . . . you foolishly think they are just meaningless doggerel now. 'Miðgarðr is the Nailed God's world,' you have said, 'stolen fair and square.' And you think the only harbingers of doom that matter anymore are the ones uttered by desert prophets and cross-kissing madmen—and they make no mention of us."

"You dance around the answer, hag! Tell her the truth, Ymir take your gnarled old bones! Tell her why!"

Dísa slowly turned her head to look from the hunched old troll-woman to Grimnir. The latter was silent now, and glowering. His single eye blazed like a beacon of hate; what it saw, Dísa could not say. "Tell me."

"Vengeance," Halla spat. "Cold, useless vengeance! He would rather give this world to the Nailed God than see the dragon arise! All over the matter of an ancient grudge between Malice-Striker and his folk, recompense for a great sacking and burning, and the fulfillment of an oath sworn over the cairn of his slain kinsfolk!"

"I understand the need for revenge," Dísa said, nodding. "But is it worth it to let the Nailed God's folk keep what they've stolen from us?"

"Oh, you know revenge, do you?" Grimnir's eyes narrowed; his lips thinned and peeled back over jagged yellow teeth. "Answer me this, then: the one who slew your mother, little bird . . . what would you do for vengeance? How blasted long would you wait to feel their hot blood spill over your hands? A day? A week? A year?"

"Longer," Dísa replied. Beside her, Halla stiffened. "I would wait my entire life, even if it meant I'd spend my dying breath knifing the swine."

"And you would let some wretched prophecy stop you?"

Dísa shook her head. "No."

Grimnir growled. "Good, then you do understand. This prophecy Halla yammers on about means nothing to me. Nothing! Not when I've waited one thousand, one hundred, and forty-nine years to see vengeance done on the wretched snake, that so-called Malice-Striker, that killed my mother, destroyed my home, and scattered the remnants of my people to the winds . . ."

11

first drew breath at Orkahaugr, *Grimnir began,* in the Kjolen Mountains. It was the last days of the Butchering Month, forty-eight years before the strife and shield-breaking that was Mag Tuiredh. *Nár!* I was still milk-drunk and foolish in those days, so when the ships launched for Èriu, Bálegyr took my wretched brother, Hrungnir, but left me behind with the other whelps and the crones! *Grimnir spat into the fire, his saliva crackling among the embers.* No matter. The she-Wolf who birthed me, Skríkja Kjallandi's daughter, stayed to keep an eye on Bálegyr's throne, and Raðbolg, her kinsman, stayed to keep those thieving little apes down in the fjord-lands in line.

I remember the night before the wolf ships put to sea. It was midsummer's eve, and there was a great council fire in the Hall of the Nine Fathers, where Bálegyr had his throne. You should have seen it, little bird! You were raised in timber and wattle; I was raised in granite and limestone, our mines, smithies, armories, and dwelling halls hacked from the mountain's innards by my sire's hands—the same hands that once fashioned trinkets of gold and iron for the kings of Jötunheimr.

The whole of your stinking village could fit in that hall. Columns of living stone stretched higher than a titan, holding up the mountain itself; shafts cut through the rock let in cold air, and hundreds of lamps hung from the branches of great trees forged from iron and bronze. Trophies dripped from the walls: banners and flayed skins, the shields of fallen foes, the hauberks of heroes slain on the field, the skulls of Jötnar and the thigh bones of trolls. And my sire's throne, carved from a block of obsidian. Two wolves—*Grimnir made an expansive gesture, his eye alight*—crouched to make the arms. And at the center of it all, a fire pit so big it could hold a brace of whole steers, spitted and dressed for the feast. Aye, the Hall was the jewel of Orkahaugr, the heart of the *kaunar* lands of Miðgarðr, and it had been for close to a thousand years.

By this time, Bálegyr was the last of the Nine Fathers—the chiefs of the *dvergar* clans chosen by the Sly One for the honor of becoming *kaunar*. Five died when the Æsir came against us in Jötunheimr, ere my people fled to Miðgarðr; two, Lútr and Hrauðnir, died in the Duel of the Four Fathers on the slopes of Orkahaugr, where Bálegyr lost an eye to Kjallandi even as he won the wolf-mantle of the North. Old Kjallandi took the exile Bálegyr offered, and his folk wandered with him. By the time of Mag Tuiredh, he'd been dead a century and more, slain fighting the cursed Romans in the Atlas Mountains, far to the south.

Skríkja was the eldest of Kjallandi's brood, but she had two brothers—Gífr and Raðbolg—who came back to the North after their father's death. Bálegyr took them in, treated them like his own stinking sons—better, even, since he had a habit of lopping off his sons' heads when they displeased him. And why not? I had twenty-two brothers, little bird. Twenty-two! And that's not counting my sisters, or the dozens of bastards he sired, or the wretched half-breeds he got on captive women. I learned early to keep my head down and toe the line, lest I wound up on the wrong side of Bálegyr's axe.

But Gífr and Raðbolg . . . the pair of them Bálegyr treated like the sons he *wished* he'd had. That night, on the eve of their journey to Èriu, the brothers quarreled over who would go with Bálegyr and who would stay behind. Neither wanted to miss the spear-shattering, but Bálegyr did not trust the fjord-men in the foothills of the Kjolen Mountains to behave themselves in his absence. He wanted a good lad at his back, one he could trust. You should have heard their howling and yammering! Some wretch proposed they wrestle for it, but Gífr refused—Raðbolg was younger and stronger; another threw out the notion that they cast axes, but Raðbolg complained Gífr's aim was better than his. Both ignored my idiot brother, Hrungnir, when he hollered they should dice for it—dice are sacred to *dvergar*, and though the bloody feast Loki made from Angrboða's monstrous afterbirth had left them twisted and scarred *kaunar,* some habits were too ingrained to break.

It was Skríkja who broke the stalemate: she bid them draw lots. That was her way, simple and direct. She prepared the draw, told them the short lot stays. Raðbolg lost. How he cursed and thundered! But not even he dared defy his sister.

Midsummer's day, in that year when the dogs of Rome put their wretched crown on four different heads, was the last time I saw my sire. They put to sea at dusk—two score wolf-prowed ships crewed by every black-hearted *kaunr* throat-slitter Bálegyr could bribe or brow-beat into joining him. He emptied Orkahaugr, leaving only the old, the sick, and the young. Skríkja stood on a tongue of rock overlooking the lake in the shadow of the mountain, a great horn in her hands. Each ship that rowed past, bound for the fjord that led to the open sea, she greeted with a thunderous blast. Bálegyr's ship came last, its keel black as pitch, its rails thick with shields and bristling with spears. Thrice did Skríkja sound that horn, thrice he answered with a howl that could split the heavens; ere the sun's last light died away, she rushed to the edge of the rocks and drew her sword—Sárklungr was its name, the dwarf-forged Wound-Thorn. She threw her arms wide and roared: *"Así att-Súlfr Bálegyr skiari tar nekumanza!"* Bálegyr is the Wolf, and he comes to devour your entrails! That's how I recall her best—a fell-handed queen girded for war, as dark and wild as the sea, bidding farewell to her king . . .

Grimnir lapsed into silence, his gaze fixed on the bed of embers. He leaned back in his seat. Memories are a bane, little bird, like a thorn lodged in your eye. Cut them out, if you can, or they'll do nothing but haunt you in your dotage. *He hawked and spat.* At any rate, summer faded away and no word reached us from Èriu. Skríkja and the old crones cast a circle and summoned all manner of birds, but none had traveled so far as the Isle of Emerald where the *vestálfar*—the cursed West-Elves—made their home. There was one night I can recall, on the cusp of the Sere Month ere the trees shed their leaves, when visions assailed her. A storm raged over the mountain. It sounded like a jötunn had hauled an anvil up the slopes of Orkahaugr. Thunder crashed and rang with the fury of a thousand hammers, and lightning set fire to the sky. Witchery was in the air that night. I could smell it.

But it was the screams that drew us, Raðbolg and me, up to the summit of the mountain. Long ago, when the *kaunar* first crawled up the slopes of Orkahaugr looking for shelter, Bálegyr had them fashion an altar of stone and on it he sacrificed the eldest of his sons to Ymir. Up there, in the wind and the sleet, we found Skríkja huddled over some wretched scrap of a girl—one of the latest thralls we'd taken from the fjord-men. Skríkja had gutted her, had her liver out, and was rooting around for her heart. She was wild-eyed. Kept saying she'd seen Bálegyr's death in the clouds, a fiery eye wreathed in darkness. Skríkja was like Gífr . . . cunning in the ways of sorcery; I had more in common with Raðbolg. Even as a pup, I trusted cold iron and what I could grasp with both hands rather than those invisible webs spun by witches and seers. So we left her to it, but I couldn't shake a sense of unease.

That was the night of the battle at Mag Tuiredh.

Grimnir leaned forward and gestured with one black-nailed finger. See, I knew something was off. I knew something had slipped. I could feel it twisting in my guts, a premonition of doom creeping up on us. But who was I? Just a know-nothing whelp, a fool with milk on his lips, that's who! But I had a mouth on me and I wasn't shy about using it. *Nár!* Even so, Raðbolg laughed when I told him we had to be on guard. He laughed, cuffed me about the head, and sent me off with a few other lads to fetch honey from the hives down by the fjord. But I knew! I knew and I was right . . . I was right . . .

Mark this, little bird: you can judge how high you stand in your enemy's esteem by the weapon he draws against you. By that measure, the one-eyed lord of Ásgarðr must have thought us lords of the earth. For what he drew against us in the days after Mag Tuiredh was a weapon without mercy, as cruel as the grave. *Niðhöggr*, it was called, the Malice-Striker. *Grimnir's voice dropped to an awed whisper.* I saw it, me and the lads Raðbolg sent to fetch the honey. Saw the dragon when it crawled out of the fjord and slithered up the slopes of Orkahaugr. This was no flying wyrm that breathed fire like you miserable Geats like to yammer on about. No, this one was a creeper, half serpent and half lizard. Longer than a wolf ship, it was—longer even than the dragon ships of the Norse—and it pulled itself along on two clawed legs. Scales of bone armored it above and below, pale as man-flesh on its belly but darkening to the colors of moss and lake mud along its back. That monstrous head . . . *Grimnir's brow furrowed at the memory. He shook, as if to rouse himself.*

The bastard paid us no mind. Why should it? We were a half-score of spitless, piss-legged whelps. My mates cowered, but I watched from the shadow of the trees as Malice-Striker scrabbled up the mountainside. That wyrm paused at the gates of Orkahaugr, its chest juddering, and from those jaws came a cloud of vapor that ran before it like storm-rack. It plunged into this froth and fume and clawed its way into the heart of the mountain.

"Up, you louts!" I said to the lads, after the sounds of steel and slaughter reached us. "Up! Were we grumbling and moaning that Bálegyr left us behind? Aye, well here's our chance to prove our mettle! Up! Put a blade in your hands and follow me!" Like an idiot, I drew my seax and charged up the mountain.

Grimnir sat back in his seat. He rubbed his jaw with the knuckles of his blade-hand. The lot of us, this was our first fight. Our first real fight. Oh, we'd scraped and scrabbled with each other, but this . . . this was different. We plunged into the wrack like dogs of war, yipping and baying. That fume, it was like breathing the steam rising from a doused forge—scalding hot and reeking of copper and rotting meat. We couldn't see a damn thing, but we charged on like a gibbering horde of fools.

We nearly tripped over the first raft of bodies. Most were thralls, worn out slatterns we'd taken in raids against the fjord-men or brought back from over the sea. Their minders were among them—a ragtag bunch of lame and crippled wretches led by a half-blooded old hag who had no legs and got herself around on the back of this cow-footed shortwit she called her son. The whole lot of them lay jumbled together, strangled by the fumes or ripped asunder by the beast's claws. Those miserable thralls bore the brunt of it, though. They couldn't run fast enough from that scaly bastard's breath, which was a pestilence to your kind. It boiled them alive or turned them into boneless sacks of flesh that leaked pus and blood.

We rolled on, my mates and me, following the dragon's wake deeper into Orkahaugr. That filthy lizard was quick for its size, and it seemed . . . guided, like the point of a spear driven by a will not its own; it knew where the heart of the mountain was and was making straight for it. None of the bodies strewn along the path gave us pause. *Nár!* We were wolves, hunting for a fresh kill. We passed lads we'd known since we were squalling babes, crushed and riven and drenched in black blood. Their gore-clotted faces cling even now to my mind. They all bore a look of surprise.

The dragon's stink drew us on. Its reeking breath hung low to the ground, like a fog. It nearly covered the ruin of a hasty barricade others had thrown up at that crossroad we called Einvigi, where we settled disputes among kin with knives and fists. The left-hand road led down to the smithies and the mines; the right took you to the bolt-holes and the lairs. Straight and you'd find yourself on a rising path that led to the Hall of the Nine Fathers and the armories—empty, now that the ships had gone to Èriu.

The bodies strewn left and right, the splintered wood . . . they told a plain tale any idiot could read: the wretch was making for the Hall.

Grimnir's nostrils flared, as if recalling a stench from long ago.

And the Hall's where the lads and me caught up to it.

You've never been in a real scrape, have you, little bird? I don't mean these games we play or the few things you learned from that old wretch, Sigrún. I mean a real fight, where the dogs are baying for your blood and the steel cuts it close to your precious head? Ha! I didn't think so. I've been party to more shield-bitings and spear-shatterings than there are Geats left in the whole of your stinking village. Half of them I can't even recall, anymore. But this one . . .

This one I remember like it happened a week gone.

Grimnir planted his feet wide and leaned forward, his elbows on his knees as he gestured with his hands—an artist painting a portrait from memory and air. We burst out into the Hall, my mates five steps ahead of me—I'd stopped to grab a spear, since it was clear my little pig-sticker would be useless. Snatched one off the wall, and a shield for good measure, and turned back around in time to see Malice-Striker's tail crush my mates like eggshells. A squalling, spitting knot of little hate-mongers with murder in their eyes one minute, and the next . . . broken, shredded corpses smeared across the stone floor. I won't lie. That caught me off guard.

I stood there, gaping like an idiot while that misbegotten wyrm tore Bálegyr's throne down. Its belly crushed the fire pit. Its clawed feet left furrows in the stone walls as it clawed its way up. Up and up, it went, its nostrils oozing clouds of poison-wrack, until it battered the hard bones of its head into the ceiling. And me, rooted to the spot with my fool mouth hanging open.

I would have died a second time, crushed under the debris raining from the ceiling, if not for Raðbolg. He snatched a handful of my hair and fairly dragged me out of the way. Slung me down, put an arrow on the nock of that great black bow of his, and whipped the cord back to his ear. *Twang!* Two more he sent after the first—and not a damn one of them did more than shatter on the plates of the bastard's belly.

But they got its attention. Ha! That thing looked down at us like we were shit-nuggets it had stepped on. And when it opened its jaws—to roar or to boil us alive—I knew there would be no third time. I felt the cold touch of the Norns' shears on the thread of what would be a wretchedly short life.

But Raðbolg, that mad whoreson, drew and loosed his last arrow. Sent that black-barbed shaft flying right down that stinking wyrm's cheese-pipe.

Grimnir laughed and sank back in his seat. Were this one of you Geats' tales, well, that would have been the end of it. Break open the mead and let's fire the corpse! But this wasn't some skald's dream. *Nár!* I watched that arrow spring off the nock; watched it sail as straight as a hymn-singer's spine . . . and watched it splinter against one of Malice-Striker's teeth! Ymir! All that did was piss it off.

Well, we were done for, weren't we? That beast came for us in an avalanche of scales and talons; eyes burning like green lamps in that ugly head, its jaws wide and spewing poisoned vapor. "Spear!" Raðbolg screamed at me. I fumbled around, and at the last moment raised the spear to meet Malice-Striker head-on.

Grimnir's eye smoldered like the banked fires of a forge; his voice dropped, becoming a hoarse whisper. That's when I saw her. Skríkja Kjallandi's daughter, the fell-handed Queen of Orkahaugr and she who gave me life. She was on the parapet above that vile wyrm, come from the summit of the mountain.

In her fist, Sárklungr. The Wound-Thorn . . .

Silence fell. Grimnir sat stock-still. A dozen heartbeats passed, then a dozen more. When once again he spoke, his words were grim and heavy, laden with the doom of his people. More than a queen, she was. She was a warrior! My sire's name was on her lips as she hurled herself off that parapet, hurled herself onto Malice-Striker's flank. Our arrows, our spears . . . useless. But Sárklungr—forged from the heart of a fallen star by the hammers of the *dvergar*—Sárklungr struck true and pierced the dragon's hide.

By Ymir! She held that hilt in a white-knuckle grip and rode the blow to the ground. You should have heard the bastard scream! Sárklungr had shorn through its bony armor behind the right shoulder and cut a furrow through its muscle and sinew. Ha! So much for Odin's vaunted dragon, I thought. Damn my eye, but I was callow and stupid back then—both traits Gífr would beat out of me over the decades to come. I was ready to dance a little jig on the wretch's grave when it decided it had had enough of our lot.

Quick as a snake, Malice-Striker spun around. Like that—*Grimnir snapped his fingers*—its tail came whipping at me, scraps of my mates' bloody flesh still hanging off it. I managed to get my shield up, ducked my head, and braced myself . . .

Grimnir chuckled. That was the wrong thing to do, little bird. I should have went as limp as a boned fish. Rode with the blow instead of fighting it. That tail . . . it was like getting hit with a battering ram. Wood splintered. The iron rim of the shield came apart and nearly took my head off; the blow drove the shield-boss into my arm, shattering the bone, and sent me flying into Raðbolg.

Grimnir's brows drew together.

Must have blacked out, because I only have bits and pieces of what happened next. I heard Raðbolg's voice like the roar of thunder. He was shouting Skríkja's name. Saw him grab up my fallen spear and thrust it under the wyrm's armor, into its wounded flank. And I heard my mother's death shriek.

Grimnir leaned back in his seat, his face a mask of scorn. He stared at his left arm, at the knots of gristle that marked the places where the bone was broken; raising his hand, he made a fist.

Skríkja's bleeding out a dozen yards away from me, ripped open from her left shoulder to her right hip, and what do I do? I lay there like a limp rag, crying over this busted arm like it meant something! *Faugh!* What happened next should have come from me. I came around long enough to realize the dragon was gone, skinned out back the way it had come. I saw Raðbolg kneeling over the slaughtered remains of Skríkja. I saw him lift Sárklungr from her limp grasp, saw him trail his hand through her blood and smear it on the blade. And I heard him howl at the heavens like a cornered wolf. "Hear me, Sly One, Father Loki!" he said, sword raised aloft. "Bear witness, O Ymir, sire of giants and lord of the frost! By this blood, the blood of my kin, I swear! I, Raðbolg Kjallandi's son, will not rest until I've brought that wretched dragon to heel! I will not rest until Niðhöggr is under my blade!"

Grimnir lowered his fist and stared into the heart of the fire pit.

EMBERS CRACKLED AND SPAT; OUTSIDE, a cold wind moaned across the ridges as the first fingers of light crept into the eastern sky. For a long moment, no one spoke. Dísa turned the tale over in her mind, while Halla and Grimnir nursed their private thoughts. Finally, the girl stirred.

"You said you've waited for vengeance these many years," Dísa said. "Did Raðbolg fail?"

Grimnir glanced sidelong at her, his eye gleaming in the ember-light. "Would we be dickering over this cursed prophecy if he had? *Nár!* For four hundred and nineteen years Raðbolg hunted Odin's little pet. We were away in the East, Gífr and me, when he finally caught up to it. Back then, the bay you call Skærvík was a peninsula—narrow spit of land rising to a set of great jutting cliffs. Malice-Striker had gone to ground in a cave beneath them. Takes a cursed long time for a wyrm's scaly hide to mend. Bastard was under there, biding his time, sneaking out by the dark of the moon to seize a few goats or raid some luckless Geat's herd of cattle. That's how Raðbolg found him. Followed a trail of gnawed hoof bones and goat horn to Malice-Striker's lair, snuck inside, and waited for the blasted thing to crawl back home."

Grimnir took up a long, fire-blackened spear and used it to stir the embers. "What went on there, under the earth, no one knows. Not a soul witnessed the death of Malice-Striker, save Raðbolg—and he died in the wyrm's death-throes. And after, the whole peninsula just . . . vanished, like some jötunn's hand had scooped it from the earth and left a puddle in its wake."

"Not a jötunn." Halla *tsked*. "The Allfather."

Dísa scowled. "Why would he do that?"

"That wretched, one-eyed wandering tosspot!" Grimnir stabbed savagely at the heart of the fire. "Didn't like that one of the *kaunar*—one of us poor plague folk—beat him at his own game! Oh, no! Didn't like that one of us had shoved a foot of dwarf-steel down the throat of his little pet, so he cheated! Sank the peninsula and sang his cursed prophecy over the ruins!"

"And stole your vengeance." Dísa understood, after a fashion. As a Geat, she was no stranger to the lure of revenge. And as the daughter of a woman slain in battle, she recognized the driving need for it, the thirst one could only assuage with the blood of a sworn enemy.

"Not for much longer," Grimnir snarled. "What is it those filthy hymn-singers say? An eye for an eye and a tooth for a tooth? Well, that dunghill rat stole from me, so I will steal from him, eh? Let old One Eye have his Ragnarök. Let him raise that cursed barrow and resurrect his precious dragon! Aye, I've sworn no oaths that might draw the eyes of Ásgarðr, so he'll be none the wiser when I slip into that stinking hole, take up Sárklungr from the dead hand of my kinsman, and cut that bastard wyrm's head off!"

Halla thrust an accusing finger at him. "You'd deny us our vengeance for the sake of your own?"

"Aye! And why not?" Grimnir's chin jutted forward, his manner savage and belligerent. "What do you even know of the world beyond your precious trees? What do you know of the ambitions of Men, their hatreds and their wars? Nothing! You've never seen the ramparts of Miklagarðr or the stews of Parisius! You've never heard the marching-song of fifty thousand men, or walked the bloody fields where the dead lie in their war rags! By Ymir, you old hag! *Thrice* have these hymn-singers gathered in their multitudes to carry their war over the sea and lay claim to their Nailed God's barrow! And a fourth time just so they could put the screws to the lords of Miklagarðr! They are like barley—reap your fill and more will arise with every passing season! *Faugh!* You could not destroy them even if that wretched wyrm came boiling out of Skærvík with a hundred offspring! So, tell me: why should I pin my hopes on a prophecy of smoke and lies when I can take the vengeance that is my right?"

"We're not saying vengeance isn't your right," Dísa piped up.

Grimnir's good eye slid to the young woman. "*We?* I forget: how is this any of your business?"

"The end comes for my world, too, does it not? That gives me a voice. See, what if you but delayed your vengeance? What would this dragon do if loosed upon the Nailed God's world?"

"Nothing!" Grimnir snapped. "Because, by the . . ." Lips writhing, he choked back an oath. "By my *hand* that scaly wretch dies ere its blasted eyes open fully on this world!"

Halla leaned forward and spat into the embers of the fire. "You're a pig-headed fool, *skrælingr*, you—"

Suddenly, Grimnir bolted upright in his seat, his good eye ablaze. His nostrils flared; his lips skinned back over his teeth. "Quiet!"

A moment later, Dísa heard it, too: three long blasts of a horn. She had a sinking feeling as she recognized it. "That's Askr's horn."

"One of your lot?"

"Aye," Dísa replied, reaching for her haubergeon. Her gaze met Halla's, and in that milky stare she saw a touch of fear reflected—neither of them had told Grimnir of Hreðel's threats for fear of what he might do. Now, that fear bubbled to the surface. "He's kinsman to my cousin's bedmate. I'll go down to the beach and see what this racket's all about."

Dísa shrugged into her mail, twisting and rolling her shoulders as it settled into place; Halla fastened Dísa's weapons' belt about her slender hips; the girl hitched at it, adjusting her sheathed seax and the Frankish axe in its leather frog—all the while trying to avoid Grimnir's suspicious glare. She caught up her helmet, shield, and short spear.

"Expecting trouble, little bird?" he said acidly, settling back in his seat. "Are these not your folk?"

"What was it you said? 'Blood's no proof against a jealous blade'?"

There was no humor in Grimnir's chuckle as she eased open the door and vanished into the rising light. He shot a suspicious glance at Halla, who moved deeper into the longhouse and away from the petrifying gleam of daylight. "I saw that look. What's she not telling me, eh?"

12

Three times more did Askr's horn sound before Dísa reached the end of the forest trail leading to the stony shingle. A niggling voice in the back of her mind preached caution, and her gut followed suit. So, rather than burst forth in full view of Askr and whomever made the journey with him, Dísa held back. She left the trail and crept silently through the undergrowth, keeping to the shadows beneath the towering evergreens so she'd have time to take the measure of what awaited her.

Askr, she saw, and Hrútr. Both were clad in wolf skins and mail. Hrútr leaned on a spear while Askr had his horn poised for a fourth blast. Auða paced alongside them, her hair drawn back in a long black braid; it twitched like a lion's tail with each sharp turn she made. She kept her gaze fixed on the trail head. Auða muttered something to Hrútr, who merely shrugged. The fourth man waited by the boat. Dísa recognized the white-haired bulk of giant Bjorn Hvítr, Bjorn the White. A bear skin hung from his shoulders, its great paws clasped around his neck. He cradled an axe in his arms.

They are clad for war, she reckoned. Not a good omen.

Auða nodded to Askr, who drew a deep breath and blew a thunderous note on his silver-chased horn. He held it for a moment, letting the sound echo across the ridges and into the hollows. It ended, and as that echo died, Dísa stepped from the shadows of the tree line and onto the shingle.

Her sudden and savage appearance took them by surprise. Auða's eyes widened; Hrútr cursed and leveled his spear at her. Askr dropped his horn to his side and clawed at the hilt of his sword. And even Bjorn Hvítr, whose temper was as mild as his curiosity, scowled at the pale-skinned apparition conjured by the horn-song.

"Cease your racket," Dísa said. She drove her spear's butt-spike into the ground, stripped off her helmet and hung it from the lug behind the broad-bladed head, and leaned her shield against it. She approached the four slowly. "I'm here. What goes, cousin?"

"We've been worried about you," Auða said. "You left Hrafnhaugr over a month ago and none have seen hide nor hair of you since. Are you well?"

Dísa stopped a dozen feet from the four; by newfound habit, she kept her distance, her carriage loose and poised to move. Though Auða was her kins-woman and she'd known the other three all her life, there was nevertheless a gulf between them. Dísa felt like a pet they'd turned loose in the wild, a dog gone feral; one that recognized her former master's smell but remained skittish. "You came all this way to ask after me? I am flattered, cousin. Truly. As you can see, I am hale and in good spirits."

"What has he done to you, girl?" This from Hrútr, who cast a scornful eye on her war-rags and ironmongery. She was lean and hard, her flesh mot-tled with bruises, purple fading to yellow; she looked like some fey spirit summoned from the fences of Hel's icy realm.

"What do you mean?"

"He doesn't know what he means," Auða snapped, glaring at Hrútr. "But since we can see with our own eyes that you are well, there's another matter we must discuss. The matter of Flóki. He's not back, either, and Jarl Hreðel is beside himself. The man is not well, cousin. Food stores run low and he does nothing to replenish them. His temper is unchecked. Even Sigrún gives him a wide berth. He wants you, Dísa. He wants you to come back to Gautheimr and explain the Hooded One's inaction. Jarl Hreðel—and a lot of us with him—feels the Hooded One has much to answer for."

Dísa bristled. "And what does Hreðel have to answer for, eh? He should have thought of this when he was busy coddling his son. Flóki seeks to be a man, his own man, is all. The Hooded One bears no blame in this, and he certainly doesn't answer to the likes of a bench-hugger like Hreðel!"

"That's enough, girl," Hrútr said. "He is your chief, and respect must be paid. Time is short. We must return."

"Then go."

Askr took a step toward her. "Auða is more patient than we are. Hreðel wants you to attend him. That was not an invitation. We will drag you back with us, if we must." The others nodded, even Auða—though she seemed reluctant.

Dísa's lips peeled back in a smile identical to Grimnir's—cold and humorless and brimming with scorn. Her dark-rimmed eyes never left Askr's as she ducked her head and spat at his feet. Dísa watched as anger suffused his features; watched as he took another step toward her . . . until Auða put out a restraining hand.

"Why are you being like this, cousin?" said the older woman.

"Why am I not abasing myself before that idiot, you mean?"

Auða's face hardened. "No! Why you are not doing your duty to your sworn lord is what I mean!"

"Oh, but I am," Dísa replied. "I am not the priestess of Hreðel, am I? No, cousin. I serve the Hooded One, and the Hooded One has spoken: let Jarl Hreðel dry his tears and act like a man whose son has fared forth to earn his war-name, not like a sulking old harridan whose lord has taken a younger wife! Go! Tell him what the Hooded One has commanded." Dísa turned away.

The gesture was calculated. She meant to draw out their true intent, to force them into playing their hand. "Call the tune," Grimnir would say, "and make your enemy dance to it." And Auða danced. Dísa could not see the sign she made to Askr, but she knew she made such a sign. She could not see the snarl of pleasure that writhed across Askr's bearded visage, but she knew he wore such a snarl. And though she willingly blinded herself by turning away, Dísa's other senses were as sharp as a fox's. She heard the crunch of stones as Askr shifted his weight to his lead foot; she heard the creak of tendons and the hissing of his breath as he committed fully to a lunge that should have ended with her hard in his grasp.

This, she heard. And, a heartbeat before Askr's fingers clamped down on her shoulder, Dísa Dagrúnsdottir moved. She sidestepped and spun; steel hissed on leather as she aired the blade of her seax. She could have killed him, then. She saw it; by the sudden fear gleaming in his eyes as he passed, Askr saw it, too. But quick as a serpent, Dísa lashed out with the pommel.

Her momentum added weight to the blow, and it connected with the back of Askr's skull. There came a dull thud. Askr stumbled. His eyes rolled back in his head as he pitched face-first onto the snow-spotted shingle.

Dísa did not stop to crow. She came around and leveled her seax at Hrútr, who took a step toward his unconscious kinsman. "Raise that spear," she growled, "and you will join him! Look at me, cousin!"

Auða, her sword half-drawn, lifted her stunned gaze from Askr to the length of razor-edged steel in Dísa's fist. Behind them, Bjorn Hvítr watched all this unfold with a thunderous scowl across his craggy brow.

"He'll have an aching head and a bruise upon his pride," Dísa said, her gaze flickering between the three. "Now take him and go, lest one of you comes to harm!"

Auða shook her head. "We have our orders, cousin. You're coming with us."

"Think again, *cousin!*"

"Enough!" Bjorn Hvítr roared. The giant Geat stalked across the shingle, axe in hand; he shouldered past Hrútr and Auða and rolled toward Dísa like an avalanche of muscle. A thrill of fear raced up her spine as she eyed his great bulk, the slabs of meat like iron plate, legs like tree trunks, and the hard-boned head tilted toward her. His brown eyes bore no trace of anger. Still, Dísa backed away. She edged toward the safety of the trees as Auða and her bedmate fanned out to either side.

"Come, girl," Bjorn said softly. "Don't make me hurt you."

Dísa bared her teeth; she stopped moving and dropped to a fighting crouch.

Suddenly, an arrow hissed from the tree line. The wind from its passing fanned the fey tangles of Dísa's hair. It pierced its target, tearing a bloody furrow through Bjorn Hvítr's flesh and taking off most of his right ear. The giant Geat howled, clutching the side of his head. Auða and Hrútr froze; Dísa risked a glance over her shoulder, and then loosed her pent-up breath in a sigh of relief when she saw a monstrous figure emerge from the trees.

She knew it was Grimnir, but he did not look like himself. Gone was his old brigandine coat. Now, he sported a hauberk of blackened mail that hung to mid-thigh, and a broad belt strung with human scalps. A wolf-skin cloak hung from his shoulders and an eerie mask and headdress hid his face from casual view. The headdress, Dísa reckoned, was made from the age-blackened skull of a huge stag. Over time, Grimnir had trimmed the antlers and carved them until he had two curling horns that came down—one on either side of his face. The mask was fashioned from a wolf's skull, rune-carved and streaked with red pigment. From one cavernous socket Grimnir's red eye gleamed even in the pale light of morning.

He stalked across the shingle, a great black bow in his hands; he had a second arrow already on the nock and the string half drawn. The hilt of his seax jutted from its scabbard on his left hip. Fear crackled before him like the lightning that presaged a storm as he drew himself up to his full height. "Are you thieves or fools?" he snarled, his voice made deep and hollow by the mask. "Either way, touch her again and I will send you as a beggar down the road to Hel!"

Dísa straightened and offered Grimnir an awkward bow. "My lord, I—"

"Be silent, little fool! We will have words later, you and I! For now, you louts will answer my question: are you thieves or fools?"

Dísa took his rebuke to heart. She kept silent and shifted her attention to Auða and the others. Though they'd never seen him, they knew they faced the Tangled God's immortal herald, the inscrutable Hooded One. Hrútr's tongue froze to the roof of his mouth. He trembled and averted his eyes. Bjorn Hvítr clutched his ruined ear and stared at his feet. Only Auða had the courage to raise her eyes to meet Grimnir's wrathful gaze.

"We are neither," she stammered, then added as an afterthought: "lord."

"Then what are you, eh? If you're not fools or thieves?"

"I am Auða of the Raven, and these are Jarl Hreðel's sworn men. He sent us to fetch her." Auða nodded at Dísa. "She must come with us. The Jarl commands it."

"Must she now?" Grimnir said. Dísa winced at her cousin's choice of words. "Hreðel *commands* it, does he? Am I to bend myself to Hreðel's will, then? Am I to let you and these so-called sworn men of Hreðel's just march up to my door and take what is mine, without so much as a 'by your leave'? Tell me, you miserable sack of bones, who is Hreðel?"

Auða frowned, plainly confused by the question. Blooms of color tinted her cheeks, her anger causing her blade hand to twitch. She glanced sidelong at the men but neither could meet her eye. "Who . . . who is Hreðel?"

"Aye, that's what I said, Auða of the Raven!"

"He's th-the Jarl . . . the Jarl of Hrafnhaugr and Chief of the Raven-Geats."

"Hrafnhaugr, eh?" Grimnir handed his bow to Dísa. She heard him take a snuffling breath as he walked closer to Auða, Bjorn, and Hrútr, smelling their fear, their anger. "So, this Hreðel: he was there when the foundations of Hrafnhaugr were laid? And when the wretched Norse tried to burn the walls and enslave the Geats in that first year, it was Hreðel's blade that cut down the Norse war-chief, eh?" Grimnir reached Askr, who groaned and struggled to rise. He caught a handful of Askr's hair and hauled him to his feet, fairly shoving him into Hrútr's grasp. Both men staggered back. "For twenty-three miserable generations of your kind, it's been Hreðel whose had the thankless task of keeping you Geats safe, is it?"

Auða licked her lips. "No."

"No? Well, if it's not Hreðel, then who was it, little bird?" Grimnir glanced back at Dísa. "Who has done these things?"

"You, lord."

"Aye, me." Grimnir rounded on Auða. Crossing the interval between them in two long steps, he put the eye sockets of his wolf-mask close to her face, his hot breath steaming in the chill air. She recoiled, her hand dropping to the hilt of her sword. "Tell me, Auða of the Raven, why should I give a Swede's fart what your precious Hreðel wants?" His gaze dropped to her hand, wrapped white-knuckle tight around her sword's leather and wire-wrapped hilt. "You think you can take my measure? The lot of you, you filthy swine, think you can take me?" His head moved slightly from side to side. Hrútr had passed his spear to Askr, who leaned heavily on it; Hrútr, too, had a hand on his sword, loosening the blade in its scabbard. On the other side of Auða, Bjorn Hvítr fingered his axe haft with a bloody hand. "You going to hew me down with that log-splitter, you dunghill rat?" Grimnir's laugh bore the chill of the grave. "Four against one, little bird! Are these fair odds among your kind?"

Dísa shrugged. "Fair enough, I think. I would ask a favor, lord. Don't kill them."

"A favor? You think you've earned that right, eh? Why did I have to find out from old Halla that their wretched Hreðel threatened to—how did she put it?—'come for my bastard head' and 'burn even the memory of me from this land'?"

"Because I knew this is what would happen!" Dísa caught the hint of movement as Hrútr bared a hand-span of steel. "Hrútr, damn your ignorant hide! Keep that up and I'll skewer you before our lord has the chance!"

"Bastard's not my lord," Hrútr said.

"Hrútr!" Auða snapped. The man stopped moving.

Grimnir swung around to face him. "I have borne the insults of your kind for long enough! It's high time I remind you lot who is the servant, here, and who is the master!"

Hrútr must have seen his doom in Grimnir's shadowed gaze, for with a curse he dragged his sword the rest of the way from its scabbard. His movements galvanized the other three—all veterans of Odin's weather, of the fume and broil of the shield wall. But as quick as they were, as skilled and as fell-handed were these journeymen of war, here they faced a master of the killer's art.

Dísa shouted a warning; before its echo reached a crescendo and died away, Grimnir was in motion. Hrútr and Askr stepped back to gain room to maneuver. But ere they took a second step, Grimnir's taloned hands knotted in each man's hair. He slammed their heads together. The *crack* of impact and both men went down, stunned.

Auða's sword rang as it cleared the mouth of its scabbard. Grimnir twisted, sidestepped the blow, and drove the hard point of his elbow into the woman's temple. She staggered. Grimnir seized her by the neck and shoved her into Bjorn Hvítr's path, her sword scraping the ground as it tumbled from her nerveless fingers. Bjorn tried to catch her with his left arm; with his right, he swung his axe. Grimnir caught that thick wrist with one hand. Hissing, he drove the first ridge of knuckles into the hollow of Bjorn's throat.

Bjorn staggered, gagging for breath. Auða's weight dragged him to his knees.

Grimnir ambled on by, deaf to their groans and slurred curses. He went to their boat, leaned over the gunwale, and drew out one of the oars: sprucecarved, its grain gone dark with age and cracked by the elements. Dísa could tell he wore a broad grin despite the concealing mask. He retraced his steps, swinging the oar to get a feel for its weight and heft. Bjorn struggled to stand; near him, Auða rolled onto her stomach and fought to get her legs under her. Dísa willed her to stay down. Of the kinsmen, Askr and Hrútr, only the latter had any fight left in him. He clawed for the fallen spear, and had risen to his knees when Grimnir reached him.

The oar whistled through the air, its tight arc ending in a dull *crack* as Grimnir broke the blade against the back of Hrútr's skull. The man pitched face-first onto the shingle and did not move.

Grimnir reversed the broken oar; a quick jab—driving the butt end into the side of Bjorn Hvítr's head, just behind the ear—took care of the thickly muscled Geat. That left only Auða. She glared up at Grimnir. "Don't—"

Grimnir kicked her in the face.

"Next time, I won't be so gentle," he said, then turned to Dísa. "And next time, you little wretch, you'd best tell me when the likes of Hreðel is running his mouth and making threats!"

"I thought it was best—"

"*Nár!* You didn't think, little bird! You had your eye fixed on the prize and wanted nothing to come between you and it!" Grudgingly, he added: "I can admire that, to a point!"

"What will you do?"

Grimnir fell silent. Turning, he hooked one thumb in his belt; the other he draped over the pommel of his seax. He looked out over the choppy waters of the Skærvík, lost in thought. His black-nailed finger tapped the cross-guard—a tuneless rhythm that punctuated his annoyance. Finally, he stirred and looked askance at her. "It's high time we put your newfound skills to good use. Get over here and grab this sack of bones. I'll get these other rats . . ."

UNDER A VEIL OF THICK gray clouds, night descended swiftly on Gautheimr, the Geat-home, which perched atop its bluff overlooking the leaden waters of Lake Vänern. The air under those carved eaves was as dark and foreboding as the twilight. A fire crackling on the stone hearth afforded little in the way of heat or light. Around tables, near braziers filled with sullen coals, the Jarl's sworn men sat in small groups; some mended or polished their war gear while others merely drank from the dwindling stocks of ale and brooded.

Closer to the doors, the Daughters of the Raven sat in a knot around Sigrún, who warmed her hands over a brazier, glaring up at the figure draped across the high seat with undisguised contempt. Hreðel drowsed in a drunken stupor, surrounded by a carpet of broken crockery jars—the last of Hrafnhaugr's stores of wine. The Jarl had not washed in days; his beard was tangled and stiff with spilled food, his hair unkempt, and he stank.

"You'd think the bastard was in mourning," Sigrún hissed. She accepted a bowl of barley stew and a wedge of coarse bread from one of the younger Daughters.

"Maybe Auða will bring him good news," Geira said. She was a scarred and knotted figure, a few years Sigrún's junior; Kolgríma had been her sister.

Sigrún sniffed. "If that fool girl, Dísa, would do her duty, we'd need not send Auða hunting for word of Flóki. Gods know, I should have drowned that one at birth and told her mother she was stillborn."

"Listen to yourself, Sigrún." Geira looked up from her meager stew. "The rest of us, we'd be proud to have a granddaughter taken to serve as the Hooded One's priestess. But you? You grouse and nitpick everything that poor girl does."

"I don't recall it being your business, Geira."

"It's all our business, old woman," Geira replied, gesturing with her spoon. "You are the eldest, but you are not our chief. Dísa is, as Kolgríma was before her. Speak civilly of her, no matter how badly it galls you, or cut that mark from your cheek and join the other old crones!"

Sigrún's face darkened; a gleam flickered in her eyes, presaging violence the way distant lightning presaged a storm. But her retort was lost when the door to Gautheimr slammed open.

A man stood on the threshold, barrel-chested and bandy-legged and sporting a bushy gray beard that flowed like moss down the craggy face of an oak. Old Hygge's son, he was, called Hygelac. He stared up at the high seat, lines of care and worry etched deep into his broad forehead as he saw the state of the Jarl. He let his gaze roam over the faces of those in attendance. There was a growing sense of urgency about him. Finally, his eyes settled on Sigrún. "Something's happened, down at the dock," Hygelac said, pointing back the way he'd come. A builder of ships and boats, Hygelac stank of the decoctions of his trade, of tar and brine, resin and oakum. "Rouse the Jarl. He needs to see this with his own eyes."

"What goes?"

"The ones he sent out? They've returned. Rouse him, lady. He needs to bear witness."

Sigrún stared at the shipwright a moment longer before motioning for Bjorn Svarti. "Wake him, if you can." Nodding, Bjorn Svarti strode up to the high seat and ascended the steps.

"Jarl," he said. Then, louder: "Jarl Hreðel!"

Hreðel stirred; he groaned and opened one eye. Suddenly, both eyes flew open. Hreðel started forward, rank breath hissing between his teeth as he grasped Bjorn Svarti's wrist. "Flóki!"

Bjorn caught him by the shoulder. "No, Jarl. It's Svarti."

"Svarti?" Hreðel blinked back tears. "I—I thought you were . . ."

"Jarl."

Hreðel cleared his throat. He nodded. "What is it, Svarti? What goes? Have they brought the girl back?"

"Hygelac has found something. He says you need to follow him to the docks."

Hreðel waved that notion aside. "I am too tired for games, Svarti. You go as my eyes and ears."

There was a resolute set to the saturnine Geat's jaw. "No, Jarl," he said. "Hygelac Hyggesson bids *you* rise and follow. He does not call for Bjorn Svarti."

Behind them, murmurs of concern rippled through Gautheimr. Had some ill befallen Auða and the lads? Hreðel listened; finally, he nodded. The Jarl grunted and heaved himself upright. "Lead on, then." He pushed away Svarti's attempt to steady him, and staggered along at the head of a procession—the Daughters falling in alongside the Jarl's sworn men, servants, and other hangers-on. On Hygelac's heels, the lot of them filed from Gautheimr.

It took less than a quarter of an hour to negotiate their way down to the dock—the same dock they'd sent Dísa off from. Heavy flakes of snow swirled down from the heavens, sizzling in the torch flames or sticking to cloaks and hoods. The woods around them seemed alive with unseen menace; hands clapped to sword hilts, and men drew their axes tighter.

"Aye," Hygelac said, shivering. "It's like Odin himself has his squinty eye upon you."

"Not the Allfather," Sigrún whispered to those Daughters in earshot. "*He's* watching us."

Old Hygge met them at the end of the trail. "Before sunset," Hygelac said, "we heard Askr's horn, my old da and me—but it was weak, like it wrenched the last breath from his lungs to sound it. We followed the noise and yonder is what we discovered."

The folk of Hrafnhaugr arrayed themselves behind their Jarl, craning to get a better look. In the trees along the water's edge, from the heaviest branches, four figures hung by their ankles. Auða and Hrútr, it was, and Askr and Bjorn Hvítr, all strung up like suckling pigs. "We did not touch them," Hygelac said, "but came to fetch you, instead."

"Ymir's blood," Sigrún said, shouldering past the Jarl to reach Auða. Bjorn Svarti followed.

"Did . . . Did *he* kill them?" Jarl Hreðel licked his lips; blood had drained from his face, and sweat beaded his brow. "Did the Hooded One do this, may the Gods ever blacken his name?" The same fear echoed from a dozen throats: "The Hooded One killed them!"

"Keep your blasphemous tongue between your teeth!" Sigrún snapped; she spun Auða around and looked her over for injuries. "She's not dead. Geira, lend me a hand!"

"Nor are these three," Svarti said. "Took a good beating, but they're breathing. Quickly, lads! Cut them down." Geira helped Sigrún while the Jarl's men saw to their own. In short order, the four were loosed and upright, groggy but alive. Auða leaned on Geira's shoulder. She spat blood.

"He . . . He wouldn't let us have her. Dísa, I mean." Auða looked over at Hreðel. "She protected you as long as she could, Jarl. She didn't tell him you'd made threats. But he found out anyway, and he means to settle the score."

"Settle?" Hreðel said. "Seems he's upped the stakes rather than settle any scores!" He turned and looked back at the folk who followed them out from Hrafnhaugr. Some were nodding; others looked petrified, as if the fabric of their world was slowly unraveling. "I say it's the Hooded One who crossed the line! We give and we give, and when we ask a simple favor we're rebuffed, our folk attacked, and we're made to live in fear? No more! I say we burn that bastard out!"

"Then what?" Sigrún said. "Say you do this thing, what then? Will you turn to the White Christ for protection from the Swedes or the Norse?"

"Why not?" Hreðel made a clumsy sign of the Cross. "What interest would the Swedes or the Norse have in us if we were like them, eh? If we knelt and prayed to the Nailed God, why would they seek to do us harm?"

"You're a fool," Auða said.

Spittle flew from Hreðel's lips as he thrust his face next to Auða's. "Am I? All he had to do was help me! Help me get my son back!"

"Dísa was right. Let Flóki go and earn his beard."

"That little traitor will pay, alongside her wretched master!" Hreðel straightened. "Men of Raven Hill! It is high time we took back what is ours! I've had my fill of being lorded over by women, and living under the threat of that devil they worship! It ends now! Tonight! Arm yourselves! I mean to cut this thorn from our side, and if that means we take to our knees and sing the hymns of the Nailed God, then so be it! I bid you, my sworn men, to stand by your oaths to serve me!"

"You'll not have the Daughters of the Raven at your side, you weak-minded fool!" Sigrún said.

Hreðel turned and stared hard at the old woman. There was a newfound purpose in the set of his jaw; his eyes glittered with righteous fervor. "Then get back to the spindle where you belong, you useless old hag! Who's with me?" The Jarl ascended the path to Hrafnhaugr without a backward glance.

Though reluctant, most of the Jarl's sworn men—some seventy-five strong—fell in behind Hreðel, Askr and Hrútr among them. Auða felt the sting of her bedmate's betrayal, but said nothing. She looked at Bjorn Hvítr, who shook his head. "I've had his measure, and I'll not take up arms against him."

The other Bjorn, Svarti, gave a solemn nod. "I must. My oath compels me, even if my heart does not." He turned and followed the cortege back to Gautheimr. The Daughters of the Raven came last; the youngest, Bryngerðr, snuffled and wiped tears from her eyes.

"What must we do?" she whispered to Geira.

"Hold to our faith and pray this madness passes."

"And look to our steel, in case it doesn't," Sigrún added.

The Daughters walked into a Gautheimr transformed. Bright flames licked the top of the hearth; torches burned in sconces, and lamps upon table. The Jarl's men were donning their war-gear, their mail and leather, wolf-headed cloaks and iron helmets. All around the hall echoed the clash and rattle of harness. Their sudden flurry of activity drew villagers from the lower terraces; they clustered around the door to watch the arming.

"Don't do this, Hreðel!" Sigrún motioned to the Daughters, who brought her mail from its stand. Another carried her round shield, its white face bearing a stylized raven in black. A third brought her spear and her raven-winged helmet. "Don't force my hand!"

"It is done!" Hreðel replied. He sat in his seat, his sword in its scabbard laid across his knees. "We've been ruled from the shadows for too long! It ends tonight! You villagers, take up arms! Unlimber your oars and draw your keels from their sheds! This night, we cross Skærvík and rewrite our destiny! Go! Spread the word! Tonight we fight for freedom!"

"No, Hreðel. Tonight you die!" Sigrún drew herself up to her full height. "I am Sigrún of the Raven, Eldest Daughter, Captain of Shield and Spear, and I challenge you, Hreðel Kveldúlfsson! Fight me, and let the Gods decide who is right!"

Ragged cheers and shouts erupted. Men paused in their arming, torn, like Bjorn Svarti, between their oaths and their hearts; their eyes flickered from Sigrún to Hreðel. The Jarl looked like a man stricken with palsy. His hands shook. To hide his tremors, he grasped his sword by scabbard and hilt and held it tight.

Before he could answer Sigrún's challenge, however, a voice from behind the villagers clustered in the doorway roared a single command: "Stop!"

All heads turned. The throng parted; gasps and whispers punctuated the scrape of hobnailed boots on stone as Dísa stalked into the heart of Gautheimr. Gone was the moody girl of fifteen summers who left here over a month before. The figure who returned was ageless, as fey and feral as a wolf, hard-eyed and snarling; her lean torso and muscular limbs bore the scars and forge-marks of the Gods' own anvil. Like Kolgríma before her, Dísa passed through the fires of an Elder World and came out the other side—its light burned in her gaze, enough to make men tremble. She reached the center of the hall.

"There is our traitor!" said Hreðel, glad for the distraction. "Come to gloat, eh? Come to witness the strife you've caused by not standing by your own people? I'll say this much for you, child: you have nerve coming here alone!"

"That is where you are wrong," Dísa replied. "I did not come alone."

A shadow rose up from behind the high seat; men had the impression of a swirling cloak, a horned and masked silhouette. A single red eye blazed as a black-nailed hand curled around Hreðel's throat and wrenched his head back. Screams erupted from the doorway of the hall.

The Jarl's sword clattered to the ground.

Led by Bjorn Svarti, a half a dozen of the Jarl's men started forward, blades rasping against scabbard chapes, spear shafts clattering. They all stopped short as the shadow drew an ancient long-seax and balanced it point-first on the heart's path, that soft hollow of flesh between Hreðel's left collarbone and neck. The threat was clear: one more step and he'd send their Jarl down the icy road to Hel's gates. The figure leaned over him and laughed, soft and menacing. "I hear you've been threatening me, you fat fool!"

AMID CRIES OF ALARM, THE Hooded One dragged Jarl Hreðel from the high seat, flinging him bodily down the short steps to land among his sworn men. Bjorn Svarti helped him to his feet; another Geat fetched a bench as Grimnir kicked away shards of crockery and settled himself into the Jarl's seat. Dísa joined him; she stood at the base of the steps, a little to Grimnir's right.

Grimnir drove the point of his seax into the arm of the seat. "Every blasted day, I walk the fences of Geat-land—through forest and fen, hill and hollow—killing any I find and leaving their heads for their mates to stumble across. Those heads tell the tale of a savage folk, you Raven-Geats, who make the piss-ant Swedes and those miserable Norse think twice before trying to raid this land! I kill and I kill and this is my thanks? You threaten me, threaten my priestess, and send an armed rabble to violate the ancient compacts? *Faugh!* Tell me why I shouldn't kill you where you stand, Hreðel Kveldúlfsson!"

"If the compacts are broken, it's you who broke them!" Hreðel sputtered. He sat heavily on the proffered bench. "We asked for a simple boon! A small thing! But you could not be bothered even to check on the well-being of the future Jarl of your followers!"

"I could not be bothered to fetch your wayward son, you mean? Who am I to stand between a lad and his war-name? Did I drag you back kicking and screaming when you went off to raid the Norse against your father's wishes?"

"That was different," Hreðel muttered. Whispers arose from the onlookers—now numbering almost three hundred, all jammed cheek by jowl in the tight confines of Gautheimr or else standing outside, listening as others relayed what was said.

"Aye," Grimnir said, leaning forward to point an accusing finger at Hreðel. "Your old da was a man about it! If the Norse got you"—Grimnir made an expansive gesture—"such was the will of the Weird Sisters, the Norns. He'd just make more sons."

"I do not have that luxury," Hreðel said, bitterly.

"And how is that any of my concern, you wretch? How is that your lad's concern?" Grimnir gestured at Dísa. "This one tells me you coddle him, is that so?" Color stained Dísa's cheeks. She looked away.

Hreðel's gaze had an edge to it. "She speaks out of turn."

"Does she?" Grimnir leaned back, directing his question to the throng of onlookers. "Does this little bird speak out of turn when she says the Jarl's son is coddled?"

Murmurs arose. But it was Sigrún who stepped forward. "She does not, lord."

Hreðel snarled and shot an accusing glance at the old woman—who moments before had been ready to spill his blood.

Sigrún met his hate-filled gaze evenly. "It is our custom that a boy on the cusp of manhood can only grow his beard after he's felt the warm and bloody rain of Odin's weather. Flóki is well into his eighteenth year and remains beardless."

Grimnir sniffed. "By what lights do you think I'd choose a beardless, unblooded boy to be the Jarl of my village? You think me that foolish?"

Hreðel's eyes snapped up, narrowing with suspicion. "The Jarl's mantle is hereditary," he said. "It passes from father to son."

"It passes from father to son, aye," Grimnir said. "But only with my blessing and only if I think the son worthy. The compact is clear. *I* choose who sits on this seat, not you!" Grimnir slapped the armrest. "This is a gift I choose to bestow, or not! You think the blood in your veins is noble and pure? That you and your sons are destined to be Jarls? Bah! Kveldúlf's grandfather was a swine-herd ere I chose him to take up the high seat!" Grimnir looked askance at Dísa. "This is what I was talking about, little bird. You lot have forgotten even what's in the cursed compact!"

"What will become of my son if he is barred from following in my footsteps?" Hreðel said. "All his life, I've groomed him to wear the wolf-mantle. I've protected him, taught him to read the runes, to sacrifice and find wisdom in the entrails; I've taught him what we recall of the compact between us."

"And you've tried to find him a wife, haven't you, you sly dog?" Grinning, Grimnir glanced from Hreðel to Dísa.

The girl knew enough not to rise to his baiting.

"It matters naught if he's to be cast adrift and forgotten."

Sigrún growled, "Then you should have better prepared him for the world out there!"

Grimnir touched the side of his bone mask. "The old hag is right. Ymir's blood, man! Where are your balls? You've dogs aplenty! You want your brat back?" Grimnir gestured to the ranks of the Jarl's sworn men. "Send one of them after him and quit grousing to me about it!"

"I'll go," Dísa said suddenly. And like a curtain, silence fell over Gautheimr. Sigrún's eyes narrowed; Hreðel snorted in contempt. But Grimnir . . . Grimnir rubbed the pommel of his seax, contemplating and calculating. He knew what drove the girl—and it was more than her admiration for Flóki. She, too, was unblooded. "You said it yourself: it's time to put to the test what I've learned from you. Send me after Flóki and the others."

Hreðel could not contain himself. The Jarl laughed and shook his head. "You? No doubt it was you who put him up to this."

"He's his own man, even if you're blind to it!" Dísa snapped. "He needs no encouragement from me."

"Svarti," Hreðel said, turning to look at the saturnine Geat. "I'd consider it a favor if you'd pick a couple of good lads and bring my son back to me."

Bjorn Svarti's face was impassive as he looked from Hreðel to his cousin, Bjorn Hvítr, before turning to the Hooded One. "By your leave?"

Grimnir chuckled. "You're a quick one, lad."

Hreðel spluttered. "You would seek his permission? Am I not your Jarl, dog?"

Grimnir came to his feet; he loomed over the assemblage, his shadow made greater by the flaring cloak, by the carved horns on his headdress. His eye blazed from the depths of his wolf-mask as he wrenched his seax free in a shower of splinters. "*Jarl?* You are nothing, swine!" he roared. "A drunkard and a fool! I take back the wolf-mantle! If you think me unkind, if you think me unfair . . . then draw your steel and we'll settle this the old way!"

Hreðel blinked. He sniffed and stared at his feet, hands trembling.

"As I thought, you dunghill rat!" Grimnir glared at the sworn men and beyond, at the throng of villagers watching this spectacle. "Any of you dare dispute my right to sit upon this seat? Step up, dogs! Step up, or keep your tongues between your rotten teeth!"

For a moment, it looked as though Hrútr might step forward, but his kinsman's hand on his arm stopped him. Askr shook his head.

Satisfied, Grimnir sat. He nodded to Dísa. "Go after him, little bird," he said. "I will decide after I meet this Flóki if he's fit to take up his father's mantle."

13

Dísa left Hrafnhaugr in the cold hours before dawn.

The night before had not been one of merriment. No songs were sung under the eaves of Gautheimr, no lies embroidered upon by drunken Geats, no calls for tests of strength or of wits. The men who drank did so in deadly earnest, silent and brooding.

Hreðel took himself off, his shame almost too much to bear. Some of his sworn men remained loyal to him and followed—Askr and Hrútr among them. The Daughters remained in the great hall, attending the needs of the Hooded One even as they gave Dísa a wide berth. Grimnir sat atop the high seat, watching. Only Berkano—gentle, mad Berkano—dared approach him. Her sister, Laufeya, waited a short distance off as Berkano sat at the foot of the seat and offered him a horn of her herb-infused mead. He sniffed it, nodded, and raised his mask a fraction. He drained the horn in three gulps. Grimnir smacked his lips and passed it back to her.

"Aye," he said, "you Otter-Geats know how to brew mead!"

"You knew our people?" Berkano said, glancing back at her sister.

Grimnir leaned back in the seat; his gaze shifted from Berkano to stern-faced Laufeya. "I hunted the Norse who burned out your folk," he said. He hitched at his belt and drew the scalps around. One he plucked from the others and held it up for the sisters to see—a red-gold mane with strips of shriveled skin still attached by the roots. "This was their chief, a black-toothed braggart who called himself Örm of the Axe."

"I remember him." Berkano shivered . . . *and recalled the screams; they echoed across the years, the sound of steel cleaving flesh, pleas of mercy; and at the center of it all, the merciless laughter of the man who led them. He was an ogre—blood-slimed and coarse-handed, and he stank of sweat, gore, and feces. She felt, once more, the wet slime of his tongue; the laughter as he violated her, then passed her to the next man. She did not fight. She did not cry out, for if she made no noise she was sure these iron men and their ogre lord would go away. They would never hurt her, her mother, or her sisters again . . .* "I remember."

Grimnir unlaced the scalp from the string and offered it to Berkano. Hesitantly, she extended her hand. Grimnir laid the scalp in her palm. Berkano cradled the mane and petted it like it was an animal. "I still dream of him . . . of what he did." Berkano closed her eyes and sobbed. Laufeya started toward her, but Grimnir warned her off with an upraised hand.

He leaned over Berkano and spoke in a harsh whisper Dísa strained to overhear. "*Nár,* girl. His bones molder on the banks of the Otrgjöld River. His shriveled soul howls from the fences of Hel's realm. I sent him there. By Ymir, let him trouble you no more."

Berkano looked up and met Grimnir's smoldering gaze without flinching. She smiled, wiped her eyes. "I will dream of that, instead," she said. Grimnir nodded and leaned back; taking that as a sign, Laufeya came and collected her sister, who showed her the scalp the same way a child would show off a prized toy.

Dísa spent the balance of the night mulling over that exchange. By every measure she knew and understood, Grimnir hated the sons of Men. He only tolerated the likes of her because there was something in it for him—in the case of the Daughters of the Raven, someone to bring him offerings of meat and of mead and, rarely, of silver. By having only one point of contact, he preserved his way of life and enriched himself in the process.

Why, then, had he shown such unaccustomed kindness to Berkano? *Or to me?*

The night wore on. Bjorn Svarti stoked the hearth, fed the glowing heart of the fire, and settled into his sleeping furs. The lads of the Jarl's sworn men who remained drew lots to see who would stand the first watch at the gate. The loser they bundled off with an extra cloak and an iron pot of embers while the rest followed Svarti's lead and sought their beds.

Sigrún dispersed the Daughters of the Raven to their homes—some still dwelled under their fathers' roofs, while older Daughters had their own houses among the folk of the first terrace. Soon, only Sigrún, Geira, and Auða remained.

Dísa came and sat next to the high seat.

Grimnir glanced down at her. "Shouldn't you be sleeping, maybe dreaming up a hare-brained plan to find this lad of yours?"

Dísa shrugged but said nothing.

Grimnir's eye narrowed. "What?"

"Do you hate my kind?"

"You have to ask?"

"You were ready to kill me, just a short month ago; ready to kill Auða and the lads today. But then, you do something like that business earlier with Berkano." Dísa nodded to where the two Otter-Geat sisters lay curled together near a brazier; Berkano still clutched the Norse scalp, and a ghost of a smile played about her lips as she slept. "It makes me wonder, is all. Wonder if your hate is real."

Grimnir was silent for a time. Then: "There was this one time, out East, beyond the lands of the Kievan Rús, when me and Gífr ran afoul of a pack of wolves. Huge, shaggy beasts, like Odin's own lap dogs. Now, Gífr hated wolves. Even though the blood of mighty Fenrir flows in our veins, he never let pass the opportunity to kill one.

"It was a hard winter, that year. Enough to make this one look like a mild spring. So they were hungry, these wolves. Bastards herded us like we were sheep. Gífr let his hate build, and when he'd finally had enough, we turned and lit into them. Ha! That was a fight, little bird! Gífr's bow sang, and the blade of my seax smoked with wolf blood. Killed all but one, a giant female. Wounded her bad. Aye, she had two of Gífr's arrows in her and I'd nearly taken off one of her forelegs at the haunch. Still, she ran. We tracked her over the snow, across a frozen river and into the hills.

"We caught up with the bitch at the mouth of a hollow. Then *she* turned and lit into *us*—nearly got old Gífr, too. I dragged her off him and split her heart with my blade." Grimnir nodded, recalling the heat of the wolf's blood as it sprayed over his knuckles. "Well, the old git was just lying there, trying to get his breath back, when we heard it . . . a cry coming from the hollow. Soft, it was. Gífr rolled over and spied a litter of wolf pups watching us. And they'd seen us kill their mother.

"Right then, Gífr decided we would ride out the winter there. Made a shelter, hunted, found water. And the old git raised those pups. He endured their bites, put up with their rage, and taught them to fend for themselves. He meant for us to take off at the spring thaw, but we had become their pack. Those mangy curs followed us back into the lands of the Kievan Rús. We raided with them, and they killed alongside us. And one by one, they died—one of old age, the rest in battle.

"Gífr sang their death-songs. The old git even wept over the grave of the last one, an old crone of a wolf. But three days after she had gone on to whatever Valhöll awaits them, Gífr put an arrow through the eye of one of her cousins, a great brute that tried to pinch a kill from us. He still hated wolves, you see, but some he hated less than others."

Grimnir raised his mask so she could see the silhouette of his face. "I hate your kind, little bird. I'd gladly set fire to the world if it meant an end to the sons of Man. But some of you I just hate less than others."

Dísa left her shield and helmet behind; she filled a small shoulder bag with whatever supplies she could find: flint and steel, a coil of braided rope, needles and twine, dried herbs and a small jar of rendered fat; she took from the Jarl's larder some hard bread, smoked fish, strips of jerky, a cloth-wrapped half-wheel of cheese, a bag of dried dates, and a flask of water. She wore a wolf-skin cloak over her mail; her sheathed seax rode her left hip, a Frankish axe her right, and she carried her short spear. When she left Hrafnhaugr, only Grimnir and the guard at the gate were conscious of her departure.

And neither said a word.

Dísa made good time. From Hrafnhaugr, she headed south toward the Horn—that broad inlet shaped like a cow's horn, where the Hveðrungr River tumbled through a rocky gorge to drain into Lake Vänern. An old bridge at the throat of the Horn marked the limits of her people's territory. Beyond the bridge, an overgrown trail eventually joined a rutted road leading farther south to Eiðar, the nearest outpost of the Swedes. Dísa reckoned she'd pick up Flóki's trail somewhere along the way.

She maintained the pace she'd learned from her morning runs with Grimnir, a long, loping stride that ate up the miles. At midday Dísa paused to drink from a freshet of water and wolf down a bit of bread and smoked fish. A cold wind blew from the north; on it, she caught the scent of ice and snow. It was nearing the end of the month called Skerpla, the Oak Month, and still there was no sign of an impending thaw. She thought of the prophecy, of *Fimbulvetr* and the ending of the world. And she wondered how long her people had until the breaking of Miðgarðr . . .

On, she ran; the day waned, and by the hour of the gloaming she caught the gleam of last light on the waters of the Horn. She pushed on until she broke through the trees and came out on a rocky beach. Only then did she stop to rest. By her estimation, she had strayed too far to the east, enough that she stood now near the mouth of the Horn. Lake Vänern was off on her left; right, the Horn curved north and narrowed, its banks rising, until the inlet became a tree-shrouded gorge. In that direction, across the glistening water, Dísa spied a curious glow—like hundreds of fires lending a ruddy tinge to the low clouds. Was Eiðar ablaze? Had Norse raiders struck over their border for plunder and slaves? The glow made Dísa vaguely uneasy, so she disdained a fire of her own, ate a cold meal, and curled up in a makeshift shelter formed of tree roots and boulders.

As her exhaustion caught up with her, Dísa fancied she could hear the roots humming to her . . .

SHE WAKES TO SMOKE AND *to ash and to the heat of crackling flames. It is familiar, if not comforting. The mail she wears is still in tatters, but her limbs are no longer heavy with exhaustion. Her dark hair is sweat-damp; her silver beads and bone fetishes clicking as she turns her head to gaze at her surroundings.*

Hrafnhaugr burns around her. She stands near the ruined gates, broken and tilting crazily on their hinges. The dead still lie in their heaps: pale and bloody-limbed Geats intertwine with bearded Danes and dark-eyed Swedes, their ragged surcoats emblazoned with the Nailed God's cross. The young woman walks from those cracked portals, down streets she had known since she was a child.

She knows the path she's on will lead to her destruction. This, she has seen before: the crazed man who flays his own flesh from his bones, the Hooded One with his wagon of severed heads, the Dragon. It is a path she is no longer beholden to walk. She turns and chooses a new direction.

The flames die; the sky overhead glows with the green lights of the North. By that emerald glow, she descends a flight of rough steps cut into an embankment and finds herself at the water's edge. A rocky beach stretches before her; surf rolls in, combers breaking in long frothy curls, crashing and hissing against the shore. Ahead, a figure waits. It bears the shape of a man, though hunched and as twisted as the staff he leans upon; he is clad in a voluminous cloak with a slouch hat pulled low. A single malevolent eye gleams from beneath the brim.

She knows him. The Grey Wanderer, he is; the Raven-God; Lord of the Gallows; the shield-worshipped kinsman of the Æsir. She knows him. She, who springs from the loins of Dagrún Spear-breaker; she, who is a Daughter of the Raven, bearer of the rune Dagaz; she, who is the Day-strider, chosen of the Gods. She, who is skjaldmær, shieldmaiden. She knows him, and she is not afraid.

"Niðing," the stranger says in a voice deeper than a tolling bell. "Useless whelp of a useless race! What you choose in this moment, now, will determine if your people survive what is to come."

"What must I choose?" she says.

The sky ripples and burns with green fire.

"To serve me." The stranger raises his head to look at the eerie lights of heaven. "Bring me the skrælingr's head, and what your heart desires most will be granted. Serve me, and I will spare your people," he says. The stranger turns and walks away. "Serve me . . ."

And with a sound like the rattle of immense bones, the stranger's cloak is borne up as by a hot breath of wind. There is only darkness beneath. And that darkness grows and spreads, becoming monstrous wings that blot out the northern lights. The darkness crawls like a serpent toward her home, toward Hrafnhaugr. It will rob the air of its breath; it will slay the living with a pestilence that rots the blood in their veins. It will crush and destroy all she holds dear.

She makes to follow, but realizes something has wrapped itself around her ankle. She glances down to see a pale and wriggling root.

It hums.

It pulls at her, gently.

"No, child," it says in a voice she recognizes. "He deceives."

"But my people," she says, struggling against the root. She looks up and sees an empty beach. Her shoulders slump. "I've doomed them."

"No." The root tugs her back; it pulls her into the embrace of more of its kind, all softly humming a lullaby of the earth. "We are all already doomed."

"Halla?"

"HALLA!"

Dísa woke with the troll-woman's name on her lips. Daylight had come, though thick clouds still obscured the face of the sun, and fat flakes of snow swirled on the cold wind. Dísa had wormed her way deeper into her bolt-hole; surrounded by roots, swathed in wolf fur, she felt warm and snug enough that she dreaded crawling forth. But crawl forth she did. Already, images from her dream were fading, leaving only longing and a sense of unease. She had to find Flóki and get back. The young woman stretched, cracking the tendons in her neck, and went to relieve herself before making a quick breakfast of bread and cheese.

As she surmised the night before, she was too far east. She'd follow the shore of the Horn, keeping to the trees, and before midday she should reach the bridge over the Hveðrungr River. She would look for some sign that Flóki and the others had passed that way—the remains of a camp, footprints, something. Nodding to herself, Dísa bolted the rest of her food, drank her fill, and set off.

An hour passed and the day brightened but did not warm. Her breath yet steamed in the chill air. But for the moaning wind, the forest along the north shore of the Horn was eerily silent. Dísa slowed her pace and moved as quietly as she could—each crackling leaf and crunching footfall like a tocsin of alarm. The wind shifted, and her nostrils caught the faint stench of a great burning.

Dísa stopped. She stood on a rocky ridgeline, the remains of an old cart road running east to west underfoot. Thickets of birch and willow stretched away north, while on the south side of the road the forest thinned as it ran to the crumbling edge of a bluff about ten feet above the shoreline. Dísa listened to the oppressive silence, bereft of the natural sounds of squirrels and birds; she snuffled the air as she'd seen Grimnir do so many times. A tree limb creaked. Dísa brought up her spear, its iron head poised to strike. Movement caught her eye.

A willow seemed to twist on the wind; in the silence, she heard a low hum. Farther off the track, another tree branch clacked—another willow, seeming to move of its own volition. Dísa recalled her dream, the gentle humming and the tree roots seeking to shield her from harm. "Halla?" she muttered, her voice profane in the absolute silence.

Dísa's gut told her she could trust the signs; on that authority, she followed the sounds of willow branches. Even so, she went warily. She carried her spear at the ready. The trees guided her to the mouth of a ravine that cut through the forest, a steaming trickle of foul-smelling water at its bottom—a hot spring. Even more than sulphur, the place reeked of death. Dísa set her jaw, teeth clenched, and as she stepped foot in that gloomy chasm, the oppressive silence suddenly lifted.

A gigantic raven screamed at her and took wing, its flight stirring the stench of putrefaction. Fear ran down Dísa's spine; she nearly backed away and ran, but the humming of the trees around her bolstered her courage—they lent her the strength of root and bole, and gave her assurances that she was not alone. Forward, she went. Cat-footed, settled into a fighting crouch. Ahead of her, in a cone of thin gray light, she saw a body. It was sitting with its back against the ravine wall, tilted to one side, its eyeless face looking up as though it sought succor from the cloud-racked sky.

An arrow stood out from beneath its left breast.

Dísa crept closer, afraid she would recognize the corpse as Flóki. While it was not Hreðel's son, she nevertheless knew that long straw-colored hair, the thin beard, even the slack face ravaged by ravens and crows. It was Eirik Viðarrson.

He'd been dead two days, perhaps three. Dísa could see that his legs were broken. She squatted on her haunches an arm's length from the corpse and glanced up. In her mind's eye, she could see him running through the forest, away from the Horn. Alone, most likely, for neither Flóki nor Eirik's brother would have left him. So, he's running, she reckoned. He's wounded—an arrow in his ribs. He's wheezing blood. He's afraid. And he makes a misstep and falls into this ravine, breaking both legs. He lives long enough to drag himself to the side of the wall. He calls for help . . . and none comes.

Dísa took hold of the white fletchings of the arrow. Placing the blade of her spear flat against Eirik's chest—to provide a counterweight—she drew the arrow from the wound with a moist sucking sound. Grimacing at the stench, Dísa rinsed it in the fetid stream and studied the head. It had a long, narrow bodkin point, good for piercing mail, with a crude cross scratched into the socket. A war arrow. But whose? Was it Swedish? Norse? Some Danish hymn-singer?

"Who were you running from, Eirik?" she muttered. "And where's Flóki?"

Near her head, the roots of an ancient ash tree hummed and rustled. Dísa looked sharply at them, and then cocked her head to one side. In the sudden silence, she heard it: crunching footsteps coming toward the ravine. She scuttled across the stream and past the corpse, pressing herself into a hollow in the far wall under an overhang of roots.

Dísa dared not breathe. Above, she heard the heavy tread come to a stop. She heard a man grunt, heard him murmur: "Whew! There you are, you bastard." His footsteps receded as he followed the ravine down to its entrance.

Dísa moved. Quickly and silently, she came out of her hiding place and sidled deeper into the ravine, away from the entrance. Here, the walls widened even as the top of the ravine grew more narrow and choked with tangled roots and debris. It was warm and dark, and it stank.

She stopped, fading into the shadows as the newcomer reached the ravine's mouth. Dísa saw a man of average size, with a golden-brown beard and hair short at the temples but long down the scalp, braided and gathered at his nape by a leather cord. He crouched and peered into the depths of the ravine.

He wore a black gambeson under a white surcoat embroidered in black with the Nailed God's symbol—a cross with flaring arms—belted around the waist. A horn with bronze fittings hung from a baldric over his shoulder. He had a falchion sheathed on his left hip; on his right, she saw a sheaf of bright cloth strips.

He rose and entered the ravine, eyes sweeping the walls, the floor. Without warning, he stopped. His eyes narrowed. From the small of his back, he drew a long-bladed knife. Dísa knew he'd spotted her footprints; he'd seen the arrow lying where she'd dropped it. No fool, he knew he wasn't alone.

"I found him like that," Dísa said suddenly, making her voice small and fearful.

He looked up, toward the back of the ravine. "Show yourself," he said, speaking Geatish with the harsh accent of the Danes. "Nice and slow."

Leaving her spear in the shadows, Dísa stepped forward, into a shaft of gray light.

The man grunted, taking in her feral appearance, her mail and seax. "What the devil? You're one of *them,* aren't you? One of those heathen Geats we've come to bring into the light of our lord, Jesus Christ."

The roots around her shivered; Dísa sensed their distress. The Nailed God's name was a poison to them, to the remaining *landvættir,* the land spirits.

"Aye," she said. "I am a Geat, of the Raven tribe. What are you?"

The man crouched beside Eirik's corpse and retrieved the arrow, tucking it into his belt. His hands went swiftly over the body, searching. "I am the bearer of glad tidings and salvation, girl. That's all you need to know."

"Don't touch him!" Dísa snapped.

The man sat back on his haunches and stared at her. "Or what? You'll dice me up with that onion slicer of yours?" He snorted. "I have fought the Saracen and the Moor, the Princes of the East. I have seen Greek fire burn the ships of Crusader kings in the straits of the Golden Horn, off Constantinople. You'll forgive me if I'm not put off by the bravado of a heathen girl."

"What are you doing here?" Dísa nodded to the strips of cloth, red and yellow, obviously torn from an old tunic.

He glanced down at them. "Surveying the trees. Marking the ones my lord will need to bridge the river, back yonder." He inclined his head in the direction of the Horn's throat.

"It has a bridge."

"Aye, it does." He shifted his weight. "But some of your folk decided to try and burn it down ere Lord Konraðr's vanguard arrived. This idiot," he nodded to Eirik's corpse, "was among them. Well, it was God's own luck that the scouts had already crossed. These dogs thought themselves safe— until they weren't. Killed one, captured two, and we'd thought this cur had escaped. Guess not, eh?"

"Who is this Konraðr and what business does he have with my people?"

"That's *Lord* Konraðr to you, bitch," the man snarled. "He's the lord of Skara, across Lake Vänern, and his business is the business of God Almighty. The Pope has commanded an end to northern heresy, and we've come to see it done!"

"A crusade." Dísa spat. "And what will happen to them, the two you captured?"

"They'll be given the same chance I'm going to give you."

"Me?"

"Aye, girl. I'm taking you back with me. Lord Konraðr's going to want to question you, himself."

"And you'll give me a chance, you say? To do what?"

The man stood. "Kiss the Cross, or hang from it." He gestured with his knife. "Drop that onion slicer, girl. Shimmy out of that mail. Come quiet and demure-like and my lord might show mercy and give you over to Father Nikulas. He could always use a good nun."

Dísa stood, staring at the man, at this Dane who'd trespassed onto the lands of the Raven-Geats. *Not trespassed,* she corrected herself. No, this one had come for war—just as the prophecy predicted. She answered him:

> "The blood-reek wafts | like dragon breath
> And hides the pallid face of Sól."

"Blast your pagan gibberish! Don't test me, girl," he said. "If I have to drag you out of there it's going to go hard on you."

Slowly, deliberately, Dísa drew her seax. The tight confines of the ravine amplified the sound of steel rasping on leather. It sounded like a dozen serpents, hissing in a cold rage. "I am a Daughter of the Raven," she said. "Bearer of the rune *Dagaz,* the Day-strider, chosen of the Norns. I am a servant of the Hooded One, immortal herald of the Tangled God. My mother was Dagrún Spear-breaker, who was *skjaldmær,* shieldmaiden of Hrafnhaugr in the land of the Raven-Geats. How are you called?"

The man ducked his head and spat. "I am He-Who-Will-Break-You if you don't quit this foolishness and come out of there."

"What is your name?"

"Why does it matter to you?" He shifted, eyes narrowed, the knife in his blade hand held loose at his side.

"I want to know the name of the first man I kill." She raised her seax, forcing his gaze to follow that rune-etched blade.

Around them, the roots hummed.

The man's face grew grim. "You think this is a game, bitch? Oh, no. The time for games is over!" He stepped toward her. "Drop—"

Dísa's free hand snapped out. Unseen, she had drawn her Frankish axe; now, she slung it side-armed. It struck the ravine wall next to the man's head, rebounding and showering him with dirt and splinters of loose scree. "God's teeth!" he swore, flinching back and protecting his eyes. "You stupid little cun—"

In that moment of distraction, when his attention was bent more upon himself than on her, Dísa struck. She struck hard and fast, as her grandmother taught her. And, as she'd learned from Grimnir, she struck to kill.

She sprang as he recovered. Her breath hissed through clenched teeth, steaming in the rancid air of the ravine. She swept her seax up—the power of her blade hand steadied by her off hand on the pommel—and felt the first four finger-lengths of the blade crunch through the bone of his chin. The blow cleft his jawbone, shattered his teeth, tore through the roots of his tongue, and wedged in his palate. He staggered, screaming through a bloody froth as he clawed at the span of steel violating his face.

The man fell to his knees, his knife forgotten. Dísa loomed over him. Her eyes were harder than iron. She watched him thrash, drowning in the blood that pumped down his throat and into his lungs. He clutched at the wall.

Of her own first kill, Auða had told her how she felt fear, remorse; she'd admitted to being sick when she realized she had taken a child's father from them, a woman's husband, a mother's son. That awesome weight of being responsible for another human's death had struck her to her knees. The second came easier, and the third, and all the killings after. But that first . . .

And yet, Dísa felt nothing. No fear, no remorse. She did not care that this nameless bastard might have had brats, or a wife, or a heartsick old mother. He had chosen to come here. He had chosen to step foot in the land of her people, bearing a message of hate none of them wanted any part of. He knew the risks—and he had underestimated her. She stared into his eyes, saw his desperation for the gift of life, and felt savage triumph.

She was ready to kill the next hymn-singing son of a bitch who crossed her path.

Snarling, Dísa seized the back of the man's head and leaned her weight into the pommel of her seax. The blade slid through the ruin of his skull and into the stem of his brain. Dísa saw the light fade from his eyes. He slumped back, fell sideways, and bled his last in that foul sulphurous trickle cutting through the floor of the ravine. The roots of the trees hummed, and then fell silent.

"Bear witness, Eirik Viðarrson," Dísa said. "Do not haunt this place. Take this soul with you and begone. Let his punishment be to serve you in the next world." She rocked the hilt of her seax back and forth, grunting as she tugged the blade free from the wreckage of the man's face. She crouched and was wiping her seax on his surcoat when a thought occurred to her. She would need to prove her kill. Prove it to Grimnir, to her grandmother. She needed a trophy. But what? An ear? A thumb? His shriveled manhood?

A slow smile spread across Dísa's face. She took up the man's own knife, got a feel for its weight, and went to work . . .

When Dísa Dagrúnsdottir left that ravine, intent on following the name-less man's trail back to his camp, she'd added a gruesome trophy to her gear: a golden-brown scalp, still damp with blood.

DÍSA CREPT LIKE A SHADOW through the woods, aided by overcast skies and a drifting fog that rolled down from the hill country west of the Horn. The man she'd killed had not come far from his camp. It lay less than a mile from the ravine. And as the sun reached its zenith, the forest came alive with the dull thump of axes, the thud of hammers, and the hiss of saws. Men shouted and called out commands as they snaked logs to the banks of the Hveðrungr River and set about repairing the half-burnt bridge.

Dísa gave them a wide berth. She slunk around the center of all the activity and came upon the banks of the Hveðrungr from the west. From her vantage, she could see the bridge was largely intact, though the end that rested on Geatish soil was charred and missing timbers. Peering across to the far bank, she suddenly apprehended the source of the lights she'd seen reflected in the clouds, last night.

An army was camped across the Hveðrungr River.

To Dísa's untutored eye, it looked like a riot of tents—hundreds of them, from canvas sheets hanging from a tripod of spears to elaborate pavilions needing ropes, poles, and pitons to stay erect. Fires burned, their smokes adding to the haze of fog. Dísa could see scores of men going about their daily routines: making food, fetching water, tending weapons and harness; grooming, repairing, praying and cursing. And upon every banner, sewn onto every surcoat and gambeson, painted on the face of every shield, she saw a black cross, the hateful symbol of the Nailed God.

Fear twisted in her gut, more for Flóki than for herself. To imagine him at the hymn-singers' mercy made her sick at her stomach. Obviously, at some point he and his lads had encountered the vanguard of the crusading army. Outnumbered, perhaps aware of why they'd come into the borderland between Geatland and Swedish territory, the four young Raven-Geats had faded back to try and hold the bridge over the river. But why hadn't they sent word back to Hrafnhaugr? Was it pride? Was this how Flóki meant to make his war-name? Now, he was either dead or captive. And Dísa could not simply run until she found out; either way, she meant to bring him home.

Since there was not yet any thaw, the Hveðrungr was not in spate. This worked to Dísa's advantage as she prowled farther west, away from the camp. A few hundred yards down the bank, she discovered a spot where boulders broke the river's surface, forming a cataract that boiled and hissed on its way to Lake Vänern. Taking a deep breath, she scotched across these, cloak flaring behind her, and faded into the undergrowth. She listened for sounds of alarm. But when no hue and cry arose, she crept nearer to the encampment, intent on working out where these hymn-singers might keep their captives.

So focused was she that Dísa almost blundered into a sentry.

It was a groan that warned her—the cracking tendons of a man stretching, moving to relieve the numbing boredom of piquet duty. Dísa froze. She sank into the shadows and peered through the foliage. Not three spear-lengths from her she spotted an older man who had the look of a Norseman about him. His hair and beard were the color of pale gold, his face scarred and weather-seamed. Beneath a cloak trimmed in fur, he wore a hauberk of dull gray mail. A watchman's horn hung from a strap over his shoulder. He turned slightly as another man came up from the camp—younger, his hair and sparse beard a reddish-brown, but also clad in war-rags and sporting a spear and shield.

The old sentry frowned. "You're early," he muttered.

"Nay," the newcomer replied. "I'm not your relief. Lord Konraðr's ordered the watch doubled. One of the surveyors has gone missing."

"Which one?"

"Haakon, I think. The lord says it's the same lot who tried to burn the bridge. We got two of theirs, so they're going to get a few of ours. Maybe use them to try and barter an exchange."

The old sentry shook his head. "Haakon's a good man. I will pray God keeps him safe among those damnable heathens."

"Amen."

Moving with agonizing slowness, Dísa inched back in the direction she'd come. She cursed under her breath, frustrated by this wall of men who fortified the camp. Dísa knew she could distract them, but to what end? She needed to infiltrate, to enter without their knowledge so she might be free to seek the hymn-singers' gaol. She studied the overcast sky, sniffed the chill air.

Night would soon fall. She could use the coming darkness to slip through cracks in the sentry wall, use it to disguise her identity once she was inside the camp. With the patience of a hunter, Dísa crept into a covert between two sentry points and waited for darkness to descend.

14

Konraðr the White knelt on a prayer bench, his ermine-fringed mantle spread out behind him. Clad in a hauberk of silver and black mail, his white surcoat sewn with a black Teutonic cross, the lord of Skara clasped a paternoster between his pale hands and prayed—for forgiveness, for the remission of sin, for victory. Most of all, though, he beseeched the Lord God, Almighty, for succor, for an end to the nightmares that plagued him.

Around him, the pavilion swayed. Night had brought a snow-laced gale down from the mountains to the west. Sleet ticked against the heavy canvas walls; the center pole, carved from the heartwood of a great oak, creaked with each gust. Flames danced in the wrought-iron brazier, its smoke curling up toward a hole where the harsh wind could snatch it away.

From the next chamber of his pavilion, he could hear the rattle of glass, the tinkle of silver implements as Father Nikulas prepared his nightly draught—a foul concoction of herbs and tinctures that, when mixed with raw Greek wine, did much to abate the fevers that had plagued Konraðr since returning from the East.

"You have the hands of a healer, my friend," Konraðr had said, after the first draught proved efficacious. "Where did you learn this art?"

Nikulas had smiled, then—a rarity for the man, who gave new meaning to the word *dour*—and replied: "From the sisters of St. Étaín, at Kincora. They raised me after my parents died in the Burning of Dubhlinn. I brought their art with me when I came to enter the Lord's service, at Lund."

But regardless of the priest's efforts to heal his war-shattered body, the fractures in his soul remained. Each night it was the same: an endless parade of screaming faces with their hot and reeking breath, their bloody hands clutching at his legs; the fetid stench of bowel and bladder, of rich marrow and foaming gore; the single, burning eye of the gray-bearded old man. *Him,* most of all. He wandered the fringes of Konraðr's dreams, clad now in a voluminous robe with a wide-brimmed hat pulled low over his features. He wandered and glared, cold guile replacing the innocence Konraðr remembered from Constantinople. That eye, wreathed in fire, caused the lord of Skara to awaken with a scream on his lips, his body bathed in a cold sweat.

"Why do I fear him now, O Lord?" Konraðr whispered, the paternoster— fifty beads of red coral, amber, and boxwood, trimmed in silver and sporting a crucifix of enameled silver—rattling as his hands trembled.

Konraðr's colorless eyes fell upon the open codex on the shelf of the prayer bench. He knew the page by sight, its illumination done in the Byzantine mode and saved from the fires of Constantinople by a learned monk in Count Baldwin's entourage. And though Konraðr could not make sense of the writing—in Greek rather than the vulgar Latin he was accustomed to—he knew it for what it was: the Gospel of Mark. In the margin, near the bottom, a fair hand had sketched an image of a storm-tossed boat, a Christ-figure in the bow depicted in red ink.

And Konraðr knew, then, that the Almighty had sent him his answer.

"*'And rising up,'*" he said, eyes closing as he recited the passage from memory, "*'he rebuked the wind, and said to the sea: Peace, be still. And the wind ceased: and there was made a great calm. And he said to them: Why are you fearful? Have you not faith yet?'*"

Konraðr sighed. The nightmares were a test of faith, and the Adversary took the shape of the old man—whose gaze had been kindly in life. The Adversary thrived on fear, and fear undermined faith. It made men question the will of God. Even the slightest crack in the righteous armor of faith gave the Adversary a toehold. Konraðr understood now. If he gave in to fear, damnation was but a step away.

"My lord?"

Konraðr stirred at the sound of the priest's voice. He crossed himself, kissed the crucifix at the end of his paternoster, and rose to his feet. Father Nikulas brought him a horn cup. Konraðr took it, saluted the priest, and drained it without pause. He felt the draught's warmth spread through his belly and limbs.

"You are troubled, my lord?" Nikulas said, taking the cup back from Konraðr. "I do not mean to pry, but I heard you reading from the Gospel of St. Mark."

"I fear, sometimes, my faith is not enough," Konraðr said, turning to look at the open manuscript. "What if I am wrong? What if this whole endeavor is nothing but a trick of the Adversary to take us further from God? What if I am cursed, in truth?"

"Then I would say you do not understand fully the words of blessed St. Mark," Nikulas replied. "Have you not faith, my lord?"

"I do."

"Then why are you fearful? Trust in your faith, and trust in the word of the Lord whose work we do. The Adversary does not want the sword of Saint Teodor brought to light, so the wretch fills your mind with doubt. What we do, here, we do for God and for king—by bringing the light of Christ to this forgotten corner of your cousin's lands, and by providing him with the tool that will win glory for the God we serve! Do not doubt, lord. Rejoice!" Father Nikulas's eyes burned with righteous fervor. "Rejoice! For we are where we can do the most good!"

Konraðr nodded. He felt new strength flood into his limbs. "You are right, Father. As always. You—"

Spectral voices whispered to him. *She comes,* they hissed. *Day-strider,* Dagaz-*bearer, raven daughter!* Konraðr turned, eyes narrowing as he sought to make sense of the clamor rising around him. *She comes!*

"My lord? What is it?"

Konraðr raised his hand, motioning Father Nikulas to silence.

"There is . . . an intruder," Konraðr said after a moment. He spoke slowly, as if in a trance. "A girl. She comes to steal back our captives. She is a Geat, but . . . but they have not seen her like, and she frightens them. There is a . . . a shroud over her, around her. Something protects her. Something not of God." The lord of Skara looked up, fixing the priest in his colorless stare. "Where are our captive Geats?"

"In the chapel tent," Nikulas replied, frowning. "Under guard. One cries for his brother, who was either slain or escaped, and will likely convert when the time is ripe. The other remains defiant. Him, we must make an example of."

Konraðr nodded. He crossed to the door-flap of his pavilion, twitched it aside, and said to the soldier on duty: "Fetch ten good lads and bid them come to the chapel tent, but quietly! Raise no alarm. Go." He turned back to Father Nikulas. "This is a little bird we must capture, for she is worth far more to us alive than dead."

THE DARKNESS, THE RISING WIND; the cold and the spitting snow, they all worked in unison to provide Dísa with the cover she needed to slip past the cordon of sentries. The camp straddled the old, overgrown road that led south, away from the territory of the Raven-Geats. It boasted no defensive works; tents grew like fungus between the bare-limbed trees. Most were dark but some glowed with lamplight from within, the snap of canvas punctuated by ripping snores and low voices. Fires crackled, and racked spear shafts chattered together in the gale.

Dísa drew her cloak tight about her, her hood slung low, and kept to the tree thickets as she wandered the fringes of the camp, looking for some sign of where they might keep their captives.

She bit back a curse.

The young woman had the sensation of a thousand eyes on her. Dísa was conscious of the fact she sported no cross upon her person, and that she looked like something that had crawled from the woods; she knew she could not pass even the most casual scrutiny. If she stepped into the open she was certain her crude disguise would fail. She'd be exposed, and the teeth of the Nailed God's dogs would rend her limb from limb. Still, she moved deeper into the camp, toward the center. There, a sprawling pavilion occupied a low hillock, a last rise before the weed-choked road descended to the bridge.

She crouched in the shadowy cover afforded by a gnarled birch grove and studied the pavilion. Near it was another, this one festooned with symbols of the Nailed God. She saw a single guard standing rigid before the curtained doorway of the larger pavilion, cloaked and muffled against the weather. Dísa frowned. The man kept glancing toward the cross-decorated tent; she saw him shake his head. He staggered as a particularly violent gust of wind threatened to topple him—in that same howling blast, Dísa saw the doorway to the Nailed God's tent ripple; in that split second, she caught sight of a knot of men standing inside with blades drawn. Her gaze flickered over two kneeling captives, both bound and gagged—Ulff Viðarrson was one, and the other was Flóki. The men seemed to be waiting, listening. A bearded and tonsured priest in a black cassock peered out before quickly securing the doorway.

And Dísa, crouching in darkness, felt the unseen jaws of a trap closing about her. She wanted to scream. *They know I'm here, but how?* She was careful not to leave a glaring back-trail; she caused no ruckus, raised no alarm. She could not fathom how they'd discovered her presence inside their camp, but the evidence was damnable—they knew *someone* was out here, and they knew who they came for.

This was foolish, she chided herself. *Better to return to Hrafnhaugr and fetch Grimnir, perhaps raise the Jarl's sworn men and attack this rabble on the road, ere they reached the village.* She stared hard at the Nailed God's tent. "Kiss their crosses, you daft bastard," she whispered. "If it keeps you alive one more day, sing their hymns and keep the Tangled God in your heart."

Slowly, Dísa made to disengage and retrace her steps from the camp.

Suddenly, a voice rang out over the keening wind. "Day-strider," it said. "*Dagaz*-bearer! Raven daughter, come out!"

From around the corner of the Nailed God's tent came a figure with skin the color of milk, his pale hair unbound; a white mantle floated on the wind. The silver in his mail caught and reflected jags of firelight. With a start, Dísa recognized him—the crucified man from her nightmares.

"Come out, Dísa Dagrúnsdottir!" he bellowed. A chill danced down her spine. Flóki or Ulff must have talked; otherwise, how could he know her name? *Damn them!* "Come out and perhaps your precious Flóki will live another day! Bring out the captives," the man said. "Bring them out. She knows they're here, and that we're using them as bait for a trap. She's a smart one, our intruder."

The priest held the door to the Nailed God's tent open while four of the men sheathed their weapons and wrestled Ulff and Flóki out into the open. Ulff, who was closer to Dísa's age, sobbed, begging for mercy through his gag. Flóki, however, remained defiant. He snarled at his captors, cursing through the knotted cloth between his jaws.

"You've come all this way from . . ." The pale man paused, as though listening to something only he could hear. "Hrafnhaugr, in the land of the Raven-Geats. I am bound for your village. Perhaps you could show me the way?"

Around them, the camp stirred. Men stepped from their tents to watch this odd display. Was their lord drunk? Had heathen spirits possessed him? But the harshly whispered truth quickly squelched such rumors; word spread from tent to tent: there was a Geat hiding among them.

The pale man hissed the growing throng of men to silence; he listened for some reply, some indicator his words had struck home. But Dísa bit her tongue; she swallowed every retort that came to her lips. He heard nothing but the rattle of the wind through naked branches. The priest stirred. "My lord Konraðr—"

"Oh no, good Father Nikulas," the man called Konraðr said. "Temper your doubts. She's out there in the darkness, near enough to hear my voice. Aren't you, little bird? You do well not to curse at me. You know to give voice to your anger would only betray you. Who taught you this? Was it your mother, Dagrún . . . Spear-breaker? No, it could not have been her, could it? She has long since shuffled off to whatever Hell you heathens are bound for."

Dísa snarled to herself. What all had Ulff or Flóki told these bastards? Did they spill the soup on every man, woman, and child inside Hrafnhaugr's walls? Ymir's blood! What did they *not* tell them? Even Grimnir's pet name . . . "No! Impossible!" she hissed under her breath, eyes growing wide. Tendrils of fear wormed through her guts. That milk-colored wretch! He had called her "little bird"—she'd heard it plain as can be—but that was a name neither Flóki nor Ulff could have known. So, how did *he* know it?

Konraðr smiled. "I know more than you could ever imagine, little bird. The wind brings me your secrets; I hear your thoughts in the chirp of insects, your dreams in the crackle of leaves. I know what it is you fear, Dísa Dagrúnsdottir."

Men were actively searching around their tents, looking for the figure their albino lord spoke to—and wondering if they followed a God-cursed madman. "Sorcerer!" she muttered. Limbs trembling, Dísa sank deeper into the well of shadows and plotted her withdrawal, back the way she'd come.

"What did you call me? *Seiðr*-man?" Konraðr considered the insult, and then shrugged it off. "I have been called worse. No! Do not run!" He snapped his fingers, gesturing for his men to bring Ulff to him. "You killed a man of mine, did you not? Poor Haakon? His ghost is here." Konraðr looked surprised. "Minus his scalp, you pitiless little beast!" Men muttered and swore.

"Where's his body, lord?" one said.

"She left him . . . in a ravine . . . with this one's brother." Ulff glanced up, eyes wide as a small glimmer of hope kindled deep inside. Konraðr crushed it like an ember. "Both dead, alas. Fear not, young Ulff." The pale lord drew his belt knife. "Fear not. She can save you with a word. Do you hear me, little bird? Speak up and Ulff Viðarrson lives!"

Flóki threw himself against his bonds, cursing and spitting through his gag. He struggled to rise, got a leg under him, but the men holding him forced him back to his knees.

Out in the darkness, Dísa clenched her fist around the shaft of her short spear until her knuckles cracked; the nails of her off hand bit into her palms. She relished the sharp jags of pain. She wanted to lash out, to kill that freakish maggot with his pale skin and reddish eyes. She longed to slash his wretched belly open and throttle him with his own entrails. But she kept still. She kept quiet. She heard Grimnir's voice echo in the back of her skull: *Make a sound and die!*

Dísa said nothing.

After a moment of silence, Konraðr *tsked*. "So be it."

He seized a handful of Ulff Viðarrson's hair, wrenched his head back; as the youth kicked and screamed around his gag, eyes glassy with terror, Konraðr sawed his knife through the tough muscle and cartilage of the young Geat's throat.

Blood spurted. Ulff writhed and snorted, froth spewing as he fought to take a breath through the wreckage of his windpipe. Steaming gore sheeted down his neck, down his chest. Konraðr held him by the hair as his struggles ebbed. Finally, as the blood slowed to a trickle, Konraðr slung him to the ground to finish dying.

"That was the blood-price for the man of mine you killed!" Konraðr roared. "Consider that account settled. Now, what will you do to save good Flóki, eh? Or will you let him die like you did poor Ulff?" He walked over to where his warriors kept Flóki on his knees, bent low to the ground. Hreðel's son glared up at Konraðr with murder in his eyes. "Will you trade your life for his?"

Tears of rage sprang unbidden to Dísa's eyes. With a soundless scream, she punched the ground with her balled fist. Thud followed thud, too low to hear; she punched until her knuckles bled and her bones threatened to crack. She loved that daft bastard. She did! She'd loved him since she was old enough to know what that sensation was that he caused in the pit of her stomach. But Dísa would not bear his children. Such was not the fate of the Hooded One's priestess. She would leave nothing of herself behind save for the fame of her name, and that fame had to be built on something. On Glory. And, in that moment of silver-bright truth, she realized to her utter shame that she loved Glory—and the promise of her name wreathed in splendor for an eternity—more than she loved anything else. Or anyone else.

She would not die for Flóki Hreðelsson, but she would kill . . .

Dísa's nostrils flared. Her lips peeled back over her teeth in a murderous snarl. She drew upon the rage seething just under the surface. Rage as red as blood, as hot as fresh-spilled gore. She called upon the spirits of the earth . . .

And though weakened by the hated symbols of the Nailed God, and by the natural barrier of the Hveðrungr River, they nevertheless heard her silent plea.

As Dísa looked on, Konraðr flinched when the fading power of the spirits struck him; this White Witch-man who meant to lead his army into the land of the Raven-Geats looked around as though he'd lost sight of something that only a moment before had appeared with great clarity. He looked confused.

Dísa chose that instant to spring. Muscular legs drove her forward a handful of steps; with a savage grunt, she hurled the spear in her right fist. Nor did she wait to see if it struck its target. Like a quick moving shadow under a windswept moon, she vanished into a night made darker by cloaking spirits.

A half a heartbeat later, Konraðr's clarity returned. "'Ware!" he cried, spinning around and pushing a stunned Father Nikulas aside. The razor-edge of Dísa's spear sliced through the flaring hem of the priest's cassock; it tore through the outer thigh of one of his mail-clad guards. The man grunted as he threw himself out of the way.

The spear thudded on impact, quivering, its blade buried deep . . . in the ground, inches from Flóki. Were it a slender javelin and not a thrusting spear, on a windless night the son of Hreðel would have joined his ancestors, slain by the merciful hand of the girl he loved. But the Norns were ever full of surprises.

He looked at the juddering spear and bellowed like a wounded animal.

Konraðr sprang up. "Sound the alarm!" he screamed. "Rouse the sentries! Do not let her escape, do you hear me? I want Dísa Dagrúnsdottir alive!"

Flóki's bellow turned to derisive laughter. He laughed as Konraðr took a step toward him and backhanded him across the mouth. Flóki laughed through the blood and the spittle soaking his gag. He laughed even as the pale lord of Skara pronounced his fate.

"Let him taste the punishment meant for Barabbas!"

"My lord?" the guard replied, puzzled.

Konraðr spat; his eyes gleamed with a red haze of cruelty as he glanced at the man. "Crucify him!"

DÍSA FLED INTO THE NIGHT and Flóki's screams followed her. The sound of his agony dogged her as she slipped from thicket to thicket; it was the screams of a wounded animal punctuated by the dull thud of hammers. What was it the man she'd killed in the ravine said? *Kiss the Cross or hang from it?* She knew Flóki would not submit, not after the maggot killed Ulff. Dísa swiped at her eyes, brushing away the tears. They were tears of shame; her face burned with it. She had failed Flóki; she'd broken her oath to fetch him back, repudiated him, and left him whole and hale in their enemies' clutches. And she let Ulff die.

Recrimination's blade stabbed deep. Sigrún would not have let this happen. Oh, no. Sigrún, her mother, even Auða would have devised some wily stratagem to fetch them all home. Grimnir would have fetched them home after killing every last man in that damned war-camp. Even Halla would have spirited them to safety. *But not me! No,* she thought, *I blundered into this like a fool and where'd that get us? The lads dead, or as good as, and me running back to find a set of skirts to hide behind!* She tasted gall.

So distracted was she by these thoughts that Dísa didn't realize how near she was to the sentry cordon. Indeed, she thought she'd passed it, stretched her pace into the loping stride of a hunting wolf, and was blindsided when a figure rose up before her.

The sentry yelped as she collided with him. They both went down, knees and elbows flashing. The sentry—a young Norseman with a short golden beard—scrabbled for his sword hilt; Dísa punched him and rolled to her feet. "Ymir take you!" she snarled, her seax flashing from its sheath. Her first blow skittered across his mail-clad shoulder. *"Faugh!"*

Dísa stepped back as he surged to his feet; she braced herself to fend off his blows. But the sentry stopped in mid-stride, sword rising to a high guard. His eyes grew wide; behind her, Dísa heard the slaughterhouse sounds of steel cleaving flesh—but she dared not look. She could not risk taking her eyes off the foeman in front of her to survey the carnage behind.

The young Norseman backpedaled; he dropped his blade, then turned and hared off toward camp. He bellowed an alarm. Dísa saw her opportunity. She snatched her Frankish axe from her belt, drew back, and hurled it with all her might. The heavy blade tumbled twice before striking edge-on at the base of the Norseman's neck. The blow split the collar of his mail shirt as the head of the axe buried itself in the hard bones of his cervical spine.

The sentry dropped.

Quick as a snake, Dísa twisted and resumed her fighting crouch, seax at the ready. The second sentry was a handful of yards behind her, but he was on his knees, his horn forgotten and his arms slack at his sides. She saw a gory crevasse of splintered bone and bits of brain where his face should have been, caused by the blade of a bearded axe that had split his head nearly to the chin.

And looming over him, with one hand on the haft of the axe—the other was a fist forged of black iron—stood a scar-faced woman with braided hair the color of wood-ash, clad in leather and mail. She nodded at the man Dísa had slain.

"Fetch your axe and follow me," she growled, "unless you want these dogs of the White Christ to find you first."

Dísa nodded; she backed away from the woman, who was easily as tall as Bjorn Hvítr, sheathed her seax, and wrenched her axe from the neck of the Norseman. He moaned weakly, clawing at the earth. Dísa struck him again, for good measure.

She turned as the woman kicked the corpse of the second sentry off her bearded axe. "I know you," Dísa said. The woman was familiar, but she could not place where she'd seen her.

The woman raised an eyebrow. "I am Úlfrún of the Iron Hand, child. Many know me, and some even live to tell the tale."

Úlfrún. Her dream, the cart of severed heads. One, she knew, was a woman called Úlfrún—and that woman had been as a mother to her. Dísa shook off her discomfiture. "I am Dísa Dagrúnsdottir."

"I know. Come."

And like shadows, the two women faded into the night.

ÚLFRÚN LED HER WEST, INTO the forested hills overlooking the Horn. She had the impression they did not run alone; twice, from the corner of her eye, she caught a flash of wolf fur. She wondered, albeit a bit late, what kind of woman she'd fallen in with. By the end of an hour, as the night grew old, they reached a camp nestled beneath an overhanging bluff, hidden from view by hurdles of thorn and yew branches woven with hides; beyond, fires warmed the air, though very little light escaped into the night.

"Coming in," Úlfrún announced, ushering Dísa in before her. Men rose from where they'd been crouched, crag-faced giants in bear-skin cloaks, heavy spears and axes at the ready; among them were smaller men, lean and feral, clad in wolf skins, the flesh around their eyes daubed black. They bared yellowed teeth in snarls of greeting.

The lot of them stared at Dísa as though Úlfrún had brought them a rabbit for their sport.

Úlfrún brushed past her and went to the far end of the camp, where a score of men were entering from a different direction—men clad in wolf fur and sporting crossbows with rune-carved stocks and iron-headed quarrels fletched with hawk feathers. They spoke in low voices to Úlfrún, some glancing in Dísa's direction. She made to move closer, so she might hear what they said, but one of the bear-men stepped into her path. He looked down at her, his eyes a gentle brown.

"What are you supposed to be, little sister?" he rumbled.

"I am a Raven-Geat," she said. Dísa tried to worm her way past him, but he stopped her with an outstretched arm.

"She will speak with you when she's ready. Brodir, I am called. Sit, drink with me, and tell me of your people. Are they all as small as you?" the bear-man said. He motioned to another, who passed him a horn cup of warmed wine. This he offered to Dísa, who accepted it with a nod.

"Most are much larger," she said. It *was* warm here, and the exhaustion of the past few days finally caught up to her. She sighed as she sat on a sawn log, near one of the fires. "Our land starts beyond the river and goes on for a day. We hunt, we till our fields, and sometimes we trade with the folk of Eiðar, or with the boat-merchants of the Swedes. We keep to ourselves. We have nothing valuable enough to draw an army. So I can't understand what the White Witch-man wants. Who is he and why does he threaten my people?"

Brodir spoke slowly, brows knitting: "A hateful bastard, that one. Konraðr the White, he is—made a name for himself off in Miklagarðr, a few years back. He's the lord of Skara, across the water, and cousin to the young king of the Swedes. As for what he wants . . ." The giant man leaned forward and tugged a leather cord from inside his shirt. On it was an amulet of silver—Mjölnir, Thor's enchanted hammer. Gently, he touched it to the raven tattoo decorating Dísa's cheek. "He wants to see an end to the Old Ways. He has called a crusade against our kind, little sister. We sons of the Bear and of the Wolf, we will answer his call!" Soft growling and hooting answered his boast.

Dísa looked from man to man, her gaze finally coming to rest on Brodir. "You are all *berserkir*?"

Brodir shrugged. "Some are; some are *úlfhéðnar,* the wolf-folk. And some are simply good men who've sworn to end the scourge of the White Christ."

"It will end soon enough," Dísa replied, staring into her wine.

Brodir looked askance at her. "You sound certain, little sister."

"She is," Úlfrún replied. The older woman joined them, taking a seat when one of her bear-men rose and moved aside for her. Another handed her a cup of wine. She drank it in three swallows, and then held it out for a refill. "She is the *Dagaz*-bearer, the Day-strider.

> "Wolf shall fight she-Wolf | in Raven's shadow;
>   an axe age, a sword age, | as Day gives way to Night.
>   And Ymir's sons dance | as the Gjallarhorn
>   kindles the doom | of the Nailed God's folk."

Dísa's eyes narrowed as she heard the words of the prophecy. "How do you know this?"

Úlfrún smiled. "I am the she-Wolf. Our pale friend, back there, is the Wolf—the Ghost-Wolf of Skara, he is called—and the Raven's shadow . . ."

"Is Hrafnhaugr," Dísa whispered. "When it speaks of the Day giving way to Night, what does it mean?"

"Aye," Brodir said. "And who are Ymir's sons?"

Úlfrún shrugged; absently, she massaged her forearm above her iron hand.

"Who can say? All we know is the prophecy is coming to pass. What we do in the next few days will kindle the doom of the Nailed God's folk. But we must push on, get in front of this rabble, and meet them at Hrafnhaugr, in the heart of the Raven-Geats' land. Will your folk fight with us?"

Dísa glanced up. "They will. But I beg a favor of you, Jarl Úlfrún: lend me a few of your men. My people expect me to return with my Jarl's son, who is at the mercy of the Witch-man's dogs. Help me free him! My friend—"

"Your friend hangs from a cross," Úlfrún said. "He'll likely be dead by sunset. If you go back now, with my help or not, all you'll accomplish is to die alongside him."

Dísa's jaw clenched. "Then at least he won't die alone. Loan me a bow, if nothing else, so I can get close enough to end his suffering!"

Úlfrún scratched and stroked her lower jaw as a man might his beard. She was of two minds, Dísa could see. A part of her wanted to err on the side of caution, to get her men to Hrafnhaugr and await the hour of the prophecy; the other part of her longed to bloody this upstart crusader's nose. She glanced between Brodir on one side and an old *úlfhéðinn* on the other, a gray-bearded man wrapped in wolf fur.

Brodir shrugged his mighty shoulders. "You and the wolf-brothers scouted their lines for a reason, lady. Why not a quick strike?"

Úlfrún leaned back and scowled. "You would risk the prophecy?"

"How can we know what risks the prophecy and what does not? Seems to me, if we succeed we say it was meant to be. But if we fail, was that not also meant to be? I leave it to the will of the Norns."

"Forne?" Úlfrún glanced at the old *úlfhéðinn,* who leaned to one side and spat.

"The more of these cross-kissers we kill here, the fewer we have to kill there." The man, Forne, nodded toward Dísa.

For a moment Úlfrún was silent. Then, nodding, she glanced over her shoulder. "Herroðr, fetch Skaðmaðr." Herroðr, the youngest man Dísa had seen among this war band—and still at least ten years her senior—brought an oiled leather sack to Úlfrún. From it, she extracted a crossbow. Its stock was fine-grained yew, carved and inlaid with ivory runes; of iron was the lock and trigger, while the bow was made of composite material: wood, horn, and sinew.

Úlfrún handed it stock-first to Dísa. "This is Skaðmaðr, the Man-slayer. She has sent three-score hymn-singers into the arms of their Nailed God, and she does not miss. Take her and free your Jarl's son—one way or the other. While you do that, we will make sure that white-skinned bastard has his hands full, won't we, boys?"

Grunts and wolf howls echoed off the stone walls of the bluff as the Sons of Úlfrún Iron-Hand girded themselves for war . . .

15

Dawn came, sunless and raw, to the Horn.

Father Nikulas pulled his cloak tighter against the chill. The priest chewed his lip as he watched the six men Konraðr had detailed to him dig three graves in the rocky soil. Haakon's body, along with the bodies of two sentries slain the night before, lay a short distance away, washed and anointed and wrapped in their cloaks, their heads covered by short lengths of linen. He considered the dead as the living hacked at the soil. Haakon they found in a ravine, as Konraðr predicted, along with a dead pagan; the other two they discovered after the chaos died down last night, on the eastern edge of the encampment. Both bore wounds from an axe or a blade, but one—the men of the burial detail had named him Egil—showed signs of having died from a significantly heavier blow.

"Our little bird had help," Konraðr had muttered. More Geats, he was sure. But how many more? And what troubles would they stir up as this small army entered the territory of the Raven tribe? Nikulas looked up, his eyes raking the forested north bank of the Horn. In truth, the priest had not expected resistance so soon. Since crossing the River of the Geats at the southern end of Lake Vänern, under the brow of a gloomy and mist-wreathed mountain locals called the Troll's Bonnet, Nikulas had felt ill at ease. Each step since, the sensation of scrutiny had grown. Something was watching them. Even here, in the company of God's anointed warriors, the priest felt naked before the great Adversary.

An Adversary whose lair was yonder, across the river.

Father Nikulas steeled himself. Somewhere in that dank annex of Hell, defended by howling and godless savages, lay a barrow; under that barrow, still wrapped in the skeletal embrace of the dragon he had slain, lay the bones of holy Saint Teodor. The Saint's hand yet clutched the hilt of his sword, whose blade had been baptized in the blood of our Savior. The crusaders' presence here not only served the King, but it served God and the Church as well. If he had to kill every pagan between here and Heaven's gates, Nikulas would see the bones of blessed Teodor enshrined in Lund. He would witness the Sword of Christ leading the King's armies to victory. And he would rejoice as the Light of Christ poured into every corner and cranny of the North, to banish the taint of ancient heathenry once and for all . . .

"Father," one of the soldiers of the burial detail said.

Nikulas blinked. He shook himself free of his reverie and looked down at the men who toiled before him. "What was that?"

"I said, is this deep enough, you think?"

Nikulas nodded. "It will do." The men clambered from the knee-deep graves and set about arranging their slain comrades' bodies. That finished, they stepped back and waited for Father Nikulas. The priest made the sign of the Cross. *"Requiem æternam dona eis, Domine,"* he began. "Eternal rest, grant unto them, O Lord. And let perpetual light shine upon them. May they rest in peace. Amen."

"Amen," the six soldiers echoed, crossing themselves.

Nikulas nodded. "If God wills it, we will see our brothers again come Judgment Day."

"Or sooner, if we get on the wrong side of a filthy pagan axe," the eldest among them said. The others chuckled. "Let's cover them up and let them sleep."

As they worked, Father Nikulas glanced back at the camp. The sound of hammers and saws echoed as work crews repaired the bridge; the rest of the army busied themselves by striking camp. Lord Konraðr wanted to be on the move before the noon hour, even if it was just a handful of miles into enemy territory.

"We should just buy them off," one of the diggers replied. "The pagans, I mean."

Nikulas turned back and stared quizzically at the six men. "Who said that?"

"I did." The speaker was a young Dane, one of the mercenaries who'd answered Konraðr's call. "Is that not what the lords of the South do when they want something? Throw gold at it until the enemy relents? We should offer gold to these pagans until they kneel before God and hand over the Saint's bones. Greed'll do our work for us."

The others snorted. "You're a right fool, Svein," the old soldier said.

"Then so are princes and kings, you old sack," Svein sneered.

Nikulas shook his head. "Salvation cannot be purchased," he said. "It must be earned through hardship and blood. Trust no man who swears fealty to God unless he has spilled his blood at the foot of the Cross."

"Well said, Father," the old crusader echoed. "We—"

Suddenly, the man fell forward, across the half-filled grave. The others laughed. "I'm the fool, but at least I have my feet under me," Svein said. Like them, Nikulas thought the old crusader had simply lost his balance. The priest moved to help him up . . . and saw the fletchings of a crossbow bolt standing out from the base of his skull.

"God's teeth!" Nikulas fell back.

"There! Over there!"

The grave detail dove for cover as bolts whined around them. Svein, who hauled Father Nikulas to his feet, screamed and cursed as a bolt punched through his thigh. "Go!" he snarled, shoving the priest away. "Go! Warn the others!"

"Pagans!" Nikulas yelled, ducking and running in a whirl of black cloth. "Pagans in the camp!"

Howling like the beasts whose skins they wore, Úlfrún's wolf-men, her *úlfhéðnar,* attacked from the south.

ON THE NORTH SIDE OF the camp, on the bridge over the Hveðrungr River, Konraðr walked the newly repaired sections. He studied the boards underfoot, testing his weight in those places where his carpenters had joined new planks to the half-charred ones. "Good work, Arngrim," he said to the captain of his engineers, a gaunt and rawboned man whose father had built ships. He passed the knowledge of adze and awl down to his son, who used it to build towers, rams, mantlets, and mines for the Ghost-Wolf of Skara. "Will it hold?"

Arngrim hemmed and hawed; he smoothed his wiry beard, knuckled the edges of his mustache. He considered the bridge with a practiced eye and after a moment, nodded. "I wouldn't want to run cavalry and a full siege train over it, but it should suffice."

"But you're not certain?"

Arngrim sucked his teeth. "I am certain, my lord. It's as solid as you please. It's just . . ." He trailed off, his face flushing.

"What?"

"You're going to think I've gone daft."

"I leave such judgments to God," Konraðr said. "Come. Out with it. What is it about this bridge that gives you pause?"

"Here, let me show you," Arngrim said. He led Konraðr to the end of the bridge nearest the camp. There, he leaned out over the wooden kerb and pointed down at the supports. "Look here," he said. Konraðr followed his lead. "This is a simple arch bridge," the engineer said. "Most of the weight is on these abutments, here, supports like this one on each bank." Konraðr nodded. He saw a rough wooden cylinder, its foundation lost amid the under-growth at the river's edge.

"And so? Looks ordinary to me."

Arngrim replied: "Aye, from up here it does. But I went down there to check for signs of rot, seeing as how this whole damned thing is wood and stays damp from the spray of the water passing under it. Here's where you're going to think I'm either an idiot or a madman: I don't think this bridge was originally made by Men."

Konraðr bit back a derisive snort. He glanced at Arngrim, then back at the abutment. His engineer was as solid a man as any he'd ever met—sober and practical, not given to flights of fancy. If *he* thought something was not right, Konraðr knew to give it an extra measure of scrutiny. "Anyone else and I would wonder what heresy had possessed your good sense."

"Anyone else, my lord," Arngrim said, "and I would carry this to my grave and never tell a soul." He gestured again at the abutment below them. "That support? It's not conventional timber mounted on a stone foundation. It's an ash tree. A living, deeply-rooted ash tree. All four of the supports that make the arch . . . ash trees. So expansive that four of the lads could not link their hands around them. And the body of the arch, that holds the road bed up? Made from intertwined branches. Oh, aye. The parts those

174

idiots burned were just old planking, half-rotted—which is the condition this whole damnable structure *should* be in: half-rotted and ready to fall into the cursed river."

Konraðr nodded. His ghosts were silent; they milled at the edges of his vision, unwilling to cross the bridge of their own volition. He wondered, then, if this would be where they parted ways. "That's why it wouldn't burn," he said. "It's living wood."

"As green as the Whale-road. You recall my old da? My father's father? He went with Lord Magnus to Halberstadt, but ended up not taking the Cross."

"Aye, I remember him. Skalli, I think was his name. Said he 'just wanted to see what the fuss was about.'"

Arngrim smiled. "That's him. Well, he was a heathen to his bones. Magnus knew and said nothing, for he valued the man before the faith. But old Skalli told me tales. Told me about bridges like this, built in the middle of nowhere. He called them the work of trolls. I called him daft. Seeing this now, I think I owe me old da an apology." Arngrim straightened. "I mean, how goes it that no one knows this land? Not a soul in Eiðar could tell us in what direction the land of the Raven-Geats lay. We had to track those four lads we came across just to get this far. And this is settled country, is it not? The King has estates along Lake Vänern's shore. Norse lords have hunting lodges up country. Fishing smacks and merchants ply these waters . . . and yet, this corner remains wild and forgotten, a road no one recalls ending in a bridge built by trolls, over a river I've never heard of? This tells me we should tread warily."

"You know what this tells me, my friend?" Konraðr said, clapping Arngrim on one broad shoulder. "It tells me we are heading in the right direction. Check it one last time. I'll head back and get the first company up and moving. We've plenty of light left and—"

The ghosts at the edge of Konraðr's vision howled their warnings a heartbeat before the albino's red eyes apprehended the threat. Cries of alarm arose from the far bank of the river, where Arngrim's work crews—the score of soldiers who doubled as carpenters and laborers—had set about dismantling their open-air workshop, taking down their treadle saws and dousing the small forge where scrap iron was turned into nails for the bridge planking.

"What deviltry?" Arngrim said.

Men scrambled for shields and spears as a line of figures shambled from the forest. At first, Konraðr thought these shaggy creatures might be trolls, come to reclaim what was theirs from the grasping hands of Man; then, he saw the bear skins, the axes and naked swords in their fists, and recognized them for what they were: *"Berserkir!"*

Konraðr was on the verge of ordering Arngrim to pull his men back to the center of the bridge when something else impinged upon his senses: shouts of alarm coming from the camp, followed by the skirling blast of a horn. The spectral voices, half heard under the clamor, suddenly changed the tenor of their warnings. *The boy,* the voices hissed, dissonant and eerie. *She wants the boy.*

"They're after the bridge!" Arngrim snarled. "What are your orders, my lord? My lord?"

But Konraðr had gone still—as motionless as a statue hewn from marble; he was not frozen in place by fear, or by indecision. Rather, his mind whirled as it processed what he could see, feel, hear, and sense: he noted how slowly the *berserkir* came, their attention focused more on wreaking havoc than killing; nor were they frothing or glassy-eyed, indicating they were not in the grips of their famed battle rage. The shouts and horn-cries of alarm from the camp, the ghostly voices fixated on "she" and "the boy" . . .

"She's a tenacious one, the little bird."

"My lord?"

"Pull back to camp!" Konraðr said, turning.

"And give them the bridge? If they get a toehold, lord, we might as well end this crusade here, fighting over timber and nails!"

"They don't want the bridge, Arngrim," the lord of Skara said. "They want us to *think* they want the bridge so we'll strip the camp bare and muster our forces here, to defend it! This is a diversion! They're striking for the chapel tent from the south! They're after the Cross!"

DÍSA CAME HARD ON THE heels of the *úlfhéðnar,* moving as quickly and as silently as the veteran wolf-warriors. This, she realized, was the work Grimnir had trained her for, to strike fast, hard, and silently; to kill, then fade into the shadows. She clutched Skaðmaðr close as she dogtrotted through the trees and around thickets of bramble and thorn, one bolt clenched in her teeth and two others in her fist. A knot of tension rippled through her guts. She realized it was apprehension; fear, even. Fear of what she had to do, should this bid to free Flóki Hreðelsson fail.

At the three graves, where Forne and his more fleet-footed pack brothers had ambushed the first of the crusaders they came across, the girl peeled off from the main assault and kept to the trees. She worked her way around until she had a clear line of sight on the cross the Witch-man, Konraðr, had ordered erected outside the Nailed God's tent. She knelt in the lee of a long-fallen tree, once an arboreal giant but now nothing but a moss-covered skeleton. She propped Skaðmaðr on the log and peered over. The knot in her guts tightened.

Dísa's breath caught in her throat at the sight of Flóki's naked body, arms stretched near to breaking, hanging from nails driven through his wrists. His head had fallen forward, his chin resting on his blood-smeared chest; his legs were bent slightly, his heels propped on a scrap of wood they'd affixed to the cross. Even above the clamor, Dísa heard him groan as he straightened his legs. He drove his head against the center stave of the cross, his mouth open in a silent scream. Dísa felt the talons of grief claw at her heart. She bit back a sob, turned it inward, and exhaled it through her flared nostrils.

She had to free him. But how? The main thrust of their assault pressed in from the south. Dísa could hear the howling of the wolf-men, the shouts of alarm; the crash and slither of steel, the dull thud of blades striking shields. Fires sprang up in that direction, black smoke drifting across the camp as Úlfrún's troops kicked over braziers or snatched brands from cook fires and flung them into tents. To the north, the attack of the *berserkir* did not draw off the main body of crusader troops as they had hoped. The Crusaders did not commit to protecting the bridge; instead, Dísa saw flashes of white—white hair, white mantle—as the lord of Skara rallied his men and formed a shield wall around the Nailed God's tent. And around Flóki.

She saw no way clear to slip in and free him. Not now. Not through a shield wall. The knot in her gut convulsed; Dísa leaned to one side, spat the bolt from between her teeth, and retched. Wiping bile from her chin, she heard a soft step as Úlfrún came alongside her. In the daylight, the older woman reminded Dísa of her grandmother, Sigrún. Both bore the scars of battle alongside the scars of a life spent proving themselves in the world of men; both had eyes as hard and cold as ice, but where Sigrún's gaze revealed a shriveled and diminished soul, Úlfrún's eyes brimmed with life.

"Give Skaðmaðr to me," she said, crouching alongside Dísa. "You go find Forne and blood your axe on Crusader skulls. Leave this to me."

"No," Dísa replied. "It must be by my hand. I owe it to him."

Úlfrún sighed. "Then, be quick about it. Do not let him linger." The older woman took one of the bolts from Dísa's hand and slotted it against the crossbow's drawn string. Its head gleamed lethal and gray in the dim sunlight. "Say his name and loose. Skaðmaðr will do the rest. I told you, the Man-slayer never misses."

Dísa nodded. She settled the crossbow's butt into the hollow of her shoulder and let the trunk of the fallen tree bear most of Skaðmaðr's weight. She tried to conjure Grimnir's face—his merciless snarl, his callousness, his casual cruelty. Instead, she kept recalling the last time she'd seen Flóki, standing in the door to Kolgríma's shack on the night he and the others fled Hrafnhaugr. He'd winked at her, smiled. *When you see me again, it will be atop a ship made of gold!* Dísa wiped her eyes, snarling as she knuckled away her tears.

"Daft bastard," she whispered.

Beside her, Úlfrún purred: "Do you have him in your sight?"

Dísa wiped her eyes again, and nodded.

"Then do it. Say his name . . ."

Her hand hovered over the trigger lever. One squeeze. Dísa exhaled, shook her head to clear it.

"Move aside," Úlfrún hissed. "We're almost out of time. There is no shame in not being able to do this thing. Put Skaðmaðr down and leave it to me, child."

"I'll do it, I said!" Dísa snapped. She returned her attention to the crossbow—and to the merciful release it offered Flóki, yonder. She drew a shuddering breath, held it, and released it in a drawn-out sigh. Dísa settled against the stock. She sighted down the firing groove, her fingers on the trigger lever. "I am no child," she whispered. "I am a Daughter of the Raven. Bearer of the rune *Dagaz,* the Day-strider, chosen of the Norns. I am a servant of the Hooded One, immortal herald of the Tangled God." Her voice cracking, she added: "And I . . . I am your death . . . Flóki Hreðelsson."

Flóki stirred; he looked up, a weary smile twisting his cracked lips as though Dísa's soft exhalation of his name reached his ears over the din. And as her hand squeezed the trigger lever, as the Man-slayer discharged its bolt with a rattle and a thunk, Dísa Dagrúnsdottir closed her eyes.

THE ATTACK ENDED AS SWIFTLY as it began as the wolf-men faded back into the undergrowth, dragging their dead and wounded with them. Smoke drifted over the crusaders' camp.

Arngrim nodded to the lord of Skara. "You were right, my lord."

Konraðr squeezed his engineer's arm and smiled. "Pray you're not there when I'm wrong, eh?" He ordered the shield wall to break ranks, save for a company of his sworn men, led by their captain, Starkad, who would stand watch around the chapel tent.

Konraðr had under his command his five hundred household troops, mailed sons of Skara who pledged themselves to their famed lord; their ranks were bolstered by mercenaries from the Danemark and by a band of Norse freebooters eager for gold and salvation. A one-eyed old pirate called Kraki Ragnarsson led the Danes, some four hundred strong, while three-hundred-odd Norsemen followed their Jarl, Thorwald the Red.

Konraðr sent Thorwald forward with a force of men to hold the bridge; Kraki, meanwhile, he set to tending the wounded and counting the dead, aided by Nikulas's monks, Brother Marten and Brother Johan. That done, Konraðr turned his attention to the corpse nailed to a cross at the heart of his camp.

They'd come for the boy. A score of his men had died while half again as many bore wounds, and for what? For a beardless lad? For the supposed love some silly girl who sought to play among men bore for him? And when she could not have him, when she realized he was beyond her grasp, Dísa Dagrúns-dottir had ended Flóki's life with a crossbow bolt through his right eye.

"God save me from that sort of love," Konraðr muttered. But as much as it pained him to admit, he knew Arngrim had been right. The pagan spirits protected their own; if not for these four boys and their foolish plan to divert a crusade ordained by God by burning the bridge, Konraðr doubted that even his scouts could have found a way in to the land of the Raven-Geats. And they would have looked like fools, or worse.

"Whatever devils this boy knelt to," Konraðr said to Nikulas as the priest joined him, "they seem set upon keeping the bones of blessed Saint Teodor—and his sword—away from we good followers of Christ."

"They will fail," Nikulas replied. "For how could they not? We have God upon our side."

"And God wills it!"

The soldiers around them took up their lord's cry: "*Deus vult!* God wills it!"

"Cut him down," Konraðr ordered, turning away. "Leave his heathen carcass for the dogs!"

"Wait!" Father Nikulas seized Konraðr's arm in an impassioned grip. The priest stared up at the cross, eyes wide. "Look!" During the affray, the clouds overhead had thinned; now, through rents and tears could be seen the blue vault of heaven. A lance of sunlight stabbed down from the firmament, piercing clouds and smoke to bathe the chapel tent and the cross before it in its golden glow. Wreathed in that light, the body on the cross assumed a sublime beauty—from the fall of his hair over his eyes to the mysterious smile forever frozen upon his lips. In that moment, Nikulas saw the face of the Redeemer. "Witness!" the priest cried. "Bear witness, O soldiers of Christ! We stand at the edge of pagan lands, but God is with us! We have lost companions, this day, but God is with us! And the army that knows God is the army that knows victory!"

"Victory!" answered the crusaders. "God wills it!"

Lord Konraðr crossed himself. He watched as Nikulas walked to one of the soldiers and took the man's spear from him. *"After they were come to Jesus,"* the priest quoted, *"when they saw that he was already dead, they did not break his legs. But one of the soldiers with a spear"*—he raised the weapon on high, its head gleaming razor-sharp in the golden light—*"opened his side, and immediately there came out blood and water."* Nikulas pierced Flóki's side, and to the wonderment of all, blood and water flowed from the wound.

Men dropped to their knees. Shouts and cries went up. Some wept openly. "It is a miracle," Nikulas declared, tossing the spear back to its owner. "In death, this pagan has been shriven by God, himself! The Almighty has absolved him of the sin of unbelief and made his soul Christian! He has given him everlasting life! Bury him, my lord! Bury him as you would bury a revered saint! For he has revealed to us the truth of our struggles this day, and in the coming days: that we are blessed in this task, and we are not alone! Forward, into the land of the wretched pagan! Forward for the power and glory of Christ Almighty! God wills it!" Nikulas stood before the army like a prophet of old, his eyes fiery, his beard a wild tangle of gold in the light that streamed from the heavens.

"Deus vult!"

PART TWO
VÍGRÍÐR

16

In the cellar beneath Grimnir's longhouse, surrounded by walls of rune-cut stone, Halla crouched over a black iron basin filled with steaming water and sought to divine the future. Wrought in the time before recorded history, the basin had come to Miðgarðr when Grimnir's folk fled from Jötunheimr—but whether as spoils of war or stolen from their master, Gífr never said. The old *kaunr* had called it the Eye of Mimir, and he'd showed her how to harness it in order to catch a glimpse of what was yet to come.

"Bastard likes to speak in riddles," he'd said, eyeing the basin as though it were a living thing. "And its answers are as clear as a slag puddle until you come to see it in hindsight. But maybe you have more patience for its bollocks than I."

Halla used the Eye sparingly over the centuries, and only when other avenues were exhausted. This night, she had to know; she had to see . . . "The Grey Wanderer walks abroad," she breathed, her words rippling the steam. "Show me."

She leaned over the Eye of Mimir and peered into its ink-black water. Halla breathed the steam, which was acrid and smelled of smoke, blood, and churned earth—the stenches of the battlefield. The smell of Vígríðr, the blood-plain where gods and giants strove and slew.

The steam wafting up from the water's surface coiled and danced, forming images in the air. Fragments of prophecy drawn in oak gall and iron, traceries of black against a fragile tapestry of air. Halla concentrated and saw . . .

. . . *eyes of hateful red glaring from stark white fur; from the black fur, eyes as blue and cold as mountain ice. Two wolves pad in circles—one black, one white—hackles raised; slaver drips from bared fangs. Their low growls promise no mercy. From above, Raven watches, head cocked. Its voice is harsh against an empty sky.*

The wolves surge together. Fangs rip; claws rend. Blood drips like rubies, jewels of life staining the snow. Raven watches. They fight, but for what? What is their prize? Is it dominance? Is it territory? Raven knows. Their prize is an illusion, a Lie driven under their skins. It is the Lie that makes them kill. It is the Lie they die for.

A silhouette watches. It is vaguely man-shaped, but it is no man; it wears the slouch hat and cloak of a wanderer, but it is no wanderer; it is one-eyed, but not Ein-eygdr. *Its smile is malice; its laugh, hate. It watches.*

The white wolf kills the black. The black wolf kills the white. Hearts beating, hot blood soaking the earth, they drag themselves toward the Lie. Howling, moaning. The Lie beckons. Raven screams the truth, but they do not hear. Raven takes wing; it tries to stem the red tide of blood as it cools and turns to an avalanche of rubies. Raven gathers them in its talons, secrets them in its feathers and protects them. But the silhouette cannot abide Raven's interference. With its wooden staff, it drives Raven away. Rubies of blood spill from Raven's wings to shatter as they strike the earth.

The ground shakes. The wolves howl their last. The silhouette waits.

Raven soars into the sun, wheels, and returns for vengeance. Black-winged, razorbeaked, it flies as true as an arrow. It pierces the figure, slicing through muscle and bone to seize its prize: the silhouette of a heart, black and beating. The man that is no man, the God that is no god, laughs, and its laughter is hatred. Its smile is malice. Its heart is doom. The silhouette crumbles like ash.

Its heart grows. It becomes vast and winged. Raven screams as a monstrous shadow devours the earth . . .

Halla shifted, suddenly aware of a tremor running deep under the earth. Dust filtered down from the roof of the cellar; ripples disturbed the surface of the water, breaking the spell cast by the Eye of Mimir. She rocked back on her haunches and waited for the trembling to subside.

Gífr had spoken the truth: the Eye of Mimir made riddles of the future. She recognized the imagery, or thought she did, of the wolves and the raven . . . these were spoken of in the prophecy. She'd expected to see the face of the dragon, the destruction of the Nailed God's world. She hoped to see the fires of Ragnarök kindled and well-burning.

And the shadows. The silhouette of a figure who was a man but not a man; a god but not a god. This was the Grey Wanderer, she reckoned, though his mortal identity remained a mystery. Lines of concern creased Halla's ancient brow as she rocked to her feet. Her limbs creaked as she climbed the steps. With each one, she felt as though she was diminishing— becoming a gnarled thing good for nursery tales, that children might take fright at but their parents would dismiss as a figment of feverish imagination.

Halla stopped at the head of the cellar steps. What if Grimnir was right? What if this feeling meant the prophecy would not change the world in any measurable way and the scourge of the Nailed God could not be stopped? Could she live in a world like that, a world bereft of the mystery and magic of her youth?

Slowly, she shuffled through the longhouse, her shoulders bowed by the weight of her years. She paid no heed to the trophies of long-forgotten triumphs, to the drifts of coin and weapons taken from dead foes, to Grimnir's throne or the banked fire in its pit. She shuffled out the door and onto the columned porch, where she stood and stared up at the nighted sky.

A full moon hung over the earth. Its bright silvery glow dimmed the other lights of heaven. But as Halla peered up at the moon, her breath caught in her throat. There was a shadow on its edge, a reddish tinge. A tremble of anticipation ran through the troll-woman's hunched frame. "Can it be?"

A voice, soft and menacing, answered her from the shadows:

"Sköll bays aloud | after Dvalin's toy."

Halla turned as a figure emerged from the darkness, a twisted silhouette leaning upon a staff of carved yew, cloak-wrapped, a low-brimmed hat drawn over its face. From beneath it, a single eye burned with the fires of Ásgarðr.

"Will you not offer hospitality to a stranger, daughter of Járnviðja?"

GRIMNIR AROSE FROM THE BENCH where he'd spent the last hours feigning sleep and crept among the warriors of Gautheimr. The hearth-fire was a bed of smoldering embers; by that ruddy glow, he moved soundlessly—though mailed and bearing arms—his body bent low to the ground, his nostrils flaring and snuffling like some beast of old, come to slake an unholy thirst. As he passed, the ground underfoot rumbled, a shudder that trembled through the bones of the earth. He stopped, listening. The men did not waken, but their snores became groans as dreams turned to nightmares of blood and slaughter.

He scrithed through the benches of the sworn men and down among the sleeping pallets of the Daughters of the Raven. A dozen of them, the eldest of the war-hags, slept fitfully among the men. He ghosted past Auða, who lay curled in a tight ball, and Geira, whose ripping snores echoed like any man's; he stepped over Thyra, who was Old Hygge's eldest daughter. Grimnir's eye gleamed with a feral light, narrowing as he caught sight of the one he was after.

Sigrún.

The old wolf-bitch lay on a rug of bear skin, her head pillowed by one lean-muscled arm. A cloak lay draped over her body from shoulder to ankle; unlike the others, she slept fully clothed in a loose tunic of russet wool and cross-gaitered linen trousers the color of cream. A naked sword rested near her blade hand, her fingers barely touching its acorn-shaped pommel. Her shield leaned against the rough wall of the longhouse, and her hauberk was close at hand, ready to snatch up and shimmy into at a moment's notice.

Grimnir, however, gave her no such moment.

Black-nailed fingers clamped over her mouth. The old woman's eyes flew open; her hand clawed for the hilt of her sword even as she came up off the bear fur. She was nearly upright when Grimnir dealt her a sharp buffet with his forearm, under her left ear. And like that, Sigrún went as limp as a boned fish.

Grimnir wasted no time. He snatched her up, threw her over his shoulder like a manikin made of twine and dry wood, and darted out the door of the longhouse. Nor did he pause there. Like a drifting shadow, he spirited her from Hrafnhaugr through the postern gate. He loped down the forested trail to the dock, skirted past it, and followed the rocky shore until they came abreast of the Skærvík mouth of the Scar—the moat-like ravine that cut the peninsula of Hrafnhaugr off from the mainland.

Here, Grimnir slung Sigrún to the ground. The moon overhead, as full and fat as a spring lamb, sported a bloody edge as a shadow slipped over it. The Wolf, Grimnir reckoned, devouring Mani, goddess of the Moon. That meant a turning of the glass—a last trickle of sand before the world shook and oceans boiled and the herald of Ragnarök emerged from its death-like slumber, or so the doggerel ran. Grimnir snarled at the harbinger of destruction and drew his seax.

It was not the same blade as the one Skríkja had given him, in the days of Bálegyr's reign over the North; the blade he'd carried on his murderous quest to avenge himself on Bjarki Half-Dane, though it was close. He had reforged it himself; its core was that ancient blade, hammered by Kjallandi from the heart of a star that had fallen on the dwarf-realm of Niðavellir. Grimnir had added steel to it, dusted it with ground scales from the wyrm's own hide—fetched from the ruin of Orkahaugr over a hundred years before—and woven into it spells of destruction. *"Hatr,"* he said. *"Hate* is your name."

"What?" The old shieldmaiden at his feet groaned from where she had fetched up against a damp and moss-grown boulder. She struggled to rise, but then satisfied herself by dragging her body into a sitting position. The light of the darkening moon touched with ruddy fire her gray locks, and they fell over her scarred face as she fixed Grimnir with a deadly glare. "By what right—" she started to say, but Grimnir cut her off with a sharp bark of laughter. He crouched just out of reach, an eerie figure in his horned headdress and wolf-skull mask. His good eye gleamed like an ember in the murk.

"By what right?" he mocked her. "Useless hag! I have been a raider, a throat-slitter, aye, and a slayer of men; I have terrorized a dozen lands, given birth to a score of wretched folk tales, and killed hundreds of your so-called heroes who'd come looking for vengeance, for glory, or just for a storied death. You dogs used to *whisper* my name for fear that saying it aloud might summon me, and not a bastard among you would dare question my right as your lord." With one black-nailed hand, Grimnir stripped off his headdress and mask. Sweat-heavy hair fell like a veil across his cheeks; he tossed his head back, bone and silver fetishes ticking together. To her credit, the old shieldmaiden did not blench at the sight of him. Grimnir leaned to one side and spat. "You do not scream and call me out as a monster?"

Sigrún wiped her hands on the thighs of her trousers. Abraded palms left swatches of blood behind. The old woman winced. "You are the Tangled God's herald. You carried the serpent banner of Angrboða in Jötunheimr, or so the legend goes. When the lords of Ásgarðr came against the children of Father Loki—mighty Fenrir, the world-encircling serpent Jörmungandr, and blessed Hel—they say it was you, lord, who led the Tangled God's armies into battle. Why should I think you'd be a blond-haired and blue-eyed son of Miðgarðr?"

Grimnir nodded, wiping his nose on his forearm and grunting to hide his sudden fit of humor. None of what she'd said was true, but he did not gainsay her. Let them reckon him older than Gífr if it kept them in line. "Those days are long gone, aren't they?" he said, after a moment. "What am I now, but a wretched shepherd, keeping a flock of prattling fools safe from the Nailed God's folk? Well, it's high time you lot remember that you live on at my pleasure! And my pleasure, now, is answers!"

"Answers to what? Why bring me out here if all you want are answers?"

"You recognize this place?"

Sigrún's eyes shifted from side to side. "It's where we found Kolgríma's body. She'd slipped and fell, yonder." The old woman indicated a place near the edge of the turgid water, slick with greenish moss.

"Oh, aye. Slipped and fell, is it?" Grimnir's lip curled in contempt. "You did her in, didn't you, you sly wretch?"

"Why would I do that? She was like a sister to me!"

"And so? Dagrún was your daughter, but that didn't stop you from sticking a knife in her gizzard, did it?"

Color drained from Sigrún's face.

"Yes," Grimnir hissed. "I already know about that little bit of wickedness. And I know it was Kolgríma who helped you get rid of the body. Is that why you dropped her over the edge of the Scar? To tie up your loose ends? *Nár!* You know it, and I know it, so don't try to play the fool and deny it!" But she did. Even as Sigrún opened her mouth to frame her innocence, Grimnir's seax flicked out. The razor-edged tip of the blade sliced through the thin cartilage of her left nostril. Sigrún hissed and flinched away, clutching at the side of her nose as blood dribbled over her lips and down her chin. "Hatr can taste your lies, hag," he said. "Think hard, ere you speak again. Think hard, for every lie you spool will cost you, and Hatr means to take its payment in blood."

Sigrún's chin jutted in defiance. "Aye, I killed Dagrún . . . that idiot wanted your head, and the glory that went along with it! She'd listened to one too many of Kolgríma's drunken yarns. I did what I had to do, back then, to keep the peace—but I did not kill Kolgríma! Why would I? What do I care if that useless sack of bones Dagrún whelped finds out what happened to her mother? You may have trained Dísa to cut throats, but I raised her! I know her limits better than you, lord!"

"Think you can take her, eh?"

"That you think I can't insults me," Sigrún said, rage thick in her voice.

"We'll see." Grimnir rocked back on his haunches. "So, if you didn't do her in, what in Hel's name was Kolgríma doing out here, at night?"

"Was she not skulking about on some errand for you? By her spoor, Bjorn Svarti thought she was looking for something."

Grimnir rose to his feet and slunk to the edge of the ravine. He moved in a low crouch, his head in motion as he swept the ground with his good eye, and stopping from time to time to snuffle at the stones and the moss. There was a sharp current in the water of the lake, here; wavelets splashed against half-submerged boulders and a breeze whistled between the sheer walls of the Scar. Grimnir straightened, a curse forming on his lips. He was about to admit defeat when he caught a ghostly scent, a whiff of something like iron boiled in brine—the Nailed God's stench.

He glanced over his shoulder at the old shieldmaiden, who had clambered to her feet. She watched him with curious intensity. "I brought you out here, away from those other swine, expecting to smell the Nailed God's reek on you, but all that sweats from your cursed pores is hatred. Hatred, and now . . ." Grimnir inhaled. "And now, fear. What are you afraid of, eh?" He gave her an opening to speak, but Sigrún remained silent. "Afraid I'd find this?"

Grimnir crept close to the wall of the ravine. He took a deep, snuffling breath; by the dim ruddy light of the eclipsing moon, he noticed a rock out of place, its edges scraped clean. He clawed at it, and it fell out easily. Grimnir cursed and flinched away from the reek rising from the niche; covering his nose and mouth with his forearm, he speared something inside it with his seax and dragged it out into the open. Burlap ripped; a thing both bright and metallic clattered to the stony floor of the ravine.

It was a standing crucifix.

Grimnir snarled and spat. He turned his head to glare at Sigrún. "Yours?" he growled.

The old woman gave a long, pent-up sigh before shaking her head. "She was curious about it, she said. Curious how something like that could have conquered the world. She was curious about its power."

"Who?"

"Kolgríma," Sigrún replied.

Grimnir exploded. Two swift steps brought him face-to-face with the old shieldmaiden; he snatched her up in one black-nailed fist, spun, and slammed her against the wall of the ravine. "You wretched hag!" Spittle flew from his lips. "Kolgríma? Kolgríma was no blasted hymn-singer! I would have known!"

Sigrún clawed at his arm. She coughed. "S-She was curious, I said! She kept it hidden away."

"How'd you find out about it?"

"She was like a sister to me. Kolgríma wanted someone to confide in. Someone close . . ."

"So she *told* you she was flirting at the edges of the Nailed God's creed?" Grimnir scoffed. He turned Sigrún loose; the old woman slumped against the ravine wall, rubbing her throat. "And, what? You killed her?"

"What if I did?" Sigrún glared at him. "You're an ungrateful bastard, do you know this? Kolgríma—aye, precious Kolgríma!—wanted to send an envoy off to the King of the Swedes! Did you know that? She wanted him to send a priest by boat, so you'd be none the wiser! She said there was change on the wind! The days of hiding would soon be over, and we'd best prepare. And the best thing *we* could do, she said . . . was kneel before the Nailed God!"

Grimnir said nothing for a moment. He stared hard at the crucifix—an altar piece as long as his forearm and wrought of heavy gold, the Nailed God's pain-racked image taunting him. Then, with a sulphurous oath, he snagged it on the point of his seax and flung it out into the dark waters of Skærvík. "Who else knows?" he said, after the splashing echo died away.

"No one. I made sure of it." Sigrún stooped and picked up Grimnir's headdress and mask. These, she held out to him.

He raised an eyebrow, chuckled darkly. "A bastard, I may be," he said, taking the items from her. "But I am not ungrateful. And Kolgríma, that hymn-singing old bat, she wasn't wrong." He gestured into the night sky with his chin, gestured at the blood-tinged moon. "The end comes. Sit, and let me tell you a tale . . ."

DÍSA CRIED IN HER SLEEP, dreaming of Flóki, until the trembling of the earth woke her. She opened her eyes, instantly alert, and listened as the vibrations faded away. She took it for what it surely was—a harbinger, an omen of the strife-filled days ahead, when the earth would split and disgorge the bones of Niðhöggr. Around her, the men of Úlfrún's war band did not stir. They slept where they dropped, wrapped in their cloaks, pressed together for warmth. Their snores came like a chorus of ripping cloth. None of them seemed to notice the reverberations deep in the bones of the earth, the rousing of a giant.

Quietly, Dísa came to her feet. She wiped her eyes. Something else disturbed her, something she could not put her finger on. She walked the perimeter of their makeshift camp, creeping past bleary-eyed sentries, as noiseless as the wind. The army of that wretched hymn-singer, Konraðr the White, was half a day and more behind them. At Dísa's urging, they made for Hrafnhaugr with all haste. "My people need time," she'd said to Úlfrún. "Time to gather provisions and reinforce the walls. Time to come to grips with a battle on their doorstep." And Úlfrún had agreed, though her men were not happy with her decision. They wanted to strike at Konraðr's column, make them pay for every inch of their advance in blood. Forne even suggested they send Dísa on alone.

"No," Úlfrún had said. "She will need our presence to convince her people this threat is real." Nor did she want to split her forces. The old wolf-warrior had cursed and stormed off, but he did as his Jarl commanded.

Dísa came to a small glade, a tear in the forest canopy caused by a felled tree. Its rotting trunk lay at the center, surrounded by weeds and bramble. The girl was surprised to see Úlfrún sitting on that fallen log. The older woman stared at the heavens, her face bathed in the light of the full moon.

Dísa came and sat beside her.

"You felt it?" Úlfrún said.

Dísa nodded. "It was Jörmungandr, the Miðgarðr Serpent, wasn't it?"

"It smells blood and strife, and it stirs," Úlfrún replied. "It is almost time."

"How can you know?" Dísa said. She followed Úlfrún's gaze and saw the ominous red shadows staining the moon's bright face. Úlfrún closed her eyes. She wore a look of soul-weary exhaustion as she massaged the stump of her missing hand.

"It is almost at an end."

Dísa looked from the moon to the silver-edged glade. She noted how the trees strained skyward, their limbs washed in moonlight; they were like the suppliants of a merciful goddess. She heard the hum of their roots, and felt their anticipation rising through the soil. They were eager for . . . what? For destruction? But their hum was not bloodthirsty, nor did she sense hatred behind their anticipation. Like an oak shedding its leaves, they were ready for the world to shed its blight, and for a new world to rise in its place.

"How long do we have?"

When Úlfrún did not answer, Dísa looked to the older woman—poised to repeat the question—and saw she'd leaned back against a thick branch. Her good hand still clutched the stump of the other, but now there was a beatific smile on her face that smoothed the lines of concern from her brow and lent her the aspect of youth. Dísa remained by her side and watched over the older woman as she slept.

"NINE TIMES NINE," KONRAÐR MUTTERED.

Sweat dripped from the lord of Skara's brow; his pale skin was splotched and ruddy, and his reddish eyes glassy as the recurring fever dug its talons into him. He reeled from his pavilion on unsteady legs, barefoot, sword in hand, clad only in breeches and a tunic. Outside, the guard snapped to attention. Konraðr waved him off as he went out into the night, shivering, his eyes wildly searching the heavens. For a moment, the warrior, one of his sworn men, made to follow, alarmed by his lord's behavior; instead, he hurried to the chapel tent, where he hoped to find Father Nikulas.

"Times nine again," Konraðr said, his breath steaming. "Nine times nine times nine again." He staggered down the line of tents where his men slept. Most were too exhausted to notice the faint trembling of the earth much less their lord's fevered rambling. The army had stopped half a day's march from the bridge and set up camp in column—a great snake of weary men, small fires, and hastily erected tents. Some of the soldiers simply crawled into tree boles or bedded down in small groups, sharing blankets and cloaks for warmth. Sentries walked the perimeter between well-stoked fires, whose feeble light was barely enough to illuminate the wall of trees hemming them in.

Arngrim's men formed the vanguard, all experienced woodsmen who picked up the faint trail left by their attackers. But for that they would have been traveling blind, lost in the heart of Raven-Geat territory.

"What is nine?" Konraðr hissed. He was delirious with fever. "Why nine?" He moved up the column toward the head of the snake. A few men watched him pass; one, an older soldier who'd served with Konraðr at Constantinople, nodded for his young tent-mate to go and fetch Arngrim.

The lord of Skara came to a break in the forest. Through naked branches of oak, ash, and elm; through the green arms of spruce and fir and giant pine, moonlight lanced from the heavens and turned the remaining crusts of snow to drifts of silver and ivory.

Here, his ghosts gathered. Pale wraiths in tattered rags still wet with the blood of their deaths. They called for Konraðr to join them. They looked up at the moon, shining above them, its light lending their siege-wasted bodies some semblance of life. A child-soldier, a boy of twelve who had died under Konraðr's blade when they breached the walls of Constantinople, laughed and clapped.

Konraðr wanted to shake him. "Boy, what is nine times nine times nine again? What does nine mean?"

The boy pointed to the moon, to the ruddy shadow consuming its bright face and turning silver to blood. When the boy spoke, his voice was legion— male, female, old and young:

> "When the years tally | nine times nine times nine,
>   again, and war-reek | wafts like dragon breath;
>   when Fimbulvetr | hides the pallid sun,
>   the monstrous Serpent | shall writhe in fury."

Konraðr swayed and fell to his knees. "Yes. Yes:

> "Sköll bays aloud | after Dvalin's toy.
>   The fetter shall break | and the wolf run free;
>   Dark-jawed devourer | of light-bringer's steed.
>   And in Vänern's embrace | the earth splits asunder."

This was how Father Nikulas found him: kneeling, shivering, muttering out of his head as the fever racked his thin frame. The bearded priest turned as Arngrim joined him. The rawboned engineer had a blanket in his fists.

"What happened to him, Father?"

"God tests him," Nikulas replied. "Tests his resolve with fevers and madness and apparitions from his days in the East."

"Will the bones of the blessed saint cure him of this affliction?"

The priest shrugged. "Perhaps. Come, help me. Let's get him back to his tent."

Arngrim started forward, and then stopped. "Father," he hissed, looking up through the interlaced branches. Nikulas followed his gaze. The priest crossed himself. In the night sky, they watched as a sinister shadow consumed the moon, like the jaws of a wolf closing on its prey.

"Do not look at it," Nikulas said. He grasped Konraðr's arm and helped the lord of Skara to his feet. "It is the Devil's moon. The great Adversary wants us to fail." Arngrim averted his eyes and looked, instead, at his lord. He wrapped the blanket around Konraðr's trembling shoulders.

"Nine times nine times nine again," he muttered, clutching Arngrim's forearm. "What is it?"

"Nine times nine times nine again?" Arngrim met Konraðr's ruddy gaze, his eyes the same hue as the blood moon. "That's seven hundred and twenty-nine, my lord."

"Wrong," Konraðr replied, pointing at the eclipsed moon. "It's now."

HALLA HEATED WINE AND SPICES in a copper pot, then poured the steaming concoction into a pair of horn cups. She handed one to the cloaked stranger, who sat now by the door of the longhouse. His good eye flitted over the treasures and trophies scattered haphazardly around the room; his gaze lingered over Grimnir's throne. Halla thought she saw a gleam of contempt.

The troll-woman sat in her accustomed place. She drank sparingly, listening as the stranger regaled her with news from faraway lands, fulfilling the customs of hospitality that called for the guest to help pass a cold winter's night by being congenial company. He told of the defeat of the German crusaders at Otepää in Estonia, and their subsequent call for help; he spoke of a great arming by the followers of the White Christ in the south, who were intent on recapturing the lands called Outremer. "I do not understand their ways," the stranger said, shaking his head. "They will journey halfway around the world to die on a barren rock because their Nailed God might have trod upon it, but they refuse to help a broken man at their feet."

Halla nodded. "The world is nothing like I remember it."

"Aye, the trackless forest," the stranger replied, his eye gleaming. "Myrkviðr, the Dark-wood, stretching from dawn to dusk. I remember

well that world. It is lost now, and forgotten by all save you and I." For an
hour and more, the stranger and Halla traded stories, remembrances of the
songs of the trees, of the laughing spirits, and of dark deeds done by moon-
less night when the sons of Man dared trespass under the emerald boughs
of Myrkviðr.

Finally, after three cups of wine, the stranger lapsed into silence. Time
passed without any accounting, then: "Do you know me, daughter of Járnviðja?" he said, placing his empty cup beside him.

"I've had word of your coming, and I know the guise you wear," Halla
replied. "The Grey Wanderer; the Raven-God; Lord of the Gallows; the
shield-worshipped kinsman of the Æsir. Your names are without number.
But I also know that the guise you wear, those names . . . they are not your
own. They were chosen for you."

"You think me some puppet, then? Some wretched *niðingr*?"

"We are all puppets, in some way." Halla, too, put her cup aside. "We
dance and caper about this stage, playing out the roles we've been given for
the grim amusement of the Gods. Playing until they see fit to cut our strings.
Then, we are puppets no longer. I have watched many such plays unfold,
stranger, but I am not familiar with yours."

"Are you not?" he replied. "Though you are but a bit player in it, you've
seen fit to add your voice to the chorus often enough:

"When the years tally | nine times nine times nine,
   again, and war-reek | wafts like dragon breath;
   when Fimbulvetr | hides the pallid sun,
   the monstrous Serpent | shall writhe in fury.

"Sköll bays aloud | after Dvalin's toy.
   The fetter shall break | and the wolf run free;
   Dark-jawed devourer | of light-bringer's steed.
   And in Vänern's embrace | the earth splits asunder.

"From the depths a barrow | rises through the water,
   the stone-girdled hall | of Aranæs, where dwells
   Jörmungandr's spawn, | the Malice-Striker.
   Its dread bones rattle | and herald an end.

"Wolf shall fight she-Wolf | in Raven's shadow;
 an axe age, a sword age, | as Day gives way to Night.
 And Ymir's sons dance | as the Gjallarhorn
 kindles the doom | of the Nailed God's folk."

Halla's milky eyes narrowed. "That's not your composition, though, is it? Nor is this a play of your devising. What are you, under that mask you wear, but some poor fool caught in a snare and made to dance?"

The stranger laughed. "Caught, indeed. I was left like offal along the Ash-Road, where the tangled branches of Yggðrasil pierce the Nine Worlds. There my master found me, broken and near death. He gave me a new purpose, lent me his *hamingja,* his luck. He has entrusted me with the plot of his play and I will see it performed." The stranger rose to his feet and came nearer to the fire. He extended his hands, warming his fingers. "But I have a thorny problem. The time for bit players is at an end. The principals are ready to take the stage. I have my Wolf, my she-Wolf, my precious little Day who gives way to Night." He glanced around the longhouse. "I even have Ymir's sons poised to dance, and Malice-Striker waiting in the wings." He turned his head and fixed Halla in his malevolent gaze. "But I seem to have one puppet too many, *niðingr.*"

"Perhaps," Halla said, clambering to her feet. "Perhaps it is my lot to join your audience."

The stranger considered this, but shook his head after a moment. "I think not. The audience should not know quite so much about the play. And you know more than you let on, don't you? Yes, I can tell from that gleam of recognition in your eyes, child of Myrkviðr. You know from whence I come. And with a well-timed word in the wrong ear you could ruin my surprise."

"Not if our purposes are aligned," Halla said. "Do we not want the same thing? To see the prophecy fulfilled? To see the Nailed God's dominion ended and the Elder World restored? Unless . . ." she looked up sharply, her milky eyes thinning to slits, ". . . unless that's not what this play is about." She recalled the Eye of Mimir; the prize the two wolves fought over, it was a lie. "The prophecy," she said slowly, backing away from the stranger. "The prophecy is a lie, isn't it?"

The stranger *tsked.* "Not a lie so much as a diversion. But come. Do not be afraid." He loomed over Halla as she moved farther from him. She came up against something unyielding—Grimnir's throne—and stopped. Still, the cloaked silhouette grew; she smelled the cold stench of Ásgarðr flowing from under the folds of his mantle as it closed over her.

Darkness. The sensation of being wrenched from her feet, stomach churning and disorienting. She can discern no up or down; neither ground below nor sky above. She has the impression of roiling smoke, flashes of fire. A howling gale pummels her ears. Through the smoke, she beholds a crucified titan. He hangs from a tree whose boughs cradle nine worlds—mighty Yggðrasil. The titan is one-eyed and fey-bearded, with a pair of giant ravens perched on his naked shoulders. She averts her gaze. Her nostrils fill with the scent of iron and blood and smoke—the fume and wrack of war. She tumbles, plummets back into darkness.

Halla fell to her knees, clutching the leaf mold as she fought against a roaring in her skull. It came from all around her; its deep intonation vibrated her diaphragm. And it only stopped when she realized it was the sound of her own scream.

Panting like a dog, she opened her eyes and glanced about. The longhouse was gone, its fire and its warmth replaced by bone-chilling cold and the damp stench of the nearby bog. The stranger's sorcery had brought her here, to the middle of the forest. She looked for the stranger but could not see him—though she felt his malignant gaze.

"If you mean to kill me," Halla's voice quavered, "do it and have done. I'll not beg."

She heard him laugh—a wheezing, humorless sound like iron scraping flint. "You think me so base as to betray the laws of hospitality? No, you'll not die by my hand. Not when I can simply let the blood of Járnviðja do the deed for me."

Instantly, she apprehended his meaning. Her head swiveled; she looked to the east, where fire touched the velvet sky, heralding the coming of dawn. Fear gibbered through Halla's brain, but the old troll-woman wasted no time. She scrambled to her feet, still unsteady, and lumbered south, toward the growing bog-reek. Halla did not know precisely where she was, but she trusted her gut; she trusted she was near enough to reach the shelter of the longhouse before the inevitable rising of the sun. Otherwise, why would that cruel bastard give her a chance?

"Hurry, child!" he said, his voice accompanied by the sudden rush of wings. "Hurry! Ere bright Álfröðull, the Elf-beam, casts her gaze upon you!"

Halla ran.

Through the rising light, through the graying of night into day, she ran; she ran till she thought her heart would burst, till her lungs burned. Down slopes carpeted in drifts of leaves, through copses and tangled webs of briar and thorn, she ran. Halla skidded around boulders and tripped over root boles; she caught herself against the rough trunks of trees, oblivious to the patches of abraded skin these collisions caused. All the while, her mind sought the touch of the *landvættir*. Against a mammoth chestnut tree—easily a century old—she felt the fleeting sensation of pity, then silence.

The old troll-woman snarled and spat. *So be it,* she said to herself, a mantra of resolve. *So be it.* She paused a moment, panting, her breath steaming in the chill air. She scanned the ground, kicked leaves aside. There, under the mold, she saw a layer of old chestnut mast, the husks and seeds gone black with rot. She snatched up a handful of weathered chestnuts and sorted them with quick flicks of her fingers until only four remained.

Just in case, she told herself, glancing up. The top of the chestnut tree gleamed with the sun's golden light. Halla licked her lips, cursed, and pushed off the craggy trunk. As she ran, her hard thumbnail scratched a symbol in each chestnut. A rune. And she prayed to Father Ymir she had the right answer—for she could feel a heaviness spreading through her legs. Her feet tingled, and her hands felt stony and hard.

Squinting against the painful light, she could just make out the path of split logs leading to the longhouse, through the trees. She was at the edge of the bog, and the house, itself, was just *there*. Safety. Home. *So close.*

Halla forced her limbs to move faster. Her breath came in gulps and wheezes as she hopped through the cold mud to clamber onto the corduroy of logs; she struggled and limped to the base of the stairs, past half-submerged skeletons and decaying corpses, spears driven upright in the bog-filth. She clawed her way up. But as she reached the head of the stairs—just a short sprint to the open door of the longhouse—the sun crested the eastern horizon.

Its unbearable light struck her full in the face.

"Ymir!" she cried, closing her eyes against the hateful glare. "Father of Frost, let my vengeance bear fruit!" And Halla, last daughter of Járnviðja, who had tasted the songs of creation under the limitless boughs of Myrkviðr, let fall the rune-etched chestnuts she'd clutched in her palm. Tendons rasped and creaked; her spine grew rigid. Her skin took on a grayish cast, like fine granite. And soundlessly, she returned to the stone from which her kind was fashioned.

17

In the chill gloaming that presaged the dawn, a mist rose from the surface of Lake Vänern. It crawled inland, wreathing the peninsula of Hrafnhaugr in gray fleece. The fog crept along—a thousand tendrils of spectral vapor that caressed the trees and brushed the tops of the tall winter grasses. Birds raised their heads from their coverts, their voices silent. Foxes and martens peered out from thickets, ever wary. There was a curious scent on the still air. It caused the deer to pause, the boar to hunker down; it drew wolf and raven as music draws a dancer. It was the stench of iron, and with it came the promise of death.

For through the mist came the stamp of feet and the rattle of harness as Úlfrún's war-band, with Dísa in the lead, drew near the rope and timber bridge that reached across the Scar.

"These trees," Dísa heard Forne mutter as they pushed through the grove of ash and willow. "Too much cover. Give me half a day and I'd burn the lot of them."

"We may not have half a day," Úlfrún replied.

Dísa saw the spirit pole loom from the mist. Approaching, she touched its base and stopped at the head of the bridge. "No enemy of Hrafnhaugr has ever made it this far," Dísa said.

Behind her, Forne whistled. "This is more to my liking. We could exact a blood price, here. How far to the gates?"

Dísa stirred. "A couple hundred yards, perhaps. The road rises and makes three sharp turns before reaching the gate."

Forne nodded. "Look here," he said, taking Úlfrún's elbow. He pointed to the far edge of the Scar. "It's higher ground, yonder. The Christians can only cross two-abreast, *and* they have to cross up a slope. A few crossbow-men and some of Brodir's trusty lads with their axes could hold this bridge till the world burns!"

"Unless they have archers," Úlfrún replied. "With enough arrows, they could keep us pinned down until they make a bridgehead. If we can hold it with a few trusty lads, they can surely take it with a few, as well."

Forne, though, merely shrugged. "Then we build a mantlet or two. Let the crossbowmen draw their fire while Brodir's lads hack through the ropes when the bridge is loaded with hymn-singers eager to meet their god." The lean wolf-warrior craned his neck to peer over the edge of the Scar. The hiss of water greeted him, waves seething against the foot of the rocks. "That'll slow the bastards down."

Brodir came to stand alongside Dísa, his bearded face tilted back to study the top of the spirit pole. "I don't recognize him," he said, nodding to the figure carved into the apex of the pole. Dísa followed his gaze.

"The Hooded One," she replied. "Herald of the Tangled God, Father Loki. He is our protector."

"A mite full of himself, is he?"

Dísa smiled. "You have no idea."

Úlfrún spared the image atop the pole a single glance before setting out across the bridge. It swayed under the combined weight of the men filing in behind her—two abreast. Some glanced down the rocky throat of the Scar at the dark ribbon of water; others stared straight ahead, gripping the ropes with fear-whitened knuckles.

Dísa and Brodir came last. Úlfrún wasted no time. Gone was the conge-niality of the last few days; she ruled these men like the iron queen she was, self-made mistress of a roving dominion that traded in blood and death. But Dísa could sense a restless desperation running beneath her stony exterior; she'd seen its like before . . . in Halla. Úlfrún, like the troll-woman, was desperate to see the prophecy fulfilled.

Dísa kept that bit of information close to her heart as she stood by, watching Úlfrún order her troops. "Forne! Send a couple of your wolf-brothers back down the trail. I want to know when the Christians are near."

Forne nodded, motioned to a pair of dark-eyed *úlfhéðnar*. The two men retraced their steps and vanished into the thinning mist. The rim of the sun had broken over the eastern horizon. Soon, it would burn away the mist to reveal the bulk of Hrafnhaugr—now just a dark silhouette looming over the peninsula.

"Herroðr," Úlfrún continued, "detail a few lads to survey this ravine. I want to know where a sound man could cross with little help. And be mindful of its depth. Ámundi," she said, looking around. A rawboned *berserkr* stood out from the others, his wild shock of hair and his beard both a fiery red, fading to gray. "You and the others guard the high ground, here. Shields at the ready, but try to stay out of sight, for now. Don't let one shit-heeled Christian step foot on Hrafnhaugr's soil ere we're ready to greet them. Understood?"

"Aye, Jarl."

"Good. Forne, you and Brodir are with me. Dísa will lead the way. Curb your tempers! These Geats are not our enemies!" she warned, turning away. "Show us to your Hooded One and let's get the fawning over with before we're up to our arses in hymn-singers."

Dísa nodded. "Follow me."

Up they went. Thrice, the road crooked back on itself as it climbed the hill to the peninsula's flat heights, where the earth and timber walls of Hrafnhaugr perched like an uneasy crown.

"Good coverage from the towers." Forne grunted. "Provided they're well-maintained. Any rot and we might as well haul the gates open and invite the kneelers inside."

"Walk the circuit of the walls," Úlfrún said. "Find me any weak points. I want to know how long we can keep the bastards out."

"Yes, Jarl."

"Find me inside when you're done."

Dísa walked on in silence. Though she'd only been gone a few days, it felt like years since last she stood here, looking up at the towers flanking the always-open gate, at the smoldering brazier on the parapet between them. And at the cloaked figure standing watch—Kjartan, this time, if that be the flash of a gilt-edged mantle.

"Who goes?" he hollered down.

"It's Dísa," the girl replied. "I bring news, and visitors. Rouse the folk, Kjartan! Sound the alarm."

As they neared the gate, a figure shuffled from a makeshift shelter erected beneath one tower. Dísa recognized him instantly. "Jarl Hreðel," she said.

"Dísa?" he said. "Is that really you? Is that my boy you bring back with you? My Flóki?"

"Come, Jarl." Dísa gestured for him to go before her as three short horn blasts split the early morning calm. "We must see the Hooded One."

"Flóki?" Hreðel reached out to touch the giant, Brodir. "Is that you, boy?"

"Nay, Jarl," Brodir rumbled. He caught Hreðel's hand and gently looped a massive arm around his shoulder—companionable, but as good as an iron chain. "Walk with us, and tell me of your boy. Flóki, is it?"

"She was supposed to bring him back to me," Hreðel muttered. "Do you know what happened to him?"

"All will be made clear," Brodir said.

As the echo of the horn blasts faded, men half-clad in their war-rags piled into the streets, blades drawn. Their women appeared at their backs, clutching spear and shield, their faces pale with sudden fear. Children cried and dogs barked.

"I did not think your people so numerous," Úlfrún said, barely loud enough for Dísa to hear. "How many?"

"There are just shy of five hundred Raven-Geats left," Dísa replied. "Twenty-four families divided into, maybe, one hundred and fifty house-holds."

"Women and children?"

Dísa glanced sidelong at her and shrugged. "Enough, though our numbers dwindle each year."

Dísa's name ran before them like a talisman. "She's back!" men cried. "Dísa's back! But where are Flóki and the others?"

"Come! Follow! I bear ill tidings for the ears of the Hooded One," Dísa replied to every hurled question. They ascended to the second terrace, and thence to the third, where Gautheimr squatted like a mist-wreathed giant. The longhouse's doors stood open; light spilled out, and a cordon of the Jarl's sworn men awaited them out front.

White-maned Bjorn Hvítr stepped to the fore. He was resplendent in his mail hauberk, its iron links worked with bronze wire; the spear in his hand would have taxed Dísa's strength to lift, and his broad round shield bore the raven insignia of Hrafnhaugr. His gaze swept over Úlfrún to fix on Brodir. But when he spoke, he addressed himself to Dísa: "What goes, girl?"

"Stand aside," she said. "I bear news for the Hooded One."

"They must leave their weapons at the door, and wait for the Hooded One to grant their petition for an audience."

Dísa felt her choler rise. "And I said stand aside! Move, Hvítr, or I will move you!"

Bjorn Hvítr blinked at the rancor in her voice. He looked down and saw *something* in her fierce gaze that gave him pause. And that mailed giant— twice her size and thrice her bulk—did as ordered. With a nod, he stepped aside and allowed them entry into Gautheimr.

The inside of the longhouse was hot and filled with light, most of it coming from the great hearth, where a cauldron of spiced wine bubbled alongside a deer haunch, roasting on the spit. Smoke and savory spices hung in the air, competing with the reek of bodies and Grimnir's own animal stench. The Daughters of the Raven were there, armed and ready, with Sigrún and Auða at their head. The sworn men filed in after Dísa; behind them came the men and women of Hrafnhaugr.

Berkano sat at the foot of the steps leading to the Jarl's chair, a lyre forgotten in her lap. She looked from the strangers who accompanied Dísa to Grimnir. And the Hooded One did not look pleased. Dísa could tell from the way he sat: legs thrown out, black-nailed hands gripping the arms of the chair, his upper body lost in shadow—save for the gleam of his eye. It burned red with hate.

"My lord, I—"

"*Nár*, little bird!" he said, his voice a harsh rasp. "I send you out to find four wayward Geats and you return with a stunted giant and some one-handed Norse harridan? What game are you playing at?"

Dísa started to reply, but Úlfrún's hand on her shoulder brought her up short. "Three hundred stunted giants, actually," she said. She walked to the center of the space before the Jarl's seat and described a slow circle, staring at the assembled Geats. Her gaze was like frosted iron, and few could meet it for long. Even Sigrún shivered and looked away. Úlfrún ended up facing the chair; raising her head, she met that glowering stare—and felt a sensation she'd long since forgotten. She felt a tremor of fear. "And we play no games, lord of Hrafnhaugr. I have more than enough men to burn this place to the ground and salt the earth with your bones, if we were enemies."

Grimnir chuckled, a cold and humorless sound. He leaned forward, snuffling the air. "Who's to say we're not, eh? You? Who are you and why do you trespass on my lands?"

It was Dísa who piped up. "This is Úlfrún of the Iron Hand, lord," she said, gesturing to the Norsewoman. "Her companion, yonder, is Brodir. She's brought her war-band to us in our time of need."

"Our what?" Grimnir snapped. "Ymir's blood! What are you yammering on about? What *time of need*?"

"There is an army bound for Hrafnhaugr," Úlfrún said. "An army of hymn-singers, Crusaders from the Swede-lands across Lake Vänern, led by the cousin of the Swedish king—Konraðr the White, he is called, the Ghost-Wolf of Skara. They've crossed the Hveðrungr River by way of the bridge, there. And they were, at most, half a day behind us." A babble of voices broke across Gautheimr, gasps and cries, oaths of protestation and calls for blood. Úlfrún spoke over them: "Their faith drives them, but so does their greed for land and wealth! And this so-called holy army is bent on your destruction, mighty Hooded One!"

"Liar!" Sigrún said, stepping in front of the assembled Daughters. "What Norse trickery is this? You might have gulled this poor girl with your lies, but we're made from sterner stuff than she! Bring your war-band! We'll send them home with their tails—"

"My Jarl does not lie," Brodir cut in. "I've seen this army."

"So have I, *Grandmother!*" Dísa snapped. She tore the scalp from her belt and held it up for all to see. "I took this from a man of theirs, and killed another to boot! I have seen their so-called Ghost-Wolf—a Christian Witch-man, is what he is! They mean to slay us all! And they will, if we sit here bickering like children!"

"Enough!" Grimnir roared.

Gautheimr fell silent.

Harness creaked as the Hooded One leaned forward. With a curt gesture, he motioned Berkano away before crooking a finger at Dísa. The girl ascended the dais and knelt before the chair—putting her at eye level with Grimnir.

"Speak."

"What she says is true," Dísa said quietly. "I swear it. They came around the lake from the south, got provisioned at Eiðar, and made for the Horn. Flóki and the lads must have run afoul of them in Eiðar, for they tried to get ahead of them and halt their advance. Idiots tried to burn the bridge over the Hveðrungr."

Grimnir grunted. "It's a troll-bridge. It won't burn until the Gjallarhorn blows. None of them thought to send word on ahead?"

Dísa glanced sidelong to where Hreðel stood. "Flóki wanted to make his war-name."

Grimnir's good eye narrowed. "Your lad didn't make it, then?"

Dísa bit back a sob, turned it into a snarl of hate. "None of them did. The hymn-singers captured Flóki and Ulff Viðarrson. I tried to get to them, to free them." Dísa shook her head, nostrils flaring. "The Witch-man's magic was too powerful. He knew I was there."

"He knew?"

Dísa nodded. "It looked like he was listening to something only he could hear. He said the wind brought him my secrets; that he could hear my thoughts in the chirp of insects, and my dreams in the crackle of leaves. Every move I made, he was ready."

"Was he now?" Grimnir hissed. "You didn't leave your precious lad to their tender mercies, did you?"

Dísa shook her head, but then shrugged. "At first, I did. But I ran across Jarl Úlfrún and her crew shadowing the kneelers. She and her lads made a diversion while I got close enough to . . . to . . ."

"Earn your war-name?"

Dísa's jaw jutted in defiance. "That I earned when I took *this* wretch's scalp!" She shook her fist, the ribbon of hair, flesh, and dried blood still clenched in her hand. "No, they killed Ulff and crucified Flóki. I ended his suffering, is all."

Grimnir caught her by the nape of the neck and drew her close, her forehead touching the center of his wolf-mask. "Then you did right by your mate, little bird. In Hel or in Valhöll, you will see him again. Now, tell his bastard father. That dunghill rat deserves to be put out of his misery. Tell them all, Ymir be damned."

Dísa drew back. She sighed, cuffed tears from her red-rimmed eyes, and glanced full at Hreðel. "There's another thing," she said, returning her gaze to Grimnir. "Úlfrún and her lads? They know of the prophecy."

"Do they now?"

"Aye. She claims she's the she-Wolf it speaks of, and that hymn-singing bastard is the Wolf, and we're standing where they fight: in Raven's Shadow."

Grimnir nodded, his face lost in the shadows of his hood—though his gleaming eye burned even brighter as it fixed on iron-handed Úlfrún. "Tell him," he said, jerking his chin in Hreðel's direction.

"Tell me? Tell me what? Is it about my son, my precious Flóki?" The old Jarl started forward, but Brodir's restraining arm brought him up short. He glanced up into the giant *berserkr*'s kind face. "My boy is out there."

Dísa pushed off the dais, straightened, and turned to face the press of Geats—Hreðel, especially. "Hearken!" she cried over their confused babble. "Hearken! I have a tale to tell . . ."

THE REVELATION OF AN INVADING army upon their doorstep brought the folk of Hrafnhaugr together. They welcomed Úlfrún's war-band into their midst, praised them as heroes and drank to their health, even as they mourned the loss of Flóki Hreðelsson, Eirik and Ulff Viðarrson, and Sigræfr the Bastard. Pyres were built around the Raven Stone, and all four were burned in effigy.

As the pyres smoldered, the sounds of hammer and axe echoed across the village. Forne found very little wrong with the walls of Hrafnhaugr. "Solid, with little rot," he told Úlfrún. "The outer surfaces of the palisade are mossy, which will make it harder to burn. There's a postern gate in the second terrace that leads down to docks at the lake's shore. It's small, and the path leading down is narrow. The main gate, now . . . that's a problem."

But it was a problem to which Forne had a ready solution. The frozen hinges had to be worked loose, the rusted iron brackets on the inside replaced, and a heavy beam found to serve as a bar. As the two Bjorns and the giant Brodir attacked the gate's hinges with mallets and pig grease, Kjartan fired up his forge. Under Forne's watchful eye, he hammered out the heavy brackets and forged nails from a supply of scrap iron. It was Old Hygge who suggested they make a beam from four weathered ship's masts, bound together with the iron hoops of broken barrels.

And while the gate was being seen to, Sigrún and Auða took stock of the armory. They sent buckets of javelins and sheaves of arrows to the towers along the wall, while Geira strung and tested the score of bows they possessed—all made from good yew, with bone nocks and cords of waxed hemp. They checked every ring of mail for rust, every shield they scrutinized for signs of rot or warping; Auða herself sharpened every spear and axe head, checked that they weren't loose in the socket or on the haft, and eyed the iron straps that protected the wood from the clash of battle.

As the morning wore on, the Daughters of the Raven distributed arms and armor to every man or woman in the village: a steel-and-leather cap, shield, and spear at the least. Most had their own arms—hauberks passed down from father to son; swords of ancient pattern with their lineages written in blood; axes that bore storied names, such as Ivar's Bane or the Dane-Hewer. Even those men not counted among Gautheimr's household troops—the Jarl's sworn men—turned out when the horns sounded assembly. Hreðel stood among them, sandwiched between Hrútr and Askr. The old Jarl wore no mail; bare-chested, his shoulders draped in a bearskin cloak and a sheathed sword cradled in his arms, he stared with red-rimmed eyes through a mask of ashes and cinder as Grimnir emerged from the longhouse.

The Hooded One was full of swagger. His mask half-raised, he peeled the flesh from a rib of venison, tossed the bone aside, and accepted a goblet of wine from the ever-attentive Berkano. This, he dashed off with lip-smacking relish before turning his eye on the assembly of Hrafnhaugr's warriors. He squinted up at the sun, its wan light shrouded by a pall of clouds.

"*Faugh!*" he said, his harsh voice like the grating of stones. "You expect me to raise your spirits? Get your dander up and send you off to the walls or to the bridge with a fiery speech about hope and victory? You got another thing coming, then!" Work around them stopped. The Daughters of the Raven, gleaming now in war-garb of steel and iron, joined with the press of men. Women from the lower terrace, shields and spears at the ready, elbowed in closer. Even the children, who'd been given javelins and small shields, bit their trembling lips and fell silent.

Dísa watched from the eaves of Gautheimr as Grimnir descended the steps. "What are you lot going to do with *hope*, eh? You can't eat it. You can't drink it. Will this hope you crave keep the spear from your gullet or the axe from your precious skull? Ha! Forget hope." Grimnir snarled and spat. "Hope is for fools. Hope is for *them*! For those soft-bellied hymn-singers who yap and whine at our door. Let them worry what tomorrow brings. Not you louts. *Nár!* You are sons and daughters of the Old Ways. Your fates are written; the Norns have spun, measured, and cut the threads of your lives. It doesn't matter if we die today, or a thousand days from today. We all die! Die in glory, you wretched bastards! Die wrapped in your foeman's embrace, your blade snuffing out his life as his pierces your heart! Die in blood, screaming at your ancestors to bear witness. Make the Choosers of the Slain weep when they come to haul your soul off to Valhöll!"

The sworn men stamped their feet, clashed spear and shield, creating a din like the thunder of steel-shod hooves. The others joined in, singly and in pairs, and the Daughters added their voices in ululating shrieks, like the deep and throaty *kraa* of their namesake, the raven. Even the children—who knew nothing of the Norns and the doom they wove for every mortal—howled like young wolves and brandished their javelins.

Grimnir strode to where Hreðel stood. "These are your swine, you wretch," he said. "You don't deserve them, but they have bled with you, and they will bleed with you again. Take them! To the wall, to the bridge, or to Hel's black hall, I care not!"

"For Flóki!" Hreðel roared.

And from four hundred throats came an answering cry: *"For vengeance!"*

AS HREÐEL ISSUED COMMANDS AND set his warriors to their posts to await the hymn-singers' onslaught, Grimnir turned and stalked back up the steps to the doors of Gautheimr. Berkano started to follow, but he waved her off. The woman bit her lip and backed away, stamping her foot in childlike petulance when he made no move to stop Dísa from joining him inside.

"What now?" Dísa said. Grimnir made no reply, though his irritation was evident from the tightness of his shoulders. He crossed the hall, ascended the dais, and sprawled across the Jarl's seat.

"Fetch me a goblet of wine." He waved her toward the hearth.

Dísa grunted. Nevertheless, she cast about; her eyes lit on a discarded horn goblet. She grabbed it up, slung the old lees from it, and dipped out a measure of spiced wine from the cauldron.

"Water won't be a problem, since our wells draw up from Lake Vänern," she said, handing the goblet to him. "But we only have perhaps a fortnight's worth of food in the larders, and that's if we practice strict rationing."

Grimnir raised his mask again, and drank the wine in three swallows. "Let them eat like kings! In a few days, none of this will matter."

"How long do we have?" Dísa recalled the dream she'd had her first night on the Horn, the dream of . . . *smoke and ash and the heat of crackling flames; it is familiar, if not comforting. Her mail is in tatters, but her limbs are no longer heavy with exhaustion . . .*

"Three days, four," Grimnir said. "We'll know when the seas boil and the earth splits asunder. That wretched wyrm's barrow will rise from the belly of Skærvík, and that sly one-eyed bastard will think he's getting the instrument of his revenge. He's in for a surprise!"

"What will Hrafnhaugr get?" Dísa said quietly.

Grimnir glanced sharply at her. He knew what she was asking: what would become of them? What would happen to their homes, to their lands, once this struggle reached its culmination? "Like I said, little bird . . . hope is for fools. Let them fight like gods of war by day, and feast like the hallowed dead by night. That is the best I can offer them."

"And what about me?"

"What about you?"

She turned away, her face to the hearth. "I watched Ulff die choking on his own blood, unable to fight back. I watched Flóki die helpless on a hymn-singers' cross, his courage be damned." She drew a long, shuddering breath. "I want your word, Grimnir. Your oath that you won't let me die screaming in a cloud of that wyrm's poisoned vapor, or crushed under its foot like I mean nothing. Let me die cleanly, blade in hand, against a foe worthy of the name." She looked to him. "Promise me a good death."

For a moment, Grimnir said nothing. He stared hard at the girl, his good eye ablaze under the shadow of his mask. Then, without pause, he pulled it off so she might see his face. Grimnir rose, descended the dais, and stood before her. Steel rasped as he drew his seax. He extended his off hand; fist clenched, he bared the underside of that arm. Grimnir nodded for her to do the same.

"I give you my oath, little bird," he said, gouging a furrow in the base of his hand. Black blood welled, and from it the stench of wet and salty iron.

Dísa emulated the gesture, her blood as rich and red as dyer's madder. She winced as he grasped her hand in his, wrist to wrist so that their blood would mingle. "You will die a *kaunr*'s death." He dragged her close, his breath reeking of wine. "But until that day comes, make sure you earn it!"

BERKANO LEFT THE STEPS OF Gautheimr and drifted down to the second terrace, where Geira and the youngest of the Daughters were busy erecting a surgery not far from the village's central well. She kept back, watching Geira direct their efforts with the efficiency of a seasoned campaigner. She reminded Berkano of her and Laufeya's mother—hard around the edges, but with kind eyes and a voice that could spin a yarn or sing a lullaby. Berkano suddenly longed to be one of those girls again. She longed to have a purpose. The Daughters of the Raven, she was sure, would not have succumbed to Örm of the Axe. They would not be afraid.

Two men brought baskets of dried herbs to the growing field hospital, while another pair rolled in a barrel of wine vinegar. Geira motioned a pair of the Daughters over and bid them separate and bunch the herbs. The two girls ambled over, looked at the baskets—with their profusion of dried petals and stems, roots and stalks—before looking at one another. Shrugging, they started in by grabbing handfuls, squeezing them together, and lashing them with twine.

"No, no," Berkano sang softly, rising from the well's kerb. "You're mixing your mayweed with your vervain." The girls looked up at her; their hands hovered over dried stems. Berkano nodded, her red hair lashing about her face like a tangled veil. "That one. That's vervain. Find all the ones that look like that and bundle them together—but not too tightly! It's best not to bruise the leaves until you're ready to steep them in wine."

Berkano crept closer until she was kneeling on the other side of the baskets from the girls. They were giggling together when Geira's ears pricked up. She turned from cutting lengths of linen into bandages and caught sight of Berkano directing the girls' efforts. The older woman smiled. "I've been looking for you, dear," Geira said. Berkano stiffened; she shot to her feet like a thief who'd been caught with her hands in the coffer. Geira's laugh put her at ease. She took Berkano by the elbow and guided her to the center of the makeshift surgery. "Can I trust you to order and make ready our supply of herbs and medicinals?"

"You . . . you want me to do this?"

Geira smiled. "Are you not herb-wise? Come, this is a task made for you. I am needed elsewhere, but I cannot leave these children without someone to watch over them. Can you do it?"

"Can . . . Can I cut bandages, too?"

"As many as you like," Geira replied.

Berkano's smile beamed like a shard of sunlight. She took Geira's apron and her cutting knife, and shooed her away.

"Come, flowers!" Berkano's singsong voice embraced the young Daughters of the Raven, most of whom had the look of frightened rabbits about them. "Come! Fetch fire, dear Bryngerðr. We must boil water, for hot water is the source of all that is good in the world! Una, that's burdock root, not vervain! Come, come!"

And this is how Laufeya found her, half an hour later: on her knees, surrounded by children, singing an old herb-woman's song extolling the virtues of the opium poppy on a world-weary soldier as they cut long strips of linen.

"Berkano," Laufeya hissed. The younger of the two Otter-Geats was clad in her traveling cloak; she had a bag under one arm, and in the other she carried Berkano's belongings.

"Feya!" Berkano said brightly. "Come, join us. We're about to make poppy poultices." She hopped to her feet and tried to coax Laufeya to follow her.

But Laufeya, dour and stern though she was ten years Berkano's junior, caught her sister by the wrist and dragged her away from the children. Laufeya's voice was like a serpent's hiss. "What are you doing? I've been looking all over for you!"

"Geira asked me to help."

Laufeya shook her head. "There's no time," she said. "We've got to be away from here."

"Who says?"

"I say!" Laufeya snapped. "We're heading north, around the lake shore. Kjartan told me there's a little market-town up in that direction. Tingvalla, he called it. We're going there, and he's going to join us, if he can. Here, take your things."

Berkano looked hurt. She made no move to take the bundle from Laufeya's hand. "We can't go. They need us here."

"Bollocks!" Laufeya spat. "Did you not hear what was said? The Nailed God's folk are coming, sister. Coming here! Remember what they did to our village? What they did to you and me? What they did to Mother? We've got to skin out now, while there's still time. Quit dawdling and let's go!"

Berkano stared down at the scalp hanging from the girdle of her skirt, and then shifted her gaze to the children who were waiting for her. She saw her own fear reflected in their eyes. She saw it, and she hated herself for it. "No," Berkano said, wrenching her hand from Laufeya's grasp. "This is our home now. We're not running away."

Laufeya leaned close to her and snatched a handful of the arm of her tunic. "Do you remember what they did to you, sister? How man after man had his way with you? Do you remember their reek? Because I do! I swore I'd never let that happen again!"

"I remember, Feya." Berkano raised her eyes and met Laufeya's pitiless gaze. "But I don't want *them* to have such a memory." She gestured over her shoulder at the young faces watching them, wondering what the sisters argued about. "I'm done running. I have no more fear of the Örms lurking out there. Let them do their worst to me if it spares just one of these flowers the same fate. You go, if you must. Find a home where you can feel safe, like we felt safe with Mama. I've found mine. I'm staying."

"Hel take you, then!" Laufeya spat, tears welling in her eyes. She turned away and stalked toward the postern gate. She felt their eyes on her—Berkano and those insipid child-warriors, the so-called Daughters of the Raven. Laufeya swore and spat. "Hel take all of you!" She knew the man on guard at the gate. He was a good man; a few tears, a tale of shame and degradation, and he'd let her slip out . . .

Why wasn't she moving then? Laufeya had stopped. She wiped her nose on her sleeve. She should go. She needed to go. The gate was *right* there! A few days' journey and she'd be somewhere new, somewhere she could start over—pose as a hymn-singer, maybe, or . . . or . . . she struggled to find an answer. But she knew the answer. She'd be alone.

Laufeya stiffened as Berkano draped an arm around her shoulder, drew her into an embrace. "This is our home now, Feya," she whispered. "I know you're afraid. So am I. But we're home." Berkano pressed her scalp into Laufeya's hand, a totem to ward off evil. The younger sister looked down at it, then met Berkano's soft gaze. She saw steel in her older sister's eyes.

Unbreakable. Unyielding. "If it comes to that," Berkano said. "I won't let Örm lay a hand on you, not this time."

Laufeya sighed. She looked once more at the postern gate. There was a rack of spears beside it, and shields. "I need a blade," she said, wiping her eyes. "If we're going to die here, I want to line our way to the meadows of Fólkvangr with the heads of Cross-men . . ."

18

The day crept by, waning into afternoon, and still there was no sign of the Crusader army. Men chafed and fretted, starting at every sound they heard from beyond the walls; women's tempers grew short as their minds wandered down dark corridors—imagining the rapine and slaughter that was to come and building it into something far worse. Even the children fussed and whined, with the youngest squirming to be let loose and the oldest experiencing that stifling sense of boredom that ran hand in hand with the first caress of mortality. Only the elders remained serene, the crones and the graybeards. Sigrún hummed a tune as she busied herself with a whetstone and her sword; Old Hygge dozed in a chair in the shadow of Gautheimr.

Dísa walked the parapet of the landward palisade. A chill breeze blew down from the north, stirring her lank hair and causing her beads and bone fetishes to click together. Out beyond the Scar, she could glimpse fallow fields among the tangled forest. The roofs of outlying farms, abandoned now, in the face of the Christian threat, still poked above the canopy—though she knew they'd become the first casualties of this invasion when the hymn-singers set fire to them.

Some of the farmers who worked those steadings stood now, with Jarl Hreðel at the bridge. The man's heartsickness and dithering had vanished; from the ashes of Flóki's effigy pyre had risen the Hreðel of old—vicious and driven. He'd given away his mail, added his sword to the pile of those held in reserve, and opted only for a shield and an axe. The shield's face he'd daubed black with ashes from the pyre—same as his face—with Flóki's name written in white.

"That's a man who is ready to die," Úlfrún said, approaching from Dísa's left. She saw the intensity of the younger girl's stare and followed it, taking in the grim silhouette that stood a dozen paces out on the gently swaying bridge, motionless and unyielding.

"He has nothing left. Nothing but his life," Dísa replied.

"You admire him."

Dísa thought about it for a moment. "I guess I do. He loves—loved—his son more than he loves himself. He would have traded his life for Flóki's, without giving it a second thought. Now, he'll give his life to avenge him. I wonder if Flóki knew the depths of his father's love . . ."

"What you take as love smacks to me of need," Úlfrún said. "He strikes me as a man who needed to live through his son, who saw himself in Flóki's eyes, and saw in Flóki a chance to right the wrongs of his own youth. Granted, I don't know him like you do."

"But that sounds like him." Dísa's lips thinned to white lines of disdain. "I'm ever the foolish girl."

"And that sounds like your grandmother, speaking her tripe through you," Úlfrún said. Dísa *harrumphed*. "You doubt me? I know of very few fools able to do what you've done. Oh, your cousin, Auða, has told me a tale or two, and I know what I've seen with my own eyes. You're no fool, Dísa Dagrúnsdottir, and whoever discounts you as merely a girl is not long for this earth."

Weaned on a diet of harsh words and harsher blows, hearing praise from one such as Úlfrún left Dísa scarlet to the ears. She ducked her head, muttered something that might have been a word of thanks, and then lifted her gaze to watch the forest with renewed intensity. Úlfrún studied her a moment longer, a smile flirting at the corners of her hard-lipped mouth, before peering with her at the land beyond the village walls.

"I thought they were biting at our heels," Dísa said after a moment, frustration heavy in her voice. "Where are they?"

"Eager to come to grips?"

The younger woman gave a small laugh. "Eager to get what's to come over with. Eager for that white bastard to show himself. I fear he's up to some deviltry. Does the waiting not gnaw at you?"

"Child," Úlfrún replied. "I have been waiting for *this* since before you, your mother, and your mother's mother were born. Waiting a few hours more?" She made a dismissive noise.

Dísa glanced sidelong at the older woman, who absently rubbed the knuckles of her iron fist. She could not reckon her age, for though she had strands of silver and gray woven through her ash-blond hair, and though she had more scars than wrinkles, Úlfrún's eyes yet gleamed with the light of youth. Could she really be older than Sigrún? No, Dísa laughed to herself. There was no way. Úlfrún spoke with the truth of poets, is all.

"What happened to it? Your hand, I mean," Dísa said, after a long pause. She inclined her head at the iron weight at the end of Úlfrún's forearm. This close, she could see runes and sigils etched into the surface of the metal; the limb had carved fingers and tendons, and old scars across the heavy knuckles. Úlfrún rapped it twice against the palisade. It struck and bounced with a dull *thock-thock*.

"I made a bargain I shouldn't have," Úlfrún said, finally. "This was the price I paid."

Dísa took the hint and dropped the matter.

"Do you think they'll come today?" she asked.

Úlfrún considered the sky, the position of the sun. "I think the Ghost-Wolf is cautious, taking his time, drawing this out. I don't think this Christian host will come until its lord has his plans laid, and not a moment before."

"Then you'd be a fool, wouldn't you?" Grimnir's harsh voice snarled from Dísa's right. Neither woman had heard his approach. He did not look at either of them; he kept his attention fixed on the belt of woods beyond the Scar. He snuffled the air, nostrils flaring, and Dísa knew he smelled something beyond what she—or Úlfrún—could scent.

"This is your little pond, *Froskr dróttin*." (*Frog-lord*, Dísa would snigger to Auða, later that evening. *She called him Frog-lord*.) "And I will accept a measure of your bile," Úlfrún growled. She turned, her cold blue eyes gleaming with the icy promise of murder. "But insult me one more time . . ."

"It's not an insult if it's true. Tell her, little bird."

Úlfrún took a menacing step toward Grimnir, but Dísa put herself between them. "What do you mean, lord?"

"You can't smell it, can you?" He tilted his head back, eye screwed tight against the sun's pale glare, and inhaled deeply of the crisp air. "Your little war's started, first blood's been claimed, and here you two stand like hens come to roost."

Dísa turned and glanced over the palisade. She could see no sign of an enemy. "What do you smell?"

"Death," Grimnir hissed. "Your Witch-man is a wily bastard. He and his rabble of kneelers and cross-kissers have sneaked up on us. Your two lads? Your so-called scouts?" Grimnir dragged a thumb across his throat. "And by the looks of it, you're about to lose a third."

Úlfrún, fuming, followed Grimnir's gesture. She saw Forne. He passed Hreðel, heading out to check on his wolf-brothers. The older woman drew a deep breath, put her thumb and forefinger in her mouth, and loosed an ear-splitting whistle. Dísa winced; Grimnir snarled and shied away. Down on the bridge, Forne heard it and turned. He looked up, eyes raking the top of the palisade until he spotted Úlfrún, who crossed her arms over her head.

Whatever message it was the gesture conveyed, Forne understood. He retraced his steps. As he drew abreast of Hreðel, he paused long enough to mutter a word. The old Jarl nodded.

"What do we do?" Dísa asked. She fairly vibrated with pent-up anticipation. Her hand cupped the pommel of her seax, caressed the hilt like she would a lover. "Should we form a shield wall? Prepare to defend the bridge?"

Grimnir chuckled. "Ready to wade into the scrum, little bird? *Nár!* For now, we do nothing."

"Nothing?" Frustration drove Dísa's voice up an octave. She turned, looking to Úlfrún for support. The older woman, though, grudgingly nodded.

Grimnir's fingers dug into the back of her neck, bringing her face back around to him. He pulled her close. "*Nothing!* Bastard thinks he's sly. Bastard thinks he's gotten one over on us. Bah! Now, he's going to spend the night trying to find a weak spot from the *other* side of the Scar while we warm our feet by the fire, have meat and wine, and you lot get a good night's rest. Let your Witch-man have the cold and the muck!"

"He's down there, then?" Úlfrún said.

Grimnir shrugged.

"Let's see if he is." Úlfrún leaned out over the village side of the palisade and bellowed: "Herroðr, fetch me Skaðmaðr!"

THE SHARP WHISTLE ECHOED EVEN among the trees. Under those eaves, under naked boughs and the thickly bristling branches of evergreens, two dead wolf-brothers lay steeping in their own gore. One died after an arrow pierced his throat and drove out the back of his neck; the other died as he turned to warn his mates on the bridge beyond the trees, his skull-split corpse still clutching a heathen's horn carved with runes of protection. The eerie whistle brought the Crusader vanguard to a halt.

These were Arngrim's men, rangers and sappers, engineers who bore the scars of Outremer on their sun-browned hides. Clad in brown wool and soft leather, their cloaks festooned with bits of bracken and fir, they daubed their faces with slashes of cinder and ash and kept to the shadows.

Arngrim was a measured and deliberate captain; Lord Konraðr wanted hard information—enemy troop disposition, fortification strengths and weaknesses, an idea of how the land might lie. Rather than undertake a reckless assault on the bridge, he instead tasked Arngrim with finding other ways across this accursed ravine. And Arngrim's mind, ever inventive, was looking for ways to bypass the bridge altogether. "Too narrow," he hissed to his adjutant, a stocky Dane men dubbed *Pétr*, the Rock. Pétr kept a waxed board and a stylus on his person, and onto this he'd transcribe his captain's thoughts in pidgin Greek. "We need to breach the ravine in multiple locations, make the heathen dogs work to defend it. Nay, friend. We cross there," Arngrim nodded to the bridge, "and we're two ropes and four axe blows away from the grave."

Pétr chewed the end of his stylus. "How?"

"We need to build a drawbridge," Arngrim said. He smoothed his beard, lost in thought. The engineer looked from the short Dane to the ravine and back again. "Wheeled drawbridges. Two of them. And two covered galleries, in case the heathens have any surprises for us."

Nodding, Pétr made a note on his waxed board. "The farms hereabout. We could dismantle them. Use the wood for frames and the wattle for cover?"

"Aye," Arngrim said. "That might do the trick. If the heathens try to fire them?"

"Wet hides?"

"Shingles of green wood might be easier."

"Agreed."

Both men paused as a third crouch-walked over to join them. From under his hood, pulled low, they caught the flash of pale white skin and milky hair. Red eyes glinted in the light of the afternoon sun.

"Lord Konraðr," Arngrim said, nodding.

"Have you found a way across this devil's chasm, my friend?" The albino lord of Skara peered at the narrow bridge, his head cocked as he seemingly listened to the rattle of limbs or the moaning wind.

"Drawbridges, lord," Arngrim replied. "We—"

A scowl creased Konraðr's pale forehead as he motioned the dwarfish Dane to silence. "They . . . they know we're here. They know their heathen brothers are dead," Konraðr said. He glared at the top of the palisade. "The she-Wolf, and my little bird . . . and someone else . . ." The lord of Skara glanced around him, as though he could see something taking place that they could not. "Why do you run?"

"Lord?" Arngrim touched Konraðr's arm. "We remain here, by your side. Perhaps you should return to Father Nikulas and leave this bit of drudgery to us."

Konraðr brushed away his captain's hand and looked him square in the eye. "Does *skrælingr* mean anything to you?"

Arngrim shook his head. "No. Pétr?"

The Dane shuddered. To Arngrim's eye, the smaller man looked as though the Devil had just trod across his grave. "Th-that word is accursed," Pétr said, making the sign of the Cross. "It signifies a creature of the Enemy! A monster—"

It was a simple thing, really. A simple thing—the flash of pale sunlight on metal—that caught Arngrim's eye; the rest lived in that intersection between experience and gut instinct. His brain wasted a fraction of a heartbeat in parsing what it was he saw: his lord rising from cover, drawn by Pétr's cryptic words; a flash from atop the palisade. His head told him it was an impossible shot to make with a crossbow, but his gut . . . instincts honed on the killing fields of Palestine drove muscle and sinew to act. Without so much as a shouted warning, Arngrim lunged for the lord of Skara . . .

And grasped only empty air.

KONRAÐR THE WHITE HAD HIS own instincts—instinct that reached out from beyond the grave to warn him of impending doom. In his mind, he heard the cacophony of ghosts, their myriad voices forming a single word of warning: *Beware!* Konraðr ducked and rolled forward into a crouch. His shield came up, and he seized Pétr by the collar of his tunic, hauling him into its shadow. The lord of Skara heard the wet crunch of bone, a gurgling cry, the heavy thud of a body . . . and the splintering of wood as a steel-tipped bolt split the boards of his shield and stopped a hand-span from his pale face. Blood dripped from the head of the dart.

"Merciful Christ!"

"Are you injured, lord?"

"Nay, good Pétr," Konraðr replied. He cast a glance over the rim of his shield, and cursed. Arngrim lay on his belly in the space Konraðr had just quitted, his head an island in a spreading pool of gore. The bolt lodged now in Konraðr's shield had first entered the back of Arngrim's skull and exited through his right cheekbone where it met the eye socket.

That eye, glazed and lifeless, stared up at the lord of Skara.

And as Pétr scrambled past and fell to his knees at his dead captain's side; as rangers converged on their position, blades drawn and arrows on the nock, Konraðr felt a new spirit move through the periphery of his vision.

"My old friend," he said quietly. The wraith turned and stared at him, his spectral gaze brimming with impatience. "You are right, as always." Konraðr surged to his feet. Roaring, he slung his riven shield away and drew his sword. "Up, lads! On your feet! These heathen bastards know we're here, so why slink and scurry? Up! Throw off those cloaks and let them see the divine cross stitched into every breast! Do it!" Konraðr snatched off his own cloak. He stalked back to where Arngrim lay, drove his sword into the ground so that the hilt formed the shadow of a crucifix on the corpse of his captain of engineers. His cloak he draped over Arn-grim's body. "Pétr," he said, motioning to a pair of nearby rangers. "These lads will get him back to the rear and entrust him to Father Nikulas." Pétr rocked back on his haunches. "I want you to get me over that cursed ravine. Can you do it?"

Pétr watched the two rangers gather Arngrim's limp form. Absently, he nodded. "Drawbridges," he said. "Two of them, he wanted."

Konraðr hauled the squat Dane to his feet. "Then build them, by God! Take all you need save time, good Pétr. I want them ready by sunrise."

The Dane rubbed his chin, and then nodded. The gesture was like striking flint to steel—it kindled a fierce light in the Rock's eyes. "Two teams, two hundred men on each. We will need axes and adzes, hammers. The forge needs to be up and running, to make nails."

"Go!" Konraðr sent the man on his way. "Sound your horns, lads! Send for my dogs of war, Thorwald and that pirate, Kraki! Summon Starkad and his noble thanes! It's time these wretched heathens see the extent of their doom!"

A dozen and more horns howled their anger into the afternoon sky.

"THAT GOT THEIR ATTENTION," ÚLFRÚN said, handing her silver-chased crossbow back to her man, Herroðr.

"And ours," Dísa replied. She glanced over her shoulder as a clamor arose inside Hrafnhaugr's walls. The sudden cacophony raised by the enemy brought villagers pouring into the streets. Men and women in their war-rags hustled to their mustering points amid the jangle of harness and the clatter of shields. A cadre of older women took the children under their wings and herded them from the lowest terrace, up to where they would shelter beneath the eaves of Gautheimr under Old Hygge's watchful eye. "How long will we keep the gate open?" Dísa said.

"Until the hymn-singers breach the ravine, at least," replied Úlfrún. Bjorn Hvítr had command of the gate, with its repaired hinges and iron-bound bar ready to fall into its new-forged brackets; just outside the gate, Brodir commanded the reserve: half the *berserkir* and half the *úlfhéðnar*, men of the Bear and of the Wolf; the rest were stationed at the bridge with Forne as their captain, alongside Bjorn Svarti and the sworn men. And Jarl Hreðel.

"What's this idiot doing?" Grimnir said, leaning out over the palisade to get a better look.

Hreðel was on the move. Alone. No man tried to stop him as he strode to the center of the bridge, well within bow shot of the enemy, and thrice clashed the haft of his axe against his shield. His voice rang clear as a church bell. "Konraðr the White!" he bellowed. "Konraðr the White! Come out, you son of a Swedish harlot! Come out and face me! *Sansorðinn,* I name you! Craven mare with a thousand riders! Come out!"

The echo faded away; silence fell. And on the far side of the bridge, Konraðr the White emerged from the trees. Grimnir eyed him closely. He saw a tall man with skin and hair both as white as mountain ice. But even at this distance Grimnir could see there was something not quite right—a distortion in the air around him, too faint for the human eye. "Little bird," Grimnir muttered. "You say he knows things he should not? That he seemed to listen to something on the wind?"

"Yes," Dísa replied. "Why?"

But Grimnir did not reply. His eye blazed with new-kindled wrath.

Below, Konraðr walked to the head of the bridge. He peered up at the spirit pole, a look of disdain creasing his broad forehead. "What hurt have I done you, old man?" he shouted.

"You killed my son!"

"I've killed many sons! What of it?" Then, the lord of Skara cocked his head to one side. Grimnir saw the distortion agitate. "You are . . . Hreðel. Poor Flóki was your son? Alas, I did not kill him!"

"You nailed him to a cross, you milk-colored sodomite!"

"And I gave him a good Christian burial after that vicious little whore Dísa Dagrúnsdottir put an arrow through his head! Did you call her out? Insult her? Offer violence upon her? No! When you've done *that,* Hreðel Kveldúlfsson, then seek me out and we will settle our grievances!" Konraðr turned.

"Coward!" Hreðel roared. "Trembler! I piss on your god, hymn-singer! I shit on your god! His love makes a woman out of you! Call down your Christ! Summon him from his whore's-nest in the sky, craven! Maybe he will face me, though more like he'll also turn his back and offer me his arse for a buggering!"

Laughter spread along the allied lines, from where they stood drawn up by the bridge. As word of what was said spread into the streets, the laughter redoubled. Men hooted and catcalled. Horns brayed, a chuckling tune like the mirth of giants.

Konraðr stopped.

Slowly, he turned back to face Hreðel. The lord of *Ska-ra* bared his teeth in a feral grin, his eyes black sockets that gleamed with red points of light. He unbuckled his sheathed sword, stripped off his gambeson and his tunic underneath until he stood as bare-chested as Hreðel. The scars etching his torso looked like eerie writing—a Witch-man's runes carved in flesh. Konraðr motioned to one of his men, who passed him a round shield and bearded axe with a long, flared head.

From the enemy side of the bridge, a chant went up. *"Ska-ra! Ska-ra!"* Spears clashed on shields, keeping time. *"Ska-ra! Ska-ra!"*

Amid the tumult, Konraðr said something to his men. A few of them, giant Danes with two-handed axes, came out from the shelter of the woods. Groans and cries arose from the walls of Hrafnhaugr as, with zealous fervor, these men laid in to the spirit pole of their ancestors. Wood chips flew; in short order they'd hacked down the heathen symbol. Konraðr nodded. With their help, he rolled the pole into the ravine.

Another warrior came forth with a cross made from two hastily lashed-together spear shafts.

Konraðr knelt a moment, lips moving as he muttered a prayer. Then, making the sign of the Cross, he rose to his feet and clashed his axe against the face of his shield.

"Ska-ra! Ska-ra!"

And like his namesake, the Ghost-Wolf came for his prey.

There was no bluster or bravado; no more taunts spilled from either man's lips—only hissing breath and creaking rope as they closed the interval and came to grips. Hreðel moved his weight from foot to foot, causing the bridge to sway. The boards groaned in protest; older boards popped and cracked, but Konraðr paid no heed.

"Flóki!" Hreðel yelled, and sprang at the lord of Skara with all the reckless courage of a Geat. Shields crashed and grated; Hreðel jabbed at Konraðr's eyes with the horn of his axe, then reeled sideways as the albino's counter caught his shield's edge and hacked a divot from the ash-daubed linden wood.

Hreðel whistled a curse through clenched teeth. He rebounded off the ropes. Wooden axe-hafts clacked as they traded blows—strike, parry, and riposte. Konraðr punched out with the iron-banded edge of his shield, driving it like a battering ram into the center boss of Hreðel's.

Back, the old Jarl staggered.

Konraðr gave him no respite. His axe darted; he hooked the left edge of Hreðel's shield with the beard of his axe and hauled it to the right, exposing the older man's left side. Again, he punched out with the rim of his own shield. This time, bone splintered as he drove it edge-on into the joint of Hreðel's shoulder, and then into his ribs.

The older man bellowed like a wounded ox. The quick, successive blows dropped him to one knee; a bloody froth sprayed from over his beard as he struggled to get his shield up and into a defensive position. The broken shoulder and ribs hampered him from bringing his axe back into play. Konraðr loomed over him.

Groans and cries went up from the allied lines. Atop the wall, Grimnir heard Dísa curse; Úlfrún said nothing. The slow, disappointed shake of her head was comment enough. From across the ravine, a clamor arose—shrieks and howls and clashing harness. Cries of *"SKA-RA! SKA-RA!"*

"Kristr á yðr alla!" the Ghost-Wolf snarled. *"Christ owns you all!"*

Before Hreðel could rise, Konraðr's axe crashed down into the juncture of the old Jarl's neck. Blood jetted as the steel blade crunched through muscle, sinew, and bone. Hreðel made a gurgling cry. His axe fell from nerveless fingers, clattered to the boards and slipped between them. The old man sagged against the ropes and sought to stem the tide of blood pumping through his fingers.

Konraðr shrugged free of his shield. He seized Hreðel Kveldúlfsson by the lank handful of hair left to him, wrenched him up, and struck again. Blood spattered the albino's milky chest. A third blow fell, and the old Jarl's head came free in a rain of gore, trailing ragged flesh and marrow-leaking vertebrae.

"Do you hear me?" Konraðr roared. His eerie red eyes flashed as he stepped over the old Jarl's headless corpse. He raised his prize. Blood spattered his arm, flecked his pale face and hair. He strode toward the line of Geats—standing now in stunned silence. At twenty yards, he stopped. With an explosive grunt, he slung Hreðel's severed head over the line of Geats. "Christ owns you all!"

For a long moment, the tableau held. Konraðr stared at the assembled Geats, who stared back in silence. Finally, he ducked his head and spat, and began to turn away.

"Wait!" a deep voice called out. Konraðr turned as a giant of a man stepped out from the enemy line. He was dark haired, and in his hands he cradled a long-hafted axe. It was Bjorn Svarti. "This Christ of yours," he said. "I'm told he practiced a type of sorcery. That he could walk on water. Is this true?"

"He was a worker of miracles," Konraðr replied truculently.

"Miracles, aye." Bjorn Svarti nodded. "But could he fly, you white-skinned whoreson?" And with an explosive curse, Svarti pivoted, raised his axe, and brought it down on the rope lashings that anchored the bridge.

Hemp parted; boards trembled.

"Run! Dog!" With each word, Svarti struck the anchor logs. The Geats cheered. Another axe-man attacked the other pole.

And Konraðr the White, Ghost-Wolf of Skara, turned and leapt over Hreðel's fallen body . . . and ran. He could feel every juddering axe blow. The ropes grew loose; the boards began to slip from their moorings. From the Crusader side of the ravine, arrows lofted skyward as archers tried to pick off the axe-wielding Geats; men roared and cursed.

Ten paces from safety, Konraðr felt the left side of the bridge give way. He threw himself forward, wrapping his right arm in the tangle of ropes as the right side of the bridge collapsed. The whole thing fell beneath him. Konraðr plummeted, breath *whuffing* from his lungs as he slammed into the wall of the ravine. He hung there a moment only, before dozens of hands pulled him to safety.

ATOP THE PALISADE GRIMNIR DOUBLED over, roaring with laughter. It was a rare thing for the humor of men to strike him as funny, and rarer still for the reverse to be true. The gallows' humor of the *kaunar*? *Nár!* Too unsettling for the likes of these piss-blooded whiteskins. Too coarse. They took their jibes and japes with civilized airs now, as stiff-necked and gelded as the hymn-singers' priests.

But that? Grimnir straightened. That was a choice bit of mockery. Dísa glanced at him, eyebrows raised in a quizzical expression. On her other side, the wolf-woman, Úlfrún, chuckled as she shook her head. She clapped a hand on Dísa's shoulder, nodded to Grimnir, and walked away. With the bridge suddenly no longer part of the defensive equation, she would doubt-less rejigger the order of battle. Bah! Let her! He had a different kettle of fish to boil.

"What?" Dísa said as his chortling ceased as quickly as it had began.

"You did not see it, did you, eh, little bird?"

"See what?"

Grimnir *chk-chk*'d his teeth. "Something protects your Witch-man, and it's not the power of his beloved Christ! It's something of our world. Something old . . ."

"I knew it!" Dísa hissed; she raised her head and peered over the palisade, looking for some glimpse of what it might be. "What can we do?"

Grimnir caught her arm and hauled her close. "First, keep your tongue between your teeth! Tell no one, not even your precious Úlfrún. I trust that one about as far as I can throw her." Dísa nodded. "Then, after these other louts have gone off to sleep, meet me by the postern gate. If we can get Halla in sniffing distance, that old hag will have an answer."

19

The Crusaders made their camp half a mile from the ravine, at the edge of a fallow field. Here, amid the stubble of last year's barley, sprang a city of tents, with well-ordered avenues and cross-streets, plazas where cook fires blazed, and alleys that led to earth-cut privies. At the center of this web stood the chapel tent, with its three-meter-high crucifix, and the pavilion complex of the lord of Skara.

As night fell, the pavilion was the center of activity. Messengers bathed in sweat came in bearing reports and left out again bearing orders. Clerks—in actuality merely soldiers of the household guard who had their letters and a steady hand—took in requests and wrote out requisitions, using waxed boards and horn-shaped styli made from carved wood with an iron tip. Quartermasters dispensed food and drink, and makeshift markets bloomed in the plazas where merchants from Eiðar who'd followed the Crusader army offered everything from preserved vegetables to barbering.

And the heart of this city, the arbiter of its laws and keeper of its customs, was Konraðr the White. The albino lord of Skara sat stripped to the waist in a plain chair, listening as a messenger reeled off a report from Pétr on the status of his war machines; as he sat and listened, Father Nikulas saw to his injured arm and shoulder—wrenched and rope-burned after the incident at the bridge. Konraðr winced as the bearded priest rotated his arm in its socket, and then applied a soothing oil to the kinked muscles.

"Tell Pétr," Konraðr said, stopping the messenger in mid-spiel, "I appreciate his attention to detail, but I simply do not have time to care how he gets this done. I only care that he has my drawbridges ready by daylight. Go!" Konraðr waved the rest of the clerks and messengers away. "All of you: leave me. Not you, good Nikulas."

The priest wiped his oily hands on a rag before taking up a stone jar of salve. This he daubed on the rope burns. Konraðr hissed at the touch of Nikulas's fingers.

"God watches over you, my lord," the priest said. "The business at the bridge could have ended poorly for us."

"Is that your way of chiding me, Father? Of telling me I should place more value on this broken vessel?"

"God spared you for a reason."

"And Arngrim?" Konraðr replied with more bitterness than he'd intended. "Did God take him for a reason, too?"

Nikulas answered him frankly: "Yes. But only God knows what that reason might be. As for you, the reason is clear: you have great works left to do. Don't squander it with games of one-upmanship and cheap theatrics."

The lord of Skara shifted in his seat, uncomfortable now. "I should have you flogged."

"I have borne the stripes of a good lashing for speaking truth to power before." Nikulas shrugged. "And I expect I will, again, ere the Almighty sends for me."

"Let us hope He waits many years to send that summons, my friend," Konraðr said, rubbing his eyes. "My tincture, if you please. I am weary, and tomorrow is set to be a day of red slaughter."

Father Nikulas nodded. Both men lapsed into silence as the priest went to a sideboard. There, in a small mortar, he crushed together a selection of dried herbs. For a long moment, the only noise inside was the soft rasp of the pestle. Konraðr's chair creaked as he shifted his weight. Then: "You're a learned man, are you not, priest?"

"Not so learned as some," Nikulas replied, "but more learned than others."

"Do you know what the word *skrælingr* means?"

The priest stopped, his pestle falling silent. Konraðr heard the sharp intake of breath, faint but distinct—the sound of a man caught off guard. Slowly, the pestle resumed its task. "Where . . . Where did you hear this word?"

"On the wind. What is it?"

Nikulas pursed his lips. "It described a hate of the Elder World. A race of night-skulking sons of Cain who would come among men by the dark of the moon, to tear their limbs off and drink their blood."

"*Was,* you say?"

"Yes, thanks be to God. They are no more."

"And you know this, how?"

Nikulas said nothing, at first. He finished his grinding, dusted off the pestle, and set it aside. "When my novitiate ended," he said, after a moment, "my first years as a monk were spent in the scriptorium at Kincora. I had a fine hand, you see, and the Abbot wanted a suitable gift produced for the Holy Father in Rome—an illuminated manuscript, a copy of *Beatus Vivere,* the Life of Our Lady of Kincora, blessed St. Étaín. A noble endeavor, this, and I focused all my efforts on it. But as I copied, I read. It was an old habit of mine.

"The saint was not a native of Ireland, you see. No, she came to us from Glastonbury, via Denmark—where she was kidnapped and her companions killed. Her captor snatched her screaming off the road of pilgrimage and made her lead him back to the south of England, to Badon on the eve of its destruction at the hands of Almighty God, and thence to Ireland. There, she fell in with partisans of Brian Mac Cennétig, and witnessed the old king's murder at the Battle of Chluain Tarbh."

"Fascinating," Konraðr said, a hint of sarcasm shading his tone. "What does any of this have to do with night-skulking sons of Cain, my priest?"

Nikulas put the ground-up herbs into a cup, added warmed wine, and stirred the mixture with a silver spoon. "Her captor," he said, bringing the cup to Konraðr, "was the last of that accursed line. The last *skrælingr.* The blessed Saint tried to bring him from the darkness and into the light of Christ, but the creature refused. After Chluain Tarbh the beast vanished, never to be seen again. That chapter of the *Beatus Vivere* ends with,

"Away sprang Bálegyr's son, | across the Ash-Road
With shoulders cloaked | in the skin of the wolf-father;
The Æsir gave chase, | goaded by Alfaðir,
And with him | came the Twilight of the Gods."

"How was her captor called? This *skrælingr*?"

"Grimnir," Father Nikulas replied.

"The Hooded One," Konraðr whispered. "He is here. Your saint's captor, her *skrælingr*—"

"Impossible!"

Konraðr drank the concoction Nikulas offered him, grimacing. "Are not all things possible under heaven? We face not only this heathen taint, my good priest, but also a cursed son of Cain. God watches." Konraðr handed the cup back and rose to his feet. He made the sign of the Cross. "The Almighty tests our hearts and our souls ere he allows Saint Teodor's sword to be revealed to us. We must prove ourselves worthy!"

For a moment, Nikulas's faith lagged. If half of what he'd read as a young monk was true—and he more than any would never dare accuse Our Lady of Kincora of so base a sin as lying—this sudden revelation was not so much a test of faith as a warning not to test God's good will. "How? How will we do this?"

The lord of Skara cocked his head to one side, adopting what had become to Nikulas a familiar stance—that of a man listening to his demons. Slowly, Konraðr nodded. "Yes. That is what we must do."

"My lord?"

Nikulas saw flames kindled deep in the albino's eerie eyes as he turned his head toward him. "God demands a sacrifice. A night-skulking son of Cain . . ."

BEHIND THE WALLS OF HRAFNHAUGR, the mood was subdued. There was no feasting, no merriment; the songs men sang were dirges for the dead, and they drank to forget rather than to buoy their tempers. Under the eaves of Gautheimr, muttered voices accompanied the meat and ale. They raised their drinking horns to Jarl Hreðel, praised Bjorn Svarti for his quick wit, and thence sought their beds—or else the silent companionship of their kin.

Úlfrún walked the circuit of the walls. It was the eve of battle. She could taste the coming blood and slaughter on the night breeze—a coppery tang that reached into her soul, taunting with promises of a gift denied. On these nights, surrounded by a host willing to die for her, she nevertheless felt alone. A chill no wolf fur or bear skin could abate seeped into her limbs. Old wounds ached. She massaged her hand where flesh met iron . . .

She runs. Her breath steams in the cold air as she pants from exertion. Fear ham-mers through her brain as she draws up, but she knows she cannot stop. Behind her, she hears the crunch of hobnailed boots, the sound of pursuit. The girl runs. Snow swirls down, through drifting smoke. She runs, and she calls upon the Gods for succor. "Help me!" she cries.

One god answers.

Ahead, a figure waits. It bears the shape of a man, though hunched and as twisted as the staff he leans upon; he is clad in a voluminous cloak with a low-brimmed hat. A single malevolent eye gleams from the shadow.

"Niðingr," the stranger says in a voice colder and deeper than a chasm of ice. "The Grey Wanderer, I am; the Raven-God; Lord of the Gallows; the shield-worshipped kinsman of the Æsir. Why do you call upon me?"

"Help," she says, choking on her fear. "Help Mama and my old da! Men . . . men have come! Men with axes!"

"They, too, call upon me. Why should I choose you over them? They offer me gold and blood. What do you offer me, little worm?"

The girl is silent. Then, "Save them. Please! I'll do anything you ask!"

The sky ripples and burns with green fire.

"Then you will serve me." The stranger raises his head to look at the eerie lights of heaven. "Without question. I have a task for you. When it is done, you'll be free. Serve me and I will spare your kin. Or refuse, I care not. But if you refuse your kin will die and you will die, and your name will be lost until the breaking of the world. Decide."

"I will serve you," she says, her voice quavering. "You have my word."

The stranger smiles, then. There is no humor, no warmth. "I have no need for your word, niðingr. Give me your hand, instead."

His touch is like ice, but the kiss of his axe-blade is colder still.

The girl screams . . .

Laughter drew Úlfrún from her reverie. She looked up and saw the light of a fire on the second terrace. It was in the lee of the Raven Stone, and around it sat a few of her lads and a few Geats. Auða and another Daughter of the Raven, Rannveig, drank from flasks and diced with Herroðr, while Forne regaled dark-haired Laufeya with tales of his home in Tróndheimr, on the Norse coast. Bear-like Brodir dozed by the fire, and across from him sat Bjorn Hvítr, drinking ale from a horn and staring thoughtfully into the fire's heart.

Herroðr caught sight of her and waved her over. "Make a space, make a

SCOTT ODEN

space," he said. Auða slid closer to Herroðr, and Úlfrún took the proffered seat. "How fares the world tonight, my Jarl?"

She could tell Herroðr was in his cups, but she offered no reproach. Merely a smile and a wink. "It is cold as a witch's tits and full of cursed hymn-singers," she said. Bjorn Hvítr stirred at this and passed his ale-horn to her.

She tossed back half the horn's contents and handed it back to him with a murmur of thanks, then wiped her lips on the sleeve of her good arm. "What is the game, and what are the stakes?"

Herroðr picked up the dice. They rattled in his palm. "High roll wins, best two out of three," he said. "And winner takes his pick."

"Or her pick," Auða said, elbowing him in the ribs.

"Why not winner takes all?" Úlfrún glanced from Auða to Rannveig. Both women turned scarlet, but Auða met her gaze with a wolfish smile.

"I like that better," she said. Forne glanced their way, eyebrows raised, but Laufeya grabbed his chin in her fingers and returned his attention to her. Even Bjorn Hvítr chuckled.

Though among friends, Úlfrún felt her melancholy deepen. Their lives were like flickers of a candle's flame to her. Soon they would drift away. Forne would find his way into the dour girl's sleeping furs, while lusty Herroðr would surely make off with both Raven Daughters. Brodir—who was the most even-tempered man she'd met in her many years—would sleep here, under the stars, and dream of a home long since turned to ash by the dynastic wars of the Norse. And what of her? A part of her thought to take Bjorn Hvítr by the hand and lead him away, to spend herself before the spear-shattering on the morrow—to remind herself what it is she fights for. But that's not what she wanted. Úlfrún wanted to crawl into the big man's arms and fall asleep, and sleep so deep and so soundly not even her dreams could find her.

Her dreams were thorns. Constant reminders of the life she'd left behind, of the life she might have lived had she not made her oath to the Grey Wanderer. She dreamed of her mama and her old da, who never saw her again after that night; of her brothers and sisters, who mourned her as one who'd died. She dreamed of the husband she'd never love, of the children she'd never bear, the grandchildren she'd never see. Thorns, every one. Pricking her, reaching beneath the flesh to pierce what remained of her soul.

No, Úlfrún reckoned. No, she would not sleep this night, either. She'd merely doze, quiet and alone and as lightly as a cat. That would keep her mind from wandering down the paths of memory. And, upon waking, she would be rested enough to kill.

A flicker of movement caught her eye. Across the fire, over the heads of Forne and Laufeya, Úlfrún saw the Hooded One emerge from the shadows, Dísa Dagrúnsdottir in his wake. They slipped through the postern gate, which yet stood ajar. "Ymir's blood," Úlfrún said. "Is there no one on guard, this night?"

"The Hooded One wanted it left open," Rannveig said. She sat with her leg touching Herroðr's thigh, and Auða, who sleeked herself like a cat in heat, added: "Besides, we discovered the hymn-singers can't fly."

Herroðr and Forne howled with laughter; Rannveig buried her face in Herroðr's shoulder as Bjorn Hvítr shook his head, a broad grin on his craggy face. Brodir stirred, chuckled in his sleep. And even Laufeya—dour Laufeya—cracked a rare and radiant smile.

"But they can swim," Úlfrún replied. She rose and went to the gate. The steep trail, a mere shadow in the darkness, wound down the side of the bluff to where a ramshackle dock extended into the star-flecked breast of Lake Vänern. "Why would he want it left open? What are they on about?"

Auða came up behind her. "With the Hooded One, who can say?"

Úlfrún followed the path down to the water. Though she could not see far into the night, her ears picked up the faint clack and hiss of oars in their locks. "Curious. Is there anything on the far bank?"

"Aye," Auða replied. "A beach and a trail leading inland, to where the Hooded One dwells."

"Gautheimr is not his home?"

"Gautheimr?" Auða shook her head. "No, for as long as I've been alive he's dwelt apart from us. The priestess—Dísa, now, and old Kolgríma before her—acts as intermediary. Our folk can go from cradle to grave and never lay eyes on the lord of our lands. We gave offerings to him through Kolgríma, a bauble here, a bit of mead there, and wrote out our grievances. He answered through Kolgríma. Whatever else can be said of him, the Hooded One is not a harsh lord, and he has kept us safe from the Nailed God's folk."

"Until now," Úlfrún said.

Auða sucked her teeth. "Aye, until now."

"I would see this lair of his," Úlfrún said. "Do you know the way?"

Auða, though, begged off. "Hard blows have taught me not to meddle in his affairs. But look here. Yonder is the Leidarstjarna, the Guiding Star." She pointed to a bright star in the Northern sky. "Keep the bow under her . . ."

Úlfrún held up her iron hand.

"Bollocks," Auða muttered. She chewed her lip. "Right. Get in. I'll row you across, but I'm not waiting around."

ROCKS SCRAPED THE HULL OF the *feræringr* as Grimnir drove the boat ashore with one last surge of the oars. He'd said nothing on the journey across Skærvík, and Dísa had been glad for the silence. She could see the lights of the Crusader camp gleaming across the water, and its nearness to the borders of Grimnir's land worried her.

"Will Halla be safe with that lot lurking about?" Dísa nodded in the direction of the glow, some miles distant.

Grimnir spared it half a glance. He'd stripped off his mask and headdress and left them on the boat's rowing bench as he sprang for the shore. Dísa followed. "Halla?" he said. "She'll not let herself get taken in by the likes of them. Leg it, little bird! We've not got all night!"

They ran. Dísa found herself not even winded as they reached the boundary stone a quarter of an hour later; nor did they pause before descending into the hollow where the longhouse lay, dark and ominously quiet. But halfway down the trail to the bog, Grimnir drew up. His spine bent double, he snuffled along the ground like a hunting wolf. His good eye blazed like an ember in the darkness.

"*Nár!*" he hissed. "I know that stench!"

Dísa heard the rasp of steel as he drew his seax.

Around them, the woods bristled with unseen menace. They went warily, Dísa watching the trail at their back. Nothing stopped them from reaching the corduroy of logs that crossed the bog, or from gaining the base of the stairs leading to the longhouse doors. A greenish glow descended from the heavens as the eerie northern lights kindled, swirling curtains that flickered and undulated. By that thinnest of lights, Dísa could see a familiar silhouette waiting at the head of the stairs.

"Halla," she said, and made to move past Grimnir.

His arm blocked her; his growled curse caused her hackles to rise.

"What is it?"

"Not Halla," he snarled. Dísa felt waves of hate radiating from him—red wrath like the coals of a forge. The figure did not move. Grimnir reached the top of the steps and came abreast of it. His black-nailed hand clenched and unclenched in an unconscious desire to kill. He reached out with his blade hand, tapped the figure on the shoulder with the flat of his seax. Steel scraped and rang as from a boulder.

Dísa saw it clearly for the first time: a stone effigy, standing facing the east, flinching; its eyes were averted, and it held one arm high and crooked as though fending off an attack. Its other hand showed fingers splayed. It was not Halla, true, but once it had been.

Dísa reeled as though someone had punched her in the gut. She fell to her knees. Grimnir circled the stone troll-woman. He snarled something in the tongue of his people, a curse or a prayer, she could not say; he sniffed, wiping his nose with the back of his blade hand.

"What . . . What was she doing outside?" Dísa said. Grimnir looked as though he wanted to stoop and stab and kill; she could see him unleashing a string of oaths, invoking forces best not mentioned in the dark and lonely places of the world. She could see him embarking on a new journey of vengeance.

But he swore nothing. It took untold force of will, but he merely ducked his head, spat, and turned away. "Off your knees, wretch," he growled, sheathing his seax. "We don't have much time."

"Are we just going to leave her?" Tears dampened Dísa's cheeks. More so than Hreðel, and even more than Flóki, this death pierced her soul. She'd had little kindness shown to her in her life, but this woman—though she was neither mortal nor human—had shown her just that: kindness. Genuine warmth. "That's not right!"

Grimnir stopped. He stood a moment, his spine rigid, and then turned back to her. When he spoke, his voice bore the sibilance of a serpent. "Right? What would you do, little fool? Cart her back to the boat? Haul her across Skærvík and set her up next to your precious Raven Stone? *Faugh!*" Grimnir caught her by the nape of the neck and hauled her to her feet. "More than six hundred years, she's dwelled on this land! Now she'll stand here till the world breaks . . ."

Grimnir trailed off. Sharp-eyed, he saw something on the ground at her feet that should not have been there. Chestnuts. Four of them. He crouched and gathered them up in his palm. Each one bore a mark, a rune.

"What?" Dísa said. "What is it?"

Grimnir shook the chestnuts, wondering what they meant. Halla had left them, he was sure of it. But why? *"Ansuz,"* he muttered, flicking the chestnut bearing the letter *A* over. Another bore the letter *I*. *"Isaz.* And a pair of *Naudiz."* Meaning two with the letter *N* scratched on them. *A-I-N-N?* That made no sense.

Grimnir's eyes narrowed. He flicked one of the chestnuts around, spelling out a new word: *N-A-I-N. Náinn?* Now that was a name he knew. A memory welled up from the unplumbed depths of Grimnir's past. *The Ash-Road. Two hundred years ago. A struggle, steel-biting and shield-breaking between the worlds:*

> The glow in Náli's eyes | was like forge-gledes,
> As bloody revenge | for his brothers burned deep;
> Under the ash he waited | and gathered his strength,
> His teeth he gnashed | and his breath was venom.

"No," Grimnir hissed. "That beardling wretch died."

"What did you find?" Dísa leaned over where she could see what it was he was doing.

Grimnir clenched his fist over the chestnuts and stood, tucking them inside his mail. "Get on! Grab what you need and let's get back. I'll have to sort out this Witch-man of yours on my own."

INSIDE, THE LONGHOUSE'S FIRE PIT was nearly cold. Dísa stirred it, digging deep to find the few embers remaining. They flared to life as the air hit them and by the resulting glow she looked around the great room. Nothing was amiss. There was no sign of a struggle. The only thing out of place was a chair by the door and a horn cup beside it.

"She had a visitor," Dísa said.

Grimnir glanced sidelong at the chair. She thought he would descend upon it with the same fury he'd shown outside, snuffling the air and revealing clues she could not fathom. But to her dismay, he merely curled his lip into a sneer of contempt—as though he knew already who the culprit was—and passed through the room. Dísa did not follow.

She stood in the center of the room and described a slow circle; with each step she tried to gather the edges of her thoughts and emotions. Dísa reckoned she'd never return here again. The place's heart had been cut out, turned to stone. Without Halla . . . the girl swore. Why so maudlin? In a matter of days none of this would matter.

In a matter of days, the world would end—or be forever changed.

Dísa found an old sack made from thrice-stitched leather, and into it she shoved an extra gambeson, tools for repairing mail, whetstones, and a few odds and ends that might come in handy after a battle: Halla's sewing kit, herbs, jars of unguents and oils, linen bandages, a jar of cobwebs. Among the detritus, she found an old shawl of Halla's. This, Dísa folded carefully and placed inside her mail.

That sack, plus a couple of axes, a sheathed sword, two spears, and another shield, she dragged out to the portico. She piled it together, turned back to the door, and nearly came out of her skin when a voice hailed her from the darkness.

"What goes, Dísa?"

The girl whirled, her hand falling to the hilt of her seax, as Úlfrún came into view, stepping around the stone figure that had been Halla. A frown creased the older woman's forehead. "What is this place?"

"How . . . ? Did you follow us?" Dísa said. She risked a glance over her shoulder; saw no sign of Grimnir. "You can't be here! You have to go!"

"It's not safe, not this far from the walls." She brushed past Dísa and peered through the open door. "And when one of the Cross-men's patrols stumble across this—and they will—you don't want them to find you here." A low whistle escaped Úlfrún's lips as she glimpsed the hoard of coin and plate, the cast-off weapons and armor, the tapestries and trophies. "Ymir's blood! Where did all this come from?"

"Please," Dísa replied. "You have to go."

"I'm not afraid of your Hooded One," Úlfrún said. "He can't hurt me."

"Then you're a precious little fool, if you believe that."

Dísa stiffened at the harsh and grating voice rising from behind her. She closed her eyes, shook her head, and then turned. Inside, cloaked in shadows not entirely natural, Grimnir sat on his throne-like chair.

"Don't harm her," Dísa said, quietly.

Grimnir chuckled. "I let you have Auða, that fool, Bjorn, and those two idiots. This one is mine."

Úlfrún put a reassuring hand on the girl's shoulder. "It is all right, I promise."

To Grimnir, she said: "Stop me if this sounds familiar, you whoreson dog! A thief and a liar, born from some Norse slattern's thighs, partners with a woman whose reputation is one of witchery. Together, they hatch a scheme to gull the folk of a village by claiming the spineless thief is . . . what? 'The Tangled God's immortal herald'? The pair of them fleece the good villagers, and raid the surrounding steadings until they amass . . . well, *this*."

As she spoke, Grimnir's good eye blazed like the coals in a hearth.

Úlfrún continued: "The woman dies, or is throttled by her confederate and he recruits a new partner—one who has lived all her life under the so-called compact forged by the thieves. Such a partner would be easy to mold." Úlfrún looked at Dísa with a mixture of pity and scorn. "You can't even see it, can you? This charlatan is playing the lot of you for fools! And what a charade it is! He claims his divine blood protects you from enemies you never see, while collecting payment from you—and, by the look of things, making a fair bit of coin from preying on your neighbors, as well. You've been gulled, child. He will try to kill me now. But I know something he does not. I—"

Steel flashed. Dísa heard the dull thud of impact, the wet crack of bone; blood splashed the piles of coin. Faster than Dísa's eye could follow, Grimnir had snatched up an axe and hurled it across the fire pit. It struck Úlfrún in the chest, splitting her sternum and cleaving the heart beneath. Her good hand clutched at the haft, pulled it free from the wreckage of her chest; eyes as hard as the grinding ice stared at Grimnir as she let the axe fall. Úlfrún swayed, fell.

"Gods below!" Dísa muttered. "What have you done?"

"You heard her! The rat predicted it," Grimnir snarled. "It must have been fate. She—"

At Dísa's feet, Úlfrún stirred. The girl gave a bleat of terror and danced away, eyes wide with fear. Úlfrún groaned. Impossibly, her limbs moved; she pushed herself to her knees, rocked back on her haunches, and smiled at Grimnir through the blood spotting her face. "I told you," she said, her voice thick. She fingered the rent in her tunic, still wet with blood. "I cannot die, you stupid man. But I can kill you!"

"What deviltry?" Dísa drew her seax, while Grimnir merely leaned back in his seat.

"A fine trick," he said. "But let me let you in on a little secret of my own . . ." Quick as a snake, Grimnir shot forward. He cleared the pit, snatched Úlfrún up by the throat, and slammed her against the longhouse wall hard enough to split open the back of her skull. "Everything you've said is wrong!"

Úlfrún glimpsed Grimnir's face for the first time—sharp and saturnine, his cheekbones heavy and his brow rough-hewn, with a jagged scar crossing the bridge of his nose, through his missing left eye, and into his hairline. It was the face of something far from human.

"S-Skrælingr!" she managed around his vise-like fingers.

"Yes!" Grimnir hissed. And with a savage twist, he snapped her neck.

He let her body slide down, a smear of blood following her to the floor, then turned and resumed his place on his chair. Dísa edged over to stand near, her seax trembling in her fist. She was pale and sweating despite the night's chill.

"What . . . what is she? A draugr?" The thought of those undead barrow-dwellers made Dísa's skin crawl.

"Someone's laid a geas on her. Reckon she can't die till she's seen some task through," he said. "Watch."

And as they looked on, broken bones grated and knit back together; Úlfrún spasmed, gasped, and sat up. She winced at the pain lancing through her head and neck, but did not try to rise. "Perhaps I was wrong," she said after a moment.

Grimnir sniffed in disdain. "Who put this thing on you, this geas, and how long have you borne it?"

"One hundred and eighty-seven years," she said, raising her iron hand. "I was nine years old when the Grey Wanderer put it upon me, saving my family from raiders and taking my hand in exchange." The iron fist fell, striking the floor with a dull thump. "I have died twenty-seven—no, twenty-nine times since that night. All because I did not wish to die once." She coughed. "Have you anything to drink?"

Dísa sheathed her seax and fetched her and Grimnir both a horn cup of wine. Grimnir sipped his, but Úlfrún took the proffered cup with a murmur of thanks and drained half its contents.

"And what does that one-eyed wretch ask of you, eh?"

"I am the she-Wolf," she said, wiping her mouth with the back of her hand. "Sworn enemy to the Wolf of Christ, that bastard out there, Konraðr the White."

"Can you not just walk through his lines and kill him, then?" Dísa asked.

"Not that simple," Úlfrún replied.

Grimnir chuckled. "It never is where that one-eyed starver of ravens is concerned."

"In a matter of days, a barrow will rise from Vänern's embrace. From it, from the skull of a dragon, I must fetch forth the sword of my ancient kinsman, Sigfroðr the Volsung. Sárklungr, the sword is called, and with it he slew the beast, Frænir. Only when I have that in my hands can I strike a last blow against the Nailed God's champion, and usher in the ending of the Christians' world." Úlfrún finished her wine, leaned back, and closed her eyes. "Only then can I die."

Dísa glanced from her to Grimnir. The girl started to say something, but Grimnir pursed his lips and gave a small shake of his head, as if to say: *let her labor under her false beliefs, no doubt put into her head by the Grey Wanderer.* Instead, he said: "I'll make a wager with you, wolf-mother." She opened one eye. "I will bet you the coin you see that your precious Konraðr is after the same thing—though he doubtless calls it the sword of some wretched saint or other."

Úlfrún scowled. "But that would mean . . ."

"Aye," Grimnir said, causing Úlfrún to belt out a stream of salty curses.

Dísa looked from one to the other. "What would it mean?"

"Think, little bird," Grimnir said. "Say there's something you're after, and you want to guarantee it winds up in your hands. Do you trust the dice those weavers of fate, the Norns, hand you, or do you sneak around and weight the knucklebones in your favor? *Nár!* The Grey Wanderer wants this sword, so he's playing sleighty and false—fire up the hymn-singers by telling them there's a pile of saintly bones and a sword out in the godless wilderness. Meanwhile, you gird the heathens' loins by telling them the same damn story, but with a twist: a storied kinsman's bones and a sword that's needed to slay these wretched kneelers."

"So, no matter who wins, he'll have his sword," Dísa said. Grimnir tapped the side of his nose with his forefinger. "Is this the source of the Witch-man's sorcery, then?"

Grimnir shrugged. "You say he hears voices?"

"I sent Forne into Eiðar to gather news," Úlfrún said. "The rumor is, Konraðr the White is haunted by the deeds he'd done away in the East. His priest is all that keeps him from cracking like an egg, they say."

"Haunted, eh?" Grimnir lapsed into silence, his eye darting as he sought to recall every scrap of lore he'd learned from Gífr, about how to command spirits and how to banish them.

Dísa stirred. "So, what now?"

"It's nigh to cock's-crow," Grimnir said. He drained his wine and shied his cup into the fire pit. An explosion of sparks billowed toward the ceiling, forming constellations of ash and ember. He stood. "Time we're getting back. Hymn-singers will be trying to cross the ravine soon. Throw up a bridge or something."

Úlfrún clambered to her feet. She stretched, rolled kinks from her shoulders, and stared wistfully at the blood-crusted tear in her tunic. "Looked like they were dismantling a few outbuildings and cutting timber. A gallery, perhaps. Maybe ladders?"

"Ha! They'll try a drawbridge, first. Mark my words."

Dísa went out first, then Úlfrún. Grimnir lingered a moment. He looked around, from the ancient ceiling beams to the hammerscale and sawdust covering the floor; from the drifts of coin and weapons to Halla's sleeping niche with its pillows and furs. "*Nár,* you gobby old hag," he muttered. "I'll make sure *he* pays."

And without a backward glance, Grimnir went out the door and into the rising light.

20

Auða and Herroðr met them at the dock.

The sun had barely cleared the cloud-wreathed eastern horizon, but by that diffuse light Dísa could see a flurry of activity in Hrafnhaugr. And from the enemy camp could be heard the blare of horns and the thunder of drums. Thick smoke rose from the direction of the nearest steadings; Dísa was sure, then, that the Crusaders had finally fired the timber and stone structures.

"Bastards are burning out the farms," she snarled.

Grimnir, who had donned his bone mask and headdress once more, tilted his head back and inhaled a lungful of smoke-laden air. "They're boiling pitch."

"What for?"

"To burn *us* out, little bird."

In the bow, Úlfrún tossed a mooring rope to Auða as the boat's hull scraped the dock. "What goes?"

But it was Herroðr who answered. "Forne sent me to find you. The Crusaders, they're massing beyond the ravine. We can see one of them standing in the open bearing a white flag. He wants to talk." Herroðr nodded to Grimnir. "And he's asking for you. By name."

"Is he now?"

"That's not all," Auða said. "They've spent the night building . . . *machines.* Accursed beasts of wood and iron, doubtless some of the Nailed God's sorcery at work. I've never seen the like of it."

Grimnir leaped onto the dock. The boards creaked ominously under his weight. He turned back and motioned to Dísa's small hoard. "Give me those two axes, a spear, and that wretched shield." He tucked one axe into his belt at the small of his back; the other he held in his shield hand. Once daubed white, the face of the shield had borne an Urnes-style serpent depicted in deep black, coiling around the boss. But age had turned white to gray, black to charcoal; the old iron boss now bled rust, so the whole now looked like an eerie eye, wounded and weeping blood. Grimnir took up the spear in his blade hand. "Show me this wretched hymn-singer who'd rather talk than fight!"

Word of Grimnir's coming sped on ahead of the little cortege. Cheers erupted, growing to full-throated roars of approbation. Dísa took note of the relief etched on many of the faces they passed. She glanced at Auða. "Did something happen last night?"

"Those idiots, Hrútr and Askr," she replied. She quickly sketched out the tale of the last few hours. When the three of them could not be found, Hrútr and Askr started spreading rumors: *they've abandoned Hrafnhaugr,* Hrútr said to the wife of Ragni the Fat, known for her loose tongue; *they've gone out to broker a deal with the chief of the hymn-singers,* Askr whispered under the eaves of Kjartan's smithy. When pressed, the cousins resorted to the boldest lie of all: *the Hooded One has succumbed to the Nailed God's power.* When the rumors reached Auða, still warm and magnanimous from her tumble with Herroðr, she went after the cousins like a vengeful spirit. "The *úlfhéðnar* and *berserkir* came with me, for they were eager to erase the stain on their Jarl's honor. Well, needless to say, that silenced those spineless gossip-mongers."

"Where are they now?"

"In the line," Auða replied, loud enough to be heard over the din. "Bjorn Svarti wanted them where he could see them."

"Good man, that Bjorn Svarti. Isn't he, my lord?" Dísa hollered to Grimnir. She could tell by the way his hackles rose and by the cock of his head that he'd heard the entire exchange. Úlfrún, too. Her eyes raking the crowd were like chips of ice hewn from the heart of a glacier.

Grimnir and his lot passed through the lowest terrace and out the gate. The bearskin-clad *berserkir* in reserve cheered them on with Brodir's deep-throated shout echoing even over the drumlike thudding of axes against shields. Near where the bridge over the Scar had stood, Bjorn Svarti had the sworn men drawn up in their serried ranks. They formed the center; on their right flank stood the common levy of Hrafnhaugr, led by Sigrún and the Daughters of the Raven, while on Svarti's left stood Forne and his wolf-cloaked *úlfhéðnar.* Úlfrún split off and joined her men.

Grimnir cut through the center like a knife, emerging alongside Bjorn Svarti. The man across the ravine was a herald; his staff was a spear to which he'd tied a scrap from a white surcoat. He raised it aloft. "Come forth, Grimnir son of Bálegyr! Come forth!"

Grimnir hawked and spat. "Your archers ready, Svarti?"

Bjorn nodded. "Say the word, my lord," he replied. "We'll send that one off to Hel's front gate."

Across the way, the herald raised his staff again. "Come forth, Grimnir son of—"

"I know my name, you dunghill rat!" Grimnir roared, stepping away from the line of his men. He stalked to the edge of the ravine, where he could better see divisions of the enemy moving through the trees. "What do you want?"

The herald, too, walked closer. He cleared his throat. "My Lord Konraðr would deign to speak with you. He—"

"Your precious Lord Konraðr can lick my hairy arse!" Laughter erupted from around him. "The time for talk is over! Now is the time for spears to shatter and shields to break! It is the axe time! The sword time! Go back to your little lordling and tell him to get on with it!"

The herald retreated. Grimnir stood still. He watched the disposition of the enemy troops and saw Norsemen, Swedes, and Danes working in unison. Once sworn enemies, they put old grievances aside and united under a cast-off rag embroidered with a black cross.

Crusaders, they called themselves. *Bah!* Grimnir saw the same thieves and killers he'd faced in the past, men who used to be honest about their skullduggery. Now they hid their deeds behind the Nailed God's skirts, confused the savage joy of battle with piety, and played the martyr when the Fates came to collect their due.

Resplendent in silver and black mail, his white surcoat sewn with a Teutonic cross, Konraðr stepped out from the trees. He walked to the place the herald had quit, leather gloves clutched in one long-fingered hand. His other rested on the pommel of a longsword.

"Ha!" Grimnir barked. "Look yonder, lads! Here's the founder of our feast now. The great lord of Skara, himself! *Faugh!* Scurry back to your shit-hole of a town, you wretch, ere I cross this ditch and take that pig-sticker away from you!"

"Grimnir son of Bálegyr," Konraðr said. "What a rough beast you are. You go by many names, I am told. *Corpse-maker* and *Life-quencher, the Bringer of Night.* Some claim you are the Son of the Wolf and Brother of the Serpent. The Irish called your kind *fomoraig,* did they not? They cursed your sire, Bálegyr, and the wolf ships that brought him to their fair isle. What did the English name you? *Orcnéas?* But to the Danes and the Norse your kind were always *skrælingar.* Accursed sons of Cain, you are . . . or were. For you are the last of your kind, are you not? Behold, men of Hrafnhaugr! Your Jarl, your Hooded One, is the last in a long line of monsters! Why do you hide your face, Grimnir son of Bálegyr? Are you ashamed of it?"

At Konraðr's revelation, Grimnir merely laughed. He reached up, stripped off his horned headdress and his wolf-bone mask, and turned to face the wall of allies behind him. There came no gasps from the throats of men; whatever they thought, they kept their emotions in check. Grinning, he swung back to face Konraðr. "You forgot, you ignorant little whiteskin, that I am also the Tangled God's immortal herald—what should I be but *kaunar,* wrought in the dark of Niðavellir from the afterbirth of great Angrboða? Did your precious spirits leave that bit out? Aye, you wretch. I know of the curse you bear, of the souls of your dead victims who haunt you."

"They tell me . . ." Konraðr cocked his head to the side. "They tell me there are malcontents among you—men who might look with favorable eyes on an offer of clemency. Yes, men of Hrafnhaugr! I make you this offer: hand over the *skrælingr!* Trade him to me, and in return I will leave you with your lives!"

"Liar!" Grimnir snarled. "You didn't come here for me, or for them!" Grimnir jabbed a thumb at the Geats behind him. "You didn't even come for your precious Nailed God! *Nár!* You came for a sword! Do those bastards know? Do they know we're going to sink a hand-span of steel into their writhing guts just so you can flash some saint's bauble under your cousin the king's nose?"

That Grimnir knew his purpose took Konraðr by surprise. "*You* know of the blessed Saint Teodor?"

"That's the wretch's name, eh?" Grimnir *chk-chk*'d his teeth. "A merry dance you've brought your lads on, if you think a saint's been loitering about these parts. Svarti!" He half-turned to face the giant Geat. "You ever see a saint's sword?"

"Aye, lord!" Bjorn Svarti grabbed his crotch and thrust his hips at the enemy. "Every morning! And every night I show it to the wenches!"

The Raven-Geats erupted in laughter.

"Enough!" Konraðr roared. "My offer stands! Bring me the beast's head and we will spare Hrafnhaugr! Think of your wives! Your children! You would die—and condemn your families to death, or worse—for this creature? He's not one of you!"

The laughter faded away. Geats up and down the line looked from the albino lord of Skara to the dark and glowering visage of the Hooded One. Grimnir turned to face them, his arms thrown wide. "Aye! Which of you dogs will take that milk-colored swine up on his offer, eh? Will it be you, Bjorn Svarti?"

Svarti shook his head.

"What about you, little bird? Will you take my head to that bastard?" Grimnir fixed his gaze on Dísa; the girl returned his stare.

"I'd rather fetch the bastard's head for you!"

"Sigrún? Auða? Taking my head might ease the sting of knowing you've served a monster all your lives!"

But both Daughters of the Raven declined. "You serve the Tangled God," Auða said. "You were chosen to bear his standard. Who are we to dispute this?"

Grimnir walked down the front rank. "What about you . . . Hrútr?" He rounded on the malcontent, who stood with his kinsman, Askr. "You spread lies about me, curse me under your breath, and likely swear by your wretched ancestors to end me! Now's your chance! Do it!" Their companions moved away from them, leaving the kinsmen to stand alone.

Hrútr glanced at Askr; he licked his lips, tightened his grip on his spear.

"Do it, I said!" Grimnir bellowed. "Strike me down and deliver my head to those hymn-singing bastards! Earn their so-called clemency!"

Hrútr took a step forward, but Askr caught his arm and stopped him from going farther. "No, lord," Askr said.

Grimnir bared jagged teeth in a snarl of disgust. "So-ho! You'll keep wagging your slippery tongues against me, but when the iron's on the anvil and the hammer's about to fall, you rats are suddenly as contrite as pinched thieves! Is that it? I guess you didn't hear me right, you piss-blooded whore-sons! I said come take my head, or I will take yours!"

Hrútr risked a sidelong glance at his kinsman. Pale and sweating, Askr gave a nearly imperceptible shrug. His hand dropped to his side; his axe slid down against his leg. He shifted, shield ready. Askr started to speak . . .

Hrútr blinked. Turned.

And lunged. His spear—seven feet of weathered ash capped with a lugged iron head as long as his forearm—darted snakelike for Grimnir's throat. Had he faced another Geat that man would have crashed to the ground then, with his life's blood spurting from a punctured neck. But what Hrútr fought was neither Geat nor man.

Grimnir was in motion even as Hrútr turned. The Geat's spear skittered off the edge of the *skrælingr*'s shield; hissing, Grimnir sidestepped Hrútr and cast his own spear point-blank into Askr's face, hurling it with every ounce of power held ready by his gnarled shoulder and its knotted muscles.

The diamond-hard blade punched through skin, teeth, and bone—entering Askr's face above his lips and left of his nose, driving through his brain to exit the back of his neck, left of his spine. Blood exploded from Askr's mouth and nose. His scream became a gurgling cry as his body tumbled back into the line of Geats.

Hrútr bellowed at the sight of his stricken kinsman. He dragged his spear around and tried to come at Grimnir's unshielded side.

The Hooded One was quicker still. Pivoting, he snatched the axe from his shield hand, rolled around Hrútr's clumsy riposte, and struck him in the apple of his throat. Gristle and bone cracked; blood fountained, spilling down the front of Hrútr's mail. The Geat's eyes widened as he sought to draw a breath through his riven throat, and ended inhaling only a rich foam of coppery gore. Grimnir left the axe there. He spun around to face the impassive Geats.

"Anyone else?"

Hrútr staggered, fell to his knees. He clutched at the ghastly wound, unable to swallow, unable to cough. He gobbled and blew froth as his lungs filled with blood.

"Anyone?"

The roar started with Bjorn Svarti, who howled as he clashed axe against shield. Dísa took up the clamor, chanting Grimnir's name for good measure. It spread through the ranks of the sworn men, and thence to the levies. Úlfrún's lot added their voices, with more wolf howls and throaty shouts of approval, steel clashing on wood.

Grimnir nodded. He knelt by Hrútr's corpse, its eyes open and sightless, and wrenched his axe free. Grimnir dipped two fingers into the wound. With Hrútr's blood, he drew a double line from his left forehead, through his empty eye socket, and down his cheek to his jawline. Then he stood and turned to face Konraðr across the ravine.

The roars and clashes swelled. Grimnir raised his bloody axe aloft, held it there for the span of a heartbeat, and then flung it down so its head carved a furrow in the earth.

"There's your answer, you cross-kissing wretch!" he called out.

Konraðr watched their savage exultation a moment longer. With a sad shake of his head, he turned away and walked into the tree line. As he vanished, a horn skirled—long and loud. Over the clamor, Grimnir heard the creak of ropes, followed by the distinctive *thump* of a beam striking a wooden frame.

And over the tops of the trees came a missile large enough to have come from the hands of a giant . . .

DÍSA HAD NEVER SEEN ANYTHING like it. The missile that lofted into the sky trailed smoke; to her, it looked like a section of a tree's trunk, sawed off into a man-high chunk. Its surface was blackened, and embers flared off it as it passed over the heads of the Geats. It struck the earthen embankment at the foot of Hrafnhaugr's walls . . . and exploded in a shower of sparks and flaming splinters of wood. Dísa flinched at the sound of it. She heard two more thumps; another pair of missiles soared over the trees. One was a second section of log; the other broke apart in midair. Stones, she realized. A mass of head-sized stones. So dumbfounded was she that she almost missed a more ominous noise: the *shhhunk* of hundreds of bows loosing in unison.

"Shields!" Grimnir roared, falling back into line alongside her. Up and down the line, men raised their shields, rims touching, and braced themselves. Dísa heard the sharp *crack* of arrows impacting, like hammers striking wood; from among the levy, she heard Auða's voice, calling on them to hold. Screams mingled with the staccato drumming. The stones struck the line between the sworn men and Úlfrún's war-band—most crashed into shields and rebounded; a handful left crippled fighters in their wake, men with broken arms or legs; a neck was snapped among the Svarti's crew, and one howling wolf-brother was abruptly silenced when a stone splintered his helmet and the skull beneath. The burning log overshot their lines and exploded on the road to the gate.

"What are those cursed things?" Dísa said, emerging from the cover of her shield.

"*Valslöngur,*" Grimnir replied. "Stone-throwers. Whiteskin bastard means to break the walls. Let him try!" In the lull between arrow storms, Grimnir stepped out. His voice boomed. "Svarti! You and Úlfrún pull your lads back to the gate! Sigrún! Make for the postern and get your lot under cover!" A narrow path ascended around to the level of the postern from where the bridge once stood, following the foundation of the walls. There, the Scar was at its narrowest, with barely fifteen feet separating the walls of the ravine. But the side nearest Hrafnhaugr had a sharp difference in elevation, its edge over ten feet higher than the enemy-held bank and screened by tangled brush and brambles. Dísa could see why he chose to send the levy that way—in the open, at the choke point that was the main gate, they were more likely to panic if the arrows continued. Grimnir's voice cracked like a whip. "Move, you wretches! Before those machines find their range!"

KONRAÐR WATCHED THE ENEMY LINES break apart, noting that the division on his left moved to the left, following the line of the wall. The albino nodded to himself. Under the trees, Starkad's archers—men of Skara's household company who learned to use the bow in the wars beyond the North—drew and loosed in volley. At their backs, through the trees, those soldiers Pétr drafted into his makeshift contingent of engineers scrambled to reload and re-align the trio of siege engines the squat Dane had constructed in the night.

Mangonels, the engineer called them. Stone-throwing traction engines. Of course, Konraðr had seen engines like these during the assault on the walls of Constantinople. Mammoth constructs with long throwing arms and bodies of heavy timber; some were powered by bundles of twisted hemp, others by counterweights, and a few—like these three—by teams of men pulling in unison.

This was what Pétr built for him? He'd wanted bridges. He'd wanted a way to cross the ravine and come to grips with the heathens. Instead, Pétr gave him rocks and burning logs! At the edges of his vision, the dead of Constantinople crept away from the machines; they remembered too well their deaths by such infernal devices—crushed by stones or strangled by burning sulphur. The lord of Skara felt their unease.

But as Konraðr looked on, sweating crewmen used long poles to roll a makeshift incendiary into position. The projectile, a five-foot section of pine that had been cored out and filled with glowing coals, was ready to launch at the walls of Hrafnhaugr. The Dane who was chief of the crew checked the sling one last time, then motioned for the ten rope-haulers to take their marks. At the count of three, they heaved with every ounce of might between them. The engine creaked ominously; the arm pivoted on its fulcrum, and the missile shot into the sky. Konraðr heard the heavy thump of the arm striking its padded stop. The incendiary whistled as it flew, rushing air acting as a forge's bellows to stoke the smoking heart of the missile. Its trajectory was a little flat. The lord of Skara followed its flight and watched it explode against the earthen embankment.

The crew chief was already at work, using a mallet to adjust the machine's windage. The next incendiary would doubtless strike full against the wooden palisade, or crest the walls to bring destruction to the first terrace of the village.

"Pétr!" he roared, slapping his gloves into the palm of his hand. "Where, in the name of Almighty God, are my bridges? Pétr!"

"Here, lord!" Pétr answered. Stripped to the waist, the squat Dane was a goatish man, his gnarled limbs covered in a pelt of fine black hair. A scrap of cloth tied above his eyes kept the sweat from blinding him, but Konraðr could tell by the redness in his features and his huffing breaths that the smaller man was nearly spent. He'd realized Arngrim's secret to rolling drawbridges was beyond him, so he turned to what he knew best: ramps and ladders and stone throwers.

Two teams of men drawn from Kraki's company of Danes threaded through the siege machines. One group carried two twenty-foot ramps made of the long central roof beams taken from the farm steadings. They had iron spikes at one end, forged from farm implements, and smaller crossbeams running their length, a foot between each. The other team carried ladders, tall enough to scale the walls of Hrafnhaugr.

Behind these teams came Kraki, himself. The chief of the Danish mercenaries was a burly man, his hair and drooping mustache more silver than
black. A tracery of old scars seamed his craggy face, and his jutting chin
looked like an axe had cleaved it. Eyes as gray and cold as the sea gleamed
now with the promise of battle. The skirts of his heavy mail hauberk rustled
as he came abreast of Konraðr.

"My war hound!" the lord of Skara said, clapping him on the shoulder.
"You have the honor of striking the heathen first. Are you and your men
ready?"

"Get us across that accursed ravine, my lord, and we'll send the Devil a
new crop of henchmen!"

"Yonder is your target," Konraðr said, pointing at the area where the enemy's division on the right flank still struggled to negotiate the narrow path.
"There is a postern gate to the left. Seize it, if you can, or escalade the walls
and gain the parapet. Raise your standard, and I will send Thorwald and his
dogs to reinforce you."

Kraki gave a sharp nod. The Dane's lips peeled back over his teeth.

"Starkad!" Konraðr called out. The captain of his household troops, a tall
and lean man with a pox-scarred face and eyes that had seen too many pyres in
far Outremer, hustled to attend him. "Direct your archers to pin down those
heathen dogs by the main gate! Keep them from venturing out to help their
mates on the left, yonder. Rain iron down upon them, good Starkad! Go!"

As Konraðr made ready to send Kraki off, Father Nikulas approached.
The priest bore a tall staff crowned with a gleaming golden crucifix; below
it hung the stark white pennon of the Crusade, bearing a black Teutonic
cross. He handed it to Kraki, who crossed himself before passing it to the
man on his right.

"Raise this above their walls, Kraki Ragnarsson!" Nikulas said. "Let
Heaven see the quality of the men who serve Him! God wills it!"

"GOD WILLS IT!"

DÍSA HEARD THE BATTLE CRY of the hymn-singers, the dull roar of men
charging across an interval. She looked back and witnessed the first of Konraðr's troops barreling out from under the eaves of the trees. Danes, by the
looks of them, a literal horde who followed a man bearing a golden cross on
a long staff. Others struggled under the weight of ramps and ladders.

They meant to bridge the Scar at its narrowest, a hundred yards downslope from the postern gate. The gate stood open; Sigrún bellowed for the men and women of the village levy to make haste, though the narrowness of the path hampered their withdrawal. Dísa could not say if she saw the threat approaching or not. But Auða surely did. As did the Geats bringing up the rear. Men stopped and milled, uncertainty leeching their courage.

The ramps, rising now, would crash down right in their midst, allowing battle-hardened Danes to swarm across and seize the path—perhaps the postern gate, as well. It would be a slaughter.

"Grimnir!" she cried out. "They're trying for the postern gate!"

Grimnir turned and snarled, venting a string of curses as, from the Crusaders' war machines, a scatter of stones the size of a man's head crashed amidst the stragglers coming up the road to the main gate.

Úlfrún and the bulk of her wolf-warriors were inside now; the *berserkir* were passing through the gate, goaded on by Brodir; last would come Svarti and the sworn men of Hrafnhaugr.

"Shields!" someone bellowed as a fresh storm of arrows hailed down from the smoky heavens. Dísa raised her shield and dropped to a crouch. Iron-heads hammered the wooden face protecting her; they grew thick upon the ground, like stalks of grain. Arrows pierced those Geats wounded by the crushing stones.

Dísa saw the Manx-Geat, Íomhar—boastful Íomhar, who never met a war tale he couldn't make his own—writhing on the ground, screaming for someone to help him. A stone had broken his ankle, and a pair of goose-feathered shafts jutted from his back. As the girl looked on, a third arrow thudded into Íomhar's back, its broad iron head splitting muscle and bone to bury itself in the Manx-Geat's heart.

Peering around the edge of her shield, Dísa cursed at the Danes who reached the edge of the ravine and threw down their ramps unchallenged. From her vantage she could see Auða chivvying men forward, slapping at them with the flat of her sword as she struggled to piece together a rear guard to screen Sigrún's withdrawal. She saw Geira come to her aid, with Rann-veig and golden-haired Hervor in tow. With two-score men, they made a semicircle around the ramp heads.

Dísa felt a lull in the deadly hail. In her gut, she knew the postern would likely fall unless someone did something. And though she was but one shieldmaiden, she was the daughter of Dagrún Spear-breaker; she was the Hooded One's right hand, and she bore the stamp of her master's hammer. Perhaps she, alone, could turn the tide. Without waiting for permission, or even for a coherent plan, Dísa sprang up and hared off back the way they'd come.

A burning log exploded against the rocky scarp a few paces to her right, showering her with embers and smoldering splinters of wood; she ducked her head and ran on. Enemy archers tracked her and loosed; she heard their laughter, their jeers, the wagers they made to the man who could bring her down. She raised her shield as she ran. An iron-headed shaft ricocheted off the iron boss; another punched through the hem of her mail and nearly tangled in her legs.

Her harness crashed and rattled with every loping stride. Dísa hurtled past the stiffening corpses of Hrútr and Askr, the latter with a spear still jutting from his head like some gruesome sapling, and pounded up the slope to where a handful of Geats milled in reserve. These were shrinking back from the ramps, their shields dropping as a prelude to a rout, but the sight of the Hooded One's priestess, her eyes alight with savage fury, brought them up short. "Ymir's blood!" she bellowed, barreling past them. "Why do you run? If those bastards scale this wall, your homes and families will burn! Will you let them take all from you? No! For the glory of the Tangled God, follow me!"

Dísa did not wait to see how they responded. Ahead, she witnessed the first of the hymn-singers scale the ramp and leap into the midst of the Raven-Geats. He was a broad-shouldered Dane, bearded and sporting a helmet with a brass boar running from crest to nasal. He caught a spear on his shield; with a roar, he swept his axe from side to side, clearing a space for his mates.

Auða lunged for him, but then stumbled back as her blade rebounded from his mail. The man grunted and thrust out with the horn of his axe. Another Dane landed alongside him, and the pair locked shields. More were scrambling up the first ramp even as the second crashed down, its iron spikes biting into the rocky earth.

Dísa came up the path; she shouldered Geats aside and slammed her shield into place beside Auða's. Iron rims grated; linden wood scraped. Auða risked a sidelong glance to see who'd joined with her. She met Dísa's fierce gaze with a snarl of approbation, and then loosed a cry of hate as the pair of them went for the Dane's unshielded side.

The path was narrow, with a grassy embankment to their right and a sheer drop into the throat of the Scar to their left. Dísa heard the dull roar of voices, the screams and war cries; she heard the crash and slither of steel and the bone-cracking impacts of axe on shield. A spear lanced over her shoulder to impale the Geat behind her. This was the scrum of the shield wall, and in it she heard the song of the valkyries.

Adding her weight to Auða's, the pair of them rammed the first Dane. He stumbled back, his heel slipping over the edge of the ravine. Dísa saw his eyes widen. She saw sudden terror bloom across his visage. He dropped his axe and clawed for Auða's shield, his fingers clamping on the edge. Unbalanced, he toppled backward—and dragged Auða after him. She had no choice but to let the shield slip from her grasp as the Dane screamed and tumbled into the Scar.

A spear jabbed up from the ramp, seeking Auða's guts. Dísa's shield caught it; the wooden shaft splintered under the impact. The second Dane, too, came at Auða, vengeance stamped on his brutal features. Dísa watched her parry the first blow of the Dane's sword. Auða thrust for his groin, overextended herself in the tight confines, and would have died under his blade had Dísa not slammed her shield rim into the knuckles of his sword hand. Bone cracked; blood spurted, and the sword dropped from his nerveless grip. The man opened his mouth to bellow a curse.

And Dísa drove the point of her spear up into the roof of his mouth. She turned loose of the weapon as the Dane's corpse fell back. Auða scrambled and came up with the man's shield. Dísa drew her Frankish axe. At their backs, the Geats finally found their courage. With roaring cries and curses, they made a wall of shields at the head of each ramp.

The air grew thick and hot with the stench of exhaled breaths and pierced bowels; a mist of blood erupted from riven throats; blades hacked at grasping hands, leaving blood-slimed stumps in their wake. Men fell under axe blows and spear thrusts, creating a treacherous morass at the feet of the defenders. Rivulets of steaming gore flowed down the path. Time held no meaning. For attacker and defender, there was nothing under heaven but that tiny strip of land at the base of the embankment. Men died for it, killed for it. It became the center of the world.

Dísa fell back, stumbling over the carpet of corpses as Rannveig took her place. Her shield arm was numb from repeated blows; though its edge had grown hacked and ragged her shield nevertheless protected her, deflecting spears and blades, axes and hurled stones. She bled from half a dozen wounds. She put her back against the embankment and struggled for breath. Near her, Auða—blood-blasted and sweating—knelt alongside Geira. She struggled to tie off a tourniquet above Geira's elbow, to slow the loss of blood from where a Danish sword had mangled her forearm. She reckoned Odin's weather had left that blade notched and dull, turning a clean blow into a welter of torn flesh and broken bone. The older woman's pain-filled eyes found Dísa's but she did not see her.

Dísa suddenly realized she stood in a lull. The Danes had pulled back; she could see through the milling Geats that the enemy was regrouping on the far side of the Scar. Rannveig took the opportunity to attack the ramp itself, but the weight of men had driven the iron spikes deep into the rocky lip of the ravine's bank. A breeze blew smoke their way. At least, she thought, the breeze was cool.

Sigrún's voice cracked through the ringing in their ears. "Move the wounded! Get them to the gate!" As Dísa nodded, she felt something behind her, touching her neck. She turned to look. A root wiggled like a blind worm through the earthen embankment. Frowning, Dísa touched it . . . and felt a shriek of alarm rising up from deep inside.

"SHIELDS!"

"TENACIOUS HEATHENS," FATHER NIKULAS SAID. The priest had hoped the first charge of Kraki's Danes would be enough to break the resolve of these Raven-Geats, but he had obviously misjudged their mettle.

"They have their good-luck charm with them, their fierce little bird to egg them on," Konraðr replied.

Nikulas sniffed. "Courage like that is wasted on these godless pagans."

"I quite agree. Starkad, clear that path while our Danish friends regroup." Then, over his shoulder, Konraðr shouted. "Pétr! My Rock!"

"Lord?"

"How precise are those mangonels of yours?"

"We have their range," Pétr said, chest swelling with pride. "We can put a missile wherever you desire, my lord."

"I desire one on that path, yonder," Konraðr said, turning back. "Make it so."

The lord of Skara motioned for Starkad; the chief of his household company nodded, turned to his cadre of archers, and raised his sword. "In volley," he bellowed. "Loose!"

EVEN AS THE CRY SPILLED from her lips, Dísa heard the tell-tale *shhhunk* of hundreds of hemp cords slapping bracers, hundreds of bow-staves snapping forward, hundreds of fletchings hissing against jute-wrapped grips. She dropped to a crouch, her ragged-edged shield canted to cover as much of her body as possible. Auða dragged a cast-off shield over Geira, and then hunkered under her own. Their eyes met as the first arrows fell.

"What was it you said when you first went to *him*? 'The old hag sends me to live a thrall's life'? Some useless thrall you are," Auða shouted. Iron-headed shafts struck the embankment with a muffled *whump;* others *thunked* against shields or ended their flight with the eerie wet *thud* of pierced flesh. The deadly hail wrenched gasps from the throats of the Geats around them. Men Dísa had known since birth screamed and died under that merciless barrage; she peeked out under the rim and saw Rannveig's body jerk beneath the impact of half a dozen shafts and pitch forward, her raven-haired corpse tumbling from the path and into Vänern's dark embrace.

Three arrows struck Dísa's shield, one cracking through the boards to stop inches from her face. "Mother of whores!" she snarled, glancing over at Auða. "Next time, remind me to keep my fool mouth shut!" The younger woman scuttled crab-like over the slain. "Let's get her inside. We can't hold here."

Auða nodded. She lifted the edge of the shield covering Geira. Dísa saw her cousin's face harden, her eyes narrowing to dagger points of ice. Reverently, she replaced the shield—as fine a warrior's death shroud as any. "I am going to kill those sons of bitches," she growled.

Dísa's lips peeled back in a snarl of hate. She could hear the Danes massing for a fresh assault, with chants of *"SKA-RA!"* and *"GOD WILLS IT!"* But, almost drowned out by the clamor and racket of Danes stoking their courage, Dísa caught a more ominous sound: the *thump* of those accursed engines.

An incendiary missile lofted over the trees. Dísa stood; she followed its smoky flight and knew the end of things was upon her. Her scream of defiance echoed to the heavens . . .

21

Kraki Ragnarsson watched the incendiary crash into the embankment, raining coals and fiery splinters of resin-soaked pine onto the narrow path. He heard the screams of the heathens, smelled the stench of their burning flesh, and knew God was with them. His Danes were the Fist of the Almighty; they were the vengeance of Heaven, set to wreak havoc among the Pagan. He raised his sword aloft. "God wills it!"

And with an answering roar, Kraki led his company of Danes up the ramps. He kept his eyes fixed straight ahead; one missed step to either side meant a sixty-foot plummet into the cold waters of Lake Vänern—likely bouncing from the narrow walls of the ravine first. The ramp creaked under his weight. It creaked, but it held. Soil and rock trickled down from beneath the ramp head, its iron spikes buried deep. Above them, the palisade walls of Hrafnhaugr loomed. He saw pale Geatish faces between makeshift embrasures, cloud-and-smoke-diffused sunlight gleaming from brass helmet crests. Arrows spat down at them in irregular intervals. One ricocheted from Kraki's helmet; another rebounded from the tightly woven links of his mail hauberk.

Snarling, the Danish captain crested the ramp and leaped onto the narrow path. He expected resistance. He held his shield at the ready, his sword unwavering; *Corpse-wand,* he called it, and etched down its damascened blade, in the letters of the Greeks, was a bit of Scripture he'd gotten from an old

Varangian at Miklagarðr: *You are my war club. With you I shatter nations; with you I bring kingdoms to ruin.*

Kraki saw no one alive. Geatish corpses lay heaped among his beloved Danes about the ramps; smoke from the burning embankment set his eyes to watering—it stank of roasted meat and singed hair. Kraki stepped forward, the churned ground underfoot a slurry of blood and other less vital fluids. He was on the verge of ordering his men to raise the standard and move up to the postern gate when a chilling scream rent the air.

Through the veil of smoke came a pair of bloodstained figures. Both were women—witches, Kraki was sure; the taller of the two limped and panted, her *whuffing* breaths like a lioness on the hunt. The left side of her face was charred, and her left eye had burst like an egg. The right eye gleamed with battle madness. The other woman was little more than a girl. She came on in eerie silence, her lips drawn over her teeth in a bestial snarl. She clutched a Frankish axe in one fist; with the other, she drew a long-seax. Both had hair as black as a carrion-bird's wings, worked with fetishes of bone and silver, and a raven tattooed on one cheek.

"The Geats send their women to do their fighting," Kraki said. He swung his sword in a figure-eight pattern, and then settled into a fighting crouch. "Come, then, hags! Come and I'll send you to hell to whore for your master!"

DÍSA DID NOT REMEMBER THE incendiary's impact. Nor did she recall the engulfing flames or the dagger-like splinters of wood; the choking embers or the cries of the wounded, burning under a blanket of smoldering debris. She only remembered Auða's scream.

It was the frustrated cry of an injured animal, wordless but expressing a world of meaning in its intensity. Dísa found her kneeling, clutching her face. She crouched beside Auða and pulled her hands away. Flames had blackened the left side of her cousin's face, charred it like meat left too long on the spit, and the eye was a ruin that leaked blood and jelly. It would never see sunlight again. In Auða's other eye, Dísa saw madness.

She understood. Dísa could hear the Danes coming up the ramps, their voices rising as they drew near. The ramps creaked under their weight. Auða stared at her with singular intensity. *If we must die,* the look in her remaining eye said, *let us call down the daughters of Odin and earn our place at the Allfather's blood-soaked table.* This, too, Dísa understood. She found her cousin's sword and pressed its hilt into her hand.

"For Hrafnhaugr, cousin," Dísa rasped, taking up her Frankish axe. Together, they rose on unsteady legs. Auða breathed hard, panting through the waves of agony that assailed her as they strode toward the first Dane to leap from the ramp.

He was a man of some consequence, Dísa reckoned from his war-rags. He wore heavy mail beneath a richly embroidered surcoat, cinched by a thick leather belt decorated with rosettes of hammered gold; of gold, too, were the chasings of his helmet, from the dragon crest running along the crown to the wide nasal and the hinged cheek pieces. The man who wore it was beardless, scarred, his cleft chin jutting forward, his bristling mustache more silver than black.

Prosperous man or poor man; jester or king . . . it made no difference to Dísa. She felt a rich vein of hate bubble up from the dark recesses of her soul—hate for the Danes and their foreign god; hate for the eager shears of the Norns, who had cut the life-strands of her folk and dyed them in blood; hate for the Witch-man and his foolish crusade; hate for the prophecy that caused all this. Dísa narrowed that hate into a lance. With it, she would kill this bastard. Kill him, then the man after him, and the next man after that. She'd keep killing until the cut of an axe or thrust of a blade sealed her fate. This was her purpose, she realized. To kill, and to die.

The man said something in harshly accented Danish. His warriors laughed. Dísa, however, ignored them. She kept her focus on a place just behind the hymn-singer's sternum, where his foul heart beat its staccato rhythm. She heard Auða growl her rage.

"Come," the wretch said, more slowly now, as he slashed the air with his sword and dropped into a fighting crouch. "Come and I'll send you to hell to whore for your master!"

And Dísa Dagrúnsdottir came, with Auða a step behind her. She skipped the last step and feinted low with her seax, drawing the Dane's shield; as he sought to parry that phantom blow, Dísa came down with her axe. She hooked the top edge of his shield.

The Dane rolled his shield, dislodging her axe and causing Dísa to stumble. With a low chuckle he punched forward, smashing the central boss full into Dísa's face. The younger woman pitched back as though a mule had kicked her. She lost her axe; the blow drove her against the smoldering embankment. She slid to one knee with thick ropes of blood starting from her nose and mouth.

Without missing a beat, the Danish chief shifted and caught Auða's sword on his. Steel rasped and rang. He pushed her away. Blow followed blow in quick succession—thrust, draw, slash, riposte; their hilts clanged together, iron grating, then sprang apart. Auða drew back and struck again. Her notched sword hammered the rim of his shield and broke. She screamed in rage . . .

Dísa heard the death-blow fall. She heard the hiss of air through the Dane's clenched teeth, the crunch and snap of mail links, the slaughterhouse sound of a blade cleaving into flesh. She shook the blood from her eyes and watched Auða fold around the Dane's sword. He'd struck her low, just above her right hip. Damascened steel cut through Auða's mail like cloth, through muscle and sinew like water, and wedged in the column of her spine. Auða shrieked—more from frustration than from pain—and tried to rake the Dane's eyes out as she crumpled to the ground. He kicked her off his sword, leaving her to bleed out while he turned his attention to Dísa.

"You must be the one Lord Konraðr calls his 'little bird,'" he said, slinging Auða's blood from his blade. He looked her up and down before snorting in derision. "My lord is easily impressed. Come. Let us finish this. I have a piss-hole of a village to sack and burn."

Dísa wiped at the blood with the back of her hand. She hawked phlegm and spat it at the Dane's feet. "Going to be hard to do," she growled, "when you're dead." She stood, her seax held loosely at her side, and walked to the center of the path. Dísa kept her off-hand side to him. "Come on, then, fat man! Or are you afraid that a girl is all that stands between you and the gates?"

Baring his teeth in a snarl of rage, Kraki Ragnarsson slung his shield away and charged.

FROM ATOP THE PALISADE, GRIMNIR watched the bull of a Dane charge the slender form of Dísa—blood-spattered from her time in the crucible of the shield wall and singed from the impact of the fiery missile. He watched, and did nothing.

"He will kill her, *skrælingr*," Úlfrún said, coming alongside him, her voice an urgent hiss. "Let me—"

"No. This is her fight, win or lose. Stay out of it! Your men, they are ready?"

"They're at the gate. Say the word and they'll drive these Danish swine into the Scar. If we go now . . ."

"When one of them dies," he replied.

"You're a cold bastard."

Grimnir grunted. "You've forgotten what it's like, is all. If you ever knew it."

"Knew what?"

His eye gleamed as he glanced sidelong at her. "How it feels to tread on Death's cloak. This lot, they're never more alive than when they're an arse-hair away from slaughter. If she lives, she'll remember this till she's called to the grave. You've died, what, twenty-nine times? This little wretch will have one death. Look around."

Úlfrún did. She could see others peering over the palisade's crenellations, their hands gripping the wood with tension-whitened knuckles. Even old Sigrún was watching, gnawing her lip out of concern for her granddaughter. "This is for them," she said, barely above a whisper.

"She wants the glory, the honor, the name. These things aren't baubles to give, only earned. She earns them now."

DÍSA COULD FEEL THEIR EYES upon her, but she did not care. She kept her attention riveted on the man who thundered up the path. Harness crashed, lungs drew smoke-laced breath, and tendons creaked as he drew his sword back. But Dísa did not seek to go toe-to-toe with him. He was a mailed behemoth, and she was no fool.

As his sword whistled down, with enough force behind it to split her from crown to crotch, Dísa dove left; she struck the ground on his off-hand side, rolled, and came up behind him. She lashed out with her seax. But she did not aim for any place covered by his heavy mail—no, that was folly; instead, as he whirled about, pivoting on his left leg, Dísa thrust her blade under the hem of his hauberk and ripped it back, the notched and jagged blade tearing through cloth, skin, muscle, and sinew. She felt it grate on bone. The Dane bellowed; his hot blood splashed across Dísa's fist. He tried and failed to latch on to her with his free hand. She came to her feet and danced out of reach of him and his long blade. He staggered toward her, dragging his injured leg, one hand clutching at the blood-slick hem of his mail while the other held his sword hilt in a death grip. His scream of rage recalled Auða's, not a handful of minutes before. At the ramps, the Crusaders answered his scream with shouts of vengeance; they wanted to be let off their leashes, but their discipline was like iron. While their captain stood, there was yet hope.

"What's wrong, Dane?" Dísa said over the clamor. "I thought you were eager to finish this? Come! Strike me down!"

Kraki took another step before sinking to one knee, his sword point-first in the ground and its cross-guard holding him upright. He glared at Dísa, spittle dripping from his chin.

From the palisade above her, Dísa heard Grimnir's voice: "Stop toying with that wretched kneeler and finish it!"

She favored the top of the wall with a sidelong glance, spat blood from her mouth, and inverted her grip on her seax. She stalked to the Danish chief, pale now and sweating despite the chill.

He raised his head, his eyes defiant.

"Any last words, wretch?"

A smile split Kraki's features—humorless and cruel. He nodded. Drawing a last deep breath, he roared: "Danes! To me!"

And like that, the hounds of war slipped their chains. Dísa backpedaled, eyes wide as a wall of iron-shod Danes bore down upon her, Kraki's dying laughter lost to the crash of mail and thunderous war cries. Dísa saw her own death reflected in their snarling visages . . .

From behind her came an answering roar. Dísa flinched as bearskin-clad giants lumbered past her, into the teeth of the Danes—and mighty Brodir led them. An axe in both fists, he was the point in a wedge of *berserkir.*

"Odin!"

The crash of these giants colliding with the Danes was like the sound of kindling snapped between fists. Men screamed, shields splintered, and bodies pitched over the edge of the ravine. All the while, the dull-throated roar of the *berserkir* was like a metronome of slaughter.

Dísa stropped the blade of her seax down her thigh, wiping the Dane's blood from it, and sheathed it. She went to where the man lay. He was on his back, one leg folded under him; he yet clung to life. Though nearly drained of blood, his hand nevertheless clawed for his sword. Dísa reached it first. She drew it from the ground. It was a fine blade, she reckoned, lighter than she'd imagined and made from patterned steel that resembled watered silk spun from shades of gray. Foreign letters ran down the blade's length.

Dísa looked at the sword, then down at the dying man. The Dane struggled to speak. Her face transformed into a mask of hate as she raised the sword and drove it point-first into the center of his chest, through mail and bone and into the blood-starved muscles of his heart.

Kraki Ragnarsson shuddered and died.

IN THE SHELTER OF THE trees, the lord of Skara flinched as though from an unseen blow. Father Nikulas watched as Konraðr made the sign of the cross; he heaved a great sigh. "You, too, my hound of war?" he muttered, shaking his head.

"My lord?"

"Recall the Danes, Starkad," he said. "Withdraw them before they are routed." To the priest, he added: "Have Thorwald attend me."

A look of utter confusion crossed Starkad's brow. "But my lord . . . they—"

"Do not test my patience," the albino lord growled. "Not this day. Order the Danes back!" Konraðr whirled and stalked off. Nikulas placed a conciliatory hand on Starkad's arm.

"Best do as he says."

The captain nodded, though his sharp glance at Konraðr's retreating back held a sour note that the priest had not seen before. As the call to withdraw echoed out from the Crusader lines, Nikulas hurried after the lord of Skara. He heard Konraðr muttering.

"She did this? You're certain? Blood of Christ! I will add this to my list of grievances against that heathen trollop! Fear not, my war hound! We will recover your body and give you a good Christian burial."

Nikulas cleared his throat. Konraðr spun around, eyes narrowed and one hand falling to his sword pommel. The priest held his hands up.

"You'd do well not to creep up on me, Nikulas," he said. "I am in a killing mood."

"So, he is dead, then? Ragnarsson?"

Konraðr nodded. "Our little bird dealt him his death wound."

"Impossible!"

But the lord of Skara merely looked at him, a withering stare made worse by his ill humor.

"I presume this means the ramps are lost?"

Konraðr shifted his gaze, looking toward where the Danes reluctantly answered the horn cry to withdraw. They streamed back without any semblance of order—the uninjured helping those bearing ghastly wounds; some pairs carried corpses between them. Among the Danes drifted the spirits of the slain. Konraðr could sense their anger, hear their ghostly clamor. They cried out for vengeance.

The lord of Skara would give it to them.

"Pétr!" he bellowed. The summons filtered through the camp, and soon the engineer hurried over, Thorwald in his wake. But for the crucifix around his bull-neck and the Teutonic cross adorning his surcoat, Thorwald the Red was indistinguishable from their pagan enemy. He wore his red hair long; his beard was twisted into two plaits, and he boasted faded rune-tattoos on his ruddy cheeks. Thorwald leaned on his spear; his was a heavy-bladed weapon stout enough to bring down a bear, and he called it Hrænðr, the Corpse-adder.

"My lord?" Pétr said.

"The ramps are lost. We will need more, if you please. And move your machines. Target the main gate and the first terrace of that God-cursed village. Burn it!" Konraðr did not wait for the engineer's reply. "Thorwald, my eagle! Have you any men among your entourage who might be both stout swimmers and capable mountaineers?"

"We are Norse, my lord," he said. "The sea and the mountains, they are our birthright. Set us a task and we will see it done!"

"Good man! We're going to take the far bank and bring this fracas to an end!"

"And the blessed saint's bones?" Thorwald said. "They are inside?"

"Somewhere, yes," Konraðr replied. He could feel Nikulas's eyes boring into him. "And we will find them!"

Thorwald nodded. "What would you have us do?"

"We need that fallen bridge repaired, and we need to get enough of our lads over to discourage the heathens from trying to retake it. But first, if we are to do this, you must scale the walls of the ravine . . ."

AN HOUR BEFORE SUNSET, THE Crusaders began their bombardment in earnest. The folk of Hrafnhaugr heard the distinct *thump* of the siege engines before the first missiles began to fall on the lowest terrace. Sections of tree trunks slammed into the palisade around the gate, cracking the wood and loosening the foundations of the wall where the wooden palings pierced the embankment. Crenels shattered, showering the Geats manning the walls with jagged splinters of wood. The next volley brought a hail of lake stones. Most were fist-sized, large enough to snap bones and break skulls; a few were massive enough to bring down a roof. One such stone, twice the size of a man's head, struck the center beam of Kjartan's smithy, bounced, and punched through the wall of Ragni the Fat's house, killing his wife.

With the fall of night, the Crusaders unleashed their incendiaries. Burning logs struck, spraying great rooster tails of sparks, embers, and flaming chunks of wood into the air to drift down into the tight streets of the terrace. Though the palisade smoldered under these repeated bursts, its mossy exterior was loath to burn. Not so the houses sheltering behind it. Men and women scrambled to fill buckets with water as a hundred small fires flared up; smoke hung like a shroud over the terrace.

And as the snap and splinter of wood continued, with the cracking thud of trunks striking the gate wall and the clatter of stones raining from the smoke-laced night sky, there came a new wrinkle: arrows. They came with the stones and the burning logs—iron-headed shafts fletched with goose feathers to fall at random. Archers stood at the edge of the Scar, at the edge of their range, and sent flights of arrows at random. Most embedded themselves in the outer surface of the palisade; a few, from the strongest bows, dropped among the Geats.

One such arrow slew old Hygge's son, Hygelac. It pierced his neck, cutting the cord of his spine and sending him headlong into the fire he was helping put out. It became his funeral pyre. Deaths like his, senseless and random, undermined the spirit of the Geats; they looked up from the spreading fires and the incessant hail of death and wondered where their protector was . . .

FROM THE DOOR OF GAUTHEIMR, Grimnir watched the lower terrace burn. That the wretched hymn-singers were concentrating their fire on the main gate and the walls around it made him think they were up to something. He glanced at Bjorn Svarti. "Double the guard at the postern, and make sure they keep a good eye on the narrows, there. Crafty buggers are up to something. I can feel it."

Svarti nodded and went to see it done.

Úlfrún, Brodir, Forne, and Herroðr sat on the benches behind him, Sigrún and the remaining Daughters of the Raven among them. Young Herroðr kept glancing their way, expecting to see Auða or Rannveig among them. Their absence cut him like a knife. Dísa sat alone. Berkano had bathed and dressed her wounds. Lines of exhaustion and grief etched her young face, giving her the appearance of years she had yet to earn. She drank ale from a horn cup.

"Lend me a boat or two," Úlfrún said. "We'll slip over to their camp by night and rid ourselves of those cursed machines."

"It won't work," Dísa replied before Grimnir could answer. "He'll know you're coming and lay a trap. Whatever it is that protects him knows our hearts better than we do."

"Aye, the little bird is right."

"So we just sit here and let that white-skinned bastard batter the gates down?" Úlfrún snapped.

"Is there a way to blind him?" This was from Sigrún. "Rob him of this second sight, or whatever it is?"

Grimnir turned away from the door. His good eye narrowed in thought as he went to where Dísa sat. He stared hard at her, but directed his words to Úlfrún. "Your man said he was haunted, is that so?"

"Forne?"

The wolf-cloaked chief of her *úlfhéðnar* nodded. "So the word was in Eiðar. Haunted by his deeds off in the East, at Miklagarðr—Constantinople, they call it now."

"And you say he seems to hear things?"

"Seemed that way to me," replied Dísa. *"The wind brings me your secrets,* he said to me. *I hear your thoughts in the chirp of insects, your dreams in the crackle of leaves."*

"Ghosts," Grimnir muttered. After a moment, he added: "Old Gífr, who was my mother's brother, he used to know things before they'd happen, too. I always chalked it up to him being witch-wise, but he told me something ere he went off to fight that hymn-singing dog, Charles Magnus. He said, 'Hold troth with your ghosts, and they will hold troth with you.' That was the sort of useless drivel the old git would spout, but here it makes sense." Grimnir gestured out beyond Hrafnhaugr's walls. "That wretch has turned whatever's haunting him into his blasted eyes and ears!"

"So, what do we do?" Úlfrún said.

Grimnir fixed his gaze on Sigrún. "Like she said, we blind the bastard."

"You can do this?"

"Not me," Grimnir said. In one black-nailed hand, he toyed with the four chestnut acorns. "But I know someone who can."

BEFORE HRAFNHAUGR CAME INTO EXISTENCE, before the foundations of Gautheimr were laid, there was the Raven Stone. Grimnir stared up at that spike of black rock. The whole thing was Gífr's work. It was he who'd found this chunk of basalt, vaguely reminiscent of a raven's feather—a bit over fourteen feet in height with one side that was broad and flat—and it was Gífr who had dragged it to the crest of the hill and raised it. Some seventy years after Raðbolg's death his elder brother had carved his epitaph.

By the dim light of the lower terrace, Grimnir could still make out the weathered runes: *Gífr Kjallandi's son raised this stone in memory of Raðbolg, his brother. He died in the wyrm's embrace.* The stylized raven at the center of the stone was Raðbolg's badge; around it wrapped the coils of the dragon, Malice-Striker.

"Stoke your fire there," he growled to Dísa. He pointed to a space opposite the flat side of the stone. "Stoke it bright! I need a well of shadow. And have someone fetch me that Christ-Dane's body. The one you killed."

"His body?"

"What does every trap need, my precious little fool?"

"Bait?" she replied.

Grimnir tapped the side of his nose. "Bait."

He watched the preparations closely; watched as men extinguished the torches along the wall facing the stone, as every living soul was ushered inside Gautheimr. It would be touch and go.

"Will this work?" Úlfrún said, echoing Grimnir's own thoughts. It was her men who brought the body of the Danish chief, a pale and near-bloodless manikin stripped of its mail. Forne carried a bucket filled with the broth of slaughter—congealed blood wrung from the fallen enemy and chunks of spear-torn viscera; a bloody thigh bone protruded from it like a hellish ladle. The chief of the wolf-brothers grimaced as he handed the bucket to Grimnir.

"I've seen it work before." Grimnir shrugged. "Or something akin to it. Put him there." He motioned to the deeper shadow opposite the fire.

Úlfrún raised an eyebrow. "But have *you* ever done this?"

"Something akin to it," he replied, fairly spitting each word. He snarled at the one-handed woman. "Get your lot ready and wait for my signal." He watched Úlfrún lead two-score of her wolf-sons, her *úlfheðnar,* out through the postern gate and down to the dock, to where a trio of boats waited to take them to the shore beyond the Scar. Grimnir heard the door to Gautheimr close with a thud; all that remained was the crash and rattle of the enemy bombardment—the whistling of incendiaries, the crunch of roofs staving in, the trembling impact of wood on wood. Bjorn Hvítr and his lads huddled in the shadow of the wall by the main gate, their eyes peeled; Bjorn Svarti had everyone else hunkered down inside the longhouse, packed cheek-by-jowl like a run of herring.

"It's time," Grimnir said, exhaling. "Keep that fire bright and hot, little bird!"

Dísa nodded. Someone had brought up the double bellows from Kjartan's smithy. She worked them slowly, each exhalation sending tendrils of flame higher. Grimnir turned back to the front of the Raven Stone. The fire cast it in deep shadow. Nodding, he dragged the bucket closer; he stirred the blood and viscera with the thigh bone—three times in one direction, then three times in the opposite direction. Thrice, he did this, chanting under his breath each time:

"I call to thee, | my ancestors,
 Who dwell beyond the pale;
 Come to this door | of earth-fixed stone
 And hear your kin-folk's plea."

At the end, Grimnir set the bone aside and hefted the bucket. With a grunt, he splashed its contents over the stone. Cold gore painted the runes, and chunks of flesh dribbled down the grooves in the carved raven. The stone's surface steamed; from it there came such stench of boiling blood and foetor that even Grimnir winced. Still, he did not falter:

"I know a hall standing | far from the sun,
 In Nástrond, under the | shadows of Niðafjoll;
 War-reek rages | and reddening fire:
 The high heat licks | against heaven itself.

"There is Bálegyr | the mightiest made
Of all the *kaunar*, | and Kjallandi next;
Lútr and Hrauðnir, | Njól and Dreki,
Naglfari and Gangr, | and fierce Mánavargr.

"Many a son of Wolf | and Serpent did they make,
To plague the deeps | of Miðgarðr;
Tjasse and Mogthrasir, | Aegir and Hræsvelgr,
Skríkja and Raðbolg, | and lore-wise Gífr.

"It is to you I call | Gífr Kjallandisson,
Plundered of life on | Miðgarðr's hateful shores;
From Nástrond, under the | shadows of Niðafjoll,
Gífr Kjallandisson, | I call out to you.

"Attend!

"Grimnir am I, | Bálegyr's son,
Alone of the *kaunar* to yet plague Miðgarðr;
I made this gate | by blood and bone,
And call you to its threshold."

The echo of Grimnir's words faded into silence—a silence punctuated by the crackle of the fire and the staccato thuds from a trio of impacts on the gate of Hrafnhaugr. The stone steamed; blood dripped and pooled at its base. Nothing.

Grimnir's lips curled in a snarl of rage. "Gífr Kjallandisson!" he roared. "Come to the door, damn your worthless hide! Gífr! I call you to this threshold! Gífr Kjallandisson!" Grimnir stooped suddenly and snatched up the blood-slimed thigh bone; cursing, he slung it at the Raven Stone. "Damn you, you old git!"

The bone struck the face of the stone . . . and vanished into it, like a pebble dropped into water. Blood splashed; concentric circles lapped across the gory surface, where gobbets of flesh now floated on this upright lake of blood. And slowly, Grimnir saw a face forming—a head and shoulders seemingly made from congealed ichor, eyeless and owning no mouth. He heard a wet exhalation.

"Why do you trouble us, | spawn of my sister's loins?
Why do you call us | to that thrice-cursed shore?
Let us here abide | in strife without end;
Till the death-note blows | fierce on Gjallarhorn."

Grimnir chuckled. "You always told me to fight fire with fire, did you not? *Faugh!* Those wretched hymn-singers out yonder have their spirits watching us. I have plots to hatch and I need them driven off. Take this"—Grimnir kicked the corpse at his feet—"as payment."

He heard a deep inhalation; a snuffling sound followed by a sharp hiss.

"More serpents there are | beneath the ash
Than these unwise apes would think;
Aye, Matteus and Markús | lurk beyond the bounds,
And with them stands | Lúkas and obscure Jóhannes.

"But while the fences wrought | by the sons of Kjallandi
Hold the Christ-god's men at bay;
No fence can stop | the fey-locked wanderer
When he comes to collect his due."

Grimnir loosed a dark chuckle. "You tell me nothing I don't already know, you useless old git. I didn't call you out for your so-called wisdom. Can you blind that sanctimonious ass, yonder, or not?"

The surface of the stone rippled, once more, as a hand and arm formed from blood reached out and caught the corpse's ankle. The body started to slide into that grisly gate, but Grimnir stopped it by slamming his heel down on the corpse's chest.

"First you blind the bastard, and then you feast."

"Trust me not, | little rat?"

Grimnir gave a short bark of laughter. "You taught me well."

There came a sudden ripping sound, as though black-nailed hands tearing through damp cloth; from the surface of the stone, something darker than the surrounding shadow detached itself. It poured around Grimnir—a shoal of deeper gloom that flowed up the wall and vanished over the top of the palisade.

Grimnir turned and watched. "Little bird," he said, motioning for Dísa. As she left the bellows and came around to his side of the stone, the young woman's face was as pale as curdled milk. "Take a torch up to the top of the wall and give Úlfrún the signal."

The girl's hands trembled as she did what Grimnir asked. For his part, the *skrælingr* turned back to the Raven Stone and sank down on his haunches. His eye gleamed like an ember in the shadow as he watched the rippling skin of blood, its surface disturbed now and again by a featureless face, by a clawed and beckoning hand.

"Skríkja," he hissed. "Your vengeance is coming."

22

Light spilled from Konraðr's pavilion.

The lord of Skara stood at the head of a long table, his captains seated at either hand. Father Nikulas sat nearest to him, on his right, with Pétr beside him; to Konraðr's left sat the hawkish form of Thorwald, and then Starkad. Both men vibrated with barely chained rage.

"You Danes," Konraðr was saying to the other captains ranked along the table—Kraki's officers, led by dour Horsten, who hailed from Roskilde and was cousin to its bishop. "You Danes will have the honor of being first across once the bridge is repaired. You will be the tip of my spear, and vengeance will be yours."

"First into the teeth of the accursed enemy," Horsten echoed with a satisfied nod.

"It should be my men, lord," Thorwald snarled, unable to contain his anger any longer. "We take the risks, we should reap the glory!"

"Aye," Starkad said. He nodded at the Danes, bloodied yet from their encounter at the postern gate of Hrafnhaugr. "They've had their chance and were found wanting! Let your sworn men have the honor—"

Thorwald snorted.

Konraðr struck the table with the flat of his palm. The albino's red eyes gleamed with a dangerous light. "Did I mumble, dogs? Because I am pale, do you mistake me for a weakling? Do you covet the high seat of Skara, Starkad? Or you, Thorwald? Then come! Evict me from it and this battle will go how you desire! No? Then keep your cursed tongues between your teeth!"

"You dare?" Thorwald started to rise, but it was a sharp word from Father Nikulas arrested the movement and caused him to resume his seat.

"God is watching!" The priest glared around the table. "You all forget yourselves, my lords! This is no lowly raid for plunder or for glory! This is the Almighty's work we do—this is *bellum sacrum,* a holy war, a Crusade to wipe this heathen filth from the North and reclaim our lost relics!"

"We know what we're here for!" Thorwald replied. He scooped up his goblet and took a long draught of wine.

"Then act like it," Nikulas hissed in reply. "There will be glory enough to go around, once we've excised this blight from our midst. And make no mistake—it is a disease, an infection of heresy! Look at yourselves. You fight over scraps, and why? Is it merely your true selves, or is it rather the base and unholy nature of this place? We stand on unhallowed ground! But for the power of the Lord, God Almighty we might succumb to it, and what then? Why, it would be as a second coming of Sodom and Gomorrah!"

"Our faith is our shield," Konraðr muttered. He looked up. "Well said, my good priest. The evil of this land plucks at my soul like a skald's fingers on the strings of a lute. Forgive my harsh words, Thorwald, and you, Starkad, but my orders stand. The Danes will be my vanguard. Come, raise your cups as brothers and toast our dead comrade. To Kraki!" Around the table, the captains lifted their goblets to Heaven and added their voices to Konraðr's. "To Kraki Ragnarsson!"

"And may God have mercy upon his soul," Horsten muttered.

"Oh, God's mercy is without question," Nikulas replied. The priest made the sign of the Cross. "Kraki died fighting the Heathen. Whatever his sins may have been, by taking the Cross he received absolution. He sits at the Lord's right hand, Horsten. All of you, and all of your men, know this: the Cross you bear, and the blood you leave behind on the field, will open the gates of Heaven. We—"

The priest's voice fades. Konraðr can plainly see Nikulas is still speaking, but no sound reaches the lord of Skara's ears. No, he corrects himself. That isn't precisely true. He can hear . . . something. He glances around, his eyes shifting from corner to corner, from face to face.

Laughter. He can hear coarse and uproarious laughter. Konraðr rises to his feet and goes to the door flap of his pavilion. He hears a woman's voice raised in song, its lyrics obscene; hands clapping in time with the off-color music. Konraðr feels his choler rise. He will make these baseborn louts pay! This is no bawdy house. This is a camp of war—and a camp of the noblest sort of war mere men can imagine. Bellum sacrum, *the priest had called it. Holy war. He shoves aside the flap, an acidic curse on his lips, and steps . . .*

. . . into the nave of that ancient cathedral the men of the east call the Great Church of Constantinople; he shuffles like a dead thing through the broken imperial door and the living follow.

None can see him. Not by the greasy orange light of the burning city, glaring in from the clerestory overhead, nor by the guttering glow of immense bonfires eating at the Greeks' holy books and wooden relics. Even to his own eye, he appears as a half-sensed shadow, a ripple of darkness glimpsed for a brief moment. But he knows he is there, even if the smoke coiling from smoldering pews has more substance than the grim and tattered wraith he has become.

A ghost of Constantinople.

He staggers on. The naked sword in his fist scrapes the blood-fouled tile underfoot as he lurches from column to column. He passes a saddled horse, spear-pierced and left to die under the sacred dome; passes a smashed reliquary, and hears laughter, again, as a horde of ragged and bloody children run past. They laugh as they kick a skull back and forth like a ball. The skull of a holy martyr. It strikes a column and shatters. The children are unperturbed. There are other reliquaries to smash open, other saints' skulls to pry loose from their gold and crystal housings.

All around, he bears witness to a thousand acts of vandalism: frescoes and mosaics defaced, images of Christ and of the Virgin Mary trodden underfoot by men—soldiers whose surcoats and gambesons sport the Cross of the Holy Father in Rome—desperate for gold and silver to repay their debt to the Venetians; he sees the doors of the Great Church, blessed Hagia Sophia, pried off their hinges and taken as spoil; men drink wine from the relics of Christ, curse and blaspheme, fornicate in the patriarch's seat with whores clad in stolen vestments . . .

He reaches the apse, and there before what is left of the great altar, the man bends his knees and collapses. Only his hands, draped over the cross-guard of his sword's hilt, keeps him upright. "Why?" he says, voice cracking as he raises his face to the altar. "Why, O Father of Heaven, do you allow this madness to continue?" His chin sinks to his breast; he closes his eyes . . .

A hard, rasping voice answers him. "Aren't you a precious sort of fool, you milk-skinned rat? What is that in your hand if not a sword?"

"I am not the Lord's retribution," the man replies. He opens his eyes. A shadow looms over him, tall and lean. He has the impression of whalebone and gristle knotted together with ropes of muscle and hard gobbets of sinew. Ruddy eyes glare down at him. "I am wreathed in sin, marked by it."

"Who better to deliver your lord's punishment? What is more difficult: staying on your knees and doing nothing, or rising and showing these swine the power and majesty of your lord, this God you kneel to?"

The man's eyes slide to the blade of his sword. There is a divine gleam to it—an urgency that lends the words of this thing a certain clarity. Still, though, he hesitates. "I am but one. They are many. Why should they listen to me?"

"Make them listen," the voice hisses. "Your blade is not the threat, little fool. It is the promise! Lop a few heads off, cut a few throats, and the rest will fall in line. Are you not a soldier of God, called upon this holy war to spread your faith? So, get off your knees, wretch, and do what you were called to do!"

The man clambers to his feet and turns.

"Do you suffer the blasphemer to live?" the shadow whispers.

"No!"

"Do you suffer the defiler, the enemy of God?"

"No!"

"Then say the words, wretch. Say the words!"

"God wills it!" the man thunders. While that phrase yet echoes under the fire-etched dome of the Great Church, blessed Hagia Sophia, the avenging spirit who was Konraðr throws himself at the men and women defiling the patriarch's seat.

His sword flashes through the smoky air.

"GOD WILLS IT!"

Konraðr convulsed. His eyes rolled back in his head; the goblet in his hand clattered to the table, splashing wine lees across its scarred boards. The albino's body went rigid. Nikulas caught him by the shoulder before he could topple from his seat. From inside his cassock, the priest produced a tube of hard leather.

"Starkad!" he called to the captain of the sworn men. "Hold his jaws apart!" Brawny Starkad did as the priest instructed, his strong fingers none too gently prying the albino lord's mouth open—far enough and long enough for Nikulas to slide the leather between them. He glanced at the men watching, their expressions running the gamut. "So he won't bite his tongue in two, or break his teeth. Come, Starkad, help me get him to his cot."

"What ails him?" Thorwald said, making the sign of the Cross. "Is he possessed?"

Nikulas smiled wearily. "Not by demons. These lingering fevers and convulsions stem from diseases he contracted off in the east, and injuries earned fighting beneath the walls of Constantinople—Miklagarðr, to you."

"Small comfort, that. But is he fit to lead us?"

A silence fell over the pavilion. Starkad started to reply, but the priest's hand on his shoulder brought him up short. Nikulas rose. He was no small man; at his full height, he and Thorwald were equals. He met the Norseman's frank stare. "You dare ask?"

Thorwald leaned forward; his eyes were cold and hard, the color of the grinding ice of his homeland. "Priest, I dare this and much more, besides. We are an army of God, and God decides who is fit to lead us. It seems to me that God has decided to punish Skara's lord for reasons only the Almighty knows. We have bled here, and we have gained nothing." He gestured to the still-rigid form of Konraðr. "Perhaps *this* is God's way of telling us to choose a new leader."

From the far end of the table, Horsten grunted his assent. "Priest?"

Nikulas sighed. "This is God's army," he said. "And the Holy Father in Rome is the chosen shepherd of God's will on earth. Do you dispute this?" The captains shrugged and shook their heads. "Then you do not dispute that I am the voice of the Holy Father in this small corner of the north? Here, now, I am the shepherd of God's will—and it is God's will that Konraðr of Skara lead His Crusade to reclaim the bones of Saint Teodor, and the sword that blessed martyr used to defeat the Devil-sent wyrm of Hell, for the glory of Christ and the King! Do you dispute this?" Nikulas roared.

Men backed away; even Thorwald motioned for peace.

"We are under attack," said Pétr—forgotten Pétr, who had watched the evening unfold in silence.

"Indeed, Brother Pétr!" Nikulas said. "We are under attack by the sin of pride! You covet glory like a lecherous man covets the virgin daughters of his neighbor! Shame, Thorwald the Red! Shame shall be your portion! We—"

"No, priest!" Pétr bellowed. He ripped aside the door flap of the pavilion;

outside, men howled in alarm as flames licked the night sky. The mangonels had fallen silent, and from the edge of camp nearest the shores of Lake
Vänern came the clash of steel. "We are under attack!"

THE WOLFLIKE SHAPES OF THE *úlfhéðnar* descended on the Crusader camp
in a silent wave. Two longboats, their oar-locks muffled, had delivered the
two-score men to a sheltered cove on Lake Vänern's shore, a rocky shingle
screened by a low hill and a tangled thicket of willow and ash. There, they
split into two groups. Úlfrún led one; Forne led the other.

The Crusaders tending the incendiaries were the first to fall. These men,
stripped to the waist and sweating, poured coals into the bored-out hearts
of pine tree trunks, each the height of a man. Nearby, axes thudded as their
mates kept the supply of trunks moving. Úlfrún watched this almost me-
chanical process for a long moment—pine trees of a certain height and girth
were marked out with strips of cloth; woodsmen felled these, and used a
team of mules to snake them over to where the engineers cleaned them up,
sawed them into pieces, and punched out their centers with awls, augers,
and reaming drills. Once the tenders poured their coals, the incendiaries had
to season for an hour and more—aided by a crew of men wielding hand
bellows—until their hearts were nearly molten with pine pitch and embers.

Several were sitting on a sled, smoldering as they awaited delivery to the
mangonels. Úlfrún grinned. These would be her target. She gave a low whistle; behind her, men clad in mail and wolf skins rose from hiding. Úlfrún led
them into the Crusaders' midst.

The first to die was a woodsman who straightened from lopping branches
off a pine log, curious at the clash of harness coming from behind him.
He turned, a frown crinkling the sweat-sheen of his brow. He glimpsed a
shadow, wolf-clad and tall, even as Úlfrún crushed his skull with one blow
from her iron hand.

Wolf howls split the night as the *úlfhéðnar* drove like a lance into the un-
protected flank of the Christians. Blood splashed; bone snapped, and men
screamed in prayer and alarm, recoiling from the savage and blood-spattered
silhouettes that suddenly appeared among them. Úlfrún kicked a shirtless
Swede into the fire, her axe snaking out to sever his leg at the knee as he
struggled to rise. The stenches of cooked blood and seared flesh mingled
with that of resin and fresh-cut pine.

"Odin!" she roared, walking through the fire over his burning corpse. Men fled from her. A short distance away, down a slight hill, she could see the first of the three infernal engines: a throwing arm housed in a frame of timber, powered by a profusion of ropes and the muscle of a dozen men. A stone the size of a dead man's torso sat in the basket at the end of the throwing arm. As Úlfrún watched, the rope-haulers pulled in unison—a mighty effort that sent the rock lofting into the night sky. Its journey would end a few hundred yards away, across the ravine, and over the palisade of Hrafnhaugr—backlit by a dozen fires burning along the lower terrace. But even as they recovered and sought to reload the basket, her lads smashed into them.

Riven bodies fell among the ropes; a head bounced, landing in the throwing basket. Its owner staggered a few steps before sinking down among the ropes. Another engineer tripped over that corpse in his haste to get away from the biting swords and axes of the heathen invaders. He screamed and writhed as a spear took him in the hip. His was not the only voice of terror. More arose, becoming cries of alarm—and that alarm spread through the Crusader camp.

Úlfrún wasted no more time. "That axe!" she bellowed, pointing to a long-handled woodsman's axe still clutched in a dead Christian's fist. "Bring it to me!" One of her men snatched it up. With Úlfrún's help, they used it to pull the first incendiary off the sled. It tipped on its side and struck the ground with a thump. Heedless of the heat rising from it, Úlfrún bellowed a warning as she put her booted heel to it, kicking it down the slope and into the siege engines. It bounced, spewing embers from one end. A pair of defenders tried to divert it with spears, but the heavy pine log smashed them to the ground and rolled over them.

The log's journey ended when it struck the heavy frame of the first mangonel. That shuddering impact, the crunch of wood on wood, knocked the engine askew even as it cracked open the incendiary, causing its near-molten heart to spill out across ropes and timbers. The machine kindled like a torch, the *whoosh* of greedy flames loud enough for Úlfrún to hear over the din. Smoke and embers billowed into the night sky.

"Again!" Úlfrún shouted. Following her lead, wolf-cloaked warriors muscled the other incendiaries off the sled and sent them tumbling down the slope toward the growing conflagration. They were not precision missiles—

not like arrows or javelins; every stone and contour of the ground set them
to bouncing. They veered off their chosen courses, rolling this way and that.
One came to rest among the Crusaders' tents, its cargo of fiery coals setting
alight canvas, cloth, and flesh. Another wobbled and slewed to a stop when
its edge bit into the soil near the second mangonel. Úlfrún led the way down
the slope after it, gesturing at the third machine with her iron hand. "Cut
the ropes on that one!"

Meanwhile, heedless of burns, she shoved the incendiary closer to the
second mangonel and struck it with her axe. "Break it open! Let the bastards
see them burn!" Úlfrún, limned by the firelight, raised her iron fist. She
meant to order her wolves deeper into the Crusader camp, but suddenly she
heard an angry hiss, felt a thudding impact that staggered her, and snarled
at the arrow that had sunk itself into her ribs. She ripped it out, heedless of
the damage. A second arrow rocked her back on her heels. Úlfrún spied the
archer, a Swede, through the smoke and waves of heat rising off the burning
mangonel. He stood on the far side—alone, as near as she could tell; he had
three more arrows thrust into the ground before him, a fourth resting on the
string. Smiling, she plucked that second arrow from the flesh of her abdomen, kissed its bloody bodkin head, and tossed it aside as she leapt forward
and charged through the wrack and ruin of the siege engines.

She loosed an ear-splitting howl.

The archer paled. She saw his lips moving; praying or cursing, Úlfrún
could not say. But he loosed a third arrow that went wide of its mark, and
then dropped his bow to claw at the mace hanging off his heavy leather belt.
He brought it up even as she struck. Úlfrún's axe bit through his upper arm
and lodged in the wall of his chest. The Swede flopped to the side; Úlfrún
wrenched him upright and kicked him free of her axe head. She saw no
other archers, but from this vantage, at the edge of the firelight, she beheld
Forne's advance.

His score of men had spiked deep into the Crusaders' camp, down a
broad avenue lined with tents, through a makeshift plaza, and toward a rich
pavilion that could only belong to the lord of Skara. They were slashing and
burning, slaying soldier and camp follower alike. But he was overextended.
He was too far from the safety of the camp's edge. And he was about to be
cut off.

"Son of a bitch!" she said, seeing a wall of mailed Crusaders pouring in behind him. Cursing, she turned and bellowed: "Herroðr! Sound the with-drawal!"

And Herroðr, blood-blasted and wild-eyed, raised a brazen horn to his lips and loosed a series of notes. Even so, it was to no avail. Iron men bearing cross-festooned shields and naked swords crashed into the rear of Forne's formation. Half a dozen of his lads went down in that first clash, taking twice their number of Christians with them. She heard Forne roaring for the rest of them to scatter, echoing her order to withdraw.

"Jarl!" Herroðr shouted. He gestured toward the third mangonel, its ropes cut but its frame not yet burning. She saw a small band of men rushing in to save the blasted machine. A small-statured Dane led them; he shouted orders, calling for a defensive cordon even as he bid men fetch water to douse the flames. He had the bearing of an engineer. Úlfrún wanted his head. She motioned for Herroðr to follow her and set off toward the little Dane at a loping run.

The diminutive engineer shaded his eyes against the harsh flames . . .

. . . And saw her bearing down on him, flanked by a handful of wolf-brothers.

The little man had time to give a bleat of fear before Úlfrún of the Iron Hand crashed into him. He stumbled back, half-drew a seax from his belt. Úlfrún's axe took him high, in the juncture of his shoulder and neck. Its blade cut sidewise, through muscle and tendon, bone and cartilage; blood fountained. The man gurgled, blowing froth from pierced lungs and a sev-ered windpipe as he fell. Úlfrún wrenched her axe free of his corpse.

"Back!" she called out. "Back to the boats! Herroðr, your horn! Sound the withdrawal again!" Úlfrún skirted the burning mangonels, retracing her path back to the crest of the hill where their attack began. There, she did a quick head-count. Three of her lads were dead, their bodies in tow; ten of the seventeen remaining bore wounds, though none severe. Nodding, she started for the boats when Herroðr gave a cry of alarm.

Úlfrún turned.

Scores of Crusaders converged on their position; hundreds more were streaming in from every corner of the camp, archers among them. She saw Danes mixing with Swedes, dour Norsemen among them. They had the foundations of a shield wall—one supported on its flanks by agile bowmen. And she saw they were herding Forne before them. Herroðr would have descended into their midst, once again, to die alongside the chief of her wolf-brothers had Úlfrún not stopped him with a sharp word.

Forne staggered and pitched forward onto his knees. He struggled to rise, but Úlfrún could see he'd taken several wounds to the body. He left a trail of blood behind him. From the enemy ranks, a giant, red-bearded Norseman, spear in hand, stepped out and strode up to Forne. He kicked him in the back with one booted foot, sending him face-first onto the ground. The Norseman reached down and stripped the wolf-headed cloak from Forne's shoulders. He gestured up the rise with his spear; Forne craned his neck, saw Úlfrún. The Norseman muttered something none of them could hear; a question, perhaps, for Forne nodded in answer. He clambered to his knees. The Norseman stepped away from him and gestured. Forne glanced over his shoulder, his gray-flecked beard bloody. The man gestured again, impatient. Forne nodded.

Suddenly, he threw his head back. From his blade-pierced body came a titanic cry: "ODIN!"

And on the rise above the Crusader camp, Úlfrún and her remaining wolves took up their brother's howl: "ODIN!"

Scowling like a man who'd been duped, the Norseman stepped in and rammed his spear in between Forne's shoulder blades. The old *úlfhéðinn* gave a choking cry that turned to a death rattle as the Norseman twisted the blade of his spear and wrenched it free.

Silence descended on the Crusader camp, save for the crackle of flames as they consumed two of the mangonels. Úlfrún stepped out from among her men. She pointed at the Norseman with her axe. "Your name, dog!"

The Norseman shook droplets of blood from his gory spear blade. "Thorwald the Red, I am called!"

"A dead man, I name you, Thorwald the Red!" Úlfrún roared. "I am Úlfrún of the Iron Hand, and by Odin, I swear I will kill you!"

"I know you, bitch of the north!" Thorwald laughed and raised his spear aloft. "And by God, I swear you can try! Hrænðr has a taste for pagan blood!"

Úlfrún felt a challenge building in her chest. Her lips writhed, eager to give it a voice. A red haze, a killing lust, danced before her eyes. She wanted to see this Thorwald dead at her feet. She wanted to taste his blood. But it was Herröðr who brought her back to the moment. Crusaders were hemming them in. He plucked at her sleeve. "We must go, Jarl, or we die here with him!"

Úlfrún nodded. And like the wolves that were their namesakes, she and her folk backed away, their eyes blazing in wrath as they vanished in the drifting smoke.

FATHER NIKULAS CROUCHED BESIDE THE supine form of his lord. Konraðr lay on his cot, naked to the waist and bathed in sweat. His limbs trembled as though from great exertion, and his heart thudded against its cage of bone. The priest shook his head—both at the scars tracing the flesh of Konraðr's torso and at the sheer futility of his disease. Was it, as Thorwald suggested, a God-sent curse, or was it merely the lingering effect of bearing so many wounds to body and soul?

Nikulas bathed Konraðr's brow with a cool compress. *"O Lord, rebuke him not in thy indignation,"* the priest quoted, *"nor chastise him in thy wrath. Have mercy on him, O Lord, for he is weak: heal him, O Lord, for his bones are troubled. And his soul is troubled exceedingly: but thou, O Lord, how long? Turn to him, O Lord, and deliver his soul: O save him for thy mercy's sake."*

Konraðr's lips trembled; under pale lids, his ruddy eyes darted to and fro. He muttered something. Nikulas leaned closer, straining to hear. Slowly, he could make out the words the lord of Skara chanted, almost like a mantra:

"G-God . . . wills it."

"God wills it!" the man booms, his sword slicing open a blasphemer's throat. He hurls the corpse aside and turns. A woman sits astride the patriarch's seat—red-lipped and lascivious, her stolen cassock slit up the sides to just under her breasts, leaving nothing to the imagination. She gyrates and grinds as if the seat is her lover's lap, beckoning to him with one crimson-tipped finger, imagining herself as the hard-fought prize he has come to claim.

"Harlot of Babylon!" he roars. Three strides bring him to the top of the dais; grunting, he strikes the woman's head from her shoulders. And suddenly, rather than a cacophony of voices there is only one. He turns, wipes the blood from his eyes, and beholds a carpet of bodies. He staggers against the patriarch's seat, but dares not sit in it.

He looks closer at the faces of the dead, expecting to see the coarse and unshaven visages of the soldiers he's killed. But there is a child—a boy of eleven, split open like a ripe fruit—and he recognizes those lifeless brown eyes. He'd killed him years before, while breaching the walls of Constantinople. And there, sprawled amid the sea of flesh, was another familiar face—the woman he'd slain, the slave of a wealthy Greek, in the vestibule of her master's home while the killing fever was upon him.

All the faces, they look familiar. He knows them. From the young soldier killed in vicious street fighting around the Blachernae Palace, to the children, a boy and a girl, who died under his blade when they would not give up their family's horse.

"Wh-what have I done?"

The specter at his shoulder chuckles, a sound like stones falling into his grave. "You've freed yourself," he snarls. "But there is one more."

From the grim shadow steps an old man, a one-eyed Varangian—half Greek and half Norse. He shuffles forward, his hands slick with blood from a belly wound. He looks around, his pale blue eyes watery with terror. He mutters something in Greek.

"Kill him, my precious fool," the specter whispers, its voice now silky and as soft as a lover's. "Come, kill him and be done."

"No!" The sword clatters from the man's hand as he rushes to the old Varangian's side. "Begone, devil! Trouble this place no longer! This is a house of God!"

"You milk-blooded little hypocrite," the specter says. "Oh, aye, it's a house of your foolish god when it serves your purpose. But what was it before, when you were slaughtering these innocents, eh? Was it a house of your so-called god, then?" The shadow-thing makes a derisive sound. "I will do you a favor, rat, though you ask none of me." Hands like smoky talons reach out and seize the old man by the throat. The remaining voice howls in rage. He feels the earth tremble, as though a jötunn were stamping its foot in indignation. He cannot move; he can only watch as the shadow-thing throttles the old man . . . or, is it an old man? Its form wavers; for half a heartbeat, he sees an ancient and wizened thing hanging from those talons, one-eyed and pale, spitting in rage. Then, with a wrench, the thing's neck bones crack and suddenly the shadow is holding an old man in its claws, dead.

"You held troth with your ghosts," the specter says, "and they with you. But those weren't yours, worm. Go and fight that wretched kinsman of mine, if you must. But know it'll be a fair fight from here on out. I have done you a favor, though I doubt you'll live long enough to appreciate it. I have seen the warp and weft of Fate, my precious little fool. Death is coming."

"Death comes for us all," the man replies. He lunges for his sword; grasping the hilt, he rises and whirls, ready to impale the shadow-thing on a yard of bright steel.

But he is alone beneath the scorched dome of the Hagia Sophia—not even his ghosts stir the smoky air.

He hears harsh laughter, a voice fading: "Not all of us, little fool."

THE CRUSADERS LET THE TWO mangonels burn; around the third, Thorwald threw up a protective cordon of soldiers. Other fires he ordered extinguished, while woodsmen tracked the intruders' retreat to the lake shore.

"Two boats," he told Nikulas. "Maybe forty men, and that she-Wolf of the north."

"What was her name?"

"Úlfrún of the Iron Hand," Thorwald replied. "I've come across her handiwork before. The king of Norway has a price on her head large enough to outfit a flotilla of ships. How is he?" The Norseman nodded to where Konraðr lay.

"He sleeps soundly now." The priest wiped his hands on a dry cloth. "He will mourn Pétr. We all will. This campaign has cost us much blood, especially the blood of friends."

"But it will be worth it, will it not? To retrieve the martyr's bones and bring his Christ-blessed sword into the light of God once more . . ."

"You sound like a priest, my friend," Nikulas said. "Yes, all this loss serves a cause greater than any one man. Any ten men. We will persevere until we remove this heathen blight from our blessed lands, and restore our relics to their rightful place. Are your men in position?"

Thorwald nodded. "They are ready."

"Give the order, then, and tell them God watches over them. Let the Heathen think we've gone quiet, that we're licking our wounds. At dawn, we will raise the bridge and bring the fight to them!"

"The Danes go first, as we agreed," Thorwald said, nodding to Horsten. "But that northern bitch is mine!"

"Agreed." Nikulas made the sign of the Cross. "God wills it!"

"God wills it!" the Crusaders answered.

DEEP BENEATH THE EARTH, THE coils of Jörmungandr, the World Serpent, twisted and writhed. The ground around Lake Vänern shuddered . . . and fell silent.

PART THREE
Ragnarök

23

Dísa woke with the stirring of the earth. She imagined the thing from the Raven Stone looming over her, its limbs made of blood and bowel, its eyes alight with the fires of hate. The young woman started, half drew her seax.

But the shadow was merely that—a shadow, cast by the crackling fire burning on the hearth. It was the shadow of a Raven-Geat who sat near it, tending the fire in silence. Dísa knew it was the cold gloom before sunrise; she sat up, rubbed the sleep from her eyes, and surveyed the grim reality of Gautheimr. Women and children slept, or tried to; men with blood-splotched bandages coughed and groaned. She heard a soft mewling coming from a small form near her. She recognized Bryngerðr, the youngest of the Daughters of the Raven. The girl lay wrapped in a fur, her face pale and sweating. Dísa knew she was deep in the grips of a nightmare.

Suddenly, the child bolted upright, eyes wide and glassy with terror. A scream formed on Bryngerðr's lips, but Dísa caught it ere she could give it a voice. "It's all right," Dísa whispered.

Bryngerðr gasped for breath and swallowed. Her eyes found Dísa's; the younger girl had seen too many deaths. Her father had died in the retreat to the postern gate; her mother, a day ago—slain by a splinter of wood that pierced her like a thrown javelin. Bryngerðr had no one left to hide behind, no one left to protect her. No one but Dísa.

"It's all right," she said again, stroking the younger girl's heavy, sweat-matted hair.

"I . . . I couldn't run," Bryngerðr whispered. "I couldn't g-get away from it. The thing in the water . . . it kept tearing pieces of me off and swallowing them. It wanted b-blood." She raised her eyes and met Dísa's concerned gaze. "We're going to die here, aren't we?"

"Not today," Dísa replied. "Go back to sleep."

"All I see are fire and death," the girl mumbled. Her eyes were heavy. She'd remember this as part of her dream, Dísa reckoned. "Fire and death." Bryngerðr's voice trailed off. Soon, she was sleeping again—more soundly than before.

"You're not going to die here," Dísa said. Rising, she first sought out Grimnir. Him, she found sprawled across the high seat of Gautheimr, snores ripping from his open mouth. The witch-work the night before had drained him. It forced him to seek sleep. And sleep, as she understood it, was an enemy of his people. Something about their blood. She left him undisturbed.

I will do this on my own.

Dísa looked around once more, seeking a familiar face. She knelt beside the man by the fire and asked a quick question. The fellow motioned outside. Dísa nodded; rising, she crossed Gautheimr and slipped out the door.

Dawn was not far off. Overnight, a mist had rolled in from the lake, lending the ruins of Hrafnhaugr an unreal quality, pearlescent and damp. She found the man she sought under the eaves of Gautheimr. Old Hygge sat by himself, his son's cloak draped over his thin shoulders. He looked like an effigy of a man carved from sacred ash wood: long-bearded, knotty; his wrinkled brown skin showed scars and tattoos in equal number. The only sign that he was himself alive was the plume of smoke he exhaled around the stem of his pipe. Dísa smelled a familiar blend of herbs, a scent that reminded her of home. Her own father had learned to smoke at Old Hygge's knee.

He glanced up at her, his ancient eyes a watery blue.

Dísa nodded to him. She made no preamble, offered no small talk: "I want to send the children, the women, and the worst of the wounded off, someplace safe. Can you take them across Skærvík and show them the way to the Hooded One's longhouse?"

Old Hygge made no reply. He looked at her a moment longer before his eyes wandered away from her face and fixed on the empty, mist-bound air over her shoulder. She wondered, then if this had not been a mistake, if the death of his son had not left his mind in tatters. Finally, though, the old sailor nodded.

Dísa mirrored the gesture. "Within the hour. I'll get them up and ready." She made to turn, but stopped when Old Hygge's hand snaked out to take hers. It was papery and thin, his grip; his skin as coarse as sand.

Around the stem of his pipe, he spoke in a voice gone soft with age: "Your mother would be proud of you, girl."

Dísa smiled. "I've known you all my life," she said, gripping his hand all the more tightly, "and I've never heard you speak."

"I've never had anything to say."

"Until now?"

"Until it was something you needed to hear," he replied. "My boy will tell her, when he sees her at the doors to Sessrúmnir, Lady Freyja's hall, or in the fields of Fólkvangr. He will tell her what you've become. And she will be filled with pride."

Dísa felt Grief's fist clench around her heart. A sob caught in her throat. She nodded again, and wiped at her eyes with the heel of one hand. "I miss her."

"We will see them, soon." Old Hygge gave her hand one last squeeze, and then he released her. He sank back into himself, his hoary head wreathed in pipe smoke as he recalled glories long past . . .

GRIMNIR WOKE TO THE CLAMOR of women and children. He pried his good eye open and glared at the folk jamming the doors to the longhouse. They'd packed their lives into baskets and bundles, into their mothers' keepsake chests and their fathers' trade-panniers. Everything they salvaged from the lower terrace and brought here for safekeeping they now carried out the doors of Gautheimr and into the misty morning.

"Where the devil are you lot going?" Grimnir croaked. He pushed himself upright on the Jarl's seat, stretched the kinks from his shoulders, and stood. "I said where are you swine going?"

It was Dísa who answered. "I'm sending them someplace safe," she said, coming up on his blind side. She bore a goblet of wine and a joint of roasted goat. He swiveled his head and fixed her with a milk-curdling stare. She continued unshaken. "The children, the older folk, the women who do not fight, and the wounded. Old Hygge is lashing three boats together to get them across Skærvík."

"What's safe yonder?" he asked as Dísa handed him the goblet of wine. He tossed it back and accepted the joint of goat, attacking it with unfeigned gusto. "More wine," he said around a mouthful of goat meat. "What's safe across Skærvík, I said?"

"Your longhouse," Dísa replied. She refilled his goblet from a clay jug of wine.

A curse stood poised on Grimnir's lips. He glared at her in silence; after a moment, he merely shrugged. "Aye," he said. "Safe a place as any. All this was your doing?"

It was Dísa's turn to shrug. She saw Bryngerðr struggling with a bale of supplies she'd gathered from the larders of Gautheimr. Dísa helped the girl hoist it onto her shoulders, and then watched as she staggered out the door under her burden. Grimnir gnawed the last strings of meat from the goat haunch. Finally, Dísa said: "We who fight are eager to die, or at least we've made peace with it. It's not fair to judge others by our standard. Those who wish to stay are welcome, but why force the women and children to die alongside their fathers, sons, and brothers? If we can get them somewhere safe, then that is our duty."

Grimnir tossed the naked bone into the fire; he licked grease from his fingers. "You surprise me, little bird." He hitched at his weapons' belt. "Come, then, let's see these louts to safety."

It took the better part of an hour to wrangle the women, children, elderly, and wounded out the postern gate and down to the dock, to where Old Hygge waited. There were tearful farewells partially glimpsed in the mist, between wives and husbands, mothers and sons; fathers embraced their daughters for the last time, while trembling-lipped sons tried to present a brave face. Dísa envied them. If she died, who would mourn her?

She turned away and saw Berkano embracing Laufeya. The Otter-Geat sisters had rarely been apart since arriving at Hrafnhaugr. When Dísa had told them one of the sisters needed to go with the boats, to tend the wounded, she'd expected a fiery standoff. But with infinite patience, Berkano—eldest by ten years, at least—took her sister by the hands and ordered her away.

"I can't leave you alone," Laufeya had said, wiping away tears. But Berkano was resolute.

"I won't be alone," she'd said. "I will have my family—my brothers and my uncles, my sisters of the Raven. The Hooded One will watch over me, just as he has these past three years. But our mothers and daughters need *you*, Feya. They need you to help soothe their hurts, just as you've soothed mine." Berkano fought back tears. She smiled at her younger sister, who seemed to crumple in on herself, broken and grief-stricken. Berkano caught her up by the shoulders. "Here, now. We're Otter-Geats, sister. The last of our people. What did Mama always say? We're always to help a neighbor in need, for one day that neighbor might be us. Well, our neighbors need help, Feya. We needed them, three years gone. Now they need us."

There, in the mist, Laufeya bit back a sob as she broke their embrace. She squared her thin shoulders and nodded; Dísa saw her take something from inside her tunic and press it into Berkano's hand. The older Otter-Geat's face lit up. It was a scalp—the chestnut-colored scalp of Örm of the Axe. "For luck," Laufeya said, then turned and clambered aboard the nearest boat.

Berkano held the scalp like an eerie pet as Old Hygge shoved off. He waved to Dísa. Men blinded by splinters of wood or boiling pine resin, their women beside them, did the rowing while Old Hygge grasped the tiller. Once he wrapped his gnarled hands around the worn spruce, the decades sloughed away. He was young again. And as the boats slowly disappeared in the lake mist, Dísa decided that was how she wanted to remember him.

Dísa's reverie was broken when Grimnir clapped her on the shoulder; he gave her a light shove back up the trail.

"Let's go, little bird."

Úlfrún met them halfway back to the postern gate. "That was a canny trick, last night," she said. "What other sorceries do you have up your sleeve?"

Grimnir grunted, looking sour. "A bit of luck, was what that was. And it took every scrap of it, at that. From here out, we're on our own. Tally up who's left, and what we have as far as food. Figure we might as well have a feast while those hymn-singers are busy praying and licking their wounds."

"We should hit them again. In force, this time," said Úlfrún. She wanted blood, especially the Norseman who'd killed Forne. "Kill the lot of them while they're praying."

"No time left," Grimnir replied as they came abreast of the postern gate.

"You felt that, last night? The roots of Miðgarðr are starting to crack. Maybe today. Maybe tomorrow, the barrow will rise from Vänern's embrace, yonder." He inclined his head back the way they'd come, toward the still waters of Skærvík.

Úlfrún followed his gaze. For a moment, she looked weary—an old woman stretched nigh to breaking by the weight of her geas. "A last day of rest, then . . ."

"What's that noise?" Dísa said. Frowning, she cocked her head to one side. Úlfrún bawled up to the guard walking the parapet above the postern.

"On the gate! Do you see anything?"

"Mist's too thick, still," the Raven-Geat answered.

"Sounds like . . . ropes creaking," Dísa said. Faintly, she heard the voices of men, calling in unison as though they were pulling the oars of a longship. "Ymir! Did that white-skinned bastard send for his fleet?"

Grimnir scowled. "Those aren't ships, little bird," he said. "Get inside." He led them into the village through the postern. "Close it up! Drop the bar and call the dogs to war, damn your hides!"

"What is it? What does the noise mean?"

Úlfrún chuckled. "It means there will be no rest."

"And it means they didn't pass the night praying and singing their cursed hymns," Grimnir added. "They're raising the bridge. Or got it raised, more like. Hel take this blasted mist! Sound the alarm, I said!"

And as the low spring sun broke over the eastern rim of the world, the Crusaders began their assault . . .

NO DEFENDING FORCE MET THE Crusaders as they streamed over the dangerously creaking bridge. For a moment, it seemed like Grimnir might lead the *berserkir* out himself, but he finally thought better of it. Úlfrún was loath to commit the backbone of her war-band merely to refuse the allied bank of the ravine. "Let them have it," she said. "One way or another, it's time we came to grips with this rabble."

Grimnir agreed. Instead, he ordered the gates shut and barred. Dísa and a mixed band of wolf-brothers and Raven-Geats would defend the postern. "They'll be coming for it, little bird," Grimnir told her. "They'll be looking to avenge that wretched Dane you killed, there."

"Let them come," she snarled.

Grimnir himself, with Úlfrún and her skin-clad *berserkir,* would defend the main gate. The two Bjorns, Hvítr and Svarti, with Sigrún and the remnants of the Daughters of the Raven, would range the parapets between the two, defending against any attempt the Crusaders might make to force their way onto the walls.

Nor did Grimnir make any grand speech as they dispersed to their positions. He merely looked each man and woman in the eye and growled, "Kill those whoreson dogs ere they kill you, and you might live to see the sun set! But if it's your lot to die, then take as many of those wretches with you as you can! Go!"

As the defenders broke ranks and made for their stations, Dísa motioned Grimnir aside. "What about the prophecy?"

"What about it?" His eyes narrowed.

"When the barrow rises . . . what part will I play?"

"How the devil should I know?"

Dísa frowned. "I am the Day that gives way to Night—"

Grimnir cut her off with a sharp motion. "Who knows what that doggerel means," he said. "I doubt even that one-eyed fool who first spake it knew what he was yammering on about! All that matters to me is getting into the barrow and cutting that wretched wyrm's head off. Everything else? The maunderings of a madman, for all I know."

"So, what do I do?"

At this, Grimnir shrugged and walked away, but over his shoulder, he said: "Stay alive and keep those blasted hymn-singers busy until the deed is done."

By the time he reached the main gate, the mist had thinned enough to reveal the extent of the enemy. His sharp eyes picked out Danes, Norsemen, and Swedes, all united by the black cross sewn to the front of their surcoats, or carried as battle standards; they streamed across the bridge, forming serried ranks in anticipation of being given the order to take the gates.

Grimnir saw no sign of the albino lord of Skara.

"That red-haired bastard?" Úlfrún said, joining him as he surveyed the faces of the enemy. He picked out the man she spoke of—a tall Norseman with a plaited beard, directing troops with a war-spear as though he were some tin-pot Allfather. "That's the one who killed Forne."

Grimnir spat over the parapet. "So that's Thorwald, eh."

"Aye." Úlfrún glanced to one side. "Herroðr . . ."

THORWALD MOVED LIKE A MAN in his element. War was in his blood; the son of a chief of the Trøndelag, as a lad he'd joined a band of *vikingr* who hired themselves out as mercenaries in the wars of their neighbors. He'd killed his first man at ten, earned his first oath-ring at thirteen; by the time he'd reached his twenties, Thorwald had won wars for half a dozen kings, from Dubhlinn to Miklagarðr. This pigsty? He'd have the gate by the afternoon and the village itself by nightfall.

"Pride is a sin," Father Nikulas had warned him as he boasted of his prowess, reciting the litany of his many victories. "Pride in killing and rapine doubly so. Tread carefully, friend Thorwald."

But Thorwald the Red was not a careful man. He was loud, a braggart who could shore up his boasts with iron fists and a jaw like carved granite. And if his foes took umbrage, they could face Hrænðr, his Corpse-adder.

Above the din, Thorwald heard his name. Someone bellowed it from the enemy walls. A smile split his grim visage as he recognized the wolf-bitch's voice.

"Thorwald the Red!"

He stepped out from the ranks of his Norsemen and raised Hrænðr aloft. "I am here, bitch of the North!" he roared. Men around him laughed. "There is still the small matter of an oath between us! Did you not swear by your heathen gods that you'd kill me?"

"I did," he heard Úlfrún reply.

The Norseman laughed. "Come out from behind your walls, then! I am right he—"

With sudden fury, Thorwald the Red's head snapped back. His body went rigid, and as his men watched, the giant chief of the Norse toppled backward to crash full length upon the earth.

A crossbow bolt stood out from his eye socket.

ATOP THE WALL, ÚLFRÚN STRAIGHTENED and handed her crossbow, Skaðmaðr, back to Herroðr. She caught Grimnir glaring at her from the corner of her eye; across the field, a sudden clamor arose from the close-ranked Norse—it was the tumult of vengeance.

Úlfrún shrugged. "What? I never said *how* I planned to kill him!"

"Well, that stirred them up," Grimnir said. "Here they come."

And across the Scar, the lone mangonel bucked and thumped, lifting a smoking incendiary into the bright morning sky and over the heads of the charging line of Crusaders . . .

FATHER NIKULAS OF LUND WAS no battle priest, not like the Archbishop, Anders Sunesen; he did his best work behind the lines, tending to the wounded and raising a litany of prayer to stiffen the spines of the men toiling in the blood and dust of the front. He was a strategist, not a tactician. And while he was no coward, neither was he possessed of some vast reserve of martial courage. Seeing the wounded—their skulls crushed, bones snapped, faces lacerated, and blood-leaking bodies riven—only confirmed a truth he long suspected: while he could goad a man to war, he wanted no part of it, himself.

He stepped from the tent where a lone surgeon worked to save the injured and poured a bowl of blood into the grass. His cassock was damp with the myriad fluids that spurted from bodies torn by steel and stone. The fighting was fierce; word had trickled back of poor Thorwald, taken by a crossbow bolt even before coming to grips with the pagans. Horsten led the assault on the main gate; Starkad, as the priest understood it, had fired the docks and was even now trying to force the postern gate.

And the mangonel to his left thumped out a slow and steady tocsin—its last crew spirited in the manner by which they worked the ropes. Stones flew like a devilish hail over the palisade, the words "For Pétr" scrawled on each one. Nikulas blessed the stones, and prayed they reaped a red harvest among the wretched heathens.

"You look a bit worse for wear, priest," Konraðr said, emerging from the tent where the injured awaited succor. Mailed and girded for war, the lord of Skara, himself, looked . . . *rested,* Nikulas thought.

"I am flush with health and good humor, my lord," the priest replied. "The hour is near."

Konraðr inclined his head to where the other priests tended the injured. "Your brothers tell me you brought Thorwald to heel and cleaved to my plan."

"It was a good plan, my lord," Nikulas said, shrugging. "And poor Thorwald ultimately paid the price for his sins, overweening pride not the least

of them. Though, I fear we will miss his prowess once we take the gates."
The priest turned and studied Konraðr with a healer's eye. "How do you
feel, my lord? That was the worst fit you've suffered since I've known
you."

"And the last."

Nikulas raised an eyebrow. "How so?"

Konraðr laid a hand on the priest's shoulder, oblivious to the reek of
blood and bowel coming from his black cassock. "*They* are gone, priest.
Where once a multitude of voices thronged inside my skull, now I hear only
one—and it is my own. This was the *skrælingr's* doing. It sent something
against me, yestereve. Something . . ."

"A devil?"

"Yes," Konraðr replied, a frown knitting his pale brows. "And no. I think
it was a thing of the Elder World, some sending from an age when men
knew not the light of Christ. It did something to me, Nikulas. Something for
its own ends, to be sure, but now . . . the wind is merely the wind, and—for
good or ill—I hear no secrets in the clamor of insects."

"Give praise to God, then, for the mystery of His ways."

Konraðr said nothing. The frown etching his brow deepened as he remembered the blood staining the walls of the Hagia Sophia. "I want the
skrælingr taken alive."

Nikulas nodded. "That blasphemous thing will be in our grasp by nightfall," he said. Konraðr knelt.

"Then bless me, Father, for I have sinned—and I will sin a thousand times
more ere the sun sets. I am bound for the gate."

On the albino's brow, the grim-faced priest drew the sign of the Cross
in blood. *"In nomine Patris, et Filii, et Spiritus Sancti,"* Nikulas said. "Fetch the
sword of Saint Teodor and end this, my son."

"If God wills it," Konraðr said, rising and drawing his sword, "I will see
it done."

And the earth trembled as the Ghost-Wolf of Skara set upon the path to
war.

BY MIDDAY, A CRACK APPEARED in the wood of the postern gate. It was a
small thing, a warping of planks between iron reinforcements, caused by the
incessant thudding of a makeshift ram. Outside, Crusaders with shields held

high protected a four-man crew armed with a pine trunk as thick as a man. From lack of space, they could not come at the gate at a full run. They could only shuffle forward, grunting as they smashed the now-splintered end of the trunk against the aged oak planks of the gate.

Dísa had a handful of archers, wolf-brothers armed with crossbows for the most part. These kept up a suppressing barrage, but it wasn't enough to discourage the Crusaders. Others hurled rocks from the parapet, though their archers made this a risky prospect.

Three times, the Crusaders came at the gate, ramming it till their men collapsed from exhaustion. Men with axes and hammers, too, tried their hand. The seasoned oak and thick iron resisted them; Dísa's boys broke skulls and sent pierced bodies back to the enemy lines. But by early afternoon, the crack had widened enough to alarm even the most optimistic of the defenders. Dísa sent for Herroðr, who brought a roof beam scavenged from a destroyed home on the first terrace, oak planks, and the last of their nails.

"How's the main gate holding?" Dísa asked him.

Herroðr shrugged and waggled his hand. "It's touch-and-go. Bastards have no lack of fire in their bellies." With a muttered curse, he gestured at the gate. Dísa turned. A Crusader had wedged his arm up to the shoulder in the crack. She could hear the hymns he sang as he clawed for the bar.

Dísa sprang at him. Her seax smashed point-first through his wrist, nailing him to the boards of the gate. The man writhed, howling like a wasp-stung dog. Her mouth set in a grim slash, Dísa drew her Frankish axe. She hacked at the bastard's arm at the shoulder, bone crunching with each blow. Blood sprayed over her face and hands. A spear tried to weasel past the dying man, who hung from the crack in the door by shreds of gristle and bloodied mail. Dísa caught the spear by the shaft and hauled it forward. She could hear men shouting: "Clear the gate!"

And she smelled pine resin.

"Back!" she hollered, barely snatching her seax and stumbling away before a gout of hot pitch splashed through the crack. From the parapet, she heard one of the wolf-brothers yell a warning: "That one! Kill that one!"

Crossbows bucked and sang; she heard a Crusader grunt . . .

. . . And a heartbeat later, a thrown torch ignited the pine resin. The sticky semi-liquid exploded, a wave of heat and flame driving before it. Black smoke guttered from the burning gate. Women with buckets of dirt rushed forward. They could extinguish the interior, but the outer face of the door would continue to burn. Given enough time, it would eat through the rock-hard oak planks and warp the iron fittings. The postern would be lost, then the wall, then the second terrace, and finally, Hrafnhaugr itself. Dísa cursed.

Through the wrack, she heard someone calling her name. Turning, she saw Berkano. The Otter-Geat looked like an apparition made of blood. "Dísa!"

"What is it?" Dísa snapped. "Spit it out, damn you! I'm neck deep in these dung-bearded pot-licking whoreson dogs!"

Berkano caught Dísa by the arm. "It's your grandmother. You'd best come. Hurry!"

Dísa Dagrúnsdottir snarled. She glanced at Herroðr, who nodded. "Go, I'll handle this," he said. Cursing, Dísa allowed Berkano to drag her away.

She led her to the third terrace, to Gautheimr. Heavy fighting at the main gate had produced a raft of casualties, and repeated attempts by the Crusaders to force their way over the walls meant a good many of the dead were Dísa's Raven-sisters. She saw Thyra, Old Hygge's eldest daughter, dead from an arrow to her breast; Káta, her Raven tattoo still fresh, lay with Isgerdr and Perthro. All three had died from spear-blows.

"Is she dead?" Dísa asked. Berkano looked back at her, her dark eyes filled with pity.

"Not yet."

Berkano led her inside, where Sigrún lay among those injured still fighting for life. Dísa bit back a curse. Rigid with agony, Sigrún's body bore a hideous patchwork of burns. Both legs were twisted and broken, likely her hips, as well. Her right hand, her blade hand, was a mass of blood-sodden bandages, and the right side of her face looked like someone had gone after her with a skinning knife. Dísa could see the bones of her skull peeking through the torn flesh of her scalp.

"What happened?"

"The jötunn-machine," Berkano said, and Dísa knew she meant the Crusaders' mangonel. "It hurled its fire-log, and she was caught by it. The impact threw her off the wall. She was asking after you."

Dísa knelt. "Sigrún?" she whispered. "G-Grandmother?"

Sigrún's eyes fluttered open. Her breathing was ragged, and it whistled through clenched teeth. With effort, she fixed her gaze on Dísa's face. Sigrún's left hand clawed for her.

"D-Dísa?"

"I'm here."

"Forgive . . . me," Sigrún whispered.

Dísa shook her head. "All is past. Auða used to tell me the world was an anvil, and I was but virgin steel. 'Your grandmother,' she would say, 'your grandmother is the hammer, sent by the Gods to mold me.' And she was right. It takes a strong arm to forge a sword."

Sigrún, though, writhed; she caught the neck of Dísa's armor and pulled at her, drawing her closer. "No! F-Forgive . . . me! I . . . I have l-lied to you!"

Dísa frowned. "About what?"

"D-Dagrún. She . . . She didn't d-die at . . . at Skagerrak."

"What?" Dísa stiffened. She caught Sigrún's hand and grasped it tight, her bones near to breaking. "What do you mean? Where did she die?"

"Here," Sigrún said. She closed her eyes. "D-Down by the b-boats."

"How?"

In a small, grief-filled voice, Sigrún said: "By my hand."

Those three words pierced Dísa to the heart, as straight and sure as if her grandmother had wielded a lance. "You?" Without thinking, Dísa's grip tightened. She splintered the bones of Sigrún's left hand, but the old woman was too far gone to feel it. "You killed my mother? Your own daughter? Why?"

"To p-protect *him*."

Rage coursed through Dísa's veins. Her fingers knotted in the old woman's hair, and she hauled her halfway off the floor. "What do you mean *protect him*? Why . . . Why did you need to protect him? From who? My mother?"

"She f-found out about him," Sigrún said. In a weak and halting voice, she told the tale—how Kolgríma had betrayed the ancient compact by revealing Grimnir's nature, and how Dagrún, eager to make a name for herself, had decided to kill the monster who'd been preying on Hrafnhaugr for generations. "F-Foolish girl! She listened to . . . to too many s-skalds. Wanted to k-kill a monster . . . the last . . . the l-last monster."

"So, you killed her, instead." A dangerous edge crept into Dísa's voice. "Killed her and made up a story to hide your crime. And now you want my forgiveness?"

Sigrún blinked. "I . . . I was p-protecting—"

"Shut that wretched hole in your face," Dísa snarled. There was a knife in her hand, suddenly, drawn from the small of her back. She'd used it at the gate; gore clotted its chape, and its blade was notched and ragged. "Where is she? Where did you bury her, you dung-eating old hag?"

Tears streamed down Sigrún's burned cheeks. "Bog," she said. "His bog. Kolgríma helped me—"

Dísa screamed; it was a feral sound, a cry of inarticulate rage and boundless grief. She did not stop to think. She did not try to rationalize. Teeth bared in a grimace of raw hate, she rammed the knife home. It slid up under Sigrún's sternum to pierce her laboring heart. "Here's my forgiveness, *niðingr!*" the girl snarled.

Rage lent Dísa's limbs a fresh vigor. Ignoring Berkano's pleas for help, Dísa rose from the corpse. She left her knife embedded in Sigrún's heart and stalked from Gautheimr. None dared step into her path, nor to console her, so fierce was the look of murder in her dark eyes.

Outside, it was near sunset. Fires burned around Hrafnhaugr as she made her way down into the decimated first terrace. She stepped over dead men and women, skirted piles of rubble that had once been the houses of her neighbors.

She found Grimnir squatting in the lee of the main gate. Like the postern, it had taken a titanic beating. Rams had warped and broken the planks, but the iron-work held. There was a lull, beyond, but she could hear the thrice-cursed Crusaders massing for another charge.

And she did not care. She did not care if the world ended, if her friends and loved ones died in a welter of blood and horror. It did not matter to her if Gjallarhorn blew and the fires of Ragnarök descended to consume the earth. Nothing mattered, save answers.

Grimnir glanced up at her approach. His nostrils flared; she saw his black-nailed hand clench around the hilt of his seax.

"Little bird," he said, spitting a gobbet of sooty phlegm in the dust.

"Did you know?" she screamed. All around, men stopped what they were doing. Úlfrún looked up from bandaging Broðir's arm; the giant *berserkr* gently motioned her aside. "Did you know? Did you know what she'd done? Did you know what happened to Dagrún?"

For his part, Grimnir was unperturbed by her display of rage. In answer, he sucked his teeth and said: "That old hag should know when to keep her wretched tongue between her teeth."

"So you did know? You lying bastard!"

Grimnir shot to his feet. "You think this is my fault? *Faugh!* Take it up with Sigrún, you little wretch!"

"I did," Dísa snarled, leaning forward. "And I put my knife through her black heart!"

Grimnir rocked back on his heels, a sardonic half-smile on his blood-blasted face. "So-ho! And you mean to do the same with me, is that it? I'm not some old woman on my deathbed, little bird."

Dísa's fists clenched, but she made no move to draw her seax. Her rage seemed to deflate, replaced by a look of betrayal. Tears dampened the corners of her dark eyes. "Why didn't you tell me? You knew, but you said nothing."

Slowly, Grimnir sank back on his haunches. He bled from a dozen cuts, his blood thick and black. "What would it have gained me?" he replied. "More to the point: what would it have gained you? What would you have done, little bird? Gone after the old hag? *Nár!* You'd have ended up alongside your mother in the bog. You were brittle iron, girl. A long way from the steel you are today."

Dísa sat. She felt hollow, used. Úlfrún started toward the girl, but Grimnir waved her off. Instead, he reached into his tunic and took out a strip of jerky. He bit a chunk off, handed the rest to Dísa. The girl accepted it and took a bite, chewing mechanically. "I boasted of my mother's prowess," she said, her voice small now. "I was proud of her. Proud she died fighting the Norse. She was Dagrún Spear-breaker, and I was her daughter . . . but who was she? Who was she, really? My father . . . did he know?"

Grimnir shrugged.

"Who was she?" Dísa sniffled.

But it was Bjorn Hvítr who answered. His voice was a deep rumble, weary. "She *was* Dagrún Spear-breaker, little one," he said. "I remember her, your age but no more, fighting with us when we stopped the Swedes at the Horn. They'd tried to push across the Hveðrungr and claim part of our lands. She was there, though Sigrún had forbid it. She earned her name in that fight, by Ymir! Broke the Swedish Jarl's spear with the edge of her shield ere she gutted him. She was the first in to any fray and the last out. You look just like her."

"She *was* at Skagerrak," Bjorn Svarti added. "I swear, I saw her on the left flank, with the Daughters of the Raven. You remember? They broke the Norse right, and she was in the vanguard. I thought that was where she fell."

"So she was a shieldmaiden," Dísa said.

"Sigrún might have told lies about her death, child," Úlfrún said. "But these brothers of the shield can tell you the truths of her life. She sounds like a mother to be proud of. You—"

Suddenly, Grimnir glanced up sharply, nostrils flaring. His good eye narrowed to a slit of baleful red fire. "It's time," he snarled.

And with no further warning, Dísa Dagrúnsdottir felt the earth suddenly rise up, and then vanish under her feet . . .

24

As a girl, Dísa had heard tales of the Miðgarðr Serpent, dread Jörmungandr, whose coils threaded around the roots of the world; she'd even felt a few tremors, its scaly muscles flexing as it moved in an endless circle through the deep places where the sun's light never shone. But nothing could have prepared her for the full, thrashing power of the beast as it sought to escape its prison.

The battle-scarred gate of Hrafnhaugr ceased to exist. Though the world spun and bucked, she could clearly see the earthen embankments sift and pour away like water; ancient wood clattered and cracked as the palisade buckled. Bereft of its foundations in the earth, the mossy pales came apart and spread along the ground like a child's game of sticks. The earth split; she heard a bellowing roar as Bjorn Svarti caught the heavy gate bar, then silence as the wooden parapet collapsed on top of him. Dísa felt herself lifted, carried in one of Grimnir's arms as he scrambled for safety.

And she could see, if for just an instant, the waters of Skærvík. Just beyond the jutting peninsula where Gautheimr sat, the lake boiled and frothed. There, a mud and weed-encrusted hillock breeched the surface like the back of an enormous leviathan. It came under the overhang that formed the third terrace, and when the two met it was like the stamping of a colossal foot.

Dísa felt herself thrown; she heard screams, rock cracking, and a sound like a hillside tumbling down the terrace.

And then Dísa knew nothing more; not until she woke to smoke and to ash and to the heat of crackling flames. Night had fallen, but the myriad fires that lit the shattered landscape relieved the darkness with their lurid glow.

She shook dust from her eyes, hacked up gobbets of mud and phlegm lodged in her throat. "G-Grimnir?" she said, her voice hollow. "Úlfrún?" Her hand found the shaft of a broken spear; she used this to support her weight, hanging by the cross-bar as she clambered to her feet. Her body was a mass of bruises, and one leg was numb from some unremembered impact. Still, nothing seemed broken. "Grimnir?"

There were bodies in the rubble around her. Some were corpses: pale and bloody-limbed Geats intertwined with bearded Danes and dark-eyed Swedes, their ragged surcoats emblazoned with the Nailed God's cross. Near as she could reckon, she was at the center of what had been the first terrace. A great pile of rubble, broken pales and slabs of bedrock, marked where the gate once stood; left would have been Kjartan's smithy and old Kolgríma's hut. Ahead of her, limned in firelight, a hill marked what would have been the second terrace . . . and the Raven Stone still crowned it, though tilted and nearly cast down. Beyond that, the foreshortened horizon revealed nothing.

"Hello?" she called out again. Through the wreathing smoke, she spied shapes moving—aimlessly shuffling through the splintered ruin of the village; she heard the sounds of her people among the fires; weeping, coughing, the groan of an injured man and a woman's voice pleading to the Gods.

The Gods, though, weren't listening.

"Grimnir? Úlfrún? Answer me!" Behind her, coming up the slope of rubble that had been the gate—the same gate men had fought and died for that day—she heard the rattle of harness. "Grimnir?"

She started toward the sound. Stopped. Overtopping the slope, she beheld a golden crucifix atop a wooden staff. Dísa backpedaled; she dropped to a fighting crouch as Konraðr the White limped over the mound of rubble where the gate once stood. He was plastered in dust, bloody from a gash to his scalp; the albino's red eyes caught the gleam of firelight and reflected it with an eerie glow. "Dísa Dagrúnsdottir, I presume," he said. A handful of his men came behind him, Danes mostly, and with them a bearded priest carrying the hymn-singers' staff, his black cassock gray with dust.

Konraðr drove the point of his sword into the rubble. "Do you yield?"

"What do your precious ghosts tell you, Witch-man?" Dísa's lips skinned back over her teeth in a *skrælingr*'s snarl. "Oh, that's right . . . you killed them all, didn't you?"

Konraðr's gave her a weary smile. "The answer is no, then? As you wish. Horsten! Yonder is the one who slew your Jarl, poor Kraki. Fetch her head for me, will you?"

A Dane in bloodied mail, his surcoat scorched and torn, peeled away from the knot of men surrounding Konraðr and stalked down the slope. He carried a long-handled axe, its bearded blade clotted with dried blood.

"That fat bastard was your Jarl, eh?" Dísa said. She kept ahold of the broken-hafted spear. "Does it make you angry that a woman killed him? *Horsten,* isn't it? But I didn't just kill your precious fool of a Jarl, *Horsten.*" Dísa backed up and circled. "*Nár!* I bled that sack of suet like a suckling pig, *Horsten!* Kept his mail," Dísa said. "And his sword, with its cursed foreign writing! But his body? Ha! That we let ripen for a few hours, then fed it to the demon we sent after your master, there—that white-skinned bastard!"

Horsten's face grew purple with rage. Roaring like a wounded lion, he sprang at Dísa; his axe whistled, struck empty air as she danced sideways, and rebounded off the broken stump of a rock-hard paling. Before he could recover, Dísa took him high, in the throat, stabbing the broad blade of the spear home with all her hate and her rage. Horsten loosed a gurgling scream, falling over rubble at his feet; Dísa bore him down. She hacked at his neck again and again, until the Dane's head came free. She stooped. Her fingers tangled in the dead man's beard.

Straightening, she threw the severed head at Konraðr's feet. "I am a Daughter of the Raven," she said, her voice rising. "Bearer of the rune *Dagaz,* the Day-strider, chosen of the Norns. I am a servant of the Hooded One, immortal herald of the Tangled God. My mother was Dagrún Spear-breaker, who was *skjaldmær,* shieldmaiden of Hrafnhaugr in the land of the Raven-Geats, and this is my home!"

"Oh, little bird," the lord of Skara said, glancing up from Horsten's mutilated head. "You shouldn't have done that. Now I have no choice. Kill her!"

And suddenly, as the six remaining Danes came for her, the ground beside the gate erupted. Dísa had the impression of a giant bear—feral and starving for blood—even as the back of Brodir's spade-like hand smashed Konraðr to his knees.

"Odin!" the *berserkr* roared.

OF ALL THE EVENTS OF his long life, one that Grimnir recalled with crystal clarity was the destruction of the walls of Badon, on the Avon River in the country of the English, some two hundred years ago. The lord of that wretched place had stolen his little hymn-singer, Étaín; to get her back, Grimnir had goaded the ancient Shepherd of the Hills, the last of an ancient race of *landvættir,* into shaking the bones of Ymir. Though he could not recall the name of Badon's lord, he could still recall down to the smallest detail the toppling of its gate towers, the firestorm caused by clouds of rock dust, the rivers of scalding water and the choking clouds of sulphur; it was an act of wholesale destruction, more cruel and wanton than anything he'd ever perpetrated. And it had all been wrought at his urging.

But as violent and awe-inspiring as that had been to watch, it was as beads rattling in a tin bucket compared to this. This was no land-spirit shaking the bones of Ymir to cause a trembling in the earth; no, this was the hand of a god, seizing the coils of the Miðgarðr Serpent, cunning Jörmungandr, and shaking it with such ferocity that the skin of the world cracked and sloughed away. Grimnir saw Gautheimr vanish; he saw the ground where it sat crumble. Carved beams, black and ancient and nearly as hard as stone, splintered like a handful of dry twigs. Grimnir heard screams from within even as the walls of the longhouse broke apart; the foundations and hearthstones followed, tumbling over the edge of the peninsula and into the churning waters of Skærvík.

As the rumbling subsided and the nape of the earth settled back on its bones, Grimnir sighted a new horizon out beyond where Gautheimr had been—through leaping flames, wreathed in smoke and dust, he saw a spit of land that had felt neither sun nor moon in over seven hundred years: a promontory once called Aranæs. Eroded down, now, by currents and tides—an island-barrow where the remains of Raðbolg Kjallandisson mingled with the bones of that accursed dragon, Malice-Striker.

A place of vengeance . . .

Grimnir did not stop to search among the rubble for Dísa, or for Úlfrún. The geas-cursed old hag would find her own way there. Of that he was certain. Nor did he offer succor to the dozens of wounded Raven-Geats he passed along the way, though they beseeched him with bloody and broken hands. He had no time. He had to reach the barrow first, to survey the surroundings and get a feel for what the deed would entail.

He scrambled to the crumbling edge of the terrace and looked over. From there, he could see the ultimate fate of Gautheimr—and the fate of those who had sheltered under its eaves. Its collapse, and the collapse of the end of the village's third terrace, had created a land bridge down to the island-barrow. Grimnir sniffed and wiped his nose on the back of his hand as he gazed upon a field of destruction.

The steep slope was thick with rubble: stone from the foundations, splintered timbers, planks, and boards, and bodies—whole and in parts, savagely ripped apart by the longhouse's impact. He recalled, then, that Gautheimr was where the injured lay. Grimnir picked his way down carefully. He paused only once, when his eye lit upon a tuft of hair lodged in the drift of rubble. Grimnir recognized it; it was the scalp he'd given to that soft-headed woman, Berkano—the scalp of Örm of the Axe. But of the Otter-Geat, he saw no sign. Grimnir prized the scalp from the ruin, tucked it into his belt, and carefully picked his way down, descending the last few treacherous feet to the island's surface.

The place had a reek to it. Grimnir wrinkled his nose and spat at the stench of corruption rising off the mud-slimed stones, a combination of rotting fish and vegetation and ancient decay. Rot-blackened tree stumps littered the island's surface, and among the rocks and pools of muddy water he could see detritus from the surface—pottery shards and rusted iron hoops from broken barrels, a ship's keel draped in clinging fronds; a bone thrust from the muck, too long to be from anything human.

Grimnir went slowly, the ground underfoot as treacherous as the descent from Hrafnhaugr's ruins. As he neared the center of the island, his ears pricked up; from ahead, he heard the hollow splash of water, as though dripping from a cave roof.

The sound came from a fissure that split the rock. It was narrow, barely wider than the span of Grimnir's shoulders, but that it led to the barrow's heart was beyond doubt. The air wafting from within was so foul that it made even a bog-dwelling *skrælingr* wince. He stood for a moment at the fissure's edge, black-nailed fists clenching and unclenching. He half-imagined himself a whelp again—hiding in the trees along the fjord while the crawling horror that was Niðhöggr, the Malice-Striker, writhed up the slopes of Orkahaugr.

Grimnir snarled and spat. Nár! *I am a whelp no longer!*

His good eye afire in the smoke-wreathed gloom of night, the last son of Bálegyr entered the fissure and sidled down into the dark. There was no labyrinth, at the end of the narrow fissure; no golden bed of treasure, only a single cavernous chamber, its far entrance still underwater—a sinister black lake that reflected a sickly blue-green glow that lit the chamber. The radiance came from patches of mold and fungi clinging to the rocky walls. By that thin light, Grimnir beheld a giant mound of bones—thigh bones and skulls, rib cages and spines. Some were animal, he reckoned, but quite a few were human. And on this eerie divan rested the remains of a giant wyrm, a fleshless skeleton inside a hide of bone-laced armored scales. His own words came back to him, told over a smoldering fire: *"a creeper, it was, half serpent and half lizard. Longer than a wolf ship, it was—longer even than the dragon ships of the Norse—and it pulled itself along on two clawed legs. Scales of bone armored it above and below, pale as man-flesh on its belly but darkening to the colors of moss and lake mud along its back. That monstrous head . . ."*

That skull, with its wide-set eyes, heavy jaws, and fangs the length of Grimnir's forearm, was pierced through its heavy brow by a sword. It was a long-hilted weapon, with an acorn-shaped pommel and a plain cross hilt, its black iron blade untouched by the centuries. Grimnir could yet see the doom-haunted runes etched into the fuller.

"Sárklungr," Grimnir hissed. To reach it, he would have to clamber up a drift of bones; instead, he knelt. There, at the edge of the dragon's grisly mound, was a skeleton unlike the others. A *kaunr* skeleton, draped in tattered lengths of corroded bronze mail, with links of gold still gleaming amid the blue-black verdigris. Its rib cage was shattered; long furrows split the bones, and one arm foreshortened, as though the dragon had bit through it.

Grimnir's nostrils flared; a heartbeat later, he heard the clatter of rocks as a foot dislodged them. His hand dropped to the hilt of his seax. A familiar voice profaned the silence. "Merciful gods," Úlfrún said, her words echoing. She cradled her axe in the crook of her arm. "This is where he died. My kinsman, Sigfroðr, this . . ."

"Faugh!" Grimnir said. "If you believe that, you're a precious sort of fool,

wolf-mother. There was never any kinsman called Sigfroðr. The wretch who took your hand and put that damnable geas on you lied."

"Oh, aye," Úlfrún replied, a dangerous glint in her pale eyes. "Because everyone lies but you, is that it? Stand aside, *skrælingr*! That sword is mine! There is a destiny that needs to be fulfilled! A reckoning between the Old Ways and the New! The prophecy—"

"Oh, aren't you all high and mighty! What are reckonings and prophecies to a lowborn guttersnipe like you?" Grimnir said. He rose from a crouch; in his hands, he held the skull of Raðbolg Kjallandisson. "You think you know the score? Tell me, then: who is your precious Grey Wanderer? Name him!"

"He is the Raven-God; Lord of the Gallows; the shield-worshipped kins-man of the Æsir; the Allfather! He is Odin!"

Grimnir laughed and shook his head. "Wrong, little fool! Oh, he might have worn the rags and hat of the so-called Grey Wanderer, that one, but it wasn't him. The one-eyed bastard-lord of Ásgarðr is innocent in all this, though I'd wager my life he approved of it. Aye, and heartily so!"

"Maybe it's you who are lying," Úlfrún said. "You want the sword for yourself, don't you, you double-crossing swine?"

"Of course I do! It belongs to me! But why didn't I just take the sword, then, if that's what I'm after?" Grimnir replied. "*Nár,* you straw-headed idiot! What happens to you if *mine* is the hand that frees Sárklungr? Do you think your geas will just let you drift along, absorbing death after death? Or do you think the one who did this to you will just heap all your many deaths on you at once for your failure? Let's find out, eh?" He reached for Sárklungr's hilt . . .

"Don't," she said, licking her lips. Her eyes flickered from the long hilt with its acorn pommel to Grimnir's saturnine visage. "Say you're telling the truth. Say it wasn't the Grey Wanderer who did this . . . then, who? And to what end?"

"My mate, Halla, figured it out, ere the sun caught her," Grimnir said. He tugged a small bag from the breast of his hauberk, unlaced it, and shook its contents out into his palm. Amid the oath-rings and fetishes were four chestnuts. Úlfrún peered closer. Each one bore a scratched rune: *Ansuz, Isaz,* and a pair of *Naudiz. A-I-N-N.* He put them in the right order with the flick of his black-nailed thumb: *N-A-I-N.* "Náinn." Grimnir spat and crushed the four chestnuts in his vise-like grip.

"Náinn?" Úlfrún glanced sidelong at him. "Who is Náinn?"

"The beardling lord who forged Sárklungr. Hammered it from the heart of a fallen star as a troth-gift for the eldest daughter of his cousin, Kjallandi." Grimnir glanced up at the hilt protruding from the wyrm's skull. "It was good work, and Kjallandi coveted it. But his eldest daughter, Skríkja—she who bore me into this world—was already pledged to another, a son of the king of Niðavellir, no less. That idiot, Náinn, took offense.

"Aye, this was back before the Tangled God came among my people, doling out platters of blood-soaked meat to the nine households he'd chosen to serve him, Kjallandi's among them. But it wasn't goat's meat or cuts of beef. *Nár!* That bloody feast Father Loki shared out was the monstrous afterbirth of Angrboða, who'd borne the mighty Fenrir, the serpent Jörmungandr, and silent Hel. Those who partook of it were forever changed." Mail jangled as Grimnir thumped his chest. "They became *kaunar*. And ere the beardlings drove my folk from Niðavellir, Kjallandi slew Náinn and took Sárklungr from him." Grimnir's voice dropped to a near-whisper, taking on a chanting cadence as he recounted the blade's history. "He drew it against the Æsir, on the fields of Jötunheimr, when the lords of Ásgarðr came to take Loki's children with Angrboða off to face the judgment of that raven-starver, Odin. And when the Allfather called for our doom, Sárklungr rode Kjallandi's hip across the Ash-Road to Miðgarðr. He killed Hrauðnir with it, on the slopes of Orkahaugr, and its point took Bálegyr's eye ere Kjallandi was defeated. He slew those cursed Romans with it, in the Atlas Mountains. And when he fell in battle, his son Gífr brought Sárklungr back to Skríkja, his sister, who was Bálegyr's wife and queen of the *kaunar*. She dealt this wretched wyrm a grievous wound with it, ere it killed her." Grimnir hefted the skull of his kinsman. "And Raðbolg, here, rammed it into the beast's skull and died for his trouble."

Úlfrún nodded slowly, taking in the enormity of the sword's lineage. Finally, she said: "If this were Náinn's doing, how so? That was no *draugr* I saw, no walking corpse animated by hate and vengeance."

Grimnir stared at the skull in his palm, stroked its forehead in silent benediction, and then laid it back down with a measure of reverence. When he straightened, anger had darkened his features. "Náinn had three sons. Two died on Sjælland, in the 999th year. The last one, a *dvergr* rat called Náli, was the wretch who opened the Ash-Road for me, when I sought Bjarki

Half-Dane. He reneged on his promise, and we came to blows. I thought the bastard was dead . . . but it was him, I'll warrant. He caused your geas."

Úlfrún shook her head. "Why? I had nothing to do with this feud. Why would a dwarf seek me out?"

"He chose you to get his father's sword back," Grimnir said with a shrug. "Likely, he expected you to take my damn fool head off somewhere along the line. Killed Halla when he realized she'd bring news of him to me. The swine's been playing us like a lute ever since."

"If I take the sword?"

"Your geas ends."

"I don't want that bastard to win," Úlfrún snarled.

"Then take it and give it to me," Grimnir said, glancing down at the skull of Raðbolg. "I have a use for it. Take it," he hissed. "Break the geas."

Úlfrún stared up at the dragon's skull, the sword spiked through its forehead. Nodding, she mounted the drift of bones. Thighs and ribs shifted and clattered around her; skulls bounced off her shins. She struggled, reaching with her good hand until her fingers brushed the pommel of Sárklungr. Úlfrún of the Iron Hand stared into the knife-toothed maw of the dragon, its thick bones gleaming in the bluish luminescence. Sweat beaded her forehead; her eyes shifted to Grimnir. "If I die, kill him with it," she said. And with a deep breath, she grasped the hilt fully and drew the dwarf-forged blade from Malice-Striker's skull.

Nothing happened.

Grimnir exhaled a breath he didn't realize he was holding. He saw no changes in the woman as she slid back down to stand beside him—she didn't suddenly age, nor did she scream as the passing of the geas inflicted twenty-nine deaths on her. She simply held the sword up, studied its rune-carved blade, still diamond sharp and free from rust. For a moment—a long moment—she pondered her future, weighed her options. She glanced from the blade to Grimnir and back again. And slowly, she held the hilt out to him.

Grimnir wasted no time. He took possession of Sárklungr, holding it with exaggerated reverence. Here was a link to his past—a sword he'd last seen centuries ago, riding the hip of his dour and single-minded kinsman, Raðbolg.

"What will you do?"

Grimnir glanced sidelong at the bones of Malice-Striker. "Unfinished business," he said. "You?"

"If she lives, I want to take the girl, Dísa. I want to show her there is a world beyond all this death."

Grimnir nodded, only half hearing. His kept his gaze fixed on the blade of the sword. "If she'll go, take her."

And thus, without another word or even a backward glance, Úlfrún of the Iron Hand turned and retraced her steps from the barrow. Grimnir waited, listening as she negotiated the fissure and emerged into the night. As her footsteps faded, Grimnir turned to the hide-covered skeleton of the wyrm. He slapped the flat of the blade into the palm of his off hand. "So much for your wretched prophecy, eh? Let's see what that one-eyed raven-starver does when his little pet shows up without its head!" Grimnir kicked aside a reef of fallen bones and was on the verge of clambering up to straddle the wyrm's spine when harsh laughter stopped him. He glared over his shoulder, good eye ablaze. He spied a figure moving in the shadows. A figure clad in a voluminous cloak and a slouch hat, who leaned on a gnarled staff. A figure whose single eye met hate with hate.

"Grimnir son of Bálegyr," it said. Its voice was like the rasp of stone on craggy iron. "My wretched cousin. There's still a small matter between us, *niðingr.* You owe me a hymn-singer."

"Náli son of Náinn." Grimnir laughed as he turned to face the figure. "I see your new master lets you wear his hand-me-downs! I'd be impressed if I didn't know that under all that mummery, you're still the same white-skinned little runt I left to die on the Ash-Road. *Faugh!* And you're right about there being a small matter between us! I owe you a death!"

"Your little troll-woman?" Náli laughed. "Touching, that you'd care for one such as her. But you were always the sort who picked up strays. Which reminds me: when I'm done with you, I'll fetch your little bird back to my master. He fancies that sort . . . the ones who break and do not bend."

"So-ho! You've still got a little fight left in you?"

Náli drew off his slouch hat. His right eye was gone, sacrificed to the All-father; the left burned as bright as a forge-glede; though still pale and black-bearded, there was a newfound strength to the set of his jaw. He threw back his cloak, revealing heavy, straight limbs under a hauberk of close-woven mail. Náli rapped his staff against the damp stone; the glamour cloaking it faded, revealing its true nature: a spear. Its ash shaft reached an arm's length beyond the crown of Náli's head, with the final quarter of the weapon being a broad, lugged blade forged from black iron and etched with doom-haunted runes. "Oh, you wretched *skrælingr*," Náli snarled, dropping into a fighting crouch. "You have no idea!"

AS DÍSA WATCHED, THE GIANT Brodir roared the Allfather's name, calling on the lord of Ásgarðr to bear witness. In response, something opened deep in the *berserkr's* soul—a doorway to a world of suffering and blood. And through this stepped a creature of nightmare. It *looked* like Brodir—kind, gentle Brodir—but Dísa could see nothing of Brodir's humanity in this ravening beast's eyes. It was a thing of cold crypts and blood-soaked fields, a shield-biter who knew nothing of mercy.

Splayed fingers seized the nearest Dane by the head. And though the man wore an open-faced helm, one convulsion of that titanic hand crushed iron and bone with equal ease. Brodir slung the dead man like a flail, beating a second Dane to his knees. The fellow raised his shield and stabbed at Brodir's legs with his notched sword. Oblivious to a ghastly wound opened in the muscle of his calf, Brodir lifted that wounded leg high and brought his heel down on the crown of the kneeling man's head. Plates of bone ruptured and vertebrae crunched as the *berserkr's* weight drove the Dane's skull down into his chest.

"ODIN!"

But Dísa did not stand idle. As the four Danes turned their attention to defending their lord—who twice tried and failed to heave himself to his feet—Dísa threaded in among them, her naked seax like a surgeon's blade in the close confines of the gate's ruins. She hamstrung one Dane and cut his throat as he fell; a second she shoved from behind. He stumbled into Brodir's path, screaming as the *berserkr* seized his head in one hand and his blade-arm in another. Slabs of hate-fueled muscle writhed; the fellow's screams turned to piercing shrieks as Brodir ripped his arm off.

A third Dane backpedaled into Dísa, his face white as a winding sheet and splashed with blood. Wild-eyed, he smashed an elbow into her face, turned to finish her off, and died when Brodir's massive fist punched him in the center of his back, driving the shards of his rib cage into his heart and lungs.

The remaining Dane turned and ran, bleating like a wolf-worried sheep.

He tumbled down the outer face of the gate ruins in his haste and vanished from sight.

That left only Konraðr and the priest. Brodir turned on them, jaws champing, spittle flecking his beard. While the lord of Skara scrambled for the hilt of his sword, the bearded priest stalked into the *berserkr*'s path. He raised his cross-topped staff, and the words that spilled from his lips bore the power of the White Christ.

"Let the Holy Cross be my light!" the priest thundered. *"Let not the Devil be my guide!"* And Brodir—giant Brodir—shrank back. Dísa watched as the huge Northman staggered, flinching as though each syllable of the priest's incantation bore a poisonous edge. *"Step back, Satan! Step back!"* The priest thrust his staff into Brodir's face. *"Get thee behind me, Satan!"*

The *berserkr* quailed. And Dísa, snarling in hate, stepped unseen around the giant's trembling body. The words dripping from the bearded priest's lips caused her eyes to water, her skin to burn. Still, she did not pause. Rage drove her, shielded her from the worst of the Nailed God's malign influence. And, in answer, Dísa Dagrúnsdottir rammed the blade of her seax into the priest's black-cassocked chest . . . and twisted.

"For Flóki, you cross-kissing son of a bitch!"

It was as though someone snuffed out a candle flame.

"S-Saints preserve me! My . . . My l-lord . . ." Nikulas reeled away, dropping his staff to clutch at the gaping wound under his sternum, as though by fingers and will alone, he could stem the freshets of blood that jetted through his hands. He stumbled and sank to his knees. "L-Lord?"

Dísa reached for the crucifix-topped staff . . .

"No!" Konraðr roared. The lord of Skara surged to his feet, sword in hand. A wild swing drove Dísa back. The girl scurried beyond the Crusader's reach and dropped to a crouch, bloody seax at the ready.

"Brodir!" she cried out in warning. The *berserkr* shook his head to clear it, and Dísa saw the fire in his eyes had abated. They were the kind, gentle eyes she recalled. Whatever had goaded his rage had faded—or been driven out by the priest's incantations. "Brodir, look out!"

A look of profound sadness crossed the giant Northman's face as a yard of bright steel bit into the thick muscles of his neck. He stumbled, clutching at the terrible wound as he turned to face his slayer. One hook-fingered hand clawed for Konraðr, a last act of defiance, but the Crusader danced aside and struck Brodir again, then a third time, and then a fourth. He struck until the *berserkr* sank down; struck until there was nothing left in that giant vessel save blood and regret.

And then, Konraðr the White came for Dísa, his manner as savage and single-minded as Grimnir's.

Dísa met him blade to blade.

Steel crashed and slithered. The pair fought in silence, their arena the smoke-wreathed ruin of Hrafnhaugr's gate. Fires guttered amid the detritus of a hundred broken lives, the burning memories of the dead providing ample light for the living. Konraðr hissed and struck. Spittle flew from cracked lips as he leaned in and tried to batter the young woman to her knees. But Dísa knew better than to let the bastard gain the upper hand through his heavier weight or his longer reach. She was canny, and she fought like a *skrælingr.*

She threw every trick, every stratagem Grimnir had taught her at the lord of Skara. She used her slight size, danced around his heavier blade, and tried to catch him low. For his part, Konraðr handled his sword like a hammer, with Dísa's arm the anvil—until he needed it to be a scalpel.

But for all the flash and thunder of their duel, it was a simple misstep that ended it. Dísa went in low, feinting left and slashing to the right. She sent him dancing back with a blow that rasped on the hem of his hauberk—that soft metallic hiss more ominous than any bellowed threat of gelding. Dísa laughed. She skipped back . . .

. . . And tripped over dead Brodir's outstretched hand.

The young woman cursed, flailed, and cursed again as Konraðr's riposte split the mail protecting the ball of her shoulder. Dísa felt hot blood and a sudden, stomach-lurching fear. Then, the pain hit her like a mallet. She stumbled back, her off hand and arm suddenly useless.

Konraðr gave her no respite. Eyes blazing, he hammered her to her knees. His booted heel kicked her seax away, the blade spinning from her grasp to clatter among the stones. Death gleamed in his reddish eyes as he drew his sword back for a last blow.

Without warning, the lord of Skara staggered and gasped as a hurled stone caught him square in the chest.

Dísa scrambled after her blade, her eyes looking wildly about for her savior. She expected to see Grimnir's choleric face; instead, through the drifting smoke came Úlfrún, axe in hand, pale eyes blazing in fury. When she spoke, her voice was the voice of the grave:

"Wolf shall fight she-Wolf | in Raven's shadow."

Konraðr stood a moment, glaring. Then, in one smooth motion he crouched and caught up a fallen shield. "So be it," he growled, straightening.

DEEP IN THE BARROW, THERE were no witnesses to the duel unfolding between *kaunr* and *dvergr,* save for the sightless eyes of the long dead. By that eerie blue glow, Náli's deadly spear darted and sang, its song one of blood and vengeance; in Grimnir's black-nailed hands Sárklungr came alive, supple and quick, the iron recognizing its own. Breath hissed through clenched teeth; iron rasped and rang.

Grimnir swayed like a drunkard, sidestepping thrusts and ducking under sweeps from the spear's weighted butt; Náli backpedaled. His advantage lay in the reach of his spear, and he strove to keep Grimnir at a distance. The choice of ground, however, worked against him. Step by step, Grimnir forced him back, until Náli's heels dislodged an avalanche of finger bones from the wyrm's pile.

The dwarf cursed; he glanced down to be sure of his footing.

Grimnir used that distraction. Snarling, he seized the shaft of the spear behind the lugged head, hauled it forward, and hacked through it. Wood splintered beneath Sárklungr's keen edge, leaving the *dvergr* with a nigh useless club. For the span of a heartbeat, Náli wondered what to do with his foreshortened spear.

Grimnir decided it for him.

Sárklungr came in low and fast; its cutting edge bit into Náli's mail over his hip. Steel rings snapped and parted. The blade sliced into cloth, skin, flesh, and bone. The black and stinking blood of the *dvergar* spilled over Grimnir's fist. With a grunt, he drew the blade back, nearly disemboweling the hapless dwarf. "Who's the *niðingr* now, you wretch?"

Náli sank down against the bones beneath the wyrm's skull. The mound shifted, until it looked like Malice-Striker's skeletal head bent over Náli's bleeding body in an attitude of concern. The *dvergr* didn't curse or rail; no threats or imprecations spilled from his slack lips. Indeed, he smiled up at Grimnir, the light in his one eye undimmed.

"I was c-certain," he said after a moment. "Certain you'd k-kill the bitch. That would have b-been easiest. But this . . . this will d-do."

"What are you yammering on about?"

Náli spat a gobbet of black blood. "You're a f-fool, son of Bálegyr, but a useful fool." He rested his cheek against the wyrm's temple. His strength ebbed. "It was n-never about . . . the sword." Thus died Náli son of Náinn.

Grimnir stared at the dwarf's corpse. In death, something ripped away from the body, something grim and cold and reeking of the frosts of Ásgarðr. *The Allfather's hamingja, his luck.* Náli's corpse took on its original form: a gnarled and twisted shadow of what he'd been under the Allfather's aegis, hunchbacked and foul. Grimnir, though, did not crow and caper in his victory. Instead, he puzzled over the dwarf's dying words. Things didn't make sense, and Grimnir had a niggling feeling he was missing something, some colossal jest leveled at him. Nevertheless, he thrust his doubts aside and readied himself to strike the last blow—the blow that would remove Malice-Striker's head from its neck.

"*This will do,* he said," Grimnir muttered. "This . . ."

Suddenly, the truth struck him. This was no duel. It was a sacrifice. Náli had meant for him to strike down Úlfrún. *But this will do!*

"Ymir's blood!" Even as Grimnir sprang forward, intent on striking the juncture of the dragon's head and neck, a feral green light kindled deep in the wyrm's left eye socket. The nightmarish head, clothed in a loose veneer of bony scales, lashed to the side, striking Grimnir in the shoulder. The blow sent him spinning; Sárklungr slipped from his grasp.

And as Malice-Striker, mighty Niðhöggr, the wyrm of Ragnarök, roused itself from its centuries-long slumber, the stones around them began to tremble and shake . . .

25

By the greasy orange light of a hundred dying fires, the Ghost-Wolf of Skara met the she-Wolf of the North.

Dísa watched them crash together. Having only one hand did not hamper Úlfrún in the least; her axe twirled and sang, as nimble as any sword. Its iron-banded haft took blows that might have snapped the handles of lesser weapons, and its bearded blade thrust as easily as it slashed. For good measure, she battered his shield with her iron hand.

But Konraðr the White was no craven bench-hugger. Forged in the crucible of the East, a veteran of the sack of Constantinople and a survivor of the rout at Adrianople, he wielded his sword with a canny skill. Edge, point, and hilt—all were tools that served a purpose, whether that be to gouge, to cut, or to batter. Nor did he ignore the iron-banded edge of his shield, or its dented central boss.

After the first clash, both grew more wary of the other. They circled, panting; Konraðr slung sweat from his reddish eyes.

"You've been gulled, Skara," Úlfrún hissed. "There were never any saints' bones, here."

"Liar!"

Úlfrún chuckled. "I was gulled, too. I came looking for a sword, left by my kinsman, Sigfroðr the Volsung, after he'd slain his cursed dragon. That was a lie."

"The sword was Saint Teodor's," Konraðr said. "The *skrælingr* has bewitched you." Konraðr came at her hard; he led with his shield, thrusting over its rim and turning her parry into a pair of whistling slashes that, had they connected, would have taken off the top of her head at the brow. Úlfrún's riposte, a stiff-armed thrust with her iron hand to the center of his shield, staggered the lord of Skara. Wood cracked and splintered; her axe forced him to relinquish the shield if he wanted to save his hide.

Úlfrún stepped back, disengaging from the fight. Panting, she watched the Crusader warily. "Let me guess: an old man with one eye told you where the sword of your blessed saint was? Who was the old man to you?"

Konraðr ducked his head and spat, hiding a sudden frown. "A ghost. The ghost of a man I'd slain in the streets of Constantinople. How—?"

"To me, he took the guise of the Grey Wanderer."

"God's teeth, you lying—"

Úlfrún chose that moment to strike. Quick as a cat, she darted inside Konraðr's guard and dealt him a blow to the stomach with the butt of her axe haft. The albino lord of Skara doubled over, his breath exploding from his lungs. As he struggled to breathe, to fight, and to survive, Úlfrún of the Iron Hand sent him sprawling with straight punch, her fingers stiffened by the handle of her axe.

Konraðr toppled sideways, dazed.

Dísa whooped and scuttled for her seax. She wanted to be there for the kill, to watch the Witch-man's blood pour out over the soil of what was once Hrafnhaugr, her home. But a sharp word from Úlfrún brought her up short. She glared at the older woman, confused.

On the ground, Konraðr clawed for his sword; Úlfrún kicked it away. The lord of Skara sighed, cuffing the blood from his split lip. He eyed her upraised axe. "End it, then, but cease your lies, bitch."

Dísa started forward, eager for the last blow to fall . . .

WHILE THE WOLVES OF PROPHECY strove and struggled on the surface, deep in the heart of the barrow Grimnir fought a battle of his own. He dove for his fallen sword, black-hilted Sárklungr. Above him, the wyrm stretched its long neck, skeletal vertebrae popping and crackling; it opened its mouth as if to speak, but all that came from that yawning darkness was a deadly foetor. It hissed at the crawling thing.

As Grimnir came to his feet, he finally understood the game. It wasn't vengeance for a slain father Náli wanted, nor was it vengeance for what befell him two hundred years ago when he and Grimnir clashed on the Ash-Road, between worlds. He'd engineered this, placing a geas on Úlfrún and haunting that hymn-singing wretch, Konraðr, because the iron blade of Sárklungr, forged from the heart of a fallen star in the dark fires of Niðavellir, kept Odin's witchery from working. That one-eyed starver of ravens wanted his wyrm back, so he'd hatched a plan . . .

Grimnir swore he saw a smile curl the bony lips of that thrice-cursed beast. It stared at him, its greenish gaze unsettling. Nevertheless, he put himself between that thing and the lake leading to the barrow's underwater exit. Sárklungr's honed edges reflected the eerie blue light. Grimnir bared his teeth in a snarl of rage. Here was the slayer of Orkahaugr, the beast who murdered his mother. "This is your tomb, wretch!" he growled. "You'll leave it over my broken corpse!"

And with an angry cough, Malice-Striker took Grimnir up on his offer.

That skeletal neck, armored by tatterdemalion scales and bony spines, snapped forward, driving its wedge-shaped head. Its jaws yawned; rows of razor-edged teeth snapped on empty air as Grimnir dove aside. Its tail flicked whiplike, made nearly weightless by the loss of its sheathing muscle and sinew. What drove the thews of the beast, now, was hate and the last shreds of sorcery culled from the Elder Age.

The son of Bálegyr skidded under that lashing tail. Sárklungr flashed; a chunk of scale sailed off—not enough to damage the wyrm, but enough to enrage it. The thing's shriek was as piercing as nails across slate. Again, its head darted around, and only a last-minute leap kept Grimnir from being bitten in half.

"Show me that blasted head," he snarled. It had no vitals, no heart or lungs; his only choices were hack it to pieces or return Sárklungr to its resting place, nestled in the bones of the beast's skull.

Malice-Striker understood him. Rising to its full extension, it kept its head out of the fray. But it needed room. It needed to feed on the rich red gore that foamed from the hearts of men. And it needed to kill this worm dancing before it.

The dragon screamed. It arched its spine, driving itself back on its thick-boned legs. It struck the wall of the barrow like a battering ram. Again and again, it pummeled the stone of its prison, until the black waters of Skærvík sprang from cracks in the wall.

Grimnir cursed. He had no target. The thing's head was out of reach and its body was a collection of bones and rotting scale knitted together and given life by sorcery. It had found a way to escape into the world and drown him, for good measure.

With a deafening shriek, it crashed one last time against the wall; Grimnir heard stone break. He heard the roar of water. But before the rising inundation could seize him, before it could sweep him into range of the beast's clashing jaws, Grimnir chose discretion over valor and dove for the fissure leading to the surface, Sárklungr clutched in a lover's embrace.

Water boiled and foamed around him, but he dragged himself from the stony heart of the barrow and collapsed against the slime-fouled stones. Overhead, an eerie curtain of green radiance played across the star-flecked heavens. The island-barrow heaved. "Ymir's blood and piss!" Grimnir scrambled to his feet, lost his balance; he tumbled and skidded, Sárklungr ringing against the stones as he slid into the cold waters of Skærvík. Though sodden cloth and mail weighted him down, he nevertheless scissored his legs and kicked back to the surface. From there, he bore witness to the emergence of Niðhöggr.

The wyrm exploded through the fissure, sending rocks and water cascading off its scaled hide. At first, its sole green eye swept the night, seeking for its ancient foe, but then its nostrils caught the war-reek of Hrafnhaugr—the stench of blood. Whatever energy animated it recognized the rich red gore, the heart-broth of weakling men that would restore its sinews and harden its armor.

The thing clambered up the slope, over the ruins of Gautheimr, and into the broken streets of Hrafnhaugr.

TO DÍSA'S DISMAY, ÚLFRÚN DID not kill the lord of Skara even though he was at her mercy. Instead, she squatted on her haunches, her axe across her knees. "Call me a liar one more time, you milky bastard, and I'll do to you what Dísa is eager to see me do! We've been gulled, I tell you. Led by the nose like a pair of sacrificial bulls, for more years than we can count."

"But if what you say is true, that means all of this . . ." A gesture from him encompassed more than the field of destruction, but the whole of the land around them.

"Was for nothing," Úlfrún finished for him. "And we fight here, now, because a hundred seasons before either of us was born, a prophecy was uttered about the breaking of the world. And it was a lie."

Konraðr shook his head, glaring sidelong at her. "No, no . . . everything spoken of in the prophecy has come to pass."

"Because *we* have made it come to pass."

Dísa charged into their conversation, her seax leveled at the lord of Skara. "Why do you yammer on? Kill him and have done, or stand aside!"

Úlfrún eyed the albino. She was a good judge of men, and the lord of Skara was a good man—for all that he was a Christian. "There's no need," she said after a moment, rising.

"He owes me a life!" Dísa hissed. Tears of rage, of frustration broke from the corners of her eyes and tracked down her cheeks. "He killed my friends! He destroyed my home, and for what? For what?"

"For the sake of war," Konraðr replied, suddenly weary. He leaned back on his off hand, reclining like a man with nothing left to fear. "For that is what warriors do, little bird."

"Don't call me that!" she screamed. "You haven't earned the right!"

Konraðr acquiesced, nodding and raising his free hand. "My apologies."

"We've all lost," Úlfrún said. For the first time, she felt the true weight of her years. "Friends, those we've loved. We've lost time we can never get back to the schemes of an Elder World."

Konraðr raised a fine-haired eyebrow. "Your *skrælingr*?"

"This wasn't Grimnir's doing," Dísa snapped. She, too, sat, straddling a broken paling with her naked seax across her lap—as though unsure if she'd kill the albino or not.

"She's right," Úlfrún said. "There was another, a dwarf called Náli. He was our old man, our Grey Wanderer. He's the one who gulled us into killing each other."

"So," Konraðr said, looking at the two women through a veil of sweat-damp white hair. "What do we do now?"

"Bury our dead. Then you go your way, Skara," Úlfrún said, glancing sidelong at Dísa. "And we'll go ours."

"I suppose I'll have to crawl to my cousin, the king, and explain why I'm not reinforcing his crusade in Estonia." Konraðr shook his head.

"You hymn-singers and your wretched crusades." Dísa spat. "Just let us live in peace."

Konraðr started to reply, but his words were lost to the wind as the ground underfoot resumed its chaotic quaking. Flames leapt; screams echoed across the ruined village. And over the women's shoulders, beyond the far edge of Hrafnhaugr where Gautheimr once stood, Konraðr the White glimpsed something that would have driven another man mad. Even so, the lord of Skara crossed himself with a trembling hand.

"Mother of God!"

Úlfrún and Dísa followed his wide-eyed gaze. Curses fell from their lips, for cresting the end of Hrafnhaugr they beheld the single burning eye and bony visage of the dread wyrm, Niðhöggr.

The Malice-Striker had awoken from centuries of slumber, and it had a terrible thirst for human blood . . .

THE SURVIVORS OF HRAFNHAUGR, THOSE scarred and bloodied souls who had endured Odin's weather, the storms of iron and stone that had left them refugees in their own land; who had emerged from the wrack to watch their friends and loved ones vanish in the ruin of Gautheimr—these three-score survivors had no fight left in them. Thus, when this hate of the Elder World pulled itself over the crumbling edge of the peninsula, half-slithering and half-crawling, none sought to meet it head-on. There was no thought of a good death or of gaining glory by slaying the beast. No, when Malice-Striker came, the last of the Raven-Geats took to their heels.

All was chaos and screaming. Shapes ran in every direction, wreathed in smoke and fume; warily, Malice-Striker dipped its fleshless head. Its jaws and teeth came up bloody as it seized one of the injured warriors and tore him in two. Its baleful green eye blazed like a torch; blood rained from its chin. It needed sweet red gore to reconstitute itself, and to fuel the sorcery that animated it. And here, there was gore in plenty.

A spear rattled off its ribs. A Geat bolted from hiding and made a run for it. The wyrm slithered forward, the weedy scales of its belly scraping themselves clean on the stones. Its jaws lashed out, snapping up the man in mid-stride. He loosed a piercing shriek. Bones crunched, blood dribbled down

Malice-Striker's naked spine as the thing mimicked eating its prey. The sorcery would remember, and the flesh would knit itself from the stringy meat and blood cascading down its bony gullet. It needed more . . .

"What do we do?" Dísa could not hide the tremble of fear in her voice as she watched the hoary beast feed on the living and on the battle-dead. Already, flesh was forming on its bones, knots and ropes of naked muscle, the roots of a tongue. "H–How do we fight it?"

"We don't. Sárklungr is the only blade that can harm it," Úlfrún said. She tightened her grip on her axe. "And Grimnir has it, if he still lives."

"We have to find him! Find Sárklungr!"

"You go. See if you can find him, or just the sword. We will hold him off." Úlfrún stood shoulder to shoulder with Konraðr, who had gone quiet. "Go!"

But Dísa did not move.

Up the slope, Malice-Striker crossed what was left of the second terrace. Its bony tail, as heavy as a battering ram, flicked out and shattered the Raven Stone; as the wyrm slither-crawled into the smoldering ruin of the first terrace, Dísa saw its head dart forward. It came up with a writhing body. Even at this distance, they heard a short, sharp scream that ended in the wet snap of bone.

"You have to run, Dísa," Úlfrún said, turning to her. "Get away from here. Start your life anew. There's a world—"

"This is my home," Dísa snapped. "Or what's left of it. I'll not run, not while you lot stand your ground. Do you take me for a piss-legged bench-hugger?"

Úlfrún straightened. "Never," she replied, her sadness palpable. "So be it. What about you, Skara? Skara?"

But Konraðr was no longer beside them. He stooped and retrieved his sword, then crossed to where Father Nikulas lay dead. He knelt by his friend. "I am sorry, my friend," he murmured. "I led you astray, subverted your sworn duty for my own ends, lied to you—though I knew it not. Now you sit among the angels, at the right hand of God. I beg you, good Nikulas, to ask God's forgiveness for my part in this." Konraðr crossed himself, and grunted as he rolled the priest's corpse aside. From beneath the body, the lord of Skara drew forth the crucifix-topped staff. "Get somewhere safe," he said, rising. "Both of you. I'll draw the beast away."

"Did you not hear me? You can't fight it . . ." Úlfrún grasped his arm.

"I don't mean to." He looked at Dísa, his expression softer. "This is my *weregild* to you, the blood-price for my deeds. Get away from here. Kneel to what gods you may, and live a good life." He looked from her to Úlfrún. "Take her and go. Go!"

"May your Nailed God be with you," Úlfrún replied. With a short, sharp nod she turned away, plucking at Dísa's arm and exhorting her to follow. The young Raven-Geat shrugged her off at first. She met Konraðr's gaze evenly.

"My people, they did not deserve this," Dísa said. "My friends, my family, my home . . . we caused you no harm, and yet you brought war to our threshold. What you do now . . . it does not absolve you of your part in this."

"No."

Dísa nodded. "Then I accept your blood-price, Witch-man, and I will weave the song of your death into the memory of Raven Hill."

Konraðr gave her the ghost of a smile. He bent his pale head. "Go, Dísa Dagrúnsdottir. Go, quickly," he said. "Ere my song reaches its crescendo."

Dísa backed away. Then, turning, she made to follow Úlfrún. Konraðr watched them vanish over the hillock of rubble marking the gates of Hrafnhaugr, then turned back to face the dragon.

The beast caught sight of him, its sinister green eye narrowing.

Konraðr hoisted the crucifix aloft.

"Praise be to God!" he roared, striding forward. *"Yea though I should walk in the midst of the shadow of death, I will fear no evils, for thou art with me. Thy rod and thy staff, they have comforted me. Thou hast trained my hands for war, my fingers for battle. Thou hast been my fortress, my stronghold and my deliverer, my shield, in whom I take refuge!"* The cross gleamed with a light of its own; the Nailed God's power coursed through the white-skinned Crusader as he reached the center of the first terrace. Here, he drove the staff into the earth and brandished his sword. *"Part thy heavens, Lord, and come down; touch thy mountains, so that they smoke. Send forth thy lightning and scatter mine enemy. Deliver me, O Lord, from the hands of the Heathen, whose mouths are full of lies and whose right hands are deceitful."* Malice-Striker recoiled, and then darted forward; the earth trembled under its charge. Konraðr bared his teeth in a fierce grimace, but he did not quail. *"And yea, though I should walk in the shadow of the Beast of Armageddon, I will fear not its evil, for thou art with me! Let thy mercy follow me all the days of my life!"*

None alive witnessed the last stand of Konraðr the White, the Ghost-Wolf of Skara; no human eye beheld his last gasp of courage amid the ruins of Raven Hill where, crucifix held aloft, he adjured the Great Serpent, and threatened it with hellfire and damnation if it did not return to the pits from whence it crawled.

And none among the living saw the beast's knifelike teeth flense the flesh from the albino's bones as it consumed him.

A DOZEN OR MORE RAVEN-GEATS pelted down the cracked and broken switchbacks, now clogged with enough splintered palings and rubble to form a ramp from the gate to the road below. Dísa and Úlfrún ran among them. But their headlong exodus slowed, finally stopping as they came near the Scar—now twice as wide as before, its edges treacherous with crumbling rock and soil. The bridge, which Thorwald's Norsemen had repaired, was now just a wreckage of frayed rope and splintered board. They were trapped, death behind them and death before.

"What do we do?" Dísa panted.

"The ropes," Úlfrún said, nodding. "From the old bridge. If we can get down to the water, maybe we'll have a chance." But Úlfrún spied the remnants of the Crusaders' advance camp. It stood hard by the ruin of the bridge, where a few men in stained surcoats, their crosses dark with mud, blood, and other fluids of war, sat in dazed silence amid tents and pavilions that were flung haphazardly about. Side by side, the women headed toward them. Small fires lit their way. By that thin light, a few hard-eyed men witnessed the Raven-Geats' flight; most ignored them—the war was over, they thought. Their lords were dead and their enemy, too. What was there left to fight over? But a few perked up at the sight of Úlfrún and Dísa approaching. Humorless smiles crept at the corners of their mouths; hands sought the reassurance of hilt and haft.

"That's her," one man said, stepping to the fore. Dísa recognized him as the Dane who had escaped Brodir's wrath. He gestured at the pair of women. "The little one, there. She's the witch who did Jarl Kraki. The other is the one-handed bitch who shot Thorwald down like a dog!"

"Peace, lads," Úlfrún said. "Help us, and we might all see the sun rise."

The jötunn lights kindled across the heavens, casting an eerie greenish radiance over the earth. Dísa could see the grim looks and bared teeth spreading through the Crusaders' ranks. She drew her seax.

"Don't do it," Dísa warned. "Listen to her!"

The Dane wiped his mouth with the back of his hand. "Let's see how tough you think you are when I take that pig-sticker from you, little girl."

Dísa's eyes narrowed. She said nothing.

"Stand back!" Úlfrún roared, hefting her axe. "We are enemies no longer! Something comes that—"

"Bitch!" The Dane who'd run from Brodir lunged for Dísa. Nor did the young woman shy away from his assault. She met him with a stiff-armed blow to the point of his chin, grabbing his beard and hauling his head to the side. Before Úlfrún could stop her, Dísa's seax flashed; blood fountained, and the Dane flopped to the earth with his throat hacked open.

She stepped over his writhing corpse and leveled her gore-slimed blade at the Dane's companions. "Listen to me, you useless sons of whores," she growled. "Something comes! Something that will kill the lot of us if we don't get off this gods-forsaken rock! Do you want to stand here and fight while our doom creeps up on us? Step forward, then, and I will oblige you! I have naught else to lose, you wretches! But if you want to see your homes, your families, then smooth your hackles and give heed!"

The Crusaders milled and muttered; finally, one stepped forward—a tonsured priest in ill-fitting mail. "I am Brother Marten," he said. "What became of Father Nikulas, do you know? And what do you mean, 'something' comes?"

Dísa and Úlfrún exchanged glances. "Your man was slain," the older woman replied. "And as for what I mean . . ." She glanced over her shoulder. "I mean that!"

"M-Mother of God!" the priest, Marten, stammered, his eyes wide as a slithering shadow crested the low hill and came through the gate, its one eye gleaming like the jötunn-lights overhead.

Screams and bellowed warnings erupted as Geats and Danes, both, caught sight of the wyrm. Malice-Striker came on like a tempest. "Down the ropes!" Úlfrún bellowed. "Get down the ropes! Otherwise, we die up here!" She grabbed Marten by the arm and propelled him toward the bridge. "Hurry, priest!" The Danish mercenaries needed no exhortation. They scrambled for the ruined bridge, shoulder to shoulder with the Geats who'd been their enemies. Men shouted and scuffled; women screamed. A Geat seized one wrist-thick cable of twisted hemp and was about to scoop up one of the women and guide her down when a gap-toothed Dane shoved him aside. Soil crumbled, and the Geat—with the woman in tow—stumbled and fell screaming over the edge of the Scar. "Christians first, you heathen bastard!" The gap-toothed Dane turned to motion for Brother Marten . . . and died with Úlfrún's axe in his chest.

"Stop!" Úlfrún of the Iron Hand roared, kicking him off the blade. The Dane's body slid into the ravine. "Marten—"

Úlfrún turned to the priest, who bared his teeth in a grimace. His fear-widened eyes saw only the bloody axe blade; his fear-deafened ears heard only the unholy scrabbling of the dragon at their heels. Brother Marten saw his death in this pale-eyed queen of the *berserkir,* with her pagan witch at her side. But God was with him . . . God was with him! Before she could strike him down, Marten punched out with the thin-bladed dagger in his fist. It caught Úlfrún under her ribs and to the left, piercing her tattered mail. She snarled; Dísa turned at the sound.

The younger woman saw Marten draw back his bloody knife; she saw Úlfrún's axe fall from her nerveless fingers. She saw her clutch at her abdomen, as though willing herself to catch and hold the spurts of bright arterial blood. And Dísa knew the score. The young Geat snarled and turned on Marten. The priest squeaked and danced back as her seax missed him by a hairsbreadth. She would have chased him down and butchered him, but Úlfrún caught her arm.

"He . . . He's not worth it," she said. "Come, run."

"Run where? It's no use." Dísa shook her head. "There's no way across." A woman loped past them and leaped out over the Scar, the Allfather's name on her lips. "Odin!" Her arms and legs cart-wheeled as Úlfrún watched her get swallowed up by the darkness of the ravine.

The dragon slithered closer—a nightmare of bone and blood under the witch lights of the North. It was ten yards away now, and coming for them. They could smell the foetor coming off its age-slimed jaws. It was the stench of death.

"Kill me," Dísa whispered, offering Úlfrún the hilt of her seax. "Do it! I don't want to die in that thing's jaws."

"No one's dying. Can you swim?" she said to Dísa. The young Geat nodded. "Good." And with a hiss of agony, Úlfrún Hakonardottir—Úlfrún of the Iron Hand, who was Jarl to the Bear-men and the Wolf-men—snatched Dísa up and leapt . . .

But as quick as she was, Malice-Striker was quicker. It smashed through the Danes and the Geats, sending their claw-ripped bodies tumbling. It bit Brother Marten's head from his shoulders as he stood before it, his dagger held by the blade like a crucifix. And it lashed out with its whiplike tail and caught Úlfrún and Dísa in midleap. Dísa felt the impact; she heard the sharp intake of breath, the hissed curse, as the wyrm's razor-edged scales and spikes of bone tore through Úlfrún's mail and laid open her back muscles.

As they tumbled and fell, Úlfrún turned loose of her. The last thing Dísa Dagrúnsdottir heard before she struck the water and knew nothing else, was Úlfrún's voice and the soft whisper of her name . . .

"DÍSA." THE VOICE CUT THROUGH the darkness. It was an old voice, a man's voice, made gravelly and harsh from the passing of years; it was a familiar voice. "Dísa Dagrúnsdottir," he said.

Dísa pried one eye open. The world swam; colors stabbed her. She closed her eyes again, and coughed up a lungful of lake water.

"Yes, girl. Get it up."

"O-Old Hygge?"

Dísa heard the ancient Geat laugh. "Aye, child."

She opened her eyes. It was near dawn, the smoke-stained sky lightening in the east. By that rising twilight, she reckoned herself in the belly of a boat. Someone had removed her mail; she lay under a tattered cloak, her gambeson still sodden. Fetishes clicked as she pushed her hair out of her eyes. Old Hygge worked the boat's tiller, while other hands manned the oars.

Women's hands. The wives and mothers, sisters and daughters she had sent to Grimnir's longhouse. All of them snuck looks at her with red-rimmed eyes, wondering why she survived and their husbands and brothers, sisters and mothers did not; she felt the burning questions in their hooded gazes, but Dísa shook her head. "Úlfrún was with me," she said to Old Hygge. "We fell together . . ."

Old Hygge shook his head. "We've found Bjorn Hvítr and Kjartan, but no others."

"The dragon?"

Old Hygge shivered. He shook his head, his lips thin and pale as he refused to even speak of the dreaded wyrm.

Dísa sank back down. She remembered the beast's tail raking Úlfrún's back; she remembered the impact with the surface of the water. And she remembered, over Úlfrún's shoulder, Malice-Striker's malignant green eye, gleaming down at them from the edge of the ravine—intelligent, ruthless, and burning with hate. "What have we done?" she muttered, closing her eyes.

Suddenly, the boat rocked violently to the port side. Old Hygge loosed a string of salty curses; the others gave bleats of fear as a black-nailed hand seized the wale. Dísa scurried over, grabbed that hand, then the scruff of coarse black hair, then the belt at his waist as she hauled Grimnir into the boat.

Bedraggled, he nevertheless clutched Sárklungr to his breast.

"Little bird," he spat, wiping his good eye.

Without warning, she threw her arms around his neck—a desperate hug that caught him off guard.

"*Nár!* Stop that," he snarled, pushing her away. Dísa sank down beside him.

"I thought you lost, as well. Everyone . . . Everyone is dead . . . Bjorn Svarti, Brodir . . . Úlfrún . . . We fell . . ." she ventured, her voice quavering.

And the tears that spilled down Dísa Dagrúnsdottir's cheeks as she named the dead would not be the last.

THAT NIGHT, ON THE BEACH leading up to Grimnir's longhouse, they built a pyre for the dead. A whole village burnt in effigy; hundreds of souls. Hundreds of ghosts. Surrounded by the women of Hrafnhaugr, by the young girls that were all that remained of the Daughters of the Raven, by Old Hygge and the crippled giant, Bjorn Hvítr; by dour Kjartan—who held the Otter-Geat, Laufeya, close—Dísa led them in the recitation of the dead. Their names floated aloft with the embers of their pyre as its flames burned low.

"The barrow sank back into the lake," Grimnir said later, as they sat near the water and listened to the lapping waves of Lake Vänern. "Took most of the peninsula with it."

"Did it take Odin's wyrm with it?" Dísa asked. She was clad now in a tunic and leggings, a cloak warding off the night's chill. A thaw was coming; she could smell it on the breeze.

"Still out there. Near as I can tell, it fed off the rest of that white-skinned bastard's army before it vanished into the lake."

"Konraðr," she said quietly, recalling the Christian's sacrifice. "His name was Konraðr. You're going after it." There was no question in Dísa's mind.

Grimnir grunted. "There's still a matter of vengeance between us. You have a piece in this now. Will you come?"

Dísa thought about it a moment, and then shook her head. "No. I've had my fill of Odin's weather," she said; then, quietly: "My people need me."

Grimnir looked hard at her but said nothing. He rose, walked to the edge of the lake. The dark waters of Skærvík lapped at the shingle. Overhead, stars gleamed like cold lanterns through rips in the clouds. Far to the north, his keen eyes beheld the crackling curtain of green fire—the jötunn-lights. Grimnir reached down and drew a knife from his boot. His lips peeled back in a snarl; he tilted his head back and let loose a deafening howl. "Hear me, Sly One, Father Loki! Bear witness, O Ymir, sire of giants and lord of the frost!" Grimnir sawed the knife across one forearm, then the other. "By this blood, the blood of my kin, I swear! I, Grimnir, son of Bálegyr, will not rest until I've brought that wretched dragon to heel! I will not rest until Niðhöggr is under my blade!"

The echo of his oath died away. The ghost-lights crackled; the stars burned. And if the old Gods heard, they gave him no sign.

ACKNOWLEDGMENTS

WHILE THE WORDS ON THE page are my own, a great many people had a hand in the creation of this book—from reading the manuscript and making suggestions, to volunteering their expertise on language, geography, and warfare, to offering a kind word of encouragement at precisely the right time. I would like to offer my heartfelt thanks:

TO MY WIFE, SHANNON, WHO keeps me grounded, encourages me, and makes sure my castles in the air have a tether to keep them from floating off. A part of her is in every woman I've ever written. She is Dísa's energy, Úlfrún's convictions, and Halla's wisdom. And she would not put up with Grimnir's guff, either.

To my agent, Bob Mecoy, for his years of wise counsel and friendship, and for understanding that working with any writer is like herding cats.

To my editor at St. Martin's, Pete Wolverton, who gives new meaning to patience—even as I give new meaning to "you'll have it tomorrow." And while his emails may be spartan, his editing notes are a master class in how to make a passable novel into a great novel.

To my beta readers this time around: Jeff Bryant, Rusty Burke, Vincent Darlage, Tom Doolan, Darrell Grizzle, Scott Hall, Josh Olive, Stan Wagenaar, and Eric Woods. Thanks for taking time out of your days to keep me honest, to listen to my whines, and to make sure I'm not spinning the dross rather than the gold.

To my friends and colleagues on social media, who answer the weirdest questions I pose without ever batting an eye. The well-thought-out answers to "How far can you chuck a severed human head?" were my personal favorites.

And, last but not least, to you, dear readers. You guys are the best.

To one and all, thank you!

ABOUT THE AUTHOR

SCOTT ODEN WAS BORN IN Indiana, but has spent most of his life shuffling between his home in rural north Alabama, a Hobbit hole in Middle-earth, and some sketchy tavern in the Hyborian Age. He is an avid reader of fantasy and ancient history, a collector of swords, and a player of tabletop role-playing games. His previous books include *Men of Bronze, Memnon,* and *The Lion of Cairo.* When not writing, he can be found walking his two dogs or doting over his lovely wife, Shannon.